POUL ANDERSON
EXPLORATIONS

A TOM DOHERTY ASSOCIATES BOOK
Distributed by Pinnacle Books, New York

Acknowledgements: The stories contained herein were first published and copyrighted as follows:

The Saturn Game: Analog, copyright ©1981, by Ziff-Davis Publishing Corporation, Inc.
The Bitter Bread: Analog, copyright ©1975, by the Conde Nast Publications, Inc.
The Ways of Love: Destinies, copyright ©1979 by Poul Anderson
The Voortrekkers: Final Stage, copyright ©1974 by Edward L. Ferman and Barry N. Malzberg
Epilogue: Analog, copyright ©1962 by The Conde Nast Publications, Inc.
Starfog: Analog, copyright ©1967 by The Conde Nast Publications, Inc.

A Tor Book

First printing: November, 1981.

ISBN: 0-523-48-517-4
Cover Art by Vincent Di Fate

Printed in the United States of America

Pinnacle Books, Inc.
1430 Broadway
New York, N.Y. 10018

TABLE OF CONTENTS

Introduction to
EXPLORATIONS
by Poul Anderson

When Jim Baen and I were first discussing this book, what should go into it, he suggested that the motif and title be "The Ways of Love." I felt this was too limited a theme, and we settled on "Explorations." Each story deals with some aspect of humanity's future movement into the cosmos, which we both hope so much will come to pass. Then Jim noticed, to our mutual surprise, that each is also a love story anyway.

On second thought, perhaps this is no coincidence. The Greeks distinguished three emotions which English lumps together as "love." Yet are the three kinds really unrelated? Might not sexual love (*eros*), love for God (*agape*), and every other sort of affection (*phile*, from which we get such words as "philosophy" and "philanthropy") spring from a common source, or even be different faces of the same mystery?

How shall we think of that emotion which drives human beings to explore?

Romanticists to the contrary, it is not universal in our species. At least, in many people it is subordinate to other desires. They are apt to resent public attention given to anything except the objects of their own yearnings. Explorers, including scientists of every description, are usually more tolerant, though this may be a matter of necessity rather than temperament.

After all, they are forever a minority, striving to get a small share of society's resources in support of their undertakings; they must compromise. Demagogues, whose claims can be unlimited, are always free to denounce them.

A case very much in point is that of the American space program. We have been told it is useless, an extravagance we can no longer afford—at any rate, until that day when the politicians have collected enough taxes, enacted enough laws, and established enough bureaucracies to abolish poverty, disease, inequality, war, crime, pollution, inflation, urban sprawl, and wrong thinking. We have also been told that the public no longer cares, that space no longer has a constituency.

Both these assertions are false.

If we put rhetoric aside for a moment and look at a few facts, it is evident that, though the space program has had it share of human inefficiencies and absurdities, it has never been a losing proposition. It has, rather, already repaid the modest investment in it, and returned a huge profit as well.

Modest? Of course. The budget of the National Aeronautics and Space Administration—for all of its varied activities—peaked at about the time of Apollo 11. Yet even in those palmy days it got less than 8 percent of the amount that the federal government spent on health, education, and welfare (a figure which takes no account of state and municipal undertakings or of private charities). It would be unkind to compare the actual accomplishments, but at least we can deny that NASA has ever taken bread out of the mouths of the poor.

Profit? Certainly. The revolution in meteorology alone, brought about by weather satellites, proves that claim. The lives saved because hurricanes can be accurately predicted offer a spectacular example. However, precise forecasts as a routine matter, year after year, are the open-ended payoff, especially for agriculture and transportation, and thus for mankind. Or think of communications. Never mind if many television shows strike you as inane; never mind, even, educational uses in primitive areas which could not otherwise be reached—the fact is that transmission over great distances was bound to come and that relaying through space is cheaper than relaying across the surface. Cash economies are mere shorthand for labor set free and natural resources conserved.

Landsats and seasats give us information by which we can make better use of those resources: for example, by identifying plant disease in remote areas, while it is still readily treatable. By examining the cosmic environment of our planet and comparing it with its neighbors, we have come to a better understanding of it: for example, studies of the chemistry of the atmosphere of Venus gave us our first clue to the menace that fluorocarbons were posing to our own ozone layer. Not much further off is a real comprehension of geophysics. The practical, humane applications of such knowledge are obvious: for example, earthquake predictions, perhaps eventual earthquake prevention. Meanwhile, astrophysics has long been a key to the full description and hence control of matter and energy; and the best place for that research is above the air. We can also expect deeper insights into how life works. Early biological experiments in space have indicated how little we know today, how badly we need to carry on studies under conditions found nowhere else. A golden age of medicine and food production may well be a result.

But, some say, can't we save money by doing this with unmanned probes, vehicles, robots, devices?

Machines are invaluable aids. Still, could they have had and shared the direct experiences of a Cook, Stanley, Lyell, Darwin, Boas, or, more recently, Cousteau, Leakey, Goodall? A human being is the only computer that continuously reprograms itself, the only sensor system that records data it is not planned to detect, the only thing that gives a damn.

Six fleeting visits to a single barren globe scarcely constitute exploration. If we stop now, it will be as if European mariners had stopped when Columbus reported his failure to reach India—which he never actually did, because he never knew how much more grand his discovery was. What he found brought legions overseas. What the astronauts have found in the tiny time granted them is astonishingly great: not material wealth, but the stuff of knowledge, whence all else arises. Shall we end the enterprise at its very beginning?

I have emphasized knowledge, that being the one absolutely certain gain. However, a permanent human presence in space should also yield nearly unlimited economic returns. As solar collectors achieve their full potential out yonder, we should have all the energy we can ever use, free, clean, inexhaustible. We should have abundant raw materials, no longer taken out of the hide of Mother Earth. We should have industries moving to locations where they cannot harm her, and entire new industries coming into existence. We should become able to abolish poverty, if not the other ills that our race keeps visiting upon itself, and abolish poverty not only in America but throughout the world. What this would mean to the spirit is incalculable.

As for the falsehood that the public has lost interest, the popularity of science fiction suffices to disprove that. We have, besides, the many thousands who undergo expense and discomfort to watch space events in person, the many millions who breathlessly follow every one on television and in the newspapers. We have a large and growing volume of mail to Washington, urging a revitalized program. (It would help mightily if *you* would send such letters, brief and respectful, to your national legislators and the President.) Oh, yes, the people care.

And so we return to the theme with which we began, love and its indivisibility. Maybe the reason why some cannot imagine what we have to gain beyond Earth is that they have not let heaven touch their hearts.

I say to them, "Go out, the next clear night. Look up."

THE SATURN GAME

I

If we would understand what happened, which
is vital if we would avoid repeated and worse
tragedies in the future, we must begin by
dismissing all accusations. Nobody was negligent;
no action was foolish. For who could have
predicted the eventuality, or recognized its
nature, until too late? Rather should we
appreciate the spirit with which those people
struggled against disaster, inward and outward,
after they knew. The fact is that thresholds exist
throughout reality, and that things on their far
sides are altogether different from things on their
hither sides. The *Chronos* crossed more than an
abyss, it crossed a threshold of human experience.
　　　　—Francis L. Minamoto, *Death*
　　　　Under Saturn: A Dissenting View
　　　　(Apollo University Communications,
　　　　Leyburg, Luna, 2057)

"The City of Ice is now on my horizon,"
Kendrick says. Its towers gleam blue. "My griffin
spreads his wings to glide." *Wind whistles among
those great, rainbow-shimmering pinions. His
cloak blows back from his shoulders; the air strikes
through his ring-mail and sheathes him in cold.* "I
lean over and peer after you." *The spear in his left
hand counterbalances him. Its head flickers palely
with the moonlight that Wayland Smith*

12

hammered into the steel.

"Yes, I see the griffin," *Ricia tells him,* "high and far, like a comet above the courtyard walls. I run out from under the portico for a better look. A guard tries to stop me, grabs my sleeve, but I tear the spider-silk apart and dash forth into the open." *The elven castle wavers as if its sculptured ice were turning to smoke. Passionately, she cries,* "Is it in truth you, my darling?"

"Hold, there!" *warns Alvarlan from his cave of arcana ten thousand leagues away.* "I send your mind the message that if the King suspects this is Sir Kendrick of the Isles, he will raise a dragon against him, or spirit you off beyond any chance of rescue. Go back, Princess of Maranoa. Pretend you decide that it is only an eagle. I will cast a belief-spell on your words."

"I stay far aloft," *Kendrick says.* "Save he use a scrying stone, the Elf King will not be aware this beast has a rider. From here I'll spy out city and castle." *And then—? He knows not. He knows simply that he must set her free or die in the quest. How long will it take him, how many more nights will she lie in the King's embrace?*

"I thought you were supposed to spy out Iapetus," Mark Danzig interrupted.

His dry tone startled the three others into alertness. Jean Broberg flushed with embarrassment, Colin Scobie with irritation; Luis Garcilaso shrugged, grinned, and turned his gaze to the pilot console before which he sat harnessed. For a moment silence filled the cabin, and shadows, and radiance from the universe.

To help observation, all lights were out except a few dim glows at instruments. The sunward ports were lidded. Elsewhere thronged stars, so many and so brilliant that they well-nigh drowned the blackness which held them. The Milky Way was a torrent of silver. One port framed Saturn at half phase, dayside pale gold and rich bands amidst the jewelry of its rings, nightside wanly ashimmer with starlight and moonlight upon clouds, as big to the sight as Earth over Luna.

Forward was Iapetus. The spacecraft rotated while orbiting the moon, to maintain a steady optical field. It had crossed the dawn line, presently at the middle of the inward-facing hemisphere. Thus it had left bare, crater-pocked land behind it in the dark, and was passing above sunlit glacier country. Whiteness dazzled, glittered in sparks and shards of color, reached fantastic shapes heavenward; cirques, crevasses, caverns brimmed with blue.

"I'm sorry," Jean Broberg whispered. "It's too beautiful, unbelievably beautiful, and . . . almost like the place where our game had brought us— Took us by surprise—"

"Huh!" Mark Danzig said. "You had a pretty good idea of what to expect, therefore you made your play go in the direction of something that resembled it. Don't tell me any different. I've watched these acts for eight years."

Colin Scobie made a savage gesture. Spin and gravity were too slight to give noticeable weight. His movement sent him through the air, across the crowded cabin, until he checked himself by a handhold just short of the chemist. "Are you calling Jean a liar?" he growled.

Most times he was cheerful, in a bluff fashion. Perhaps because of that, he suddenly appeared menacing. He was a big, sandy-haired man in his mid-thirties; a coverall did not disguise the muscles beneath, and the scowl on his face brought forth its ruggedness.

"Please!" Broberg exclaimed. "Not a quarrel, Colin."

The geologist glanced back at her. She was slender and fine-featured. At her age of forty-two, despite longevity treatment, the reddish-brown hair that fell to her shoulders was becoming streaked with white, and lines were engraved around large gray eyes. "Mark is right," she sighed. "We're here to do science, not daydream." She reached forth to touch Scobie's arm, smiled shyly. "You're still full of your Kendrick persona, aren't you? Gallant, protective—" She stopped. Her voice had quickened with more than a hint of Ricia. She covered her lips and flushed again. A tear broke free and sparkled off on air currents. She forced a laugh. "But I'm just physicist Broberg, wife of astronomer Tom, mother of Johnnie and Billy."

Her glance went Saturnward, as if seeking the ship where her family waited. She might have spied it, too, as a star that moved among stars, by the solar sail. However, that was now furled, and naked vision could not find even such huge hulls as *Chronos* possessed, across millions of kilometers.

Luis Garcilaso asked from his pilot's chair: "What harm if we carry on our little *commedia dell' arte?*" His Arizona drawl soothed the ear. "We won't be landin' for a while yet, and everything's on automatic till then." He was small, swart, deft, still in his twenties.

Danzig twisted the leather of his countenance into a frown. At sixty, thanks to his habits as well as to longevity, he kept springiness in a lank frame; he could joke about wrinkles and encroaching baldness. In this hour, he set humor aside.

"Do you mean you don't know what's the matter?" His beak of a nose pecked at a scanner screen which magnified the moonscope. "Almighty God! That's a new world we're about to touch down on—tiny, but a world, and strange in ways we can't guess. Nothing's been here before us except one unmanned flyby and one unmanned

lander that soon quit sending. We can't rely on
meters and cameras alone. We've got to use our
eyes and brains." He addressed Scobie. "You
should realize that in your bone, Colin, if nobody
else aboard does. You've worked on Luna as well
as Earth. In spite of all the settlements, in spite of
all the study that's been done, did you never hit
any nasty surprises?"

The burly man had recovered his temper. Into
his own voice came a softness that recalled the
serenity of the Idaho mountains whence he hailed.
"True," he admitted. "There's no such thing as
having too much information when you're off
Earth, or enough information, for that matter."
He paused. "Nevertheless, timidity can be as
dangerous as rashness—not that you're timid,
Mark," he added in haste. "Why, you and Rachel
could've been in a nice O'Neill on a nice
pension—"

Danzig relaxed and smiled. "This was a
challenge, if I may sound pompous. Just the same,
we want to get home when we're finished here. We
should be in time for the Bar Mitzvah of a great-
grandson or two. Which requires staying alive."

"My point is, if you let yourself get buffaloed,
you may end up in a worse bind than—Oh, never
mind. You're probably right, and we should not
have begun fantasizing. The spectacle sort of
grabbed us. It won't happen again."

Yet when Scobie's eyes looked anew on the
glacier, they had not quite the dispassion of a
scientist in them. Nor did Broberg's or
Garcilaso's. Danzig slammed fist into palm. "The
game, the damned childish game," he muttered,
too low for his companions to hear. "Was nothing
saner possible for them?"

II

Was nothing saner possible for them? Perhaps not.

If we are to answer the question, we should first review some history. When early industrial operations in space offered the hope of rescuing civilization, and Earth, from ruin, then greater knowledge of sister planets, prior to their development, became a clear necessity. The effort must start with Mars, the least hostile. No natural law forbade sending small manned spacecraft yonder. What did was the absurdity of as much fuel, time, and effort as were required, in order that three or four persons might spend a few days in a single locality.

Construction of the *J. Peter Vajk* took longer and cost more, but paid off when it, virtually a colony, spread its immense solar sail and took a thousand people to their goal in half a year and in comparative comfort. The payoff grew overwhelming when they, from orbit, launched Earthward the beneficiated minerals of Phobos that they did not need for their own purposes. Those purposes, of course, turned on the truly thorough, long-term study of Mars, and included landings of auxiliary craft, for ever lengthier stays, all over the surface.

Sufficient to remind you of this much; no need to detail the triumphs of the same basic concept throughout the inner Solar System, as far as Jupiter. The tragedy of the *Vladimir* became a reason to try again for Mercury . . . and, in a left-handed, political way, pushed the Britannic-American consortium into its *Chronos* project.

They named the ship better than they knew. Sailing time to Saturn was eight years.

Not only the scientists must be healthy, lively-minded people. Crewfolk, technicians, medics, constables, teachers, clergy, entertainers, every element of an entire community must be. Each must command more than a single skill, for emergency backup, and keep those skills alive by regular, tedious rehearsal. The environment was limited and austere; communication with home was soon a matter of beamcasts; cosmopolitans found themselves in what amounted to an isolated village. What were they to *do*?

Assigned tasks. Civic projects, especially work on improving the interior of the vessel. Research, or writing a book, or the study of a subject, or sports, or hobby clubs, or service and handicraft enterprises, or more private interactions, or— There was a wide choice of television tapes, but Central Control made sets usable for only three hours in twenty-four. You dared not get into the habit of passivity.

Individuals grumbled, squabbled, formed and dissolved cliques, formed and dissolved marriages or less explicit relationships, begot and raised occasional children, worshipped, mocked, learned, yearned, and for the most part found reasonable satisfaction in life. But for some, including a large proportion of the gifted, what made the difference between this and misery was their psychodramas.

— Minamoto

Dawn crept past the ice, out onto the rock. It was a light both dim and harsh, yet sufficient to give Garcilaso the last data he wanted for descent.

The hiss of the motor died away, a thump shivered through the hull, landing jacks leveled it, stillness fell. The crew did not speak for a while. They were staring out at Iapetus.

Immediately around them was desolation like that which reigns in much of the Solar System. A

darkling plain curved visibly away to a horizon
that, at man-height, was a bare three kilometers
distant; higher up in the cabin, you saw farther,
but that only sharpened the sense of being on a
minute ball awhirl among the stars. The ground
was thinly covered with cosmic dust and gravel;
here and there a minor crater or an upthrust mass
lifted out of the regolith to cast long, knife-edged,
utterly black shadows. Light reflections lessened
the number of visible stars, turning heaven into a
bowlful of night. Halfway between the zenith and
the south, half-Saturn and its rings made the vista
beautiful.

Likewise did the glacier—or the glaciers?
Nobody was sure. The sole knowledge was that,
seen from afar, Iapetus gleamed bright at the
western end of its orbit and grew dull at the
eastern end, because one side was covered with
whitish material while the other side was not; the
dividing line passed nearly beneath the planet
which it eternally faced. The probes from *Chronos*
had reported the layer was thick, with puzzling
spectra that varied from place to place, and little
more about it.

In this hour, four humans gazed across pitted
emptiness and saw wonder rear over the world-
rim. From north to south went ramparts, battlements, spires, depths, peaks, cliffs, their shapes
and shadings an infinity of fantasies. On the right
Saturn cast soft amber, but that was nearly lost in
the glare from the east, where a sun dwarfed
almost to stellar size nonetheless blazed too fierce
to look at, just above the summit. There the silvery
sheen exploded in brilliance, diamond-glitter of
shattered light, chill blues and greens; dazzled to
tears, eyes saw the vision glimmer and waver, as if
it bordered on dreamland, or on Faerie. But
despite all delicate intricacies, underneath was a
sense of chill and of brutal mass; here dwelt also

the Frost Giants.

Broberg was the first to breathe forth a word.
"The City of Ice."

"Magic," said Garcilaso as low. "My spirit could
lose itself forever, wanderin' yonder. I'm not sure
I'd mind. My cave is nothin' like this, nothin'—"

"Wait a minute!" snapped Danzig in alarm.

"Oh, yes. Curb the imagination, please." Though
Scobie was quick to utter sobrieties, they sounded
drier than needful. "We know from probe trans-
missions the scarp is, well, Grand Canyon-like.
Sure, it's more spectacular than we realized,
which I suppose makes it still more of a mystery."
He turned to Broberg. "I've never seen ice or snow
as sculptured as this. Have you, Jean? You've
mentioned visiting a lot of mountain and winter
scenery when you were a girl in Canada."

The physicist shook her head. "No. Never. It
doesn't seem possible. What could have done it?
There's no weather here . . . is there?"

"Perhaps the same phenomenon is responsible
that laid a hemisphere bare," Danzig suggested.

"Or that covered a hemisphere," Scobie said.
"An object seventeen hundred kilometers across
shouldn't have gases, frozen or otherwise. Unless
it's a ball of such stuff clear through, like a comet.
Which we know it's not." As if to demonstrate, he
unclipped a pair of pliers from a nearby tool rack,
tossed it, and caught it on its slow way down. His
own ninety kilos of mass weighed about seven. For
that, the satellite must be essentially rocky.

Garcilaso registered impatience. "Let's stop
tradin' facts and theories we already know about,
and start findin' answers."

Rapture welled in Broberg. "Yes, let's get out.
Over *there*."

"Hold on," protested Danzig as Garcilaso and
Scobie nodded eagerly. "You can't be serious.
Caution, step-by-step advance—"

"No, it's too wonderful for that." Broberg's tone shivered.

"Yeah, to hell with fiddlin' around," Garcilaso said. "We need at least a preliminary scout right away."

The furrows deepened in Danzig's visage. "You mean you too, Luis? But you're our pilot!"

"On the ground I'm general assistant, chief cook, and bottle washer to you scientists. Do you imagine I want to sit idle, with somethin' like that to explore?" Garcilaso calmed his voice. "Besides, if I should come to grief, any of you can fly back, given a bit of radio talk from *Chronos* and a final approach under remote control."

"It's quite reasonable, Mark," Scobie argued. "Contrary to doctrine, true; but doctrine was made for us, not vice versa. A short distance, low gravity, and we'll be on the lookout for hazards. The point is, until we have some notion of what that ice is like, we don't know what the devil to pay attention to in this vicinity, either. No, we'll take a quick jaunt. When we return, then we'll plan."

Danzig stiffened. "May I remind you, if anything goes wrong, help is at least a hundred hours away? An auxiliary like this can't boost any higher if it's to get back, and it'd take longer than that to disengage the big boats from Saturn and Titan."

Scobie reddened at the implied insult. "And may I remind you, on the ground I am the captain? I say an immediate reconnaissance is safe and desirable. Stay behind if you want—In fact, yes, you must. Doctrine is right in saying the vessel mustn't be deserted."

Danzig studied him for several seconds before murmuring, "Luis goes, however, is that it?"

"Yes!" cried Garcilaso so that the cabin rang.

Broberg patted Danzig's limp hand. "It's okay, Mark," she said gently. "We'll bring back samples for you to study. After that, I wouldn't be surprised but what the best ideas about procedure will be yours."

He shook his head. Suddenly he looked very tired. "No," he replied in a monotone, "that won't happen. You see, I'm only a hardnosed industrial chemist who saw this expedition as a chance to do interesting research. The whole way through space, I kept myself busy with ordinary affairs, including, you remember, a couple of inventions I'd wanted leisure to develop. You three, you're younger, you're romantics—"

"Aw, come off it, Mark." Scobie tried to laugh. "Maybe Jean and Luis are, a little, but me, I'm about as other-worldly as a plate of haggis."

"You played the game, year after year, until at last the game started playing you. That's what's going on this minute, no matter how you rationalize your motives." Danzig's gaze on the geologist, who was his friend, lost the defiance that had been in it and turned wistful. "You might try recalling Delia Ames."

Scobie bristled. "What about her? The business was hers and mine, nobody else's."

"Except afterward she cried on Rachel's shoulder, and Rachel doesn't keep secrets from me. Don't worry, I'm not about to blab. Anyhow, Delia got over it. But if you'd recollect objectively, you'd see what had happened to you, already three years ago."

Scobie set his jaw. Danzig smiled in the left corner of his mouth. "No, I suppose you can't," he went on. "I admit I'd no idea either, till now, how far the process had gone. At least keep your fantasies in the background while you're outside, will you? Can you?"

In half a decade of travel, Scobie's apartment had become idiosyncratically his—perhaps more so than was usual, since he remained a bachelor who seldom had women visitors for longer than a few nightwatches at a time. Much of the furniture he had made himself; the agrosections of *Chronos* produced wood, hide, fiber as well as food and fresh air. His handiwork ran to massiveness and archaic carved decorations. Most of what he wanted to read he screened from the data banks, of course, but a shelf held a few old books, Childe's border ballads, an eighteenth-century family Bible (despite his agnosticism), a copy of *The Machinery of Freedom* which had nearly disintegrated but displayed the signature of the author, and other valued miscellany. Above them stood a model of a sailboat in which he had cruised Northern European waters, and a trophy he had won in handball aboard this ship. On the bulkheads hung his fencing sabers and numerous pictures—of parents and siblings, of wilderness areas he had tramped on Earth, of castles and mountains and heaths in Scotland where he had often been too, of his geological team on Luna, of Thomas Jefferson and, imagined, Robert the Bruce.

On a certain evenwatch he had, though, been seated before his telescreen. Lights were turned low in order that he might fully savor the image. Auxiliary craft were out in a joint exercise, and a couple of their personnel used the opportunity to beam back views of what they saw.

That was splendor. Starful space made a chalice for *Chronos*. The two huge, majestically counter-rotating cylinders, the entire complex of linkages, ports, locks, shields, collectors, transmitters, docks, all became Japanesely exquisite at a distance of several hundred kilometers. It was the solar sail which filled most of the screen, like a turning golden sun-wheel; yet remote vision could also appreciate its spiderweb intricacy, soaring and subtle curvatures, even the less-than-gossamer thinness. A mightier work than the Pyramids, a finer work than a refashioned chromosome, the ship moved on toward a Saturn which had become the second brightest beacon in the firmament.

The doorchime hauled Scobie out of his exaltation. As he started across the deck, he stubbed his toe on a table leg. Coriolis force caused that. It was slight, when a hull this size spun to give a full gee of weight, and a thing to which he had long since adapted; but now and then he got so interested in something that Terrestrial habits returned. He swore at his absent-mindedness, good-naturedly, since he anticipated a pleasurable time.

When he opened the door, Delia Ames entered in a single stride. At once she closed it behind her and stood braced against it. She was a tall blonde woman who did electronics maintenance and kept up a number of outside activities. "Hey!" Scobie said. "What's wrong? You look like—" he tried for levity—"something my cat wouldn've dragged in, if we had any mice or beached fish aboard."

She drew a ragged breath. Her Australian accent thickened till he had trouble understanding: "I . . . today . . . I happened to be at the same cafeteria table as George Harding—"

Unease tingled through Scobie. Harding worked in Ames' department but had much more in common with him. In the same group to which they both belonged, Harding likewise took a vaguely ancestral role, N'Kuma the Lionslayer.

"What happened?" Scobie asked.

Woe stared back at him. "He mentioned . . . you and he and the rest . . . you'd be taking your next holiday together . . . to carry on your, your bloody act uninterrupted."

"Well, yes. Work at the new park over in Starboard Hull will be suspended till enough metal's been recycled for the water pipes. The area will be vacant, and my gang has arranged to spend a week's worth of days—"

"But you and I were going to Lake Armstrong!"

"Uh, wait, that was just a notion we talked about, no definite plan yet, and this is such an unusual chance—Later, sweetheart. I'm sorry." He took her hands. They felt cold. He essayed a smile. "Now, c'mon, we were going to cook a festive dinner together and afterward spend a, shall we say, quiet evening at home. But for a start, this absolutely gorgeous presentation on the screen—"

She jerked free of him. The gesture seemed to calm her. "No, thanks," she said, flat-voiced. "Not when you'd rather be with that Broberg woman. I only came by to tell you in person I'm getting out of the way of you two."

"Huh?" He stepped back. "What the flaming hell do you mean?"

"You know jolly well."

"I don't! She, I, she's happily married, got two kids, she's older than me, we're friends, sure, but there's never been a thing between us that wasn't in the open and on the level—" Scobie swallowed. "You suppose maybe I'm in love with her?"

Ames looked away. Her fingers writhed together. "I'm not about to go on being a mere convenience to you, Colin. You have plenty of those. Myself, I'd hoped—But I was wrong, and I'm going to cut my losses before they get worse."

"But . . . Dee, I swear I haven't fallen for anybody else, and I, I swear you're more than a body to me, you're a fine person—" She stood mute and withdrawn. Scobie gnawed his lip before he could tell her: "Okay, I admit it, a main reason I volunteered for this trip was I'd lost out in a love affair on Earth. Not that the project doesn't interest me, but I've come to realize what a big chunk out of my life it is. You, more than any other woman, Dee, you've gotten me to feel better about the situation."

She grimaced. "But not as much as your psychodrama has, right?"

"Hey, you must think I'm obsessed with the game. I'm not. It's fun and—oh, maybe 'fun' is too weak a word—but anyhow, it's just little bunches of people getting together fairly regularly to play. Like my fencing, or a chess club, or, or anything."

She squared her shoulders. "Well, then," she asked, "will you cancel the date you've made and spend your holiday with me?"

"I, uh, I can't do that. Not at this stage. Kendrick isn't off on the periphery of current events, he's closely involved with everybody else. If I didn't show, it'd spoil things for the rest."

Her glance steadied upon them. "Very well. A promise is a promise, or so I imagined. But afterward—Don't be afraid. I'm not trying to trap you. That would be no good, would it? However, if I maintain this liaison of ours, will you phase out of your game?"

"I can't—" Anger seized him. "No, God damn it!" he roared.

"Then goodbye, Colin," she said, and departed. He stared for minutes at the door she had shut behind her.

Unlike the large Titan and Saturn-vicinity explorers, landers on the airless moons were simply modified Luna-to-space shuttles, reliable but with limited capabilities. When the blocky shape had dropped below the horizon, Garcilaso said into his radio: "We've lost sight of the boat, Mark. I must say it improves the view." One of the relay microsatellites which had been sown in orbit passed his words on.

"Better start blazing your trail, then," Danzig reminded.

"My, my, you *are* a fussbudget, aren't you?"

Nevertheless Garcilaso unholstered the squirt gun at his hip and splashed a vividly fluorescent circle of paint on the ground. He would do it at eyeball intervals until his party reached the glacier. Except where dust lay thick over the regolith, footprints were faint, under the feeble gravity, and absent when a walker crossed continuous rock.

Walker? No, leaper. The three bounded exultant, little hindered by spacesuits, life support units, tool and ration packs. The naked land fled from their haste, and even higher, ever more clear and glorious to see, loomed the ice ahead of them.

There was no describing it, not really. You could speak of lower slopes and palisades above, to a mean height of perhaps a hundred meters, with spires towering farther still. You could speak of gracefully curved tiers going up those braes, of lacy parapets and fluted crags and arched openings to caves filled with wonders, of mysterious blues in the depths and greens where light streamed through translucencies, of gem-sparkle across whiteness where radiance and shadow wove mandalas—and none of it would convey anything more than Scobie's earlier, altogether inadequate comparison to the Grand Canyon.

"Stop," he said for the dozenth time. "I want to take a few pictures."

"Will anybody understand them who hasn't been here?" whispered Broberg.

"Probably not," said Garcilaso in the same hushed tone. "Maybe no one but us ever will."

"What do you mean by that?" demanded Danzig's voice.

"Never mind," snapped Scobie.

"I . . . think . . . I . . . know," the chemist said. "Yes, it is a great piece of scenery, but you're letting it hypnotize you."

"If you don't cut out that drivel," Scobie warned, "we'll cut you out of the circuit. Damn it, we've got work to do. Get off our backs."

Danzig gusted a sigh. "Sorry. Uh, are you finding any clues to the nature of that—that thing?"

Scobie focused his camera. "Well," he said, partly mollified, "the different shades and textures, and no doubt the different shapes, seem to confirm what the reflection spectra from the flyby suggested. The composition is a mixture, or a jumble, or both, of several materials, and varies from place to place. Water ice is obvious, but I feel sure of carbon dioxide too, and I'd bet on ammonia, methane, and presumably lesser amounts of other stuff."

"Methane? Could they stay solid at ambient temperature, in a vacuum?"

"We'll have to find out for sure. However, I'd guess that most of the time it's cold enough, at least for methane strata that occur down inside where there's pressure on them."

Within the vitryl globe of her helmet, Broberg's features showed delight. "Wait!" she cried. "I have an idea—about what happened to the probe that landed." She drew breath. "It came down almost at the foot of the glacier, you recall. Our view of the site from space seemed to indicate that an avalanche buried it, but we couldn't understand how that might have been triggered. Well, suppose a methane layer at exactly the wrong location melted. Heat radiation from the jets may have warmed it, and later the radar beam used to map contours added the last few degrees necessary. The stratum flowed, and down came everything that had rested on top of it."

"Plausible," Scobie said. "Congratulations, Jean."

"Nobody thought of the possibility in advance?" Garcilaso scoffed. "What kind of scientists have we got along?"

"The kind who were being overwhelmed by

work after we reached Saturn, and still more by data input," Scobie answered. "The universe is bigger than you or anybody can realize, hotshot."

"Oh. Sure. No offense." Garcilaso's glance returned to the ice. "Yes, we'll never run out of mysteries, will we?"

"Never." Broberg's eyes glowed enormous. "At the heart of things will always be magic. The Elf King rules—"

Scobie returned his camera to its pouch. "Stow the gab and move on," he ordered curtly.

His gaze locked for an instant with Broberg's. In the weird, mingled light, it could be seen that she went pale, then red, before she sprang off beside him.

Ricia had gone alone into Moonwood on Midsummer Eve. The King found her there and took her unto him as she had hoped. Ecstasy became terror when he afterward bore her off; yet her captivity in the City of Ice brought her many more such hours, and beauties and marvels unknown among mortals. Alvarlan, her mentor, sent his spirit in quest of her, and was himself beguiled by what he found. It was an effort of will for him to tell Sir Kendrick of the Isles where she was, albeit he pledged his help in freeing her.

N'Kuma the Lionslayer, Béla of Eastmarch, Karina of the Far West, Lady Aurelia, Olav Harpmaster had none of them been present when this happened.

The glacier (a wrong name for something that might have no counterpart in the Solar System) lifted off the plain abruptly as a wall. Standing there, the three could no longer see the heights. They could, though, see that the slope which curved steeply upward to a filigree-topped edge was not smooth. Shadows lay blue in countless small craters. The sun had climbed just sufficiently high to beget them; a Iapetan day is more than seventy-nine of Earth's.

Danzig's question crackled in earphones: "Now are you satisfied? Will you come back before a fresh landslide catches you?"

"It won't," Scobie replied. "We aren't a vehicle, and the local configuration has clearly been stable for centuries or better. Besides, what's the point of a manned expedition if nobody investigates anything?"

"I'll see if I can climb," Garcilaso offered.

"No, wait," Scobie commanded. "I've had experience with mountains and snowpacks, for whatever that may be worth. Let me study out a route for us first."

"You're going onto that stuff, the whole gaggle of you?" exploded Danzig. "Have you completely lost your minds?"

Scobie's brow and lips tightened. "Mark, I warn you again, if you don't get your emotions under control we'll cut you off. We'll hike on a ways if I decide it's safe."

He paced, in floating low-weight fashion, back and forth while he surveyed the jökull. Layers and blocks of distinct substances were plain to see, like separate ashlars laid by an elvish mason . . . where they were not so huge that a giant must have been at work. . . The craterlets might be sentry posts on this lowest embankment of the City's defenses . . . .

Garcilaso, most vivacious of men, stood motionless and let his vision lose itself in the sight. Broberg knelt down to examine the ground, but her own gaze kept wandering aloft.

Finally she beckoned. "Colin, come over here, please," she said. "I believe I've made a discovery."

Scobie joined her. As she rose, she scooped a handful of fine black particles off the shards on which she stood and let it trickle from her glove. "I suspect this is the reason the boundary of the ice is sharp," she told him.

"What is?" Danzig inquired from afar. He got no answer.

"I noticed more and more dust as we went along," Broberg continued. "If it fell on patches and lumps of frozen stuff, isolated from the main mass, and covered them, it would absorb solar heat till they melted or, likelier, sublimed. Even water molecules would escape to space, in this weak gravity. The main mass was too big for that; square-cube law. Dust grains there would simply melt their way down a short distance, then be covered as surrounding material collapsed on them, and the process would stop."

"H'm." Broberg raised a hand to stroke his chin, encountered his helmet, and sketched a grin at himself. "Sounds reasonable. But where did so much dust come from—and the ice, for that matter?"

"I think—" Her voice dropped until he could barely hear, and her look went the way of Garcilaso's. His remained upon her face, profiled against stars. "I think this bears out your comet hypothesis, Colin. A comet struck Iapetus. It came from the direction it did because of getting so near Saturn that it was forced to swing in a hairpin bend around the planet. It was enormous; the ice of it covered almost a hemisphere, in spite of much more being vaporized and lost. The dust is partly from it, partly generated by the impact."

He clasped her armored shoulder. "*Your* theory, Jean. I was not the first to propose a comet, but you're the first to corroborate with details."

She didn't appear to notice, except that she murmured further: "Dust can account for the erosion that made those lovely formations, too. It caused differential melting and sublimation on the surface, according to the patterns it happened to fall in and the mixes of ices it clung to, until it was washed away or encysted. The craters, these small ones and the major ones we've observed from above, they have a separate but similar origin. Meteorites—"

"Whoa, there," he objected. "Any sizeable meteorite would release enough energy to steam off most of the entire field."

"I know. Which shows the comet collision was recent, less than a thousand years ago, or we wouldn't be seeing this miracle today. Nothing big has since happened to strike, yet. I'm thinking of little stones, cosmic sand, in prograde orbits around Saturn so that they hit with low relative speed. Most simply make dimples in the ice. Lying there, however, they collect solar heat because of being dark, and re-radiate it to melt away their surroundings, till they sink beneath. The concavities they leave reflect incident radiation from side to side, and thus continue to grow. The pothole effect. And again, because the different ices have different properties, you don't get perfectly smooth craters, but those fantastic bowls we saw before we landed."

"By God!" Scobie hugged her. "You're a genius."

Helmet against helmet, she smiled and said, "No. It's obvious, once you've seen for yourself." She was quiet for a bit while still they held each other. "Scientific intuition is a funny thing, I admit," she went on at last. "Considering the problem, I was hardly aware of my logical mind. What I thought was—the City of Ice, made with starstones out of that which a god called down from heaven—"

"Jesus Maria!" Garcilaso spun about to stare at them.

Scobie released the woman. "We'll go after confirmation," he said unsteadily. "To the large crater you'll remember we spotted a few klicks inward. The surface appears quite safe to walk on."

"I called that crater the Elf King's Dance Hall," Broberg mused, as if a dream were coming back to her.

"Have a care." Garcilaso's laugh rattled. "Heap big medicine yonder. The King is only an inheritor; it was giants who built these walls, for the gods."

"Well, I've got to find a way in, don't I?" Scobie responded.

"Indeed," *Alvarlan says.* "I cannot guide you from this point. My spirit can only see through mortal eyes. I can but lend you my counsel, until we have neared the gates."

"Are you sleepwalking in that fairytale of yours?" Danzig yelled. "Come back before you get yourselves killed!"

"Will you dry up?" Scobie snarled. "It's nothing but a style of talk we've got between us. If you can't understand that, you've got less use of your brain than we do."

"Listen, won't you? I didn't say you're crazy. You don't have delusions or anything like that. I do say you've steered your fantasies toward this kind of place, and now the reality has reinforced them till you're under a compulsion you don't recognize. Would you go ahead so recklessly anywhere else in the universe? Think!"

"That does it. We'll resume contact after you've had time to improve your manners." Scobie snapped off his main radio switch. The circuits that stayed active served for close-by communication but had no power to reach an orbital relay. His companions did likewise.

The three faced the awesomeness before them. "You can help me find the Princess when we are inside, Alvarlan," *Kendrick says.*

"That I can and will," *the sorcerer vows.*

"I wait for you, most steadfast of my lovers," *Ricia croons.*

Alone in the spacecraft, Danzig well-nigh sobbed, "Oh, damn that game forever!" The sound fell away into emptiness.

III

To condemn psychodrama, even in its enhanced form, would be to condemn human nature.

It begins in childhood. Play is necessary to an immature mammal, a means of learning to handle the body, the perceptions, and the outside world. The young human plays, must play, with its brain too. The more intelligent the child, the more its imagination needs exercise. There are degrees of activity, from the passive watching of a show on a screen, onward through reading, daydreaming, storytelling, and psychodrama . . . for which the child has no such fancy name.

We cannot give this behavior any single description, for the shape and course it takes depend on endlessly many variables. Sex, age, culture, and companions are only the most obvious. For example, in pre-electronic North America little girls would often play "house" while little boys played "cowboys and Indians" or "cops and robbers," whereas nowadays a mixed group of their descendants might play "dolphins" or "astronauts and aliens." In essence, a small band forms; each individual makes up a character to portray, or borrows one from fiction; simple props may be employed, such as toy weapons, or any chance object such as a stick may be declared something else such as a metal detector, or a thing may be quite imaginary, as the scenery almost always is. The children then act out a drama which they compose as they go along. When they cannot physically perform a certain action, they describe it. ("I jump real high, like you can do on Mars, an' come out over the edge o' that ol' Valles Marineris, an' take that bandit by surprise.") A large cast of characters, especially villains, frequently comes into existence by fiat.

The most imaginative member of the troupe dominates the game and the evolution of the story line, though in a rather subtle fashion, through offering the most vivid possibilities. The rest, however, are brighter than average; psychodrama in this highly developed form does not appeal to everybody.

For those to whom it does, the effects are beneficial and lifelong. Besides increasing their creativity through use, it lets them try out a play version of different adult roles and experiences. Thereby they begin to acquire insight into adulthood.

Such playacting ends when adolescence commences, if not earlier—but only in that form, and not necessarily forever in it. Grown-ups have many dream-games. This is plain to see in lodges, for example, with their titles, costumes, and ceremonies; but does it not likewise animate all pageantry, every ritual? To what extent are our heroisms, sacrifices, and self-aggrandizements the acting out of personae that we maintain? Some thinkers have attempted to trace this element through every aspect of society.

Here, though, we are concerned with overt psychodrama among adults. In Western civilization it first appeared on a noticeable scale during the middle twentieth century. Psychiatrists found it a powerful diagnostic and therapeutic technique. Among ordinary folk, war and fantasy games, many of which involved identification with imaginary or historical characters, became increasingly popular. In part this was doubtless a retreat from the restrictions and menaces of that unhappy period, but likely in larger part it was a revolt of the mind against the inactive entertainment, notably television, which had come to dominate recreation.

The Chaos ended those activities. Everybody knows about their revival in recent times—for healthier reasons, one hopes. By projecting three-dimensional scenes and appropriate sounds from a data bank—or, better yet, by having a computer produce them to order—players gained a sense of reality that intensified their mental and emotional commitment. Yet in those games that went on for episode after episode, year after real-time year, whenever two or more members of a group could get together to play, they found themselves less and less dependent on such appurtenances. It seemed that, through practice, they had regained the vivid imaginations of their childhoods, and could make anything, or airy nothing itself, into the objects and the worlds they desired.

I have deemed it necessary thus to repeat the obvious in order that we may see it in perspective. The news beamed from Saturn has brought widespread revulsion. (Why? What buried fears have been touched? This is subject matter for potentially important research.) Overnight, adult psychodrama has become unpopular; it may become extinct. That would, in many ways, be a worse tragedy than what has occurred yonder. There is no reason to suppose that the game ever harmed any mentally sound person on Earth; on the contrary. Beyond doubt, it has helped astronauts stay sane and alert on long, difficult missions. If it has no more medical use, that is because psychotherapy has become a branch of applied biochemistry.

And this last fact, the modern world's dearth of experience with madness, is at the root of what happened. Although he could not have foreseen the exact outcome, a twentieth-century psychiatrist might have warned against spending eight years, an unprecedented stretch of time, in as strange an environment as the *Chronos*. Strange it certainly has been, despite all efforts—limited, totally man-controlled, devoid of countless cues for which our evolution on Earth has fashioned us. Extraterrestrial colonists have, thus far, had available to them any number of simulations and compensations, of which close, full contact with home and frequent opportunities to visit there are probably the most significant. Sailing time to Jupiter was long, but half of that to Saturn. Moreover, because they were earlier, scientists in the *Zeus* had much research to occupy them en route, which it would be pointless for later travelers to duplicate; by then, the interplanetary medium between the two giants held few surprises.

Contemporary psychologists were aware of this. They understood that the persons most adversely affected would be the most intelligent, imaginative, and dynamic—those who were supposed to make the very discoveries at Saturn which were the purpose of the undertaking. Being less familiar than their predecessors with the labyrinth that lies, Minotaur-haunted, beneath every human consciousness, the psychologists expected purely benign consequences of whatever psychodramas the crew engendered.

— Minamoto

Assignments to teams had not been made in advance of departure. It was sensible to let professional capabilities reveal themselves and grow

on the voyage, while personal relationships did
the same. Eventually such factors would help in
deciding what individuals should train for what
tasks. Long-term participation in a group of
players normally forged bonds of friendship that
were desirable, if the members were otherwise
qualified.

In real life, Scobie always observed strict
propriety toward Broberg. She was attractive, but
she was monogamous, and he had no wish to
alienate her. Besides, he liked her husband. (Tom
did not partake of the game. As an astronomer, he
had plenty to keep his attention happily engaged.)
They had played for a couple of years, their bunch
had acquired as many as it could accommodate in
a narrative whose milieu and people were
becoming complex, before Scobie and Broberg
spoke of anything intimate.

By then, the story they enacted was doing so,
and maybe it was not altogether by chance that
they met when both had several idle hours. This
was in the weightless recreation area at the spin
axis. They tumbled through aerobatics, shouting
and laughing, until they were pleasantly tired,
went to the clubhouse, turned in their wingsuits,
and showered. They had not seen each other nude
before; neither commented, but he did not hide his
enjoyment of the sight, while she colored and
averted her glance as tactfully as she was able.
Afterward, their clothes resumed, they decided on
a drink before they went home, and sought the
lounge.

Since evenwatch was approaching nightwatch,
they had the place to themselves. At the bar, he
thumbed a chit for Scotch, she for pinot
chardonnay. The machine obliged them and they
carried their refreshments out onto the balcony.
Seated at a table, they looked across immensity.
The clubhouse was built into the support frame on

a Lunar gravity level. Above them they saw the sky
wherein they had been as birds; its reach did not
seem any more hemmed in by far-spaced, spidery
girders than it was by a few drifting clouds.
Beyond, and straight ahead, decks opposite were a
commingling of masses and shapes which the
scant illumination at this hour turned into
mystery. Among those shadows the humans made
out woods, brooks, pools, turned hoar or agleam
by the light of stars which filled the skyview
strips. Right and left, the hull stretched off beyond
sight, a dark in which such lamps as there were
appeared lost.

Air was cool, slightly jasmine-scented, drenched
with silence. Underneath and throughout,
subliminal, throbbed the myriad pulses of the
ship.

"Magnificent," Broberg said low, gazing
outward. "What a surprise."

"Eh?" asked Scobie.

"I've only been here before in daywatch. I didn't
anticipate a simple rotation of the reflectors
would make it wonderful."

"Oh, I wouldn't sneer at the daytime view.
Mighty impressive."

"Yes, but—but then you see too plainly that
everything is manmade, nothing is wild or
unknown or free. The sun blots out the stars; it's
as though no universe existed beyond this shell
we're in. Tonight is like being in Maranoa," *the
kingdom of which Ricia is Princess, a kingdom of
ancient things and ways, wildernesses, enchantments.*

"H'm, yeah, sometimes I feel trapped myself,"
Scobie admitted. "I believed I had a journey's
worth of geological data to study, but my project
isn't going anywhere very interesting."

"Same for me." Broberg straightened where she
sat, turned to him, and smiled a trifle. The dusk

softened her features, made them look young. "Not that we're entitled to self-pity. Here we are, safe and comfortable till we reach Saturn. After that we should never lack for excitement, or for material to work with on the way home."

"True." Scobie raised his glass. "Well, skoal. Hope I'm not mispronouncing that."

"How should I know?" she laughed. "My maiden name was Almyer."

"That's right, you've adopted Tom's surname. I wasn't thinking. Though that is rather unusual these days, hey?"

She spread her hands. "My family was well-to-do, but they were—are—Jerusalem Catholics. Strict about certain things; archaistic, you might say." She lifted her wine and sipped. "Oh, yes, I've left the Church, but in several ways the Church will never leave me."

"I see. Not to pry, but, uh, this does account for some traits of yours I couldn't help wondering about."

She regarded him over the rim of her glass. "Like what?"

"Well, you've got a lot of life in you, vigor, sense of fun, but you're also—what's the word?—uncommonly domestic. You've told me you were a quiet faculty member of Yukon University till you married Tom." Scobie grinned. "Since you two kindly invited me to your last anniversary party, and I know your present age, I deduced that you were thirty then." Unmentioned was the likelihood that she had still been a virgin. "Nevertheless—oh, forget it. I said I don't want to pry."

"Go ahead, Colin," she urged. "That line from Burns sticks in my mind, since you introduced me to his poetry. 'To see oursels as others see us!' Since it looks as if we may visit the same moon—"

Scobie took a hefty dollop of Scotch. "Aw, nothing much," he said, unwontedly diffident. "If you must know, well, I have the impression that being in love wasn't the single good reason you had for marrying Tom. He'd already been accepted for this expedition, and given your personal qualifications, that would get you in too. In short, you'd grown tired of routine respectability and here was how you could kick over the traces. Am I right?"

"Yes." Her gaze dwelt on him. "You're more perceptive than I supposed."

"No, not really. A roughneck rockhound. But Ricia's made it plain to see, you're more than a demure wife, mother, and scientist—" She parted her lips. He raised a palm. "No, please, let me finish. I know it's bad manners to claim somebody's persona is a wish fulfillment, and I'm not doing that. Of course you don't want to be a free-roving, free-loving female scamp, any more than I want to ride around cutting down assorted enemies. Still, if you'd been born and raised in the world of our game, I feel sure you'd be a lot like Ricia. And that potential is part of you, Jean." He tossed off his drink. "If I've said too much, please excuse me. Want a refill?"

"I'd better not, but don't let me stop you."

"You won't." He rose and bounded off.

When he returned, he saw that she had been observing him through the vitryl door. As he sat down, she smiled, leaned a bit across the table, and told him softly: "I'm glad you said what you did. Now I can declare what a complicated man Kendrick reveals you to be."

"What?" Scobie asked in honest surprise. "Come on! He's a sword-and-shield tramp, a fellow who likes to travel, same as me; and in my teens I was a brawler, same as him."

"He may lack polish, but he's a chivalrous knight, a compassionate overlord, a knower of sagas and traditions, an appreciator of poetry and music, a bit of a bard . . . Ricia misses him. When will he get back from his latest quest?"

"I'm bound home this minute. N'Kuma and I gave those pirates the slip and landed at Haverness two days ago. After we buried the swag, he wanted to visit Béla and Karina and join them in whatever they've been up to, so we bade goodbye for the time being." Scobie and Harding had lately taken a few hours to conclude that adventure of theirs. The rest of the group had been mundanely occupied for some while.

Broberg's eyes widened. "From Haverness to the Isles? But I'm in Castle Devaranda, right in between."

"I hoped you'd be."

"I can't wait to hear your story."

"I'm pushing on after dark. The moon is bright and I've got a pair of remounts I bought with a few gold pieces from the loot." *The dust rolls white beneath drumming hoofs. Where a horseshoe strikes a flint pebble, sparks fly ardent. Kendrick scowls.* "You aren't you, with . . . what's his name? . . . Joran the Red? I don't like him."

"I sent him packing a month ago. He got the idea that sharing my bed gave him authority over me. It was never anything but a romp. I stand alone on the Gerfalcon Tower, looking south over moonlit fields, and wonder how you fare. The road flows toward me like a gray river. Do I see a rider come at a gallop, far and far away?"

After many months of play, no image on a screen was necessary. *Pennons on the night wind stream athwart the stars.* "I arrive. I sound my horn to rouse the gatekeepers."

"How I do remember those merry notes—"

That same night, Kendrick and Ricia become lovers. Experienced in the game and careful of its etiquette, Scobie and Broberg uttered no details about the union; they did not touch each other and maintained only fleeting eye contact; the ultimate goodnights were very decorous. After all, this was a story they composed about two fictitious characters in a world that never was.

The lower slopes of the jökull rose in tiers which were themselves deeply concave; the humans walked around their rims and admired the extravagant formations beneath. Names sprang onto lips, the Frost Garden, the Ghost Bridge, the Snow Queen's Throne, *while Kendrick advances into the City, and Ricia awaits him at the Dance Hall, and the spirit of Alvarlan carries word between them so that it is as if already she too travels beside her knight.* Nevertheless they proceeded warily, vigilant for signs of danger, especially whenever a change of texture or hue or anything else in the surface underfoot betokened a change in its nature.

Above the highest ledge reared a cliff too sheer to scale, Iapetan gravity or no, *the fortress wall.* However, from orbit the crew had spied a gouge in the vicinity, forming a pass, doubtless plowed by a small meteorite *in the war between the gods and the magicians, when stones chanted down from the sky wrought havoc so accursed that none dared afterward rebuild.* That was an eerie climb, hemmed in by heights which glimmered in the blue twilight they cast, heaven narrowed to a belt between them where stars seemed to blaze doubly brilliant.

"There must be guards at the opening," *Kendrick says.*

"A single guard," *answers the mind-whisper of Alvarlan,* "but he is a dragon. If you did battle with him, the noise and flame would bring every warrior here upon you. Fear not. I'll slip into his burnin' brain and weave him such a dream that he'll never see you."

"The King might sense the spell," *says Ricia through him.* "Since you'll be parted from us anyway while you ride the soul of that beast, Alvarlan, I'll seek him out and distract him."

Kendrick grimaces, knowing full well what means are hers to do that. She has told him how she longs for freedom and her knight; she has also hinted that elven lovemaking transcends the human. Does she wish for a final time before her rescue? . . . Well, Ricia and Kendrick have neither plighted nor practiced single troth. Assuredly Colin Scobie had not. He jerked forth a grin and continued through the silence that had fallen on all three.

They came out on top of the glacial mass and looked around them. Scobie whistled. Garcilaso stammered, "J-J-Jesus Christ!" Broberg smote her hands together.

Below them the precipice fell to the ledges, whose sculpturing took on a wholly new, eldritch aspect, gleam and shadow, until it ended at the plain. Seen from here aloft, the curvature of the moon made toes strain downward in boots, as if to cling fast and not be spun off among the stars which surrounded, rather than shone above, its ball. The spacecraft stood minute on dark, pocked stone, like a cenotaph raised to loneliness.

Eastward the ice reached beyond an edge of sight which was much closer. ("Yonder could be the rim of the world," Garcilaso said, and *Ricia replies,* "Yes, the City is nigh to there.") Bowls of different sizes, hillocks, crags, no two of them eroded the same way, turned its otherwise level stretch into a surreal maze. An arabesque openwork ridge which stood at the explorers' goal overtopped the horizon. Everything that was illuminated lay gently aglow. Radiant though the sun was, it cast the light of only, perhaps, five thousand full Lunas upon Earth. Southward,

Saturn's great semidisc gave about one-half more Lunar shining; but in that direction, the wilderness sheened pale amber.

Scobie shook himself. "Well, shall we go?" His prosaic question jarred the others; Garcilaso frowned and Broberg winced.

She recovered. "Yes, hasten," *Ricia says*. "I am by myself once more. Are you out of the dragon, Alvarlan?"

"Aye," *the wizard informs her*. "Kendrick is safely behind a ruined palace. Tell us how best to reach you."

"You are at the time-gnawed Crown House. Before you lies the Street of the Shieldsmiths—"

Scobie's brows knitted. "It is noonday, when elves do not fare abroad," *Kendrick says* remindingly, commandingly. "I do not wish to encounter any of them. No fights, no complications. We are going to fetch you and escape, without further trouble."

Broberg and Garcilaso showed disappointment, but understood him. A game broke down when a person refused to accept something that a fellow player tried to put in. Often the narrative threads were not mended and picked up for many days. Broberg sighed.

"Follow the street to its end at a forum where a snow fountain springs," *Ricia directs*. "Cross, and continue on Aleph Zain Boulevard. You will know it by a gateway in the form of a skull with open jaws. If anywhere you see a rainbow flicker in the air, stand motionless until it has gone by, for it will be an auroral wolf . . . ."

At a low-gravity lope, the distance took some thirty minutes to cover. In the later part, the three were forced to detour by great banks of an ice so fine-grained that it slid about under their bootsoles and tried to swallow them. Several of these lay at irregular intervals around their destination.

There the travelers stood again for a time in the grip of awe.

The bowl at their feet must reach down almost to bedrock, a hundred meters, and was twice as wide. On this rim lifted the wall they had seen from the cliff, an arc fifty meters long and high, nowhere thicker than five meters, pierced by intricate scrollwork, greenly agleam where it was not translucent. It was the uppermost edge of a stratum which made serrations down the crater. Other outcrops and ravines were more dreamlike yet ... was that a unicorn's head, was that a colonnade of caryatids, was that an icicle bower. . . ? The depths were a lake of cold blue shadow.

"You have come, Kendrick, beloved!" *cries Ricia, and casts herself into his arms.*

"Quiet," *warns the sending of Alvarlan the wise.* "Rouse not our immortal enemies."

"Yes, we must get back." Scobie blinked. "Judas priest, what possessed us? Fun is fun, but we sure have come a lot farther and faster than was smart, haven't we?"

"Let us stay for a little while," Broberg pleaded. "This is such a miracle—the Elf King's Dance Hall, which the Lord of the Dance built for him—"

"Remember, if we stay we'll be caught, and your captivity may be forever." Scobie thumbed his main radio switch. "Hello, Mark? Do you read me?"

Neither Broberg nor Garcilaso made that move. They did not hear Danzig's voice: "Oh, yes! I've been hunkered over the set gnawing my knuckles. How are you?"

"All right. We're at the big hole and will be heading back as soon as I've gotten a few pictures."

"They haven't made words to tell how relieved I am. From a scientific standpoint, was it worth the risk?"

Scobie gasped. He stared before him.

"Colin?" Danzig called. "You still there?"

"Yes. Yes."

"I asked what observations of any importance you made."

"I don't know," Scobie mumbled. "I can't remember. None of it after we started climbing seems real."

"Better you return right away," Danzig said grimly. "Forget about photographs."

"Correct." Scobie addressed his companions: "Forward march."

"I can't," *Alvarlan answers.* "A wanderin' spell has caught my spirit in tendrils of smoke."

"I know where a fire dagger is kept," *Ricia says.* "I'll try to steal it."

Broberg moved ahead, as though to descend into the crater. Tiny ice grains trickled over the verge from beneath her boots. She could easily lose her footing and slide down.

"No, wait," *Kendrick shouts to her.* "No need. My spearhead is of moon alloy. It can cut—"

The glacier shuddered. The ridge cracked asunder and fell in shards. The area on which the humans stood split free and toppled into the bowl. An avalanche poured after. High-flung crystals caught sunlight, glittered prismatic in challenge to the stars, descended slowly and lay quiet.

Except for shock waves through solids, everything had happened in the absolute silence of space.

Heartbeat by heartbeat, Scobie crawled back to his senses. He found himself held down, immobilized, in darkness and pain. His armor had saved, was still saving his life; he had been stunned but escaped a real concussion. Yet every breath hurt abominably. A rib or two on the left side seemed broken; a monstrous impact must have dented metal. And he was buried under more weight than he could move.

"Hello," he coughed. "Does anybody read me?" The single reply was the throb of his blood. If his radio still worked—which it should, being built into the suit—the mass around him screened him off.

It also sucked heat at an unknown but appalling rate. He felt no cold because the electrical system drew energy from his fuel cell as fast as needed to keep him warm and to recycle his air chemically. As a normal thing, when he lost heat through the slow process of radiation—and, a trifle, through kerofoam-lined bootsoles—the latter demand was much the greater. Now conduction was at work on every square centimeter. He had a spare unit in the equipment on his back, but no means of getting at it.

Unless— He barked forth a chuckle. Straining, he felt the stuff that entombed him yield the least bit under the pressure of arms and legs. And his helmet rang slightly with noise, a rustle, a gurgle. This wasn't water ice that imprisoned him, but stuff with a much lower freezing point. He was melting it, subliming it, making room for himself.

If he lay passive, he would sink, while frozenness above slid down to keep him in his grave. He might evoke superb new formations, but he would not see them. Instead, he must use the small capability given him to work his way upward, scrabble, get a purchase on matter that was not yet aflow, burrow to the stars.

He began.

Agony soon racked him, breath rasped in and out of lungs aflame, strength drained away and trembling took its place, he could not tell whether he ascended or slipped back. Blind, half suffocated, Scobie made mole-claws of his hands and dug.

It was too much to endure. He fled from it—

His strong enchantments failing, the Elf King brought down his towers of fear in wreck. If the spirit of Alvarlan returned to its body, the wizard would brood upon things he had seen, and understand what they meant, and such knowledge would give mortals a terrible power against Faerie. Waking from sleep, the King scryed Kendrick about to release that fetch. There was no time to do more than break the spell which upheld the Dance Hall. It was largely built of mist and starshine, but enough blocks quarried from the cold side of Ginnungagap were in it that when they crashed they should kill the knight. Ricia would perish too, and in his quicksilver intellect the King regretted that. Nevertheless he spoke the necessary word.

He did not comprehend how much abuse flesh and bone can bear. Sir Kendrick fights his way clear of the ruins, to seek and save his lady. While he does, he heartens himself with thoughts of adventures past and future—

—and suddenly the blindness broke apart and Saturn stood lambent within rings.

Scobie belly-flopped onto the surface and lay shuddering.

He must rise, no matter how his injuries screamed, lest he melt himself a new burial place. He lurched to his feet and glared around.

Little but outcroppings and scars was left of the sculpture. For the most part, the crater had become a smooth-sided whiteness under heaven. Scarcity of shadows made distances hard to gauge, but Scobie guessed the new depth as about seventy-five meters. And empty, empty.

"Mark, do you hear?" he cried.

"That you, Colin?" rang in his earpieces. "Name of mercy, what's happened? I heard you call out, and saw a cloud rise and sink . . . then nothing for more than an hour. Are you okay?"

"I am, sort of. I don't see Jean or Luis. A landslide took us by surprise and buried us. Hold on while I search."

When he stood upright, Scobie's ribs hurt less. He could move about rather handily if he took care. The two types of standard analgesic in his kit were alike useless, one too weak to give noticeable relief, one so strong that it would turn him sluggish. Casting to and fro, he soon found what he expected, a concavity in the tumbled snowlike material, slightly aboil.

Also a standard part of his gear was a trenching tool. Scobie set pain aside and dug. A helmet appeared. Broberg's head was within it. She too had been tunneling out.

"Jean!"—"Kendrick!" She crept free and they embraced, suit to suit. "Oh, Colin."

"How are you?" rattled from him.

"Alive," she answered. "No serious harm done, I think. A lot to be said for low gravity . . . . You? Luis?" Blood was clotted in a streak beneath her nose, and a bruise on her forehead was turning purple, but she stood firmly and spoke clearly.

"I'm functional. Haven't found Luis yet. Help me look. First, though, we'd better check out our equipment."

She hugged arms around chest, as if that would do any good here. "I'm chilled," she admitted.

Scobie pointed at a telltale. "No wonder. Your fuel cell's down to its last couple of ergs. Mine isn't in a lot better shape. Let's change."

They didn't waste time removing their backpacks, but reached into each other's. Tossing the spent units to the ground, where vapors and holes immediately appeared and then froze, they plugged the fresh ones into their suits. "Turn your thermostat down," Scobie advised. "We won't find shelter soon. Physical activity will help us keep warm."

"And require faster air recycling," Broberg reminded.

"Yeah. But for the moment, at least, we can conserve the energy in the cells. Okay, next let's check for strains, potential leaks, any kind of damage or loss. Hurry. Luis is still down underneath."

Inspection was a routine made automatic by years of drill. While her fingers searched across the man's spacesuit, Broberg let her eyes wander. "The Dance Hall is gone," *Ricia murmurs*. "I think the King smashed it to prevent our escape."

"Me too. If he finds out we're alive, and seeking for Alvarlan's soul—Hey, wait! None of that!"

Danzig's voice quavered. "How're you doing?"

"We're in fair shape, seems like," Scobie replied. "My corselet took a beating but didn't split or anything. Now to find Luis . . . Jean, suppose you spiral right, I left, across the crater floor."

It took a while, for the seething which marked Garcilaso's burial was minuscule. Scobie started to dig. Broberg watched how he moved, heard how he breathed, and said, "Give me that tool. Just where are you bunged up, anyway?"

He admitted his condition and stepped back. Crusty chunks flew from her toil. She progressed fast, since whatever kind of ice lay at this point was, luckily, friable, and under Iapetan gravity she could cut a hole with almost vertical sides.

"I'll make myself useful," Scobie said, "namely, find us a way out."

When he started up the nearest slope, it shivered. All at once he was borne back in a tide that made rustly noises through his armor, while a fog of dry white motes blinded him. Painfully, he scratched himself free at the bottom and tried elsewhere. In the end he could report to Danzig: "I'm afraid there is no easy route. When the rim collapsed where we stood, it did more than produce a shock which wrecked the delicate formations throughout the crater. It let tons of stuff pour down from the surface—a particular sort of ice that, under local conditions, is like fine sand. The walls are covered by it. Most places, it lies meters deep over more stable material. We'd slide faster than we could climb, where the layer is thin; where it's thick, we'd sink."

Danzig sighed. "I guess I get to take a nice, healthy hike."

"I assume you've called for help."

"Of course. They'll have two boats here in about a hundred hours. The best they can manage. You knew that already."

"Uh-huh. And our fuel cells are good for perhaps fifty hours."

"Oh, well, not to worry about that. I'll bring extras and toss them to you, if you're stuck till the rescue party arrives. M-m-m . . . maybe I'd better rig a slingshot or something first."

"You might have a problem locating us. This isn't a true crater, it's a glorified pothole, the lip of it flush with the top of the glacier. The landmark we guided ourselves by, that fancy ridge, is gone."

"No big deal. I've got a bearing on you from the directional antenna, remember. A magnetic compass may be no use here, but I can keep myself oriented by the heavens. Saturn scarcely moves in this sky, and the sun and the stars don't move fast."

"Damn! You're right. I wasn't thinking. Got Luis on my mind, if nothing else." Scobie looked across bleakness toward Broberg. Perforce she was taking a short rest, stoop-shouldered above her excavation. His earpieces brought him the harsh sound in her windpipe.

He must maintain what strength was left him, against later need. He sipped from his water nipple, pushed a bite of food through his chow-lock, pretended an appetite. "I may as well try reconstructing what happened," he said. "Okay, Mark, you were right, we got crazy reckless. The game—Eight years was too long to play the game, in an environment that gave us too few reminders of reality. But who could have foreseen it? My God, warn *Chronos!* I happen to know that one of the Titan teams started playing an expedition to the merfolk under the Crimson Ocean—on account of the red mists—deliberately, like us, before they set off . . . ."

Scobie gulped. "Well," he slogged on, "I don't suppose we'll ever know exactly what went wrong here. But plain to see, the configuration was only metastable. On Earth, too, avalanches can be fatally easy to touch off. I'd guess at a methane layer underneath the surface. It turned a little slushy when temperatures rose after dawn, but that didn't matter in low gravity and vacuum . . . till we came along. Heat, vibration—Anyhow, the stratum slid out from under us, which triggered a general collapse. Does that guess seem reasonable?"

"Yes, to an amateur like me," Danzig said. "I admire how you can stay academic under these circumstances."

"I'm being practical," Scobie retorted. "Luis may need medical attention earlier than those boats can come for him. If so, how do we get him to ours?"

Danzig's voice turned stark. "Any ideas?"

"I'm fumbling my way toward that. Look, the bowl still has the same basic form. The whole shebang didn't cave in. That implies hard material, water ice and actual rock. In fact, I see a few remaining promontories, jutting out above the sandlike stuff. As for what *it* is—maybe an ammonia-carbon dioxide combination, maybe more exotic—that'll be for you to discover later.

Right now . . . my geological instruments should help me trace where the solid masses are least deeply covered. We all carry trenching tools, of course. We can try to shovel a path clear, along a zigzag of least effort. Sure, that may well often bring more garbage slipping down on us from above, but that in turn may expedite our progress. Where the uncovered shelves are too steep or slippery to climb, we can chip footholds. Slow and tough work; and we may run into a bluff higher than we can jump, or something like that."

"I can help," Danzig proposed. "While I waited to hear from you, I inventoried our stock of spare cable, cord, equipment I can cannibalize for wire, clothes and bedding I can cut into strips, whatever might be knotted together to make a rope. We won't need much tensile strength. Well, I estimate I can get about forty meters. According to your description, that's about half the slope length of that trap you're in. If you can climb halfway up while I trek there, I can haul you the rest of the way."

"Thanks," Scobie said, "although—"

"Luis!" shrieked in his helmet. "Colin, come fast, help me, this is dreadful!"

Regardless of pain, except for a curse or two, Scobie sped to Broberg's aid.

Garcilaso was not quite unconscious. In that lay much of the horror. They heard him mumble, "—Hell, the King threw my soul into Hell, I can't find my way out, I'm lost, if only Hell weren't so cold—" They could not see his face; the inside of his helmet was crusted with frost. Deeper and longer buried than the others, badly hurt in addition, he would have died shortly after his fuel cell was exhausted. Broberg had uncovered him barely in time, if that.

Crouched in the shaft she had dug, she rolled

him over onto his belly. His limbs flopped about and he babbled, "A demon attacks me, I'm blind here but I feel the wind of its wings," in a blurred monotone. She unplugged the energy unit and tossed it aloft, saying, "We should return this to the ship if we can." Not uncommonly do trivial details serve as crutches.

Above, Scobie gave the object a morbid stare. It didn't even retain the warmth to make a little vapor, like his and hers, but lay quite inert. Its case was a metal box, thirty centimeters by fifteen by six, featureless except for two plug-in prongs on one of the broad sides. Controls built into the spacesuit circuits allowed you to start and stop the chemical reactions within and regulate their rate manually; but as a rule you left that chore to your thermostat and aerostat. Now those reactions had run their course. Until it was recharged, the cell was merely a lump.

Scobie leaned over to watch Broberg, some ten meters below him. She had extracted the reserve unit from Garcilaso's gear, inserted it properly at the small of his back, and secured it by clips on the bottom of his packframe. "Let's have your contribution, Colin," she said. Scobie dropped the meter of heavy-gauge insulated wire which was standard issue on extravehicular missions, in case you needed to make a special electrical connection or a repair. She joined it by Western Union splices to the two she already had, made a loop at the end and, awkwardly reaching over her left shoulder, secured the opposite end by a hitch to the top of her packframe. The triple strand bobbled above her like an antenna.

Stooping, she gathered Garcilaso in her arms. The Iapetan weight of him and his apparatus was under ten kilos, of her and hers about the same. Theoretically she could jump straight out of the hole with her burden. In practice, her spacesuit was too hampering; constant-volume joints allowed considerable freedom of movement, but not as much as bare skin, especially when circum-Saturnian temperatures required extra insulation. Besides, if she could have reached the top, she could not have stayed. Soft ice would have crumbled beneath her fingers and she would have tumbled back down.

"Here goes," she said. "This had better be right the first time, Colin. I don't think Luis can take much jouncing."

"Kendrick, Ricia, where are you?" Garcilaso moaned. "Are you in Hell too?"

Scobie dug heels into the ground near the edge and crouched ready. The loop in the wire rose to view. His right hand grabbed hold. He threw himself backward, lest he slide forward, and felt the mass he had captured slam to a halt. Anguish exploded in his rib cage. Somehow he dragged his burden to safety before he fainted.

He came out of that in a minute. "I'm okay," he rasped at the anxious voices of Broberg and Danzig. "Only lemme rest a while."

The physicist nodded and knelt to minister to the pilot. She stripped his packframe in order that he might lie flat on it, head and legs supported by the packs themselves. That would prevent significant heat loss by convection and cut loss by conduction. Still, his fuel cell would be drained faster than if he were on his feet, and first it had a terrible energy deficit to make up.

"The ice is clearing away inside his helmet," she reported. "Merciful Mary, the blood! Seems to be from the scalp, though; it isn't running any more. His occiput must have been slammed against the vitryl. We ought to wear padded caps in these rigs. Yes, I know accidents like this haven't happened before, but—" She unclipped the flashlight at her waist, stooped, and shone it downward. "His eyes are open. The pupils—yes, a severe concussion, and likely a skull fracture, which may be hemorrhaging into the brain. I'm surprised he isn't vomiting. Did the cold prevent that? Will he start soon? He could choke on his own vomit, in there where nobody can lay a hand on him."

Scobie's pain had subsided to a bearable intensity. He rose, went over to look, whistled, and said, "I judge he's doomed unless we get him to the boat and give him proper care almighty soon. Which isn't possible."

"Oh, Luis." Tears ran silently down Broberg's cheeks.

"You think he can't last till I bring my rope and we carry him back?" Danzig asked.

"'Fraid not," Scobie replied. "I've taken paramedical courses, and in fact I've seen a case like this before. How come you know the symptoms, Jean?"

"I read a lot," she said dully.

"They weep, the dead children weep," Garcilaso muttered.

Danzig sighed. "Okay, then. I'll fly over to you."

"Huh?" burst from Scobie, and from Broberg: "Have you also gone insane?"

"No, listen," Danzig said fast. "I'm no skilled pilot, but I have the same basic training in this type of craft that everybody does who might ride in one. It's expendable; the rescue vessels can bring us back. There'd be no significant gain if I landed close to the glacier—I'd still have to make that rope and so forth—and we know from what happened to the probe that there would be a real hazard. Better I make straight for your crater."

"Coming down on a surface that the jets will vaporize out from under you?" Scobie snorted. "I bet Luis would consider that a hairy stunt. You, my friend, would crack up."

"Nu?" They could almost see the shrug. "A

crash from low altitude, in this gravity, shouldn't do more than rattle my teeth. The blast will cut a hole clear to bedrock. True, then surrounding ice will collapse in around the hull and trap it. You may need to dig to reach the airlock, though I suspect thermal radiation from the cabin will keep the upper parts of the structure free. Even if the craft topples and strikes sidewise—in which case, it'll sink down into a deflating cushion—even if it did that on bare rock, it shouldn't be seriously damaged. It's designed to withstand heavier impacts." Danzig hesitated. "Of course, could be this would endanger you. I'm confident I won't fry you with the jets, assuming I descend near the middle and you're as far offside as you can get. Maybe, though, maybe I'd cause a . . . an ice quake that'll kill you. No sense in losing two more lives."

"Or three, Mark," Broberg said low. "In spite of your brave words, you could come to grief yourself."

"Oh, well, I'm an oldish man. I'm fond of living, yes, but you guys have a whole lot more years due you. Look, suppose the worst, suppose I don't just make a messy landing but wreck the boat utterly. Then Luis dies, but he would anyway. You two, however, you should have access to the stores aboard, including those extra fuel cells. I'm willing to run what I consider to be a small risk of my own neck, for the sake of giving Luis a chance at survival."

"Um-m-m," went Scobie, deep in his throat. A hand strayed in search of his chin, while his gaze roved around the glimmer of the bowl.

"I repeat," Danzig proceeded, "if you think this might jeopardize you in any way, we scrub it. No heroics, please. Luis would surely agree, better three people safe and one dead than four stuck with a high probability of death."

"Let me think." Scobie was mute for minutes

before he said: "No, I don't believe we'd get in too much trouble here. As I remarked earlier, the vicinity has had its avalanche and must be in a reasonably stable configuration. True, ice will volatilize. In the case of deposits with low boiling points, that could happen explosively and cause tremors. But the vapor will carry heat away so fast that only material in your immediate area should change state. I daresay that the fine-grained stuff will get shaken down the slopes, but it's got too low a density to do serious harm; for the most part, it should simply act like a brief snowstorm. The floor will make adjustments, of course, which may be rather violent. However, we can be above it—do you see that shelf of rock over yonder, Jean, at jumping height? It has to be part of a buried hill; solid. That's our place to wait . . . . Okay, Mark, it's go as far as we're concerned. I can't be absolutely certain, but who ever is about anything? It seems like a good bet."

"What are we overlooking?" Broberg wondered. She glanced down to him who lay at her feet. "While we considered all the possibilities, Luis would die. Yes, fly if you want to, Mark, and God bless you."

—But when she and Scobie had brought Garcilaso to the lodge, she gestured from Saturn to Polaris and: "I will sing a spell, I will cast what small magic is mine, in aid of the Dragon Lord, that he may deliver Alvarlan's soul from Hell," *says Ricia.*

IV

No reasonable person will blame any inter-planetary explorer for miscalculations about the actual environment, especially when *some* decision has to be made, in haste and under stress. Occasional errors are inevitable. If we knew exactly what to expect throughout the Solar System, we would have no reason to explore it.

— Minamoto

The boat lifted. Cosmic dust smoked away from its jets. A hundred and fifty meters aloft, thrust lessened and it stood still on a pillar of fire.

Within the cabin was little noise, a low hiss and a bone-deep but nearly inaudible rumble. Sweat studded Danzig's features, clung glistening to his beard stubble, soaked his coverall and made it reek. He was about to undertake a maneuver as difficult as rendezvous, and without guidance.

Gingerly, he advanced a vernier. A side jet woke. The boat lurched toward a nosedive. Danzig's hands jerked across the console. He must adjust the forces that held his vessel on high and those that pushed it horizontally, to get a resultant that would carry him eastward at a slow, steady pace. The vectors would change instant by instant, as they do when a human walks. The control computer, linked to the sensors, handled much of the balancing act, but not the crucial part. He must tell it what he wanted it to do.

His handling was inexpert. He had realized it would be. More altitude would have given him more margin for error, but deprived him of cues that his eyes found on the terrain beneath and the horizon ahead. Besides, when he reached the glacier he would perforce fly low, to find his goal. He would be too busy for the precise celestial navigation he could have practiced afoot.

Seeking to correct his error, he overcompensated, and the boat pitched in a different direction. He punched for "hold steady" and the computer took over. Motionless again, he took a minute to catch his breath, regain his nerve, rehearse in his mind. Biting his lip, he tried afresh. This time he did not quite approach disaster. Jets aflicker, the boat staggered drunkenly over the moonscape.

The ice cliff loomed nearer and nearer. He saw its fragile loveliness and regretted that he must cut a swathe of ruin. Yet what did any natural wonder mean unless a conscious mind was there to know it? He passed the lowest slope. It vanished in billows of steam.

Onward. Beyond the boiling, right and left and ahead, the Faerie architecture crumbled. He crossed the palisade. Now he was a bare fifty meters above surface, and the clouds reached vengefully close before they disappeared into vacuum. He squinted through the port and made the scanner sweep a magnified overview across its screen, a search for his destination.

A white volcano erupted. The outburst engulfed him. Suddenly he was flying blind. Shocks belled through the hull when upflung stones hit. Frost sheathed the craft; the scanner screen went as blank as the ports. Danzig should have ordered ascent, but he was inexperienced. A human in danger has less of an instinct to jump than to run. He tried to scuttle sideways. Without exterior vision to aid him, he sent the vessel tumbling end over end. By the time he saw his mistake, less than a second, it was too late. He was out of control. The computer might have retrieved the situation after a while, but the glacier was too close. The boat crashed.

"Hello, Mark?" Scobie cried. "Mark, do you read me? Where are you, for Christ's sake?"

Silence replied. He gave Broberg a look which lingered. "Everything seemed to be in order," he said, "till we heard a shout, and a lot of racket, and nothing. He should've reached us by now. Instead, he's run into trouble. I hope it wasn't lethal."

"What can we do?" she asked as redundantly. They needed talk, any talk, for Garcilaso lay beside them and his delirious voice was dwindling fast.

"If we don't get fresh fuel cells within the next forty or fifty hours, we'll be at the end of our particular trail. The boat should be someplace near. We'll have to get out of this hole under our own power, seems like. Wait here with Luis and I'll scratch around for a possible route."

Scobie started downward. Broberg crouched by the pilot.

"—alone forever in the dark—" she heard.

"No, Alvarlan." She embraced him. Most likely he could not feel that, but she could. "Alvarlan, hearken to me. This is Ricia. I hear in my mind how your spirit calls. Let me help, let me lead you back to the light."

"Have a care," advised Scobie. "We're too damn close to rehypnotizing ourselves as is."

"But I might, I just might get through to Luis and . . . comfort him . . . Alvarlan, Kendrick and I escaped. He's seeking a way home for us. I'm seeking you. Alvarlan, here is my hand, come take it."

On the crater floor, Scobie shook his head, clicked his tongue, and unlimbered his equipment. Binoculars would help him locate the most promising areas. Devices that ranged from a metal rod to a portable geosonar would give him a more exact idea of what sort of footing lay buried under what depth of unclimbable sand-ice. Admittedly the scope of such probes was very limited. He did not have time to shovel tons of material aside in order that he could mount higher and test further. He would simply have to get some preliminary results, make an educated guess at which path up the side of the bowl would prove negotiable, and trust he was right.

He shut Broberg and Garcilaso out of his consciousness as much as he was able, and commenced work.

An hour later, he was ignoring pain while clearing a strip across a layer of rock. He thought a berg of good, hard frozen water lay ahead, but wanted to make sure.

"Jean! Colin! Do you read?"

Scobie straightened and stood rigid. Dimly he heard Broberg: "If I can't do anything else, Alvarlan, let me pray for your soul's repose."

"Mark!" ripped from Scobie. "You okay? What the hell happened?"

"Yeah, I wasn't too badly knocked around," Danzig said, "and the boat's habitable, though I'm afraid it'll never fly again. How are you? Luis?"

"Sinking fast. All right, let's hear the news."

Danzig described his misfortune. "I wobbled off in an unknown direction for an unknown distance. It can't have been extremely far, since the time was short before I hit. Evidently I plowed into a large, um, snowbank, which softened the impact but blocked radio transmission. It's evaporated from the cabin area now. I see tumbled whiteness around, and formations in the offing . . . . I'm not sure what damage the jacks and the stern jets suffered. The boat's on its side at about a forty-five degree angle, presumably with rock beneath. But the after part is still buried in less whiffable stuff—water and CO_2 ices, I think—that's reached temperature equilibrium. The jets must be clogged with it. If I tried to blast, I'd destroy the whole works."

Scobie nodded. "You would, for sure."

Danzig's voice broke. "Oh, God, Colin! What have I done? I wanted to help Luis, but I may have killed you and Jean."

Scobie's lips tightened. "Let's not start crying before we're hurt. True, this has been quite a run of bad luck. But neither you nor I nor anybody could have known that you'd touch off a bomb underneath yourself."

"What was it? Have you any notion? Nothing of the sort ever occurred at rendezvous with a comet. And you believe the glacier is a wrecked comet, don't you?"

"Uh-huh, except that conditions have obviously modified it. The impact produced heat, shock, turbulence. Molecules got scrambled. Plasmas must have been momentarily present. Mixtures, compounds, clathrates, alloys—stuff formed that never existed in free space. We can learn a lot of chemistry here."

"That's why I came along . . . . Well, then, I crossed a deposit of some substance or substances that the jets caused to sublime with tremendous force. A certain kind of vapor refroze when it encountered the hull. I had to defrost the ports from inside after the snow had cooked off them."

"Where are you in relation to us?"

"I told you, I don't know. And I'm not sure I can determine it. The crash crumpled the direction-finding antenna. Let me go outside for a better look."

"Do that," Scobie said. "I'll keep busy meanwhile."

He did, until a ghastly rattling noise and Broberg's wail brought him at full speed back to the rock.

Scobie switched off Garcilaso's fuel cell. "This may make the difference that carries us through," he said low. "Think of it as a gift. Thanks, Luis."

Broberg let go of the pilot and rose from her knees. She straightened the limbs that had threshed about in the death struggle and crossed his hands on his breast. There was nothing she could do about the fallen jaw or the eyes that glared at heaven. Taking him out of his suit, here, would have worsened his appearance. Nor could she wipe tears off her own face. She could merely try to stop their flow. "Goodbye, Luis," she whispered.

Turning to Scobie, she asked, "Can you give me a new job? Please."

"Come along," he directed. "I'll explain what I have in mind about making our way to the surface."

They were midway across the bowl when Danzig called. He had not let his comrade's dying slow his efforts, nor said much while it happened. Once, most softly, he had offered Kaddish.

"No luck," he reported like a machine. "I've traversed the largest circle I could while keeping the boat in sight, and found only weird, frozen shapes. I can't be a huge distance from you, or I'd see an identifiably different sky, on this miserable little ball. You're probably within a twenty or thirty kilometer radius of me. But that covers a bunch of territory."

"Right," Scobie said. "Chances are you can't find us in the time we've got. Return to the boat."

"Hey, wait," Danzig protested. "I can spiral onward, marking my trail. I might come across you."

"It'll be more useful if you return," Scobie told him. "Assuming we climb out, we should be able to hike to you, but we'll need a beacon. What occurs to me is the ice itself. A small energy release, if it's concentrated, should release a large plume of methane or something similarly volatile. The gas will cool as it expands, recondense around dust particles that have been carried along—it'll steam—and the cloud ought to get high enough, before it evaporates again, to be visible from here."

"Gotcha!" A tinge of excitement livened Danzig's words. "I'll go straight to it. Make tests, find a spot where I can get the showiest result, and . . . how about I rig a thermite bomb? . . . No, that might be too hot. Well, I'll develop a gadget."

"Keep us posted."

"But I, I don't think we'll care to chatter idly," Broberg ventured.

"No, we'll be working our tails off, you and I," Scobie agreed.

"Uh, wait," said Danzig. "What if you find you can't get clear to the top? You implied that's a distinct possibility."

"Well, then it'll be time for more radical procedures, whatever they turn out to be," Scobie responded. "Frankly, at this moment my head is too full of . . . of Luis, and of choosing an optimum escape route . . . for much thought about anything else."

"M-m, yeah, I guess we've got an ample supply of trouble without borrowing more. Tell you what, though. After my beacon's ready to fire off, I'll make that rope we talked of. You might find you prefer having it to clean clothes and sheets when you arrive." Danzig was silent for seconds before he ended: "God damn it, you *will* arrive."

Scobie chose a point on the north side for his and Broberg's attempt. Two rock shelves jutted forth, near the floor and several meters higher, indicating that stone reached at least that far. Beyond, in a staggered pattern, were similar outcrops of hard ices. Between them, and onward from the uppermost, which was scarcely more than halfway to the rim, was nothing but the featureless, footingless slope of powder crystals. Its angle of repose gave a steepness that made the surface doubly treacherous. The question, unanswerable save by experience, was how deeply it covered layers on which humans could climb, and whether such layers extended the entire distance aloft.

At the spot, Scobie signalled a halt. "Take it easy, Jean," he said. "I'll go ahead and commence digging."

"Why don't we together? I have my own tool, you know."

"Because I can't tell how so large a bank of that pseudo-quicksand will behave. It might react to the disturbance by a gigantic slide."

She bridled. Her haggard countenance registered mutiny. "Why not me first, then? Do you suppose I always wait passive for Kendrick to save me?"

"As a matter of fact," he rapped, "I'll bargain because my rib is giving me billy hell, which is eating away what strength I've got left. If we run into trouble, you can better come to my help than I to yours."

Broberg bent her neck. "Oh. I'm sorry. I must be in a fairly bad state myself, if I let false pride interfere with our business." Her look went toward Saturn, around which *Chronos* orbited, bearing her husband and children.

"You're forgiven." Scobie bunched his legs and sprang the five meters to the lower ledge. The next one was slightly too far for such a jump, when he had no room for a running start.

Stooping, he scraped his trenching tool against the bottom of the declivity that sparkled before him, and shoveled. Grains poured from above, a billionfold, to cover what he cleared. He worked like a robot possssed. Each spadeful was nearly weightless, but the number of spadefuls was nearly endless. He did not bring the entire bowlside down on himself as he had half feared, half hoped. (If that didn't kill him, it would save a lot of toil.) A dry torrent went right and left over his ankles. Yet at last somewhat more of the underlying rock began to show.

From beneath, Broberg listened to him breathe. It sounded rough, often broken by a gasp or a curse. In his spacesuit, in the raw, wan sunshine, he resembled a knight who, in despite of wounds, did battle against a monster.

"All right," he called at last. "I think I've learned what to expect and how we should operate. It'll take the two of us."

"Yes . . . oh, yes, my Kendrick."

The hours passed. Ever so slowly, the sun climbed and the stars wheeled and Saturn waned.

Most places, the humans labored side by side. They did not require more than the narrowest of lanes—but unless they cut it wide to begin with, the banks to right and left would promptly slip down and bury it. Sometimes the conformation underneath allowed a single person at a time to work. Then the other could rest. Soon it was Scobie who must oftenest take advantage of that. Sometimes they both stopped briefly, for food and drink and reclining on their packs.

Rock yielded to water ice. Where this rose very sharply, the couple knew it, because the sand-ice that they undercut would come down in a mass. After the first such incident, when they were nearly swept away, Scobie always drove his geologist's hammer into each new stratum. At any sign of danger, he would seize its handle and Broberg would cast an arm around his waist. Their other hands clutched their trenching tools. Anchored, but forced to strain every muscle, they would stand while the flood poured around them, knee-high, once even chest-high, seeking to bury them irretrievably deep in its quasi-fluid substance. Afterward they would confront a bare stretch. It was generally too steep to climb unaided, and they chipped footholds.

Weariness was another tide to which they dared not yield. At best, their progress was dismayingly slow. They needed little heat input to keep warm, except when they took a rest, but their lungs put a furious demand on air recyclers. Garcilaso's fuel cell, which they had brought along, could give a single person extra hours of life, though depleted as it was after coping with his hypothermia, the time would be insufficient for rescue by the teams from *Chronos*. Unspoken was the idea of taking turns with it. That would put them in wretched shape, chilled and stifling, but at least they would leave the universe together.

Thus it was hardly a surprise that their minds fled from pain, soreness, exhaustion, stench, despair. Without that respite, they could not have gone on as long as they did.

At ease for a few minutes, their backs against a blue-shimmering parapet which they must scale, they gazed across the bowl, where Garcilaso's suited body gleamed like a remote pyre, and up the curve opposite to Saturn. The planet shone lambent amber, softly banded, the rings a coronet which a shadow band across their arc seemed to make all the brighter. That radiance overcame sight of most nearby stars, but elsewhere they arrayed themselves multitudinous, in splendor, around the silver road which the galaxy clove between them.

"How right a tomb for Alvarlan," *Ricia says in a dreamer's murmur.*

"Has he died, then?" *Kendrick asks.*

"You do not know?"

"I have been too busied. After we won free of the ruins and I left you to recover while I went scouting, I encountered a troop of warriors. I escaped, but must needs return to you by devious, hidden ways." *Kendrick strokes Ricia's sunny hair.* "Besides, dearest dear, it has ever been you, not I, who had the gift of hearing spirits."

"Brave darling . . . . Yes, it is a glory to me that I was able to call his soul out of Hell. It sought his body, but that was old and frail and could not survive the knowledge it now had. Yet Alvarlan passed peacefully, and before he did, for his last magic he made himself a tomb from whose ceiling starlight will eternally shine."

"May he sleep well. But for us there is no sleep. Not yet. We have far to travel."

"Aye. But already we have left the wreckage behind. Look! Everywhere around in this meadow, anemones peep through the grass. A lark sings above."

"These lands are not always calm. We may well have more adventures ahead of us. But we shall meet them with high hearts."

Kendrick and Ricia rise to continue their journey.

Cramped on a meager ledge, Scobie and Broberg shoveled for an hour without broadening it much. The sand-ice slid from above as fast as they could cast to down. "We'd better quit this as a bad job," the man finally decided. "The best we've done is flatten the slope ahead of us a tiny bit. No telling how far inward the shelf goes before there's a solid layer on top. Maybe there isn't any."

"What shall we do instead?" Broberg asked in the same worn tone.

He jerked a thumb. "Scramble back to the level beneath and try a different direction. But first we absolutely require a break."

They spread kerofoam pads and sat. After a while during which they merely stared, stunned by fatigue, Broberg spoke.

"I go to the brook," *Ricia relates.* "It chimes under arches of green boughs. Light falls between them to sparkle on it. I kneel and drink. The water is cold, pure, sweet. When I raise my eyes, I see the figure of a young woman, naked, her tresses the color of leaves. A wood nymph. She smiles."

"Yes, I see her too," *Kendrick joins in.* "I approach carefully, not to frighten her off. She asks our names and errands. We explain that we are lost. She tells us how to find an oracle which may give us counsel."

They depart to find it.

Flesh could no longer stave off sleep. "Give us a yell in an hour, will you, Mark?" Scobie requested.

"Sure," Danzig said, "but will that be enough?"

"It's the most we can afford, after the setbacks we've had. We've come less than a third of the way."

"If I haven't talked to you," Danzig said slowly, "it's not because I've been hard at work, though I have been. It's that I figured you two were having a plenty bad time without me nagging you. However—Do you think it's wise to fantasize the way you have been?"

A flush crept across Broberg's cheeks and down toward her bosom. "You listened, Mark?"

"Well, yes, of course. You might have an urgent word for me at any minute."

"Why? What could you do? A game is a personal affair."

"Uh, yes, yes—"

Ricia and Kendrick have made love whenever they can. The accounts were never explicit, but the words were often passionate.

"We'll keep you tuned in when we need you, like for an alarm clock," Broberg clipped. "Otherwise we'll cut the circuit."

"But—Look, I never meant to—"

"I know," Scobie sighed. "You're a nice guy and I daresay we're overreacting. Still, that's the way it's got to be. Call us when I told you."

*Deep within the grotto, the Pythoness sways on
her throne, in the ebb and flow of her oracular
dream. As nearly as Ricia and Kendrick can understand what she chants, she tells them to fare west-
ward on the Stag Path until they met a one-eyed
graybeard who will give them further guidance;
but they must be wary in his presence, for he is
easily angered. They make obeisance and depart.
On their way out, they pass the offering they
brought. Since they have little with them other
than garments and his weapons, the Princess gave
the shrine her golden hair. The knight insists that,
close-cropped, she remains beautiful.*

"Hey, whoops, we've cleared us an easy twenty
meters," Scobie said, albeit in a voice which
weariness had hammered flat. *At first the journey,
through the land of Narce, is a delight.*

His oath afterward had no more life in it.
"Another blind alley, seems like." *The old man in
the blue cloak and wide-brimmed hat was indeed
wrathful when Ricia refused him her favors and
Kendrick's spear struck his own aside. Cunningly,
he has pretended to make peace and told them
what road they should take next. But at the end of
it are trolls. The wayfarers elude them and double
back.*

"My brain's stumbling around in a swamp, a
fog," Scobie groaned. "My busted rib isn't exactly
helping, either. If I don't get another nap I'll keep
on making misjudgments till we run out of time."

"By all means, Colin," Broberg said. "I'll stand
watch and rouse you in an hour."

"What?" he asked in dim surprise. "Why not
join me and have Mark call us as he did before?"

She grimaced. "No need to bother him. I'm
tired, yes, but not sleepy."

He lacked wit or strength to argue. "Okay," he said, stretched his insulating pad on the ice, and toppled out of awareness.

Broberg settled herself next to him. They were halfway to the heights, but they had been struggling, with occasional breaks, for worse than twenty hours, and progress grew more hard and tricky even as they themselves grew more weak and stupefied. If ever they reached the top and spied Danzig's signal, they would have something like a couple of hours' stiff travel to shelter.

Saturn, sun, stars shone through vitryl. Broberg smiled down at Scobie's face. He was no Greek god, and sweat, grime, unshavenness, the manifold marks of exhaustion were upon him, but—For that matter, she was scarcely an image of glamour herself.

Princess Ricia sits by her knight, where he slumbers in the dwarf's cottage, and strums a harp the dwarf lent her before he went off to his mine, and sings a lullaby to sweeten the dreams of Kendrick. When it is done, she passes her lips lightly across his, and drifts into the same gentle sleep.

Scobie woke a piece at a time. "Ricia, beloved," *Kendrick whispers, and feels after her. He will summon her up with kisses—*

He scrambled to his feet. "Judas priest!" She lay unmoving. He heard her breath in his earplugs, before the roaring of his pulse drowned it. The sun glared farther aloft, he could see it had moved, and Saturn's crescent had thinned more, forming sharp horns at its ends. He forced his eyes toward the watch on his left wrist.

"Ten hours," he choked.

He knelt and shook his companion. "Come, for Christ's sake!" Her lashes fluttered. When she saw the horror on his visage, drowsiness fled from her.

"Oh, no," she said. "Please, no."

Scobie climbed stiffly erect and flicked his main radio switch. "Mark, do you receive?"

"Colin!" Danzig chattered. "Thank God! I was going out of my head from worry."

"You're not off that hook, my friend. We just finished a ten hour snooze."

"What? How far did you get first?"

"To about forty meters' elevation. The going looks tougher ahead than in back. I'm afraid we won't make it."

"Don't *say* that, Colin," Danzig begged.

"My fault," Broberg declared. She stood rigid, fists doubled, features a mask. Her tone was steady. "He was worn out, had to have a nap. I offered to wake him, but fell asleep myself."

"Not your fault, Jean," Scobie began.

She interrupted: "Yes. Mine. Perhaps I can make it good. Take my fuel cell. I'll still have deprived you of my help, of course, but you might survive and reach the boat anyway."

He seized her hands. They did not unclench. "If you imagine I, I could do that—"

"If you don't, we're both finished," she said unbendingly. "I'd rather go out with a clear conscience."

"And what about my conscience?" he shouted. Checking himself, he wet his lips and said fast: "Besides, you're not to blame. Sleep slugged you. If I'd been thinking, I'd have realized it was bound to do so, and contacted Mark. The fact that you didn't either shows how far gone you were yourself. And . . . you've got Tom and the kids waiting for you. Take my cell." He paused. "And my blessing."

"Shall Ricia forsake her true knight?"

"Wait, hold on, listen," Danzig called. "Look, this is terrible, but—oh, hell, excuse me, but I've got to remind you that dramatics only clutter the action. From what descriptions you've sent, I don't see how either of you can possibly proceed solo. Together, you might yet. At least you're rested—sore in the muscles, no doubt, but clearer in the head. The climb before you may prove easier than you think. Try!"

Scobie and Broberg regarded each other for a whole minute. A thawing went through her, and warmed him. Finally they smiled and embraced. "Yeah, right," he growled. "We're off. But first a bite to eat. I'm plain, old-fashioned hungry. Aren't you?" she nodded.

"That's the spirit," Danzig encouraged them. "Uh, may I make another suggestion? I am just a spectator, which is pretty hellish but does give me an overall view. Drop that game of yours."

Scobie and Broberg tautened.

"It's the real culprit," Danzig pleaded. "Weariness alone wouldn't have clouded your judgment. You'd never have cut me off, and— But weariness and shock and grief did lower your defenses to the point where the damned game took you over. You weren't yourselves when you fell asleep. You were those dream-world characters. They had no reason not to cork off!"

Broberg shook her head violently. "Mark," said Scobie, "you are correct about being a spectator. That means there are some things you don't understand. Why subject you to the torture of listening in, hour after hour? We'll call you back from time to time, naturally. Take care." He broke the circuit.

"He's wrong," Broberg insisted.

Scobie shrugged. "Right or wrong, what difference? We won't pass out again in the time we have left. The game didn't handicap us as we traveled. In fact, it helped, by making the situation feel less gruesome."

"Aye. Let us break our fast and set forth anew on our pilgrimage."

The struggle grew stiffer. "Belike the White Witch has cast a spell on this road," *says Ricia.*

"She shall not daunt us," *vows Kendrick.*

"No, never while we fare side by side, you and I, noblest of men."

A slide overcame them and swept them back a dozen meters. They lodged against a crag. After the flow had passed by, they lifted their bruised bodies and limped in search of a different approach. The place where the geologist's hammer remained was no longer accessible.

"What shattered the bridge?" *asks Ricia.*

"A giant," *answers Kendrick.* "I saw him as I fell into the river. He lunged at me, and we fought in the shallows until he fled. He bore away my sword in his thigh."

"You have your spear that Wayland forged," *Ricia says,* "and always you have my heart."

They stopped on the last small outcrop they uncovered. It proved to be not a shelf but a pinnacle of water ice. Around it glittered sand-ice, again quiescent. Ahead was a slope thirty meters in length, and then the rim, and stars. The distance might as well have been thirty light-years. Whoever tried to cross would immediately sink to an unknown depth.

There was no point in crawling back down the bared side of the pinnacle. Broberg had clung to it for an hour while she chipped niches to climb by with her knife. Scobie's condition had not allowed him to help. If they sought to return, they could easily slip, fall, and be engulfed. If they avoided that, they would never find a new path. Less than two hours' worth of energy abode in their fuel cells. Attempting to push onward while swapping Garcilaso's back and forth would be an exercise in futility.

They settled themselves, legs dangling over the abyss, and held hands and looked at Saturn and at one another.

"I do not think the orcs can burst the iron door of this tower," *Kendrick says,* "but they will besiege us until we starve to death."

"You never yielded up your hope erenow, my knight," *replies Ricia, and kisses his temple.* "Shall we search about? These walls are unutterably ancient. Who knows what relics of wizardry lie forgotten within? A pair of phoenix-feather cloaks, that will bear us laughing through the sky to our home—?"

"I fear not, my darling. Our weird is upon us." *Kendrick touches the spear that leans agleam against the battlement.* "Sad and gray will the world be without you. We can but meet our doom bravely."

"Happily, since we are together." *Ricia's gamin smile breaks forth.* "I did notice that a certain room holds a bed. Shall we try it?"

Kendrick frowns. "Rather should we seek to set our minds and souls in order."

She tugs his elbow. "Later, yes. Besides—who knows?—when we dust off the blanket, we may find it is a Tarnkappe that will take us invisible through the enemy."

"You dream."

Fear stirs behind her eyes. "What if I do?" *Her words tremble.* "I can dream us free if you will help."

Scobie's fist smote the ice. "No!" he croaked. "I'll die in the world that is."

Ricia shrinks from him. He sees terror invade her. "You, you rave, beloved," *she stammers.*

He twisted about and caught her by the arms. "Don't you want to remember Tom and your boys?"

"Who—?"

Kendrick slumps. "I don't know. I have forgotten too."

She leans against him, there on the windy height. A hawk circles above. "The residuum of an evil enchantment, surely. Oh, my heart, my life, cast it from you! Help me find the means to save us." *Yet her entreaty is uneven, and through it speaks dread.*

Kendrick straightens. He lays hand on Wayland's spear, and it is though strength flows thence, into him. "A spell in truth," *he says. His tone gathers force.* "I will not abide in its darkness, nor suffer it to blind and deafen you, my lady in domnei." *His gaze takes hold of hers, which cannot break away.* "There is but a single road to our freedom. It goes through the gates of death."·

She waits, mute and shuddering.

"Whatever we do, we must die, Ricia. Let us fare hence as our own folk."

"I—no—I won't—I will—"

"You see before you the means of your deliverance. It is sharp, I am strong, you will feel no pain."

She bares her bosom. "Then quickly, Kendrick, before I am lost!"

He drives the weapon home. "I love you," *he says. She sinks at his feet.* "I follow you, my darling," *he says, withdraws the steel, braces shaft against stone, lunges forward, falls beside her.* "Now we are free."

"That was . . . a nightmare." Broberg sounded barely awake.

Scobie's voice shook. "Necessary, I think, for both of us." He gazed straight before him, letting Saturn fill his eyes with dazzle. "Else we'd have stayed . . . insane? Maybe not, by definition. But we'd not have been in reality either."

"It would have been easier," she mumbled.

"We'd never have known we were dying."

"Would you have preferred that?"

Broberg shivered. The slackness in her countenance gave place to the same tension that was in his. "Oh, no," she said, quite softly but in the manner of full consciousness. "No, you were right, of course. Thank you for your courage."

"You've always had as much guts as anybody, Jean. You just have more imagination than me." Scobie's hand chopped empty space, a gesture of dismissal. "Okay, we should call poor Mark and let him know. But first—" His words lost the cadence he had laid on them. "First—"

Her glove clasped his. "What, Colin?"

"Let's decide about that third unit, Luis'," he said with difficulty, still confronting the great ringed planet. "Your decision, actually, though we can discuss the matter if you want. I will not hog it for the sake of a few more hours. Nor will I share it; that would be a nasty way for us both to go out. However, I suggest you use it."

"To sit beside your frozen corpse?" she replied. "No. I wouldn't even feel the warmth, not in my bones—"

She turned toward him so fast that she nearly fell off the pinnacle. He caught her. *"Warmth!"* she screamed, shrill as the cry of a hawk on the wing. "Colin, we'll take our bones home!"

"In point of fact," said Danzig, "I've climbed onto the hull. That's high enough for me to see over those ridges and needles. I've got a view of the entire horizon."

"Good," grunted Scobie. "Be prepared to survey a complete circle quick. This depends on a lot of factors we can't predict. The beacon will certainly not be anything like as big as what you had arranged. It may be thin and short-lived. And, of course, it may rise too low for sighting at your distance." He cleared his throat. "In that case, we two have bought the farm. But we'll have made a hell of a try, which feels great by itself."

He hefted the fuel cell, Garcilaso's gift. A piece of heavy wire, insulation stripped off, joined the prongs. Without a regulator, the unit poured its maximum power through the short circuit. Already the strand glowed.

"Are you sure you don't want me to do it, Colin?" Broberg asked. "Your rib—"

He made a lopsided grin. "I'm nonetheless better designed by nature for throwing things," he said. "Allow me that much male arrogance. The bright idea was yours."

"It should have been obvious from the first," she said. "I think it would have been, if we weren't bewildered in our dream."

"M-m, often the simple answers are the hardest to find. Besides, we had to get this far or it wouldn't have worked, and the game helped mightily . . . . Are you set, Mark? Heave ho!"

Scobie cast the cell as if it were a baseball, hard and far through the Iapetan gravity field. Spinning, its incandescent wire wove a sorcerous web across vision. It landed somewhere beyond the rim, on the glacier's back.

Frozen gases vaporized, whirled aloft, briefly recondensed before they were lost. A geyser stood white against the stars.

"I see you! Danzig yelped. "I see your beacon, I've got my bearing, I'll be on my way! With rope and extra energy units and everything!"

Scobie sagged to the ground and clutched at his left side. Broberg knelt and held him, as if either of them could lay hand on his pain. No large matter. He would not hurt much longer.

"How high would you guess the plume goes?" Danzig inquired, calmer.

"About a hundred meters," Broberg replied after study.

"Uh, damn, these gloves do make it awkward

punching the calculator . . . . Well, to judge by what I observe of it, I'm between ten and fifteen klicks off. Give me an hour or a tadge more to get there and find your exact location. Okay?"

Broberg checked gauges. "Yes, by a hair. We'll turn our thermostats down and sit very quiet to reduce oxygen demand. We'll get cold, but we'll survive."

"I may be quicker," Danzig said. "That was a worst case estimate. All right, I'm off. No more conversation till we meet. I won't take any foolish chances, but I will need my wind for making speed.'

Faintly, those who waited heard him breathe, heard his hastening footfalls. The geyser died.

They sat, arms around waists, and regarded the glory which encompassed them. After a silence, the man said: "Well, I suppose this means the end of the game. For everybody."

"It must certainly be brought under strict control," the woman answered. "I wonder, though, if they will abandon it altogether—out here."

"If they must, they can."

"Yes. We did, you and I, didn't we?"

They turned face to face, beneath that star-be-swarmed, Saturn-ruled sky. Nothing tempered the sunlight that revealed them to each other, she a middle-aged wife, he a man ordinary except for his aloneness. They would never play again. They could not.

A puzzled compassion was in her smile. "Dear Friend—" she began.

His uplifted palm warded her from further speech. "Best we don't talk unless it's essential," he said. "That'll save a little oxygen, and we can stay a little warmer. Shall we try if we can sleep?"

Her eyes widened and darkened. "I dare not," she confessed. "Not till enough time has gone past. Now, I might dream."

THE BITTER BREAD

I

Seven years have gone since last we on Earth had news of *Uriel* in heaven, and I do not think we ever shall again. Whether they died or triumphed or their wild hunt still runs between the stars, yon crew has eternally left us. Should they after all return, it will surely be only briefly, with word and image for mankind and maybe, maybe a smile recorded for me.

That smile must then travel here, first in a shipboard tape, then in a code beamed through the sky, the censor, the global comweb to my house on Hoy. I shall never more see space. Three years ago the directors required me to retire. I am not unhappy. Steep red and yellow cliffs, sea green in sunlight or gray under clouds until it breaks in whiteness and thunder, gulls riding a cold loud wind, inland the heather and a few gnarly trees across hills where sheep still gaze, a hamlet of rough and gentle Orkney folk an hour's walk away, my cat, my books, my rememberings—these things are good. They are well worth being often chilled, damp, a wee bit hungry. It may even be for the best that the weather seldom gives me a clear look at the stars.

Also, eccentric though I was to spend my savings on this place, rather than enter a Church lodge for senior spacemen, nobody will trouble to come here and examine my scribblings. Are they found after I am dead, they should not hurt my

sons in their own careers. For one thing, I have
always been openly kittle. The Protectorate must
needs allow, yes, expect a measure of oddness
among its top-rank technos. Of course, my papers
would be deemed subversive and whiffed. So I put
them each night in a box under a flagstone I have
loosened, wondering if some archeologist
someday may read them . . . and smile?

In the main, though, you archeologist, I write
for myself, to bring back years and loves: today,
Daphne.

When she sought me out, I had lately been ap-
pointed head of the *Uriel* relief mission. To
organize this, I had taken an office in New
Jerusalem, high up in Armstrong Center where my
view swept across city roofs and towers, on over
the Cimarron to the wheat-bronze Kansas plain
beyond. That day was hard, hot, cloudless. The
cross on the topmost spire of the Supreme Church
blazed as if its gold had gone incandescent, and
flitfighters on guard above the armored bulk of
the Capitol gleamed like dragonflies. Though the
room was air-conditioned, I could almost feel the
weather beyond my window, a seethe or crackle
amongst steady murmurs of traffic.

My intercom announced, "Mrs. Asklund, sir." I
muttered a heartfelt "Damn!" and laid down the
manifest I'd been working on. I'd forgotten that,
somehow, the wife of *Uriel*'s navigator had
obtained a personal appointment. Hadn't I
overmuch to do, in ghastly short time, without
soothing distraught females? Eidophone
conversations with two other crewmen's wives
had been difficult—when at least they were
accepting God's will in Christian fortitude, and
wanted only to ask about sending messages or
gifts to the men they would never remeet in his
life. "Aweel, remind her I've but a few minutes to

spill, and let her in," I ordered.

Then Daphne came through the door, and everything was suddenly a bright surprise.

She was tall. A gown of standard dark modesty did not hide a fine figure. The skirt swished around her ankles with the sea-wind vigor of her stride. Green-eyed, curve-nosed, full-mouthed, framed in coils of mahogany hair, her face wasn't pretty, it was beautiful. I saw there not sorrow but determination. When she stopped before my desk, folded her hands and bowed her head above them to me, the salutation had scant meekness. Yet her voice was low and mild, the English bearing a slight accent: "Captain Sinclair, I am Daphne Asklund. You are kind to receive me."

We both knew I did so because she had pulled wires. However, I could say no less than, "Please sit down, sister. I'd call this a pleasure were the occasion not sad. How can I be of help to you?"

She settled herself and spent a few seconds studying my grizzle-topped lankiness, almost like a friendly challenge, before she curved her lips upward a very little and answered, "You can hear me out, sir. What I'll propose isn't quite as fantastic as it will sound."

"The whole business is fantastic." I leaned back in my own chair and reached for my pipe. "Uh, I do sympathize. I'm affected too. Matthew King was my classmate at the Academy, and we were always close friends afterward."

"But you don't know Valdemar?"

"Your husband? Not really, I fear. The Astronautic Corps is small enough that we have occasionally been at the same conference or the same refresher training session; but it's big enough that we didn't get truly acquainted. He did . . . does impress me well, Mrs. Asklund."

"*Uriel*'s skipper is your friend. Its navigator is my husband. I hope you can imagine the difference," she said: no hint of self-pity, simply remarking on a fact.

I am not sure why, already then, I let go my reserve and told her, "Yes. My wife died only last year."

Her look softened. "I'm sorry. My aplogies, Captain Sinclair. I've been too snarled in my personal troubles to—Well." She straightened. "Val is not departed, though. He . . . they all face years, decades of . . . endless trial." Exile, imprisoned in a metal shell ahurtle among the stars— perhaps at last madness, murder, horror beyond guessing, till a lone man squatted among dead bones—she did not mention these things either.

I gathered myself to speak bluntly. "We'll do what we can for them. That's the duty I'm on, and you will forgive me if it leaves scant attention to spare for anybody Earthbound. I—I am told clergy are counseling the wives to—Well, they expect the Pastorate will soon permit, aye, encourage dissolution of any unions involved, and the ladies be free to remarry. Has not your minister spoken to you of this?"

She met my plainness with hers. "No. I am not a Christian. My maiden name was Greenbaum."

"What?"

"I'm not a good Jewess either, I admit. Haven't been to temple in years—that would have handicapped Val too much, professionally—but I could never bring myself to convert. Nor did he want me to." She left tacit the obvious, that his faith was probably mostly on his lips. Reading history, I have seen how tolerance has grown in the World Protectorate since its early days after the Armageddon War. But the time will be long yet before a professed non-Christian, not to mention an outright unbeliever, gets a spaceman's berth.

Daphne Asklund's background did help explain why her husband was aboard *Uriel*. The Corps doesn't exactly have a policy of giving its deviant members the most hazardous assignments. But they tend to volunteer for these, in the hope of advancement despite their social disadvantages or for deeper personality reasons. And then the tendency is to choose them from among qualified applicants, in compassion or a silent hope they may be more original and resourceful than average, or (I suppose) now and again a less honorable motive. Matt King, for instance, when young and foolish, had fathered a bastard. Or—I, commanding the relief mission, did not belong to the Absolute Christian Church but to a remnant of the old Kirk of Scotland; and kinfolk of mine, before I was born, were involved in the European Insurrection.

"Well," I said. "Well." My pipe and tobacco busied my hands. "Best we come to business. What do you want of me that lower echelons can't arrange for you? And why this visit, instead of a message or a phone call?"

"Only you can give me what I am after," she replied, "and you would not do it for a stranger. I don't expect you to say yes the first time."

You take for granted there will be more times, I thought. "Go on."

She drew breath. "Let me first describe myself. I hold full North American citizenship"—which had opened the ears of men who could grant access to me, a client national—"but was born and raised in Caribbea. My father was stationed there as an engineer for the Oceanic Power Authority. I grew up swimming, diving, sailing, hiking; or we'd hop to the Andes and mountaineer. I still do such things—did, with Val. My father got me entry to the University of Mexico, where I took a degree in microbiotics. Afterward I was an assistant to Sancho Dominguez—yes, I helped him develop his improvements in balanced life-support systems for spacecraft. That was how I met Val. He was on the team that tested them, and came to the laboratory for conferences. After we married, I had to resign my job—you know how spacemen get moved around, also on Earth—but Dr. Dominguez keeps me on retainer as a consultant and has called me in on several problems. That's the main reason we put off having children, social stigma be damned."

An oath on a woman's tongue seemed not altogether wrong: when tears glimmered forth on her eyelashes. Did the golden cross throw too harsh a light, or had she all at once felt that now they would have no children ever? She blinked, lifted her head, and went on defiantly:

"A peculiar life, hasn't it been? Almost like a female's before Armageddon." She flushed, though her tone stayed crisp. "Except for their moral looseness, of course. But please understand, sir—check me out later on—in spite of my sex, I'm athletic, used to handling emergencies, scientifically skilled, a specialist in the very thing your expedition is chiefly concerned with—

"Captain Sinclair, I want to go along."

It happened that our propaganda department had completed the official film on this task, and screened it that afternoon for me and my staff prior to release. I invited Daphne to join us. "Frankly, the reaction of a wife may show us changes we ought to make," I said. Hesitating: "You may prefer to wait, and watch at home when it's 'cast. They've doubtless included shots of your husband."

"Could I wish not to see those?" she answered.

On our way to the auditorium, I explained the need for a dramatic presentation. Spiritual relations were no great problem. The Church could scarcely object to an errand of mercy. A few

canons had expressed fear that men spending a
lifetime shipbound, no chaplain among them,
might fall into despair, curse God, yes, commit the
sin against nature. But unless we let them starve,
or slaughtered them, that risk must be taken. And
in truth, the temptation was their opportunity: to
smite Satan, bear witness, win sainthood.

As for temporal authorities, the Protector
himself had approved our undertaking. He had
more interest in science than Enoch IV before him
or, for that matter, David III today. Out of disaster
we could pluck a farther-ranging exploration of
the galaxy than anyone had awaited for generations. We might even find that long-sought
dream, New Eden, the planet so like a virgin Earth
that full-scale colonization is possible. Rumors
reaching me said some of the Council had warned
against that. Start men moving freely outward,
and what heresies, what libertinisms and
rebellions, might they soon spawn? However, at
present the opposition didn't appear too strong.

The public was what we must convince, at any
rate a sufficient minority. "Every special interest
protests resources going to space research instead
of it," I remarked. "You can't imagine the
pressure. I didn't myself, in spite of being in the
Corps, until I got this administrative post. The
journalistic media don't report major disputes.
That doesn't mean they don't exist."

"But if our rulers—" Hastily: "If most of the
government endorses what we do, who cares
about mobs?" she asked. I was to learn that she
didn't lack charity for the humble of Earth, save
when they threatened her man. And then her anger
blasted mainly at their ignorance. ("Can't they
listen? Why, just what's been learned out there
about repairing radiation damage should have
each soul of the millions that crater dust has
blown across, down on his knees in thanks.")

I shrugged. "The Protectorate is only total in theory. In practice, it rests as much on being the compromise maker, the broker, between nations, races, classes, faiths, as it does on military force."

"Faiths?" she half scoffed. "When it keeps an established Church?"

"Och, wait, sister. You're educated, you know the Articles. The Absolute Christian Church is recognized as advisory to the government, no more. Membership in it can't be compelled. If nothing else, that would be politically impossible. Think of your own case."

"Ye-e-es. Still, you're aware what communicancy means in practice. And everything the Church calls a sin, the Protectorate has made universally illegal, under stiff penalties."

I stared. "Do you object? Besides murder and theft Well, would you want lads and lasses free to fornicate? Your husband free to commit adultery? Or . . . forgive me . . . under his present circumstances, worse?"

Her nostrils flared. "He never would!"

"There, you see, the thought makes you indignant. Doesn't that prove you share the same moral code?"

"True," she sighed. "Mosaic principles. As internalized in me as in anybody, no doubt. I simply wonder if God wants us to shove them on others at gunpoint. Wasn't righteousness more meaningful before Armageddon, in those parts of the world where people were let choose for themselves? Where they could individually seek the truth, make their lives as they saw fit, why, it sounds trivial, but when women in particular could wear whatever they liked—Oh, never mind. Here we are, aren't we?"

I was relieved. We had been alone in the corridor, she hadn't spoken loudly, and hers weren't forbidden questions. But if a zealot had overheard, an embarrassing scene would have followed. Her chance of joining my expedition would have dropped to zero. I wasn't sure why I feared that, when I had insisted the idea was impossible.

Though the auditorium was uncrowded. Daphne sat next to me. As the room went dark and the showing started, she caught my hand and did not let go.

Our proppas had used minimum fake effects, where necessary to bridge gaps. They had ample real data to work with. Men aboard the associated vessels, *Abdiel*, *Raphael*, and *Zephon*, had taken excellent shots both before and after the catastrophe. In *Uriel* they kept cameras going too, and later transmitted what these recorded. Aimed almost at random, the lenses were cruelly honest. Our producers had not much more to do than choose sequences and add occasional explanatory narration.

I see, hear, all but feel and taste and smell the story around me now.

A thousand light-years hence, stars throng blackness, jewel-hued, icy sharp, marshalled in alien constellations. The galactic band and the clouds that cleave its silver are less changed to sight—except dead ahead, where a haze grows as the ships near, until it fills a quarter of heaven. White and flame-blue at its heart, the nebula roils outward to edges which are a lacework formed of molten rainbows.

Instruments take over, seeing and projecting what vision cannot. In the middle of that majestic chaos, two things which have been suns whirl crazily about each other. One, hardly bigger than Earth although more massive than Sol, has no light of its own, but flings back the fury of its huge companion's death. There are no words to tell of this. And yet the image is a ghost, a mathematical

construct. Men who looked straight upon the
reality would die before they knew they had been
blinded.

Narrator: "Here crews have stood watch and
watch for a score of years, ever since astronomers
predicted that the blue giant would soon explode.
Here was our chance to observe a supernova close
at hand. Who could tell what we might learn? So
little could we predict about this newest wonder
of God's, that unmanned probes by themselves
were insufficient. We could not tell what observations to program them for. Only man has the
flexibility to see the unforeseeable.

"And what about its companion, a neutron star
orbiting almost in contact? How was this
possible? It must once have undergone the same
throes, perhaps even more violent. But an outburst like that should drive the members of a pair
apart, not together.

"We think probably there was a third member,
also a giant, which blew up at about the same
former time. Itself escaping, it took such a path
that the second body was drawn close in toward
the still steadily shining first. Friction with ex-
pelled gases must have helped shorten the orbit.

"Our investigators have searched for that third
object. Its remnants cannot have traveled far, in
cosmic terms. But they must be very feebly
shining, or altogether dark, collapsed into a ball
the size of a planet. We have not found them. God
made the universe too big; let us put down our
pride."

The tone cools: "Now that the last of the trio has
erupted, the system is indeed breaking apart.
Losing immense quantities of mass, the supernova
must spiral away from the neutron star, and vice
versa, to conserve angular momentum. But
friction, again, hinders this retreat. It had scarcely
begun when *Uriel* arrived, to relieve *Zophiel* on the
regular three-month rotation plan.

"Certain persons question the sense of traveling a light-millennium, weeks at top quasispeed, for so short a season of duty. But we have no choice. The radiation around a recent supernova is too intense. Even under superdrive, a ship gets some of it, and a percentage of that comes through the heaviest shielding. Nor can the crew make accurate studies, entirely while moving faster than light. Much of their work must be done in normal state, at true velocity. Of course, then they extend magnetohydrodynamic fields well beyond the hull, control a plasma cloud, and enjoy quite effective protection. But no protection is perfect, unless it be divine. In view of propable cumulative dosage, the rule has been that three months is the maximum safe exposure time.

"In *Uriel*'s case, the period was greatly lessened."

The screen has been carrying diagrams and cartoons to clarify this physics for the layman. Next leaps forth a view from the observation bridge of a craft already on station, yes, I glimpse an officer whom I recognize, Ludwig Taube, aboard *Abdiel*. Cameras always record arrivals, to have information should misfortune occur. The scanning is Solward, whence the newcomer is expected. Those who wait will get no advance warning—what signal could outpace light?—but they have no reason to think King is off schedule, give or take a few hours. And, in a corner of the screen, see! The lean shape flashes into sight, into existence within the framework of relativity. It drifts off scene. Tracking, the camera catches and centers it. Stars appear to stream past; *Uriel* is moving swiftly across their field. Those in a cone ahead of the vessel show a flicker, their light rippled by its thrust drive as it decelerates. Taube's words: "What a hellbat of an intrinsic. I wonder why."

More drawings and narration explain: "—conservation of energy. A ship about to enter super-drive has a certain definite velocity—speed and direction—with respect to any other given object in the universe, including its destination. Crossing space with inertia nullified does not change that velocity, nor do gravitational wells affect it significantly . . . as a rule. In ordinary procedure, we try to match this so-called intrinsic to the intrinsic of the target, as closely as feasible, before staring the nonrelativistic part of our journey. Else we might have to spend too much fuel at the far end of the trip, where it can't readily be replaced. Not even the tanks of a fusion engine can carry enough for more than about five thousand kilometers per second of delta-V—that is, total velocity changes, both speedups and slowdowns, added together in the course of a mission . . . " Old hat. I noticed acutely how warm and tightly gripping was Daphne's hand.

Switch back to intership transmission. Matt King's blocky face appears, reporting to over-commander Cauldwell aboard *Zephon*. "Sorry about our excess V. I thought I had our vector well calculated."

"Don't fret," his superior smiles. "You're within acceptable limits—barely, but nevertheless within, praise God. Given the uncertainty and variability of parameters, you've done OK."

Jump to a date weeks later, Cauldwell before the board of inquiry on Earth. His features are worn and strained, a tic plagues his mouth, he speaks roughly: "Gentlemen, the guilt is mine. I should have weighed the possibility that the trouble was due to a fault developing within *Uriel*, worsening till a breakdown must occur."

"But nothing ominous had registered on their gauges en route, had it?" says the presiding officer. I know him. He is a man who, in the fear of the Lord, strives to be just. "We realize how

intricate a thing a spaceship is. The least careless-
ness in maintenance can plant the seed of a
terrible surprise."

"Father, forgive me," Cauldwell groans toward
the infinite. "I should have thought seriously
about that and ordered them straight home."

"Thus canceling their scientific projects:
forever, because the stellar system would not have
remained long in that particular state," declares
the president. "No, Admiral, your decision was
correct. Note well that King did not request an
abort, nor any of his men. Our task is to track
down whatever technician homeside was
negligent, and find out what he did wrong." Pause.
"The Pastorate will set his penance."

Narrator: "Seven men aboard *Uriel*—"

Singly, they go past us. Captain Matthew King,
commanding. Lieutenant Commander Valdemar
Asklund, navigator and first officer. Lieutenant
Jesse Smith, chief engineer. Lieutenant Blaise
Policard, second engineer and supervisor of life-
support systems. That is all the crew which one of
our marvelous wanderers needs, and each has
been taught in addition how to assist the
scientists. Those are not members of the Corps,
though naturally in fine physical shape and sent
through basic astronautical training. Nikolai
Vissarionovich Kuzmin has planned especially to
study nuclear reactions as they gutter out in the
bared kernel of the ruptured star, Ioannes
Venizelos gas and radiation dynamics in the
nebula, Sugiyama Kito the gravity waves as con-
figurations change. We see their lives, wives,
parents, children—

Daphne, and I because of her, saw Valdemar
Asklund as if he were alone.

He is a tall young man, lean, blond, narrow-
faced, crinkly-eyed, readily smiling. His grays
always seem the least bit rumpled, tunic open at

the throat and bare of the ribbon to which he is entitled for his role in the daring rescue of *Michael*.
His English carries the rise and fall of surf against
the cliffs of that fjord where he was born. He was
an indifferent student and barely got accepted
into the Corps, but thereafter did brilliantly. Yet
he is no spacegoing machine. He loves what
remains of Earth's outdoors; he reads widely, with
a special fondness for the comedies of Aristo-
phanes, Shakespeare, Holberg, and Yarbro; he
paints, plays chess and tennis, can cook a tasty
meal or mix a powerful drink (that's a minor point
against him, of course), is a genial host and sought-
after guest; influenced by his wife, he is deep into
the music of Beethoven and has been learning the
piano; he has likewise been pondering and quoting
old American writings like the Declaration of
Independence (good), though he omits the
Churchly glosses upon them (bad); he keeps a
seemingly unlimited supply of jokes for both stag
gatherings and polite company; the more I see, the
better I like him. And . . . those glimpses of him
and Daphne which the filmmakers were able to
dig out of this newsfile or that private album . . .
appearances, frolics, the little possessions which
turned their series of apartments into a single
home—how happy they made each other!

Return our scene to space. Vessels extrude gang
tubes, men cross between and cheerily fraternize,
the chaplain aboard *Zephon* holds a special
service for these seven who have gone weeks without hearing the Word from an ordained mouth.
But time is fleeting. Captains and scientists
confer. The four vessels will proceed in formation
to the fringes of the nebula. Thence *Uriel* will
plunge further, to conduct its first set of planned
experiments.

The little fleet glides on superdrive to the initial
goal. The three which will wait there, making dif-

ferent observations as they free-float in normal
state, are sufficiently distant from the core—a
quarter light-year—that their hulls and low-
intensity MHD fields guard personnel from harm.
Fading fast as it expands, today the burst sun
gives them hardly more heat and X-rays than they
would get in the orbit of Venus; the blast of
leptons has already gone past this region, the
baryons and ions have not yet reached it, the thin
light-haze around is mainly due to excited interstellar gas.

Uriel leaves them. The recorded transmission
includes sight of Asklund at his work. He reads off
a string of figures, then abruptly grins, his head
haloed in stars, waves, calls, "So long and
cheerio."

Daphne's nails bit blood out of my hand. I did
not stir.

Briefly back under superdrive, *Uriel* slips close,
close to the inferno before reverting to normal
state, visibility, vulnerability. From protector
nozzles gushes a cloud of plasma, which a height-
ened field wraps around the hull like a faintly
shimmering cocoon. This will ward off not only
the hurricane of charged particles, but the lethal
photons . . . most of them. Should the dose aboard
approach a safe limit, the ship will flee, faster
than light.

These events must be shown in reconstruction.
No outside lens, were any that close, could have
spied a work of man against the nebular blaze. No
message beam, were any receiver that close, could
have pierced the wild electricity around. What we
see is an impressionistic view, the craft large till it
suddenly whirls off, dwindles to sight, vanishes
amidst fire. Next, as if given the eyes of angels, we
see the greater globe white-hot and still
collapsing,the lesser burnt-out and compressed
though now ashimmer, whipping in seconds

through their orbit. And we see a dot which images *Uriel*. That dot plunges in.

Closeups: Needles abruptly aswoop across dials, numbers in screens changing too fast to follow, frantic chatter of printout; afterward men, whose resoluteness is a cage for horror.

Narrator: "Without warning, power failed. Engineers Smith and Policard could barely squeeze out the ergs to maintain radiation shielding. Nothing could be spared for either thrust or superdrive. The collapse of the MHD field for half an instant would mean death. There was nothing to do but work—find the cause of the trouble and make repairs—while *Uriel*, helpless, was hauled in like a comet by the gravity of two suns both heavier than Sol itself.

"The orbit had been established beforehand, to swing safely wide of the hot companion, slightly nearer the cold. Nobody had expected to continue in the path for long—certainly not till it almost grazed the sun-clinker. But this is what happened."

A scarlet thread grows behind the dot, marking its track through space. At first, time on the screen is compressed. *Uriel* had a high intrinsic in the direction of the double, whose mass accelerated it ever more furiously. Nevertheless the ship took days, terrible days to reach apastron.

Later, time is necessarily stretched. For close in, speed increases, increases, increases, dizzily beyond what the simple attraction of matter for matter can wreak. *Uriel* sweeps around the side of the neutron star opposite the late supernova, a moment in shadow which saves the men, since radiation is forcing itself past their screens in such amounts that every danger signal shrills. Acceleration climbs to better than half a million gees, five hundred kilometers per second per second. Thus the ship departs spaceward in the wink of a quantum, too swiftly for its re-exposure to the starblast to kill. The acceleration tumbles down again; but by then, *Uriel* is coursing on the heels of light.

Narrator: "Bodies as massive as these two, spinning as fast, generate forces according to the laws of general relativity which act like a kind of negative gravity. That is what seized our unhappy men. They felt no drag, no pressure; they were in free fall throughout, and did not come within the effective tidal action zone. But their intrinsic mounted to more than fifty times what their thrust drive could possibly shed before fuel was exhausted. They were, they are trapped in the speed they have gained."

I meant to write down everything we saw, the pictures taken on board, the forlorn gallantry of men who toiled, suffered, prayed, endured, never really expecting survival nor, maybe, really wanting it. But I cannot.

I will merely write of scenes toward the end, that Daphne and I watched while she wept, my arm around her. The faulty powerplant has been repaired. The medication against radiation exposure is taking effect. The interior of the ship is cool again, scorch and sweat are gone from the air, pseudogravity generators once more provide stable weight, guardian fields scoop interstellar gas aside in an invisible bow wave so that rays no longer seethe through bodies; and a great silence has fallen.

In awe, the seven stand on their observation bridge. Lengths are shrunken, masses swollen, time dilated. Doppler shift has muffled nearly all stars fore and aft, though a few glint wanly still. Aberration has turned the rest into a single eldritch constellation girdling enormous night.

By no other light than that, Captain King leads his men in thanksgiving. "The heavens declare the glory of God: and the firmament sheweth his handy-work . . . For I will consider thy heavens, even the works of thy fingers; the moon and the stars, which thou has ordained. What is man, that thou art mindful of him: and the son of man, that thou visitest him?"

But Asklund stands erect, looking outward as if into the face of a foe.

Afterward they resume stations, start the superdrive; automatic optical compensators give them an illusion of being back in a familiar universe; they run toward rendezvous with their fellows.

Narrator: "In the inertialess condition, a difference of intrinsic does not manifest itself. Taking due precautions, crews from the spared vessels boarded *Uriel*, offered consolation, taped messages to bring home."

Some words are stammered, some stilted, some tearful. Asklund smiles almost wryly into the camera, though tenderness dwells in his voice: "—Daphne, darling, do you remember that old, old ballad I translated for you, about the dead knight who returns to his sweetheart? Do you remember what he tells her?

"For every time you're weeping
And sad your mood,
Then is my coffin filled inside
With clotted blood . . .

"But every time you're singing
And have no grief,
Then is my coffin filled inside
With rose and leaf . . .

"Please give me that gift. Live. Let me know and be glad that you're happy. Because I'll be alive myself, don't forget. This is no coffin. We can have good and useful lives, if people will help. If you will help, Daphne, by not mourning but living—" There is a little more.

Narrator: "*Uriel* stayed on cruise while the men recovered fully from their ordeal. Meanwhile the Astronautic Corps debated what is best for them. A plan is ready, a mission in progress."

Daphne swallowed hard before she whispered in my ear: "And Sinclair, I'm going too!"

Not till she returned from training did I learn, in part, how she got her way. The recommendation she magicked out of me was not enough, however hard I wrangled.

Director Jarvis: "Nonsense. The trouble and expense of teaching a one-shot rookie, when we've got career men? And a woman? Great Scott, just imagine the plumbing problems!"

Secretary Wardour: "Well, yes, it wouldn't hurt the Corps to perform a well-publicized act of compassion. But what kind of mercy is this, letting them meet for a couple of weeks in a crowded hull, her spacesuit always between them?"

Pastor Benson: "Propriety first. It would be extremely difficult, at best, for a sole woman to travel and work among men, in close quarters, without occasionally revealing what should not be revealed. Morality second. She could not help arousing lust. Oh, I realize nothing untoward would happen. But minds would stray from godliness—from concentration on temporal duties also, perhaps, in that dangerous environment. Religion third but foremost. Might not the unexpected, stunning sight of her, an attractive female, briefly among men condemned to lifelong celibacy —not only her husband but the whole seven, young and virile—might that not weaken their resolve to accept the will of God? Might the memory not haunt them until at last they despair of his grace and fall into the Devil's claws?"

I was astounded when the OK came through. But I had been too busy to see much of Daphne or hear her schemes. And she was promptly whisked off to Luna base for two intensive months, while the load on me redoubled. You don't casually gather a crew, hop into a craft, and take off for the deeps. Look what happened to *Uriel*, where everybody supposed that everything had been checked out. The operation which I headed involved more unknowns yet.

Maybe you, archeologist, wonder why. In your ultrasophisticated astronautics (if God has not closed down technological civilization, lest we make an idol of material progress) what could be simpler than to lay alongside, both vessels in superdrive, and transfer cargo? Why, you may know how to kill such speed and let its victims rejoin the human race.

But we— Well, *Uriel* already had systems for recycling air and water. However, they were not completely adequate. Nobody had expected them to be in continuous use for half a century. They would degrade, poisonous organics would accumulate, unless we added refinements and ancillaries. And we couldn't simply plug in the new stuff. We had to do considerable rebuilding. Likewise, the ship had carried six months' worth of food. We would install closed-ecology units that would feed the men indefinitely, indeed yield a large surplus. But this too we couldn't merely dump aboard. It must be integrated with everything else. For a single example of our needful planning, remember that health and sanity required we leave the crew reasonable elbow room.

And while we labored, we must take elaborate precautions to assure no substantial number of atoms from *Uriel* got aboard our own ship. A few nanograms would destroy us, the moment we reverted to normal state and they took off at their light-like intrinsic velocity. There wouldn't be an explosion unless the mass was really gross, up in the milligrams or whatever. But from end to end of our hull would go a fatal wave of radiation.

Obviously, *Uriel* can never leave the inertialess state. It must always keep moving at a quasispeed which outruns light—a modern incarnation of that eerie ancient legend, the Flying Dutchman. (What did *its* crew ever do, to merit their damnation?) Even if we invented a means to slow it, it would first have to enter normal state—would it not?—and our gift of supplies and machinery would annihilate it in a brief burst that might rival a nova.

Fortunately, fuel is no problem. The demands of life support are modest, those of keeping an inertialess body moving are less. Tanks topped off by us ought to serve for more years of exploration than those men have left in their bodies.

You may not believe me, in your hypothetical age of universal enlightenment, but fools have actually asked why *Uriel* didn't backtrack, once its superdrive was operational again, and let the double star undo what was wrought. Evidently, for them the narration was futile when explaining that a velocity is a direction as well as a speed. And, to be sure, Asklund calculated that at the rate yon companions are moving apart, already then they could no longer accelerate an infalling object in anything near the fashion they handled him.

Less crackpot was the suggestion that the ship find a safe, solitary and cold neutron star, go normal near its surface, and let gravity act as a brake, repeating this process until the intrinsic was down to a reasonable figure. This would work, but only corpses would be aboard at the end of it. The difficulty is that every such star known to us is surrounded by too much gas—whether left over from its death throes or drawn in later from the interstellar medium—through too vast a volume. Deceleration would necessarily be at a low rate, especially at first. During the time required, more hard synchrotron radiation would be generated by the passage of the vessel's own shielding fields, and leak through, than life can tolerate.

Another double of precisely the right characteristics, or any of several more exotic and hypothetical things, could reverse the effect, yes. While we have not publicized the fact, *Uriel* spent what months were possible on minimum rations, before reserves got hopelessly low, seeking just such a deliverance. The hunt was foredoomed, of course. Recall the sheer size of space, and guess at the probabilities. Then think what spirit was in those men, that they tried.

Further search is pointless. The equipment of survival, which we have given our comrades, has a differential intrinsic of almost three hundred thousand kilometers per second: to the best of our present-day knowledge and imagination, irrevocable.

Why is my dictascribe trudging through elementary physics? Don't I want to remember how Daphne came back to me?

She protested the two-week furlough granted our crew before departure. They were edging starvation in that ship. I told her the custom was vital. We dared not go to space tired, tense, unrefreshed by our loves. We would meet our deadline, which King and Cauldwell had determined between them a thousand light-years from home. Let her not fear.

"Yes, I've been told," she said. "I'm sorry I grew impatient."

"You have a downright duty to enjoy yourself." I wagged a finger at her. "Where will you go, if I may ask?"

"Well," she said, "my parents have passed away, I haven't anybody close, I'd like to, oh, bid Earth good-bye. Luna was magnificent but stark. Doesn't the Corps maintain a wilderness resort?"

"Aye," I answered, and changed my mind about visiting my sons.

Autumn descends early upon the Grant Tetons. Except for the lodge staff, we had this part of them to ourselves. During the days we tramped their trails, canoed on their lakes, dared their glaciers, found nooks of sunlit warmth and sat down to wonder at their birds, beasts, trees, and distances. Evenings we attacked dinner, surprised at how often we japed and laughed; afterward we took our ease before a stone fireplace, in dimness that burning pine logs made flickery fragrant, and talked more seriously, traded memories, thoughts, and—shyly at first—dreams.

I will sketch a single hour, soon after we arrived. We left in the morning for a hike to the peak above. Our path took us through a wood where leaves glowed in crystalline sunlight, scarlet maple, golden birch, fallow aspen. Between their slim trunks we saw how the mountain slanted toward a dale where a brook went rushing, and how on the far side the range lifted anew in white and violet purity. The sky was like sapphire. The air was chill in our nostrils, smoky when we breathed out, sweetened by faint odors of soil and damp and life. Sometimes a raven went "Gruk!" or a squirrel streaked up a bole and chattered at us; twice a flock of geese passed overhead, their calls drifting down; else our footfalls resounded through holy quietness.

We stopped a while to rest. The ground was soft beneath us. Daphne sat looking outward, arms clasped around knees, cheeks flushed from our climb. The warmth of her went over me in a wave. Her hair, tumbling from a headband and across her shoulders, shimmered as bronze does, or heavy silk.

She said at last, low, maybe to herself, "Val

spoke of this country a lot. We were going to pay a visit together. But something always made us postpone. We didn't really understand that we weren't immortal. So now it seems we never will come."

"You will," I promised.

"I . . . won't be able to. I'm temporarily associated, not actually in the Corps."

"I can bring guests."

She turned her head and gave me a grave smile. "Thank you, Alec. You're kinder to me than is right. But no. I've seen what it costs, and won't have that sort of money."

"Eh?" I was startled, having read the dossier on her which Personnel compiled. "I thought your parents left you quite well off."

"They did. Everything's gone for a bribe, though."

"What?"

She chuckled. "Poor shockable Alec! Nobody told you? Oh, not strictly a bribe. I informed the Pastorate that if it would approve my going in your gang, and pressure an acceptance through secular channels, I'd donate my inheritance to the Church. I dropped a strong hint that otherwise I'd endow a synagogue. They huffed and puffed, but in the end—" She shrugged. "I'll spare you the list of my other blackmails, browbeatings, bluffs, and deceits."

"Lass, lass," I whispered, "how can it mean that much to you, squinting at him through a helmet visor?"

"It does."

I gathered courage to say, "He himself begged you to put him behind you."

She looked back toward the snowpeaks. "I don't think I can. 'In plenty and in want; in joy and in sorrow; in sickness and in health; as long as we both shall live.'" Her hands, groping about, closed on a fallen dry branch. "I . . . suppose . . . I'm more of a monogamist . . . in my way . . . than he is." The noise was startlingly loud when the branch snapped. "But he does love me!"

A deer bounded into sight. Our gaze followed, enchanted. "He loves Earth also," she ended, "and he's been forever shut away. Shouldn't I bring him what touch—what remembrance I can?"

To hurt him the worse? Have you thought how selfish you maybe are? I barely halted my tongue, and hunched appalled. What good would lie in lashing out at her craziness? The fault was mine. I should have stood on my veto at the beginning. Now we were locked in. She was precision-fitted for a crucial role. Quite rightly, the directors would not allow me to substitute her backup for any reason less than a medical emergency. Nor would she ever forgive me.

Whereas—Very well, keep silence, let her get that adieu out of her system. *Afterward*—

"You find this a bonny land, do you not?" I asked rhetorically.

She nodded. "I'll never forget," she murmured.

"You need not hanker," I told her. "When we return to Earth—" My heart slammed. "We can come here. Whenever we're both free. No matter money. I draw a good wage, and nobody depends on me anymore."

"Oh, Alec!" For an instant I glimpsed tears. For another instant her arms were around me, her face buried in my shoulder. Then she leaped up. "C'mon, lazylegs!" she cried, and we were on our way again.

We made rendezvous beyond Mars, where *Uriel* had lately been flying a prearranged exact circle. Knowing position and quasispeed of the exiles, my instruments, automatons, and I brought *Gabriel* carefully closing in. When the two counterinertial

fields, extending a few kilometers beyond either
hull, began to mesh, I saw ghostlike waverings
across the Milky Way. As we neared, our objective
solidified. Having reached the same phase, an
optic screen showed it not far off, as real among
the stars as we were . . . or as unreal, in this mass-
annulled condition we shared.

"Synchronism achieved," I mumbled into the
intercom, and sank back in my pilot chair. The
process had been slow, trying, dangerous because
of the short range within which mutual detection
was possible; inside our fields, we still had inertia
with respect to each other if not to the outside
cosmos, and a collision would wreck us both. I
smelled the sweat rank on me, heard breath and
pulse rattle, felt the separate stiffnesses and aches
in a body no longer young.

"How are they?" rang Daphne's voice. "May we
see?"

I decided I wasn't ready for the boneyard yet,
and switched the telereceivers aft into the visual
compensator circuit. A buzz of excited talk
reached me vaguely, from my men. They were five
altogether besides her, excellent fellows, who had
treated her with awkward chivalry while we
rehearsed and at last ran outward from Earth
orbit. I wish them well. But none of them
especially matters.

"Maintain stations," I ordered. "I'll try for
contact." Right off, I saw my mistake. "I'll make
contact," I amended. They must not be dead or
insane over there! My fingers stumbled across the
com panel. *Gabriel* to *Uriel*, come in."

"*Uriel* to *Gabriel*." The screen flashed color.
Matt King stared forth. His eyes and cheeks were
sunken back among the bones of his face, and he
spoke in a hoarse whisper; but he was clean,
closely groomed, crisply uniformed. My worst
fears drained out of me. "Welcome, welcome." He
managed a shaky smile. "You're skippering the

mission, are you, Alexander Sinclair, you old rascal? What a pleasant surprise."

"How is everybody?" I barked.

"Basically healthy, praise God. Weak but functional, and we got out of the habit of hunger six months ago. Morale is, um, not bad. We do hope you've brought steaks and champagne! When do you expect you can board?"

"We need rest, and I want a complete final checkout of every system . . . Let's say in twenty-four hours. I'm sorry it cannot be sooner. Uh, I wonder if Valdemar Asklund could come to your pickup?"

"Why, well, yes, if you wish."

"Will you report to the command bridge?" I said into the intercom. No reason to state who.

She arrived just as Asklund's hollowed-out countenance appeared. Through a minute or more, they were dumb. I might not leave my post until relieved by Roberts, my first officer; but I glowered at the optic screens. In one of them, its radiance stopped down for the sake of my vision, the sun looked shrunken and cold; in another, Earth shone deep blue, loveliest of the stars and somehow more distant-seeming than any else; in the rest gleamed inhuman hordes and the immensities between.

Finally I heard Asklund sigh, "Daphne, why?"

"To be with you," she wept.

"When we can't even touch? I . . . we're going away as soon as—Oh, my dearest, I worked for weeks on a message to record for you, and now— no words—" I heard him weep too.

Presently she said, "I'll be busy, you realize. I'm responsible for the core parts of your food-cycling equipment. But you can assit me, and—and Captain Sinclair did promise we'd have chances, a compartment where we're by ourselves, or a private line—"

To talk.

We used no gang tube. A handful of air molecules, diffusing from *Uriel* to *Gabriel*, would bring the same doom on us. Instead, we kept the ships as far apart as synchronicity allowed, and jetted across in spacesuits which we wore during an entire shift. This handicapped us infernally. Sheer bulk got in its own way. Gloved fingers, being clumsy, must often operate specially designed manipulators. Speech was via sonic amplifiers, likewise a nuisance. But there was no help for it; and, to be sure, as we instructed them in the requirements, our outcast comrades became quite skillful teammates. Returning to our vessel to eat and sleep, we paused outside the entry lock and practiced elaborate rotations and contortions while an infrared beam boiled off whatever atoms might cling to our suits, and well-nigh baked us. Those were the more obvious physical discomforts.

And they were not what made us long to finish and be gone. No, it was what *Uriel*'s men said, generally with Spartan mildness, and their eyes upon us, and the way they handled the letters, pictures, tapes, mementos we brought them.

I remember a talk out of many which King and I had. We were off duty, seated in our cabins, using an exclusive frequency. This is standard on spacecraft, whose captains may have to reach a grim decision. We let Daphne and her husband into these cubicles at a regular hour out of the twenty-four.

King poured whiskey from a bottle, my smuggled gift, raised the tumbler, and toasted. "Here's to our noble selves." I responded in kind. He didn't show it, really—indeed, having begun to flesh out since we brought abundant food, he looked better than erstwhile—but he had let himself become a trifle drunk.

"Or skoal, my navigator would say," he added.

I let the drink glow down my throat. The leastmost cheer felt large. What had I around me? Three meters by two of room, gray-painted metal, bunk, locker, chair, desk, reference works, Bible, a file of favorite books and a microreader for them, a small musical library and player, a harmonica that I occasionally tootled on, pipes and tobacco, photographs of Meg who was dead and our sons who were grown—that, and starriness outside.

But I could go walk on planets of yon suns, including a planet named Earth.

"Your pronunciation is wrong, Matt," I tried to laugh.

"How do you know?" he bridled. A ventilator muttered around his words.

"Well, ah, Daphne Asklund told me I had it wrong, and taught me a closer approximation." I took a second swallow, much sooner than I had intended.

He peered at me. "Why did she make you bring her?"

"What? Why did I? I've explained. She told you herself. She saw how to join her husband this brief while—unless when you return to the Solar System—and since she could in fact carry her share of the load, I had no heart to refuse her."

The image of his head shook from side to side in the cramped screen. "Don't evade my question, Alec. It wasn't about your motive—that's pathetically obvious—but hers. Nobody who wasn't . . . terrifyingly . . . strong and clearheaded could have swung what she did. I know how these things work as well as you do; I can make the same estimate of the barriers she had to break down, the powerful men she had to outface and outsmart. Such a person doesn't do such a thing for an orgy of sentimentalism that can only agonize her man. Then *why?*"

"Who knows what drives a soul?" I counterattacked. "Do you understand yours? I don't mine. How is Asklund taking it?"

"How does he strike you? I've been meaning to get your outside opinion, Alec, to check my impression. We'll spend the rest of our mutual life together; I'd better have an accurate judgment of him."

I needn't stop to ponder, having done that in uncounted wakeful nightwatch hours. "He was knocked off his orbit at first, I'd say. But he appears to have recovered fast. I don't see him much, you ken, and almost always in public, at work. He's calm, competent—rather withdrawn, I think. They both are."

"He wears a stout mask." The lines deepened around King's mouth. "I gauge him as being under the tightest, breaking-point control."

"Is that uncanny?"

"No, I suppose not. My other men—she's causing them trouble too, not as intense but nevertheless trouble."

"Psychological disturbance was foreseen and allowed for. Still, what is she to them? A bulgy suit like everybody's from *Gabriel*. A face in the visor, a voice out of a speaker, aye, those are female. But men throughout history, in military units or monasteries, have seen more of women, and not been tantalized beyond endurance."

"Soldiers expected to get home; monks expected to keep vows they'd made. We're neither. Already Blai—an astronaut has admitted to me being in love with her. I myself—" King tossed off a mouthful and quirked a smile. "Oh, we'll get over our emotions, our itch, that is. But frankly, I'm thankful this will soon end. Please don't let her join in the next rendezvous."

Wordlessness hummed between us.

"Have you decided where you will go first?" I blurted. We'd brought a bundle of recommendations from different scientists, but the *Uriel* crew had taken no opportunity thus far to study these. King had mentioned how, in the months of their hunt for a savior star, they discussed every imaginable possibility and contingency. What else was there for them?

And what else had they to do in the years that remained, but range the galaxy, and, from time to time, bring us tales of their discoveries? A radio capsule, shot free of the counterinertial field, could summon our people to a meeting. Though we dared not accept any physical record, we could make copies.

But we could merely request and recommend, never command. They were untouchable.

"A shakedown cruise," he answered. "To the Orion Nebula. You know what a lot of unsolved puzzles it holds, and . . . we'd like to see new suns being formed. Then, when we're reasonably sure of our ship and ourselves—the long jump. Clear to galactic center."

I was not altogether surprised. Nevertheless— "Already?" For that would be a voyage of years; and opinion continues divided as to whether, beyond the vast dust clouds which hide it from our probings, the heart of the Milky Way is a hell of radiation or—

"The Elders," he capped my thought.

Surely we are not the solitary species who fare between the stars. God is too generous for that. Far out in this fringe of a spiral arm, barely starting to fumble around off our home shores, we must be like cavemen on a raft, compared to races ahead of us which, maybe, are not burdened by original sin, not plagued by the Devil or a myriad lunacies. Half our astronomers think the middle regions are clear, the suns close together but old and benign, the likeliest hearths of beings whose recorded history runs for multiple millions of years—

—and who might even know how to lift the curse

off *Uriel*.

"What have we to lose?" King said.

To that same room came Daphne, at the close of our mission.

When I heard her knock, I soared from the chair where I had been grinding at return-trip calculations, hit my knee on the desk, and in the pain swore at myself for a lubberly old gowk. Aloud, I called, "Enter." She came through in her pride and gentleness, and I forgot about hurting.

"The captain summoned me," she uttered formally. Her eyes were the green of Earth's living seas.

"Aye. Please shut the door. Sit down." I gestured her to the chair. As she brushed past, touching me, I scented her warmth afresh, after these many days in spacesuits or a crowded mess or a bunk alone. When she was seated, her gaze must travel too far to meet mine. So I perched on a corner of my desk, swung the foot that was free of the deck, and speculated at the back of my mind whether this made me seem younger.

Did she, regardless, bear dread behind her face? I studied closely. She blinked, drew a long breath, then eased back and smiled. "Everything I've worked on checks out swab-O," she said. "And my fellows tell me they're satisfied."

I nodded, while fighting my throat.

"What can I do further?" she asked, neither wondering nor defying but quietly helping me along.

"You—" I tried again. "You are in a, an unco situation, lass. I couldna but see— Well, tomorrow mornwatch we go to *Uriel* for . . . we canna call't a celebration—a speech or twa—and—"

She said (how kindly!), "You wonder if Val and I have any special last request, don't you, Alec?"

"I've seen your glove seek him."

She laid her hand across mine where it clenched
the desk edge. Is not a woman's hand twice beautiful on the knobbly hairy paw of a man? "If we
could go off by ourselves, to Matt King's cabin or
wherever, a while, we'd be grateful."

"You know you can that." I snapped after air.
"Why I called you here . . . I'm not quite sure. I
thought, 'twill be a hard farewell. And he, Val, he
does trust you'll build a life of your own
afterward. I want you to, to know you have a
friend here who cares for you very much, Daphne.
How can I be of service?"

"Oh, Alec, Alec." Suddenly she kissed me, and
fled crying.

At last I slept.

We would have been mad to leave *Gabriel* long
unattended, on automatics. Nor could anybody
stand much ceremony. But rightness required
that, together, we see directly through our visors
our comrades for whom we had toiled and clasp
them good-bye in our armored arms, and wish
them godspeed till death or a miracle delivered
them.

Crossing over, I flew as near as might be to
Daphne. She was half a shadow, half a shimmer,
amidst the stars and silence around. I heard
naught save a radio hiss in my earphones, a thrum
of thrust, my heart knocking. At breakfast, some
of us had been boisterous and some bleak; she had
been unreadable; now none talked. Did we feel
guilt, that soon we would know blueness, clouds,
rain, leaves in the wind? Myself, did I do wrong to
hope?

The sternest realism I could muster warned she
would remarry, if she did, for convenience and
companionship. Well, I dared not want more.

My boots thudded on *Uriel*'s hull.

We cycled through the lock. At the inner valve

waited Matthew King, Jesse Smith, Blaise Policard, Nikolai Kuzmin, Ioannes Venizelos, Sugiyama Kito, Valdemar Asklund. No longer grimy in coveralls, no longer starved, and no longer looking forward to human advent, they stood in dress uniforms as if on parade; and I saw that these brave, decent men were unsure how they might comfort us.

"Welcome," King said. Walking down the corridor, he took me around the waist. After half a second I was ashamed that I was shocked. He did have womanless years before him, but I was his old friend, and muffled away from the very air he breathed, and due to depart in an hour. Next I noticed that, while Daphne and Asklund were side by side, they had not embraced as they did when first she boarded. Their faces were as shut as her helmet.

What had she told him, in the privacies we gave them?

Though we fourteen had fractional room to move around in the mess, we quickly took places at its table. By prearrangement, *Uriel*'s crew had set out glasses and the last bottle of champagne. They would drink for both and we, homeward bound after this was done, would pray for both.

King stood up, klinged thumbnail on goblet, and said: "Mrs. Asklund and gentlemen, we cannot reckon or repay what we owe you. I speak less of your help which will let us live on—that was rendered in the tradition of the Corps—than of your spirit, your generosity—"

I, rising to respond, said: "Brothers, forgive a, a wee bit of dramatics. From your wives, children, parents, your kin and closest well-wishers on Earth, we brought what they gave us to bring you. But we held back one small thing for each till now, whatever they felt would be extra special—"

We tried together to stay calm, and even I hardly

saw the Asklunds excuse themselves and leave.

"—we will never forget," I was saying: "mankind will never forget," when they made re-entry, bare hand in hand. She wore her undergarb, and carried high her head and the unbound ruddy hair.

I am a starship captain, therefore disciplined into command of myself. I roared the chaos around the table back to order. Matt King came to my help. Daphne and Valdemar waited calmly.

Jezebel, harlot of outlaws, wandering Jewess—what pain did the curses give her, give them, when *Uriel* returned for the first and last time to report wonders? What freedom have they found to keep them away ever since, if death does not? And what interior victory, readiness of both to give ungrudging love, must he and she have won before at last, in sight of us all, she kissed her man full upon the mouth?

III

THE WAYS OF LOVE

Ten of their years before, we had seen that being come through the transporter into our ship and die. This day we stood waiting upon his world, and as we waited, we remembered.

The *Fleetwing* was bound for Prime of that constellation for which she was named. She would not —will not—arrive there for many lifetimes, though already she had fared, at more than half the speed of light, while Arvel swung six hundred and twelve orbits around Sarnir. So deep is the universe. She was, indeed, the farthest out of all our ships, and Rero-and-I reckoned it an honor when we were assigned a term of service within her.

Not that we expected anything spectacular. Rather, it should be the opposite. Until the starcraft reach their goals, they are doing little but patiently traveling. A change of crew is almost like a casual rite. You and your mate go to the mattercasting station on Irjelan. The pair whom you are to relieve come back and inform you of conditions aboard. That seldom takes long and, as a rule, is done at ease, above a brazier of smokeleaf in the elders' lounge. (Yet you see Arvel shining green among the stars, over this scarred face of her outer moon, and feel what your duty will mean.) Soon you two give the others a farewell twining of tendrils and make your way to the appropriate sender unit. The flash of energy which scans and disintegrates your bodies, atom by atom, you do not feel; it goes too swiftly, as fast as the modulated tachyonic beam which then leaps across the light-years. At the end, the patterns which are you are rebuilt in new atoms, and there you are for the next ninety-six days.

.You do maintenance, perhaps minor repair; you record scientific observations and perhaps program new ones; you might start the engine for a course correction, though rarely when the target sun is still remote; none of it takes much effort. Your true job is to stand by against improbable emergencies. Sometimes a vessel in transit gets used as a relay station by a couple or a party bound for too distant a world to make it in a single jump. Then they stop for a short visit. This would happen in *Fleetwing*, she being on our uttermost frontier and bound onward into strangeness.

Rero-and-I welcomed the isolation. Our usual work was challenging. We had been pilot and chief engineer on a series of exploratory boats in several different planetary systems, which meant assisting the teams after landing them. Perforce, we became a pair of jackleg xenologists. This in turn involved us in the proceedings of the Stellar Institute back on Arvel, its rather hectic social rounds as well as its data evaluations. We couldn't plead family needs when we would have preferred to stay home, since both our children were young adults. Nor did we want more; an infant would ground us. We enjoyed too much what we did in space. Its price was that we had too little life for ourselves.

Thus we were glad of aloneness wherein to meditate, read, watch classic choreodramas on tape, really get to know certain music and fragrances, be altogether at leisure in our lovemaking. And so it went for seven and thirty days.

Then the alarm whistled, the warning panels flashed, we hastened to the receiving chamber. As we floated waiting in free fall, I sensed how both my hearts knocked. Rero's body and mine worked to cool us down from the heat of our excitement; we hung in a mist and our odors were heady, we gripped hands and wished we could join flesh. What cause had anyone to seek us out? A messenger, telling of catastrophe?

He materialized, and we knew the disaster was not ours but his.

Our first shock at his appearance blent with the pain that sent us hurtling back, a-gasp. A puff of the atmosphere in his ship had come through with him. I recognized the lethal acridity of oxygen. Fortunately, there was not more than our air renewers could clean out in a hurry. Meanwhile he died, in agony, trying to breathe chlorine.

We returned to attend his drifting corpse. Silence poured in from the unseen dark, through the barren metal around us, as if to drown our spirits. We looked long upon him—not then aware that he was male, for the human genitals are as peculiar as the human psyche. His odors were salt and sour, few and simple. We wondered if that was because he was dead. (It wasn't, of course.) After we had carefully, reverently opened his soiled coverall and inner garments, we spent a while trying to see what kind of beauty might be his. He looked grotesquely like us and unlike us: also a biped, larger than Rero, smaller than me, with five digits to a hand, no part truly resembling anything of ours. Most striking, perhaps, was the skin. Save for patches of hair and a scattering of it everywhere else, that skin was smooth, yellowish-white, devoid of color-change cells and vapor vents. I wondered how such a folk expressed themselves, their deepest feelings, to each other. (I still do.) Eeriest to me, somehow, were the eyes. He had two, the same as us, but in that tendrilless, weirdly convoluted visage their blindness glimmered white around blue . . . blue.

Rero whispered at last: "Another intelligent race. The first we've met that explores too. The very first. And this one of them had to come through to our ship unprotected, and die. How could it happen?"

I sent look and fingers along the body, as gently as might be. His aura was fading away fast. Oh, yes, I know it's only infrared radiation; I am not an Incarnationist. Nevertheless, that dimming after death is like a sign of the final wayfaring. "Emaciation may be normal to the species, and the society may be careless about cleanliness," I said in my driest tone. "I doubt both, though, and suspect that here has been a terrible accident consequent upon an earlier misfortune." Meanwhile I thought the old goodbye: *God take home your soul, God shelter it in the warmth of His pouch and nourish it with the milk of Her udder, until that which was you has grown and may go free.*

Rero joined me in speculations which proved to be essentially correct. Since the truth has never become as widely known on Arvel as it should be, let me set it briefly forth.

The *Southern Cross* was likewise among the oldest and farthest-out vessels from her world. She likewise was bound for the brightest star in the constellation for which she was named, the same as we desired; humans call that sun Alpha Crucis. Like us, they use mattercasters to alternate the watches in space. This craft had chanced to pass near enough a burnt-out black dwarf that they changed her program and put her in orbit around it for scientific study. Four males went to initiate this. Unforeseen factors, chiefly the enormous magnetic field of the object, wrecked both their ion drive and their transmitter. Two of them died in the effort to make repairs. The two survivors were starving when at last they had put together a primitive caster. Not knowing its constants with exactness, they must vary the tuning until they got the signal of a receiving station. When they did, David Ryerson rushed impulsively through. It chanced that he had not tuned to a human-built circuit, but to ours aboard *Fleetwing*.

Soon I warned Rero: "We must respond, and fast, before whoever is at the other end switches to a different code and we lose contact."

"Yes," she agreed. Her aura flamed with eagerness, though at the same time her touch honored the dead. "By the dawn, what a miracle! A whole race as advanced as us, but surely knowing things we don't—a whole transporter network linked to ours—O unknown friend, rejoice in your fate!"

"I'll armor myself and take the reamins along," I said. "That ought to demonstrate good will."

"What?" Her smells, vapor cloud, color-change cells gone black, showed horror. She clutched my arm till claws dug in. "Alone? Voah, no!"

I drew her to me. "It will be a gray fire to depart from you, Rero, my life, not knowing if . . . if I condemn you to widowhood thereby. Yet one of us must, and one must stay behind, to tend the ship and bear the news home if the other cannot. I think female agility won't count for much, when yonder hull isn't likely to be bigger than this, and male strength may count for a little."

She did not resist long, for in fact her common sense exceeds mine. It was only that *I* had to say the word first. We did not even stop to make love. But never have I seen a red more pure than was in her glance upon me when we embraced.

And so I, protected against poison, entered the transmitter and emerged on the *Southern Cross* with David Ryerson's body in my arms. His shipmate, Terangi Maclaren, received it in awe. Afterward, Rero-and-I helped him find the tuning for a station maintained by his race, and he trod across the gulf between, bearing death and glory.

—There followed the dozen years—ten of Earth's—that everyone knows about, when commissions from the two species met in neutral spots; when a few representatives sent to either planet brought home bewilderment; when meanwhile the scientists jointly hammered out sufficient knowledge that they could guess how vast was their ignorance. My wife and I were concerned in this effort, not merely because first contact had chanced to be ours, but because our prior experience with sophonts had given us a leap ahead. To be sure, those were all primitives, whereas now Arvel was dealing with a civilization that sundered the atom, rebuilt the gene, and colonized across interstellar distances. Here too, however, we were well equipped, she to seek converse with fellow pilots, I with fellow engineers.

Accordingly, when the Earthfolk, to whom ten is a special number, decided to celebrate the decade with ceremonies, and invited Arvelan participation, it was natural that Rero-and-I go. Apart from symbolism, we might be of practical use. Thus far the two breeds had shared hardly anything except those technical endeavors. The time was overpast for agreements. Most obviously, though not exclusively: If we could combine our mattercaster webs, then we would each have access to about twice as much space as before, twice the wealth, twice as many homesites—

No, not really. In that respect, Arvel would gain less, inasmuch as the Sarnirian System has a cosmically unusual distribution of elements. Planets where photosynthesis liberates chlorine are more rare than those where it liberates oxygen, not to mention additional requirements. (My brother mariner, David Ryerson, with calcium instead of silicon in his bones . . . .) Many people in our families and tribes felt ungenerous about this, wanted compensation for the difference. Meanwhile on Earth—well, that is what I wish to relate, if I am able. Certainly both sides were haunted: *How far can we trust them? They command energies which can break a world apart.*

Ostensibly present for harmless rituals, Rero-and-I meant to talk privately, informally with powerful humans, helping lay the groundwork for a conference that could arrive at a treaty. That was our plan, when eagerly we agreed to go.

It made our disappointment the fierier, after we had been on Earth for a time. And in this wise it happened that we stood on a terrace waiting to be borne to a secret rendezvous.

Once a fortress in a frightful age, later remodeled and enlarged to hold the masters of the globe, that complex called the Citadel dwells magnificently among those mountains called the Alps. From the parapet we looked down steeps and cliffs which tumbled into a valley. Beyond it the heights lifted anew, a waterfall ashine like a drawn blade, a blue-shadowed whiteness blanketing peaks, the greenish gleam of a solid mass. This is a chill planet where water often freezes, a sight which can be lovely. The sun stood close to midday in a wan heaven, its disc seeming slightly larger than that of Sarnir above Arvel but its light muted. Not only does it give off less ultraviolet, the air absorbs most of what there is. Yet Rero-and-I had learned to see beauty in soft golden-hued luminance, in a thousand shy tints across eldritch landscapes.

"I wish—" Wind boomed hollowly around Rero's voice. She broke off, for she had no real need to speak her thought. Through the transparent sealsuit, face-tendrils and skin-language said for her how she would joy to inhale, smell, drink, taste, feel, take the wholeness of this plan unto herself. Impossible, of course, unless she first hooked into a pain inhibitor; and then she would have a bare moment for the orgasm of body comprehension, before the oxygen killed her. Poor David Ryerson, had he known what awaited him he might at least have died observing, not bewildered.

I took her by the hand, glove in glove. My own desire was as strong as hers, but directed toward her. She saw that, and saucily flexed her sex organ at me . . . but the rest of her declared longing rather than humor. Imagine for yourself and your mate: the entire time you spend outside an Arvel-conditioned suite, which is most of the time, you are enveloped apart from each other!

"Do you think Tamara Ryerson will be present?" I asked, more for the talk than out of curiosity.

"Who?—Ai, yes, David Ryerson's widow," Rero said. We had met her just once, at a welcoming ceremony which included Terangi Maclaren. This was at the beginning of our visit, and no opportunity came to converse with either of them. An omen—for when had we since gotten to link minds in fullness and candor with anybody? "I'd hardly expect that." My wife paused. "Although, now you mention it, we might well try to seek her out later. What does widowhood mean to her? That could give us a clue to the whole psychology of these beings."

"I doubt that, from a single sample" I answered. "However . . . n-n-n-n . . . one sample is better than none. Maybe Vincent Indigo can arrange it." A short, brightly-clad human came out of a doorway. "Name the Illwisher and you'll sense his heat."

My use of the proverb was figurative. Our

Citadel-appointed guide, liaison, arranger, and general factotum had been tirelessly helpful. True, we soon got a feeling of being rushed from spot to spot, person to person, event to event, with never an instant free for getting acquainted. But when we complained of this to him—

"Good day, Sir Voah, Lady Rero," he said with a salute. "I'm sorry I'm late. If we're to get you away from here unbeknownst, you can't be seen leaving. A Guards officer was inspecting the area and I had to wait till he finished."

Our throatstrings could not form his kind of sounds very clearly, but a minicomputer passed our words through a transponder which corrected that. I admired the device. In spite of more experience with aliens, we Arvelans had never developed anything as good for this purpose. On their side, human members of the study group had expressed immense interest in some of our construction technology. What might our peoples not accomplish together, if they would allow themselves? "It is in order, then, on the island of Taiwan?" I asked.

Vincent Indigo nodded. "Yes, the Maclarens are ready for you. It'll be dark there and the house has big, well-shaped grounds. We can set you down and take off again afterward without being noticed. Come on, we'd better not dawdle here."

As we strode over the flagstones, I could not help fretting. This world was so full of mysteries, riddles less of nature than of the soul. "How long can we stay? You weren't certain about that."

"No, because it depended on what arrangements I could make. The idea is to get you together with him for completely free conversation—no officials around, no busybodies, no journalists. And it has to stay secret that you did, or the whole project is spoiled from the start, right? Knowing you'd be questioned about it afterward would inhibit things, no matter how well-meant the questions. Voah, my friend, you can't escape being a first-magnitude celebrity."

If you want to feel our problem, consider those few sentences. I can hardly translate the key words; you notice what archaic and foreign terms I am borrowing, in search of rough equivalents. *Officials*: Not parents, not tribal elders, not Speakers for an Alliance or their executive servants—no, agents of that huge bloodless organization called a "government," which claims the right to slay whomever resists the will of its dominators. *Busybodies:* Without sanction of kinship, custom, or dire need, certain humans will still thrust themselves into affairs. *Journalists:* Professional collectors and disseminators of news recognize no bounds upon their activities except for what is imposed by the government; and is that limitation not odd in itself? *Celebrity:* Lest the foregoing make Earthfolk seem repulsive, let me say that they have a wonderful capacity for giving admiration, respect, yes, a kind of love to persons they have never met individually and to whom they have no kinship whatsoever.

I pass over the fact that Indigo addressed me alone, ignoring Rero. That might be a simple peculiarity of language, when it was I who had spoken to him.

"Twenty-four hours looks reasonable," he told me—a rotation period of the planet, slightly longer than Arvel's. "The Protector is making an important speech tomorrow, you see, which'll draw everybody's attention away from you."

"Indeed?" said Rero. "Should we not join in heeding your . . . your head of state?"

"If you want." Indigo gave a very Arvelan-like shrug. "However, I'm told it'll be on internal matters — currency stabilization, ethnic discontents, revolutionary sentiment on certain colonial worlds and how we should quell it—nothing which makes any difference to you, I should think."

"I don't know what *I* should think," she blurted, and gave up. What we had heard hovered on the edge of making sense but was never quite seizable, like a chant in a dream. Could we ever win enough understanding of these creatures that we would dare trust them?

Indigo led us down a staircase hewn from the rock, to a lower level where a hangar stood open. Despite lessened weight there, I was glad to see that end of our walk. The water-circulation unit felt heavy on my back. Humans who come to Arvel have an advantage over us in that regard, needing less life support apparatus. Their survival depends more on maintaining a particular range of temperatures than it does on maintaining a temperature differential.

We climbed into the spearhead craft which waited for us and reclined into specially modified seats. An attendant connected our suits to a pair of full-cycle biostatic units in the rear of the cabin, greatly increasing our comfort. "Relax, friends," Indigo urged. "This is a suborbital jet, you remember. We'll reach Taiwan in an hour."

"You are kind to us," Rero said. Calm and cool, her gratitude laved me as well.

The human's beaky countenance crinkled in what he could have called a smile. It is a large part of their meager body language. "No, no, milady," he replied. "I get paid for assisting you."

"But is this not . . . unauthorized, is that the word? Don't you risk trouble for yourself, if your elders accuse you afterward of having acted un-wisely?"

The bars of hair above his eyes drew together. "Only if something goes wrong and they find out. I admit it could happen, though it's very unlikely.

As I've tried to explain to you, we have antisocial elements on Earth, criminals, political or religious fanatics, lunatics. They could make you a target. That's why the Citadel's had you closely guarded and kept you to a strict itinerary. But since this is a secret trip, we ought to be safe, and I do want to oblige you whenever possible.''

The aircraft rolled forth and lifted easily, as if on a quite ordinary flight. Not until we were in the stratosphere did she unleash her entire strength. Then stars blinked into view, the planet became many-marbled immensity, we soared above a continent which dwarfed any upon Arvel until we began slanting down again toward the ocean east of it. Silence prevailed among the passengers. Indigo puffed nervously on a series of smoke-sticks, the cabin attendants watched a television show, the crew were elsewhere. I knew no reason to be taut, but my hearts thudded ever more loud and I saw that Rero felt the same. To the minute degree that sight and touch, nothing more, permitted, we spent most of the journey making love.

Night was young over the island, Earth's single moon rising full. The Maclaren home stood by itself, likewise on a mountain though one that held trees and gardens to the top. Our craft descended silently, as a glider, probably unnoticed save by a traffic control computer or two. For lack of a proper landing strip such as its size required, it employed a straight stretch of road which bore no traffic at this hour. I admired the pilot's skill. More did I admire Indigo's, in gathering information and making arrangements. To do that when the Protector's spies seemed to be everywhere struck me as remarkable.

The flyer halted by an upward-bending side road. Our man peered through a window. "He's here, waiting," he said. "Go on out. Fast, before somebody else happens by. We've got to scramble. I'll be back for you at this time tomorrow evening."

We had already been unplugged from the biostats and had restarted our portable units. They could maintain us that long, though not much more. Food would be dried rations shoved through a helmet lock, drink would be water sucked from a tube, waste release would be into an aspirator, rest would be uneasy and sexual intercourse nil. However, if we could achieve real converse, it would be worth everything. We scrambled forth with eagerness making our auras dance. The flyer taxied off at once, rounded a curve, and vanished. After a moment we heard a rumble and saw it take off above the shoulder of the mountain, an upward meteor.

Terangi Maclaren stood shadowlike in the dim light, save for his own deep-colored radiation. "Welcome," he said, and briefly clasped our gloves. We'll have to walk; those rigs of yours wouldn't fit in my car. Follow me, please." I decided he was this curt because he likewise was anxious to get us hidden.

Trees turned the drive into a gut of darkness. We switched on our flashlights. "Can you do without those?" Maclaren asked. "That blue-white isn't like anything a local person would use."

Rero-and-I doused them. "Suppose we link hands and you lead us," she suggested. When we had done this, she wondered, "Are you indeed worried about the possibility of our being observed? Can you not deny curiosity seekers access to your—" She groped for a word. They do not seem to have kin-right on Earth. "Your property?"

"Yes, but gossip might reach the wrong ears," he explained. "That could bring on trouble."

"Of what kind? Surely you do nothing . . . unlawful? . . . in receiving us."

"Technically no." By now I believed I had learned the nuances of the human voice sufficiently well to hear bitterness in his. "But the Citadel has ways to make things unpleasant. For instance, you may recall I'm an astrophysicist. These days I'm directing a survey in detail of the stars we have access to—expensive. By hinting that funds might otherwise be cut off, a bureaucrat could get me dismissed. And I do have independent means, but I'm a little old to go back to playboying."

Footfalls resounded loud on the pavement, through a rustle of leaves in a sea breeze. I toiled up the mountainside under a burden of gear, in a cramped loneliness of my own scents and no other. The night of Earth pressed inward.

"Of course," Maclaren went on after a while, "I may be borrowing grief. It's no secret that I'm strongly in favor of close relationships with Arvel. To date, that hasn't caused many obstacles to get thrown in my way—though it hasn't been exactly smoothed for me either. My talking to you in private needn't necessarily alarm the Protector and his loyalists. It might even encourage people in the government who agree with me. I just can't tell. Therefore, let's be as cautious as practical.

"Besides," he added, "there are individuals, yes, organizations that hate the idea of making alliance with you. They could do something rash, if they knew you were here unguarded."

Indigo had intimated the same. Rero-and-I had failed to understand. *"Why?"* I asked into the darkness. "Yes, I realize many will be wary of us because we are an unknown quantity. We have their kind on Arvel. In fact, frankly, sir, the pair of us came largely in hopes of learning more about your kind."

"A hope that has been frustrated," Rero put in. "We have become convinced we are deliberately being hurried along and kept busy, in order that we will return home still ignorant . . . or down-right suspicious."

"Terangi Maclaren," I said, "you speak as if more is involved than exaggerated prudence. You give the impression that certain humans want to isolate humanity from us on principle."

"That is the impression I meant to give," he replied.

Through my glove I felt how his clasp tightened. I returned the tension to him, and Rero shared it with me.

"I'm not sure how clear I can make the situation," Maclaren said with care. "Your institutions are so utterly unlike ours—your beliefs, your ways of looking at the universe and living in it, everything—Well, that's part of the problem. For instance, the Hiroyama Report. Do you know about that? Hiroyama tried to find out what your major religions are. Her book created a sensation. If a powerful, scientifically oriented culture can hold that God is love . . . with sex apparently the major part of love—well, that defies a lot of old-established Terrestrial orthodoxies. Heresies spring up, which provokes reaction. Oh, yes, Hiroyama did mention that Arvelans practice monogamy and fidelity, or so she thought. She couldn't be sure, because their spokesmen never described this as a moral requirement. Therefore the new human cults, most of them, go in for orgies and promiscuity."

Though we had encountered curious sexual patterns elsewhere, Rero still faltered in surprise: "Mating for life—what else can we do?"

"Never mind now," Maclaren said bleakly. "It's a single example of why some groups on Earth would like to ring down the curtain forever on contact with Arvel. And by extension, with any other high-level civilization we may come upon. For practical purposes, what matters is why the Protector fears alliance, and his followers do.

"You see, the Citadel already has a nearly impossible job, trying to keep control over the human race, including settlers on the colonial planets and the societies they're developing. Disaffection, subversion, repeated attempts at rebellion—You mean you Arvelans have never had similar woes?"

"Why should we?" I asked in my bemusement.

Did the vague ruddiness of his aura show him nodding? "I'm not too surprised, Voah-and-Rero." (He was that familiar with our mores. Hope blossomed small within me.) "Since you don't have anything we could call a proper government, you avoid its troubles and costs. To be sure, we're a different breed; what works for you probably wouldn't for us. Just the same, already quite a few thinkers are wondering aloud and in print if we really need a state sitting on us as heavily as the Citadel does. Given close, ongoing relationships with you, the next generation may well decide we don't need the Citadel at all.

"Besides that, well, simply doubling the space available to us, the number of planets we can occupy, that alone will soon make us ungovernable as a whole. We'll explode in a million different directions, and God Himself can only guess at the ultimate consequences. But a single thing is certain. It will bring down the Protectorate.

"Oh, our present lord can doubtless live out his reign. His son after him . . . maybe, maybe not. His grandson: impossible. And he isn't stupid. He knows it.

"At the same time, the Dynasty does still command powerful loyalties. A lot of people fear change for its own sake—not altogether unreasonably. They have a big stake in the existing order of things, and would like to pass it on to their children.

"Others—well, for them it's more emotional,

down in the marrow, therefore more strong and
dangerous. I don't know if you can imagine, Rero-
and-Voah, what grip the Dynasty has on a man
whose fathers served it these past three hundred
years. What are *your* mystiques?"

We didn't try to answer that. The thought gave
me a faint shock: that I too probably lived by
commitments so deep-seated that I didn't know
they could override my reason. I heard Rero say,
"You yourself would open the portal wide
between our races, would you not, Terangi
Maclaren? And surely many are with you."

"Right," he told us. "In and out of the government, there's a mighty sentiment in favor of going
ahead. We feel stifled, and we want to let in a clean
wind we can hear blowing . . . . Yes, it's a delicate
balance of forces, or a multi-sided political
struggle, or whatever metaphor you prefer. I do
believe Arvelans and Earthlings are overdue for
getting some real depth-psychological empathy
with each other. That ought to clear away sus-
picion, ought to give the movement for freedom
overwhelming strength." His tones, hitherto low,
lifted. "How glad I am you came here."

The drive debouched on a level stretch of
ground, the woods yielded to openness, and we
were again out in light. To Maclaren, with his
superior night vision, the view must have been
magnificent, for even I found it beautiful. On our
right the mountain rose further, on our left it
plunged downward, in frosted shadowiness where
here and there gleamed yellow the windows of a
home. Far off on the seashore, a village twinkled
in countless colors. Beyond reached the ocean,
like living obsidian bridged by moonglade. Across
the sky glimmered the galaxy. Everywhere else
were individual stars, each of them a sun.

Maclaren led us among flowerbeds and across a
wide stretch of lawn, to his house. It was low and
rambling, the roof curved high; it had been built

largely of timber, according to a pattern that I felt must be ancient in these parts; I wished very much that I could savor it with unmuffled senses. A lantern lighted a verandah. As we mounted this, the main door opened. A female human stood in the glow that poured out from behind her.

We knew her at once. Not being sure we would, Maclaren said, "Do you remember my wife, from the program we were on together when you arrived? Tamara." In the flicker of bright and black across Rero's skin, I saw my own shock mirrored. New as we then were to Earth, we had not caught any mention of Tamara's closeness to Maclaren. His wife? But she was David Ryerson's widow!

We were inside the house before I was enough past my agitation to see that Maclaren had noticed it. Perhaps Tamara had too. Her manner was most gentle as she bowed her head above her hands laid together and murmured, "Be welcome, honored guests. It grieves us that we cannot offer refreshment. Is there any way we can minister to your needs or comfort?"

I saw that seats were provided to fit us in our sealsuits. Otherwise the room was long and lovely. Strange environment does not change the laws of harmonius proportion; swirls of wood grain in the floor, hues and textures of vegetable mats, were foreign but serene; a crystal bowl on a table held a stone and a flower, beneath a scroll of calligraphy that we did not have to read in order to admire; bookshelves breathed forth a promise; windows gave outlook on the night land, the sea, and the cosmos. A music player lilted notes of a piece that Rero-and-I had long ago told human members of the commission we enjoyed; the form is called *raga*. An incense stick burned, but of course I could only smell the manifold acridities of my own confined flesh.

"You are kind," Rero said. "Still, are you not

being overly formal? Voah-and-I came in hopes of . . . of close understanding."

"Then why don't you sit?" Maclaren invited. He and Tamara waited till we had. She perched forward in her chair, fingers twined on her lap. In a long skirt and brief blouse, her skin was golden-brown, her form abstractly pleasing to us. Framed by flowing blue-black hair, her eyes were like the bright darkness outside. Maclaren was tall for an Earthling, he stood with half his torso raised above Rero while his head reached well up on my chest. Seated, he assumed an attitude as casual as his tubular garments, lounged back with ankle over knee—but his gaze never left us and I recognized gravity on his face.

"What had you in mind, Rero-and-Voah?" he began.

We were silent a while, until I trilled a laugh of sorts and admitted, "We are seeking what questions to ask, and how."

Tamara confirmed my guess about her perception when she inquired, "What surprised you on the verandah?"

Again we must hesitate. Finally Rero said, "We do not wish to give offense."

Maclaren waved a hand. "Let that be taken for granted on both sides, hm?" he suggested. "We might well drop something ourselves that you don't like. In that case, tell us, and we'll all try to find out why, and maybe we can get a little enlightenment from it."

"Well, then " Regardless, Rero must summon her courage. "Tamara Ryerson, is that your proper name now? You are wedded to Terangi Maclaren?"

"Why, yes, for the past eight years," the human female replied. "Didn't you know?"

I tried to explain that the information had gone by us because of its alienness. Astonished in her turn, she exclaimed, "Doesn't it seem natural to you? Terangi and David were friends, shipmates. When Terangi came back, he found me alone with my baby, and helped me—at first for David's sake, but soon—Would you consider it wrong?"

"No," I said hastily. "We Arvelans also differ in our customs and beliefs, from culture to culture."

"Although," Rero added, "none of our kind would remarry . . . that quickly, I think. A young person who was widowed might remarry, but after several years."

"An older one?" Tamara asked softly.

"As a rule, they go asexual—celibate, if I remember your word aright," I told her. Fearing she might regard that as cruel: "This had been an honorable estate in every country and era. In civilized milieus, institutions have existed, such as . . . lodges, would you call them? . . . to give the widowed a solid place, a new belongingness."

"Why can't they remarry, though?"

"Few societies have actually forbidden remarriage at any age. It's just that few persons want to, who've had a mate for a long while."

Maclaren made a chuckling noise. "And yet, as far as I can tell," he remarked, "you Arvelans are hornier than us humans, which is saying a lot."

I exchanged a look, a handclasp, and a sexual signal with Rero.

"What makes the difference?" Tamara wondered. "Sorrow?"

"No, sorrow wears away, if I use that word correctly," I answered, doubtful whether I did. (Afterward that doubt was to grow. Do they indeed mourn as we do?) "But think, please. Precisely because of the close relationship, personalities have blended. Remarriage involves changing one's entire spirit, that originally developed in young adulthood after the first wedding. Not many individuals want to become somebody quite different. Of those who might wish to, not many dare attempt it."

Sensing Tamara's puzzlement, Rero said in her most scientific manner:

"It has long been obvious that sexual dimorphism is greater among Arvelans than among Earthlings. In your species, the female both carries the child to term and nurses it afterward. Among us, she carried the fetus a much shorter time, then delivers it and gives it to the male, who puts it in his pouch. There it has shelter and temperature differentials till it has matured enough to venture forth. However, the mother does provide nourishment for the infant from special glands—milk, is that your word? This means the male must always be close to her, to hand the infant over for feeding. It means, too, that he must be large and strong. That leaves her free, in an evolutionary sense, to become small but agile. Our presapient ancestors hunted in male-female teams, as savages did within historical times. Civilizations have not changed that basic partnership; most work has always been organized so as to be done by mated couples. The interdependence goes beyond the physical into the psyche. Among the primitive peoples, the widowed have generally pined away. A large part of our history and sociology has turned on the provision of various means to give the asexual a survivor's role."

"Oh, yes, Tamara knows that." Did Maclaren sound annoyed, as if his wife had been insulted? "We've both followed the reports of the study teams."

"No, wait, dear." Her fingers brushed across his. "I think Rero—Rero-and-Voah are trying to tell us how it *feels*." Her vision met ours. "Maybe we can tell you how it feels in us," she said. "Maybe that's part of the knowledge you're searching for."

She rose, crossed to where Rero sat, and squeezed the armored shoulder. Immediately realizing, she gave me the same gesture. "Would you like to see our children?" she asked. "There's the oldest, David's and mine. These are two more, Terangi's and mine. Will you believe that he loves them equally?"

Memory rushed over me of *The Adopted Son*. I have merely read it in translation. Somehow, though, across oceans and centuries, Hoiakim-and-Ranu's genius has come through to me. I think that from their poetry I know what it meant to live in a land where the nursing or pouching of an infant not one's own was not the highest form of devotion and sacrifice, but was actually taboo. It may be that from this I have an inkling of how deep goes the caring for our young.

Except . . . is this what she intends to say? I wondered.

"I wish you could cuddle them," Tamara said. "Well, they're asleep anyhow. You'll meet them properly tomorrow. What a gorgeous surprise for them!"

She activated a scanner to show us their rooms. I was touched and fascinated: the chubbiness of the small, the lengthening limbs of the oldest. Rero paid more heed to the adults. In our language she asked me, "Is my impression right, that in his mind they are secondary to her?"

"I have no idea," I confessed. "I'm wondering how they will feel about each other—the five of them—after the children are grown."

"And what is intrinsic, what cultural?"

"Impossible to say, darling. It could be that in them, parental emotions are potentiated by close association with the offspring, and in most human societies the mother enjoys more of this than the father does . . . . "

The bit of intimacy went surprisingly far to ease things between us four. If we could not share smokeleaf, food, drink, odors, prayers, we could share parenthood. For a while Tamara was quite eagerly gossiping with Rero-and-me about our respective households. At last Maclaren said:

"Do you know, I suspect we may already be verging on an insight that's never been reached before." He paused; I saw him quiver where he sat. "Sure, sure, naturally we've gotten endless speculation on Earth, and doubtless on Arvel. How basic is the psychosexual element to any intelligent race? But it's been pretty dry and abstract. Here, tonight—well, we won't solve that problem, but might we not make a start on it? I've a wild guess as to how all your institutions, in all your cultures, may spring from your reproductive pattern. Might you be able to make a guess like that about us? It could tell us things about ourselves that've been mysterious through the whole of our history."

I thought for a span before I replied, "If nothing else, Terangi Maclaren, your guesses about us ought to reveal something about you."

He leaned forward. His hands made gestures. His tone held eagerness:

"With you people, the nuclear family—*really* nuclear—has got to be the basis of everything, everywhere and everywhen. It's the indissoluble unit . . . and I wish you could give me an idea of what the indissoluble unit is among humans.

"Your history, what little of it we know here on Earth—never a nation-state. Usually clans, that might keep their identities for many centuries . . . forming tribes, that might keep their identities, for a few centuries . . . but the families endure. They trace themselves back to mythic ages.

"More parochialism than on Earth, progress a local affair, few changes ever happening at once over your entire planet, obsolete and evil matters persisting till late dates in corners of the world.

However, no nationalism; variety not getting ground down into uniformity; if nothing like democracy, then also nothing like absolutism; eventually, gradually, a union of the whole species on a loose and pragmatic foundation; no public passions, even for good causes, but no public lunacies either—

"In religion . . . when monotheism came along, God was bisexual—no, I suppose 'supersexual' would be a better word, but sexual for certain. At the same time, in everyday life, orderly sex relationships are the norm, taken for granted— therefore you don't have to worry about regulating that, you can make moral investments different from ours—"

The door flew open. A weapon came through.

Three men, likewise armed, crowded behind the automatic pistol of their leader. The whole group wore nondescript coveralls and hoods to mask their faces. Behind them I made out the raindrop shape of a little aircraft parked on the lawn. Engrossed in talk, we had none of us heard its whispering as anything but a night wind.

We sprant to our feet. "What the hell?" ripped from Maclaren.

"Vincent Indigo!" Rero-and-I cried together.

He was taken aback at our recognition of him. Unequipped for much conscious details. He rallied at once, chopped air with his firearm, and snapped: "Silence. Not a peep out of you. The first that starts trouble, we'll shoot." A pause. "If you cooperate, nobody need get hurt. If you don't the kids might suffer too."

Tamara gasped and clutched at her husband. He laid an arm around her waist. Rero-and-I joined in a look of longing. We couldn't touch.

"We're taking the Arvelans away," Indigo said. "A kidnapping. The government ought to pay a fancy sum for their release. I'm telling you this so you'll see we don't mean worse and it's to your advantage to be good. Sir and Lady Maclaren, we're going to disable your phone and your car, to keep you from giving the alarm before we're a safe distance off. We don't want to do you more harm than that, and won't if you stand quietly where you are. As for you two . . . creatures, we don't want to harm you either. No ransom for a corpse, eh? We'll take care of you if you behave yourselves. If you don't—well, a bullet doesn't need to kill you by itself. It only needs to make a hole in your sealsuit.

"Quiet, I said!" he ordered as Maclaren's mouth stirred. To his followers: "Get busy."

They grunted assent. One attacked the telephone. Not content to break its connection, he put a shot through the screen. The hiss of the pistol, the crack of splintered glass sounded louder than they were. He used the scanner to make sure the children had not roused, then rejoinded Indigo in keeping watch on us. Meanwhile his companions had gone back inside, evidently to the garage for their own task of demolition. I had noticed tools hung at their waists. This was a carefully planned operation.

Stupefaction left me; anger seethed up. *Vincent Indigo! The rest are unknowns—he must have left the official craft when it landed at a nearby airport to wait for tomorrow, and met them—Was he always a criminal, who slithered his way into public service, or was it the chance he saw which corrupted him?*

No matter. He dares endanger Rero!

Beneath the fury, a logical part of me was baffled. *His actions don't make sense. Probably he supposes, probably rightly, that his name didn't register on the Maclarens when we uttered it. Voice transponders or no, we do have a thick accent.*

Nevertheless, can he really hope that his part in this business will remain hidden? He has to return us if he wants to collect his price, and we'll denounce him—

Is he insane, to overlook that? Are his accomplices, too? He never struck me as irrational. But what is sanity ... in a human?

My glance went to Maclaren and his wife. Over the years I have learned in slight measure to read expression, stance, aura in that race. Fear had largely departed from them, now that it appeared there was no direct physical threat. He stood a-scowl with thought, and a cold wrath was coming over him. She was regarding us, her guests, with a horrified pity. Though they remained in bodily contact, that was not where their attention lay.

It would have been for Rero-and-me, of course, if we could have touched. But we could simply hold gloves and make forlorn skin-signs.

The two men re-entered and reported their task done. "Fine," Indigo said. "Let's get going. You"—he pointed at the human prisoners—"stay indoors. You"—that was us—"go on out."

The four kidnappers moved cautiously, two ahead of us, two behind, while we shuffled forth. Moonlight glimmered on early dew. The stars looked infinitely far. The lights of the village and of neighboring houses looked farther still. Most distant was the yellow glow from the home we had left.

Rero attempted speech in our language. Since our hosts could no longer hear it, Indigo did not forbid. Her words hurried: "Beloved, what do you suppose we should do? How can we trust them? They must be crazy to believe they can carry this off and go unpunished."

So her thought had paralled mine to that extent: hardly a surprise. Mine leaped onward. "No, they

can reason, in a twisted fashion," I said. "Else
they wouldn't have the kind of preparation and
discipline they do. Perhaps they have a secure
hiding place ready, or a change of identities, or
whatever. The risk would still appear enormous to
me—considering that we represent a whole
planet, won't the Citadel bend every effort to
hunting them down?—but what do we know of the
ins and outs of Earth?" I clamped her fingers in
mine, hard. "Best we stay calm, alert, bide our
time. The ransom will surely be paid. If the Protector won't, then I expect those people who want
alliance with our kind will subscribe to the sum
demanded."

We reached the aircraft. Its door stood ajar
above us. "Go on in," directed Indigo. His men
drew closer.

We could not enter side by side in our bulky
equipment. As it happened, I went first, climbing
up a short extruded ladder. Cabin lighting was
weak but sufficient. My gaze traveled aft, and I
stopped short in the entrance.

"You have only one biostatic unit!" I protested.
My hearts began to gallop. A roaring rose in my
head.

"Yes, yes, we've no room for two," Indigo said
impatiently. "Either of you can plug into it if you
like. The othe can last in his suit, or hers, till we
get where we're bound. There we have an Arvel-
conditioned chamber."

My look sought Rero's. Though her countenance
was a blur in the moonlight, her aura throbbed
red. Mine did too. She spoke in our language: "If
that is true, why need they bother with a unit at
all? They only mean to keep one of us alive. Not
both."

"Alive as a hostage." My words sounded remote,
a stranger's. "This is not a capture for money."

And rage took us into itself.

She at the thought that I might have to die, I at the thought that she might have to die, went aflame. You can imagine; but in these peaceful years of ours, you cannot know.

We were no longer persons, we were killing machines. Yet never had our awarenesses been more efficient. I believe I saw each dewdrop upon each blade of turf around the feet of those who would let Rero perish. I knew that my suit and its gear made me awkward, but I knew also that they were heavy. I gauged and sprang.

A man stood beside the ladder. My boots crashed on his skull. He went down beneath my mass, we rolled over, he lay broken, I lumbered up and charged at the next nearest. Rero was entangled with a third man Indigo danced about. He hadn't fired immediately for fear of hitting a comrade. He would in a moment, I knew, and Rero-and-I would be dead.

Dead together.

A form hurtled from the verandah, across the lawn, toward us. Utterly astounded, I did not slay him with whom I grappled. I only throttled him slack while I stared.

Maclaren. Maclaren had abandoned his wife to come help us.

He caught Indigo by surprise, from behind— grabbed the pistol wrist, threw his left arm around the man's neck, put a knee in the back.

I mastered myself and went to aid Rero. Despite her weight of apparatus, her small form was bounding back and forth, in and out, fast enough for her enemy to miss when he shot. Him I did pluck apart.

The moon stood higher when calm had returned to us. It had to the Maclarens earlier. In him it took the form of sternness, in her of a puzzled half-compassion, as we loomed above Vincent Indigo.

He huddled in a chair, a blot upon that beautiful room, and pleaded with us.

"Certainly I'm going to take your flyer and fetch the police," Maclaren said. "But before then, in case the Citadel tries to cover for you, I want the facts myself." He realigned his audiovisual recorder. "Several copies of this tape distributed in the right places—You were acting for the Protector, weren't you?"

Wretchedness stared back. "Please," Indigo whispered.

"Shall I break a few bones?" I asked.

"No!" Tamara exclaimed. "Voah, you can't talk that way. You're civilized!"

"He would have let Rero die, wouldn't he?" I retorted.

My wife's arm went around me. Through my sealsuit, I imagined the pressure, and the same desire kindled in us both. How long till we could appease it? I heard the force she must use to stay reasonable as she counselled in our language: "Better we be discreet. Two men killed in a fight, that's condonable. But it wouldn't speak well for us, in human ears, if we injured helpless prisoners."

I subsided. "Correct," I said, "though does he need to know this?"

The spirit had gone out of Indigo anyhow. His aura flickered bluish-dim. He dropped his glance to the floor and mumbled, "Yes, that was the idea. Trying to make the Arvelans break off negotiations because they'd decide our race is too—oh, too unstable to be safe around. It couldn't be done officially, when so many dupes are putting on pressure for a treaty conference."

Maclaren nodded. "We were supposed to think it was the work of a criminal gang," he said. "Which it was indeed. A criminal gang in the Citadel, running the government. When that news breaks, I hope to see them not just out of office, but on trial."

"No!" Anguish whipped through Indigo. He raised eyes and hands, he shuddered. "You can't! Not the Protector—the *Dynasty*—God alive, Maclaren, can't you understand? That's what we've been trying to save. Would you let it crumble? Would you leave us defenseless before a pack of monsters?"

Silence grew until at last Maclaren said, from the bottom of his throat, "You actually believe that, don't you?"

"He does, he does," Tamara cried through tears. "Oh, the poor fool! Don't be too hard on him, Terangi. He was acting out of . . . out of love . . . wasn't he?"

Love, for such an object? Rero-and-I shared horror.

"I don't know as how that excuses him," Maclaren said grimly. "Well, we have his admission. Let the courts decide what to do with him and the rest. It won't matter."

He straightened, I saw him easing muscle by muscle, and he said to us: "What does matter is that the plot failed. I suppose there'll have to be a lot of behind-the-scenes bargaining, compromises, pretenses that certain individuals never were involved—political expediency. Not too important. What is important is that we can use the scandal to bring down the whole clique that's wanted to lock us up in a hermit kingdom. We will be leaguing with Arvel." Wonder trembled in his voice. "We truly will."

Truly? passed through Rero-and-me.

"Your doing!" Tamara hugged us both where we stood. "If it hadn't been for your courage—"

"Why, there was no courage," Rero told her. "If we had gone meekly along, one of us would have died. What had we to lose?"

The knife that had formed within my soul flashed out of its sheath. "We would have been killed—which ought to have served the purpose reasonably well—if you had not intervened, Terangi Maclaren," I said, as if each word were being cut out of me.

He didn't notice my mood, in his pleasure, as he replied, "What else could I do, after the fighting began?" He hesitated. "It wasn't just your lives, Voah-and-Rero, though of course they meant a great deal. It was realizing that your race might well be provoked into withdrawing from ours. And that would have been about the most terrible loss humanity had ever had. Wouldn't it?"

"Your wife was endangered," I declared.

"I knew that," he said. They gripped hands, those two. Nevertheless he could tell me while she listened and nodded: "We both did. But we had the whole world to think about."

Rero-and-I do recommend making a pact, sharing transporter networks, conducting what trade and cultural exchange are possible. In our opinion, this will bring benefits outweighing any psychic harm of the kind that some fear. We can even suggest precautions to take against troublous influences.

Above all, O people of Arvel, never pity the beings on Earth. If you do, then sorrow will drown you. They know so little of love. They cannot ever know more.

THE VOORTREKKERS

—And he shall see old planets change
and alien stars arise—

So swift is resurrection that the words go on
which had been in me when last I died. Only after
pulsebeats does the strangeness raining through
my senses reach my awareness, to make me know
that four more decades, and almost nine light-
years, have flowed between me and the poet.

Light-years. Light. Everywhere light. Once, a
boy, I spent a night camped on a winter mountain-
top. Then it entered my bones—and how can
anyone who has done likewise ever believe otherwise?—that space is not dark. Maybe this was
when the need was born in me, to go up and out
into the sky.

I am in the sky now, and of it. Around me stars
and stars and stars are crowding, until there is no
room for blackness to be more than a crystal
which holds them. They are all the colors of
reality, from lightning through gold to the
duskiest rose, but each one singingly keen.
Nebulae are flung among them like veils and
clouds, where great suns have died or new worlds
are whirling to birth. The Milky Way is a cool
torrent, here cloven by the thunderstorm masses

of galactic center, there open a-glint toward end-lessness. I magnify my vision and trace the spiral of our sister maelstrom, a million and a half light-years hence in Andromeda.

Sol is a small glow on the edge of Hercules. Brightest is Sirius, whose blue-white luminance casts shadows of fittings and housings across my hull. I seek and find its companion.

This is not done by optics. The dwarf is barely coming around the giant, lost in glare. What I see, through different sensors, is the X-radiation; what I snuff is a sharp breath of neutrinos mingled with the gale that streams from the other; I swim in an intricate interplay of force-fields, balancing, thrusting, while they caress me; I listen to the skirls and drones, the murmurs and melodics of a universe.

At first I do not hear Korene. If I was a little slow to leave Kipling for these heavens, so I am to leave them for her. Maybe it's more excusable. I must make certain at once, as much as possible, that we are not in danger. Probably we aren't, or the automatons would have restored us to existence before the scheduled moment. But auto-matons can only judge what they were designed and programmed to judge, by people nine light-years away from yonder mystery, people most likely dust, even as Korene and Joel are surely dust.

Joel, Joel! Korene calls from within me. *Are you there?*

I open my interior scanners. Her principal body, the one which houses her principal brain, is in motion, carefully testing every part after forty-three years of death. For the thousandth time, the beauty of this seat of her consciousness strikes me. Its darkly sheening shape is only humanlike in the way that an abstract sculpture might be on far, far Earth—those several arms, for instance, or the

dragonfly head which is not really a head at all—
and only this for functional reasons. But something about the slimness and grace of movement
recalls Korene who is dust.

She has not yet made contact with any of the
specialized auxiliary bodies around her. Instead
she has joined a communication circuit to one of
mine.

Hi, I flash, rather shakily, for in spite of studies
and experiments and simulations, years of them, it
is still too tremendous to comprehend, that we are
actually approaching Sirius. *How are you?*

Fine. Everything okay?

Near's I can tell. Why didn't you use voice?

*I did. No answer. I yelled. No answer. So I
plugged in.*

My joy gets tinged with embarrassment. *Sorry.
I, uh, I guess I was too excited.*

She breaks the connection, since it is not ideally
convenient, and says, "Quite something out
there?"

"You wouldn't believe," I respond by my own
speaker. "Take a look."

I activate the viewscreens for her. "O-o-o-ohh; O
God," she breathes. Yes, breathes. Our artificial
voices copy those which once were in our throats.
Korene's is husky and musical; it was a pleasure
to hear her sing at parties. Her friends often urged
her to get into amateur theatricals, but she said
she had neither the time nor the talent.

Maybe she was right, though Lord knows she
was good at plenty of other things, her astronautical engineering, painting, cookery, sewing
fancy clothes, throwing feasts, playing tennis and
poker, ranging over hills, being a wife and mother,
in her first life. (Well, we've both changed a lot
since then.) On the other hand, that utterance of
hers, when she sees the star before her, says everything for which I can only fumble.

From the beginning, when the first rockets roared into orbit, some people have called astronauts a prosaic lot, if they weren't calling us worse; and no doubt in some cases this was true. But I think mainly it's just that we grow tongue-tied in the presence of the Absolute.

"I wish—" I say, and energize an auxiliary of my own, a control-module maintainer, to lay an awkward touch upon her—"I wish you could sense it the way I do, Korene. Plug back in—full psycho-neural—when I've finished my checkouts, and I'll try to convey a little."

"Thanks, my friend." She speaks with tenderness. "I knew you would. But don't worry about my missing something because of not being wired up like a ship. I'll be having a lot of experiences you can't, and wishing I could share them with you." She chuckles. *Vive la différence.*

Nonetheless I hear the flutter in her tone and, knowing her, am unsurprised when she asks anxiously, "Are there . . . by any chance . . . planets?"

"No trace. We're a long ways off yet, of course. I might be missing the indications. So far, though, it looks as if the astronomers were right who declared minor bodies cannot condense around a star like Sirius. Never mind, we'll both find enough to keep us out of mischief in the next several years. Already at this range, I'm noticing all kinds of phenomena which theory did not predict."

"Then you don't think we'll need organics?"

"No, 'fraid not. In fact, the radiation—"

"Sure. Understood. But damn, next trip I'm going to insist on a destination that'll probably call for them."

She told me once, back in the Solar System, after we had first practiced the creation of ourselves in flesh: "It's like making love again."

They had not been lovers in their original lives.
He an American, she a European, they served the
space agencies of their respective confederations
and never chanced to be in the same cooperative
venture. Thus they met only occasionally and
casually, at professional conventions or celebra-
tions. They were still young when the interstellar
exploration project was founded. It was a joint
undertaking of all countries—no one bloc could
have gotten its taxpayers to bear the cost—but
research and development must run for a generation before hardware would become available to
the first true expeditions. Meanwhile there was
nothing but a few unmanned probes, and the inter-
planetary studies wherein Joel and Korene took
part.

She retired from these, to desk and laboratory,
at an earlier age than he did, having married Olaf
and wishing children. Olaf himself continued on
the Lunar shuttle for a while. But that wasn't the
same as standing on the peaks of Rhea beneath the
rings of Saturn or pacing the million kilometers of
a comet, as afire as the scientists themselves with
what they were discovering. Presently he quit, and
joined Korene on one of the engineering teams of
the interstellar group. Together they made
important contributions, until she accepted a
managerial position. This interested her less in its
own right; but she handled it ferociously well,
because she saw it as a means to an end—
authority, influence. Olaf stayed with the work he
liked best. Their home life continued happy.

In that respect, Joel at first differed. Pilots on
the major expeditions (and he got more berths
than his share) could seldom hope to be family
men. He tried, early in the game; but after he
realized what a very lonely kind of pain drove a
girl he had loved to divorce him, he settled for a

succession of mistresses. He was always careful to explain to them that nothing and nobody could make him stop faring before he must.

This turned out to be not quite true. Reaching mandatory age for "the shelf," he might have finagled a few extra years skyside. But by then, cuts in funding for space were marrow-deep. Those who still felt that man had business beyond Earth agreed that what resources were left had better go mostly toward the stars. Like Korene, Joel saw that the same was true of him. He enrolled in the American part of the effort. Experience and natural talent equipped him uniquely to work on control and navigation.

In the course of this, he met Mary. He had known a good many female astronauts, and generally liked them as persons—often as bodies too, but long voyages and inevitable promiscuity were as discouraging to stable relationships for them as for him. Mary used her reflexes and spirit to test-pilot experimental vehicles near home.

This didn't mean that she failed to share the dream. Joel fell thoroughly in love with her. Their marriage likewise proved happy.

He was forty-eight, Korene sixty, when the word became official: The basic machinery for reaching the stars now existed. It needed merely several years' worth of refinement and a pair of qualified volunteers.

It *is* like making love again.

How my heart soared when first we saw that the second planet has air a human can breathe! Nothing can create that except life. Those months after Joel went into orbit around it and we observed, photographed, spectroanalyzed, measured, sampled, calculated, mainly reading what instruments recorded but sometimes linking ourselves directly to them and feeling the input as

once we felt wind in our hair or surf around our
skins—

Why do I think of hair, skin, heart, love, I who
am embodied in metal and synthetics and ghostly
electron-dance? Why do I remember Olaf with this
knife sharpness?

I suppose he died well before Korene. Men
usually do. (What does death have against women,
anyway?) Then was her aftertime until she could
follow him down; and in spite of faxes and diaries
and every other crutch humankind has invented, I
think he slowly became a blur, never altogether to
be summoned forth except perhaps in sleep. At
least, with this cryogenic recall of mine which is
not programmed to lie. I remember how aging
Korene one day realized, shocked, that she had
nothing left except aging Olaf, that she could no
longer see or feel young Olaf except as words.

Oh, she loved him-now, doubtless in a deeper
fashion than she-then had been able to love him-
then, after all their shared joy, grief, terror, toil,
hope, merry little sillinesses which stayed more
clear across the years than many of the big events
—yes, their shared furies and frustrations with
each other, their few and fleeting intense involvements with outsiders, which somehow also were
always involvements between him and her—she
loved her old husband, but she had lost her young
one.

Whereas I have been given him back, in my
flawless new memory. And given Joel as well, or
instead, or—Why am I thinking this nonsense?
Olaf is dust.

Tau Ceti is flame.

It's not the same kind of fire as Sol. It's cooler,
yellower, something autumnal about it, even
though it will outlive man's home star. I don't
suppose the unlikenesses will appear so great to
human eyes. I know the entire spectrum. (How

much more does Joel sense! To me, every sun is a once-in-the-universe individual; to him, every sunspot is.) The organic body/mind is both more general and more specific than this . . . like me *vis-à-vis* Joel. (I remember, I remember: striding the Delphi road, muscle-play, boot-scrunch, spilling sunlight and baking warmth, bees at hum through wild thyme and rosemary, on my upper lip a taste of sweat, and that tremendous plunge down to the valley where Oedipus met his father . . . Machine, I would not experience it in quite those terms. There would be too many other radiations, forces, shifts and subtleties which Oedipus never felt. But would it be less beautiful? Is a deaf man, suddenly cured, less alive because afterward his mind gives less time to his eyes?)

Well, we'll soon know how living flesh experiences the living planet of Tau Ceti.

It isn't the infinite blue and white of Earth. It has a greenish tinge, equally clear and marvelous, and two moons for the lovers whom I, sentimental old crone, keep imagining. The aliennesses may yet prove lethal. But Joel said, in his dear dry style:

"The latest readouts convince me. The tropics are a shirt-sleeve environment." His mind grinned, I am sure, as formerly his face did. "Or a bare-ass environment. That remains to be seen. I'm certain, however, organic bodies can manage better down there than any of yours or mine."

Was I the one who continued to hesitate because I had been the one more eager for this? A kind of fear chilled me. "We already know they can't find everything they need to eat, in that biochemistry—"

"By the same token," the ship reminded, not from intellectual but emotional necessity, "nothing local, like germs, can make a lunch off them. The survival odds are excellent," give the

concentrated dietary supplements, tools, and the
rest of what we have for them. "Good Lord,
Korene, you could get smashed in a rock storm,
prospecting some wretched asteroid, or I could
run into too much radiation for the screens and
have my brain burned out. Or whatever. Do we
mind?"

"No," I whispered. "Not unendurably."

"So *they* won't."

"True. I shouldn't let my conscience make a
coward of me. Let's go right ahead."

After all, when I brought children into the
world, long ago, I knew they might be given
straight over to horror; or it might take them later
on; or at best, they would be born to trouble as the
sparks fly upward, and in an astonishingly few
decades be dust. Yet I never took from them, while
they lay innocent in my womb, their chance at life.

Thus Joel and I are bringing forth the children
who will be ourselves.

He wheels like another moon around the world,
and his sensors drink of it and his mind reasons
about it. I, within him, send forth my auxiliary
bodies to explore its air and waters and lands;
through the laser channels, mine are their labors,
triumphs, and—twice—deaths. But such things
have become just a part of our existence, like the
jobs from which we hurried home every day.
(Though here job and home go on concurrently.)
The rest of us, the most of us, is linked in those
circuits that guide our children into being.

We share, we are a smile-pattern down the
waves and wires, remembering how chaste the
agency spokesman made it sound, in that first
famous interview. Joel and I had scarcely met
then, and followed it separately on television. He
told me afterward that, having heard the spiels a
thousand times before, both pro and con, he'd
rather have gone fishing.

(Neither was especially likable, the commentator small and waspish, the spokesman large and Sincere. The latter directed his fleshy countenance at the camera and said:

"Let me summarize, please. I know it's familiar to you in the audience, but I want to spell out our problem.

"In the state of the art, we can send small spacecraft to the nearer stars, and back, at an average speed of about one-fifth light's. That means twenty-odd years to reach Alpha Centauri, the closest; and then there's the return trip; and, naturally, a manned expedition would make no sense unless it was prepared to spend a comparable time on the spot, learning those countless things which unmanned probes cannot. The trouble is, when I say small spacecraft, I mean small. Huge propulsion units but minimal hull and payload. No room or mass to spare for the protection and life support that even a single human would require; not to mention the fact that confinement and monotony would soon drive a crew insane."

"What about suspended animation?" asked the commentator.

The spokesman shook his head. "No, sir. Aside from the bulkiness of the equipment, radiation leakage would destroy too many cells en route. We can barely provide shielding for those essential items which are vulnerable." He beamed. "So we've got a choice. Either we stay with our inadequate probes, or we go over to the system being proposed."

"Or we abandon the whole boondoggle and spend the money on something useful," the commentator said.

The spokesman gave him a trained look of pained patience and replied: "The desirability of space exploration is a separate question, that I'll be glad to take up with you later. If you please, for the time being let's stick to the mechanics of it."

" 'Mechanics' may be a very good word, sir," the commentator insinuated. "Turning human beings into robots. Not exactly like Columbus, is it? Though I grant you, thinkers always did point out how machine-like the astronauts were . . . and are."

"If you please," the spokesman repeated, "value judgments aside, who's talking about making robots out of humans? Brains transplanted into machinery? Come! If a body couldn't survive the trip, why imagine that a brain in a tank might? No, we'll simply employ ultra-sophisticated computer-sensor-effector systems."

"With human minds."

"With human psychoneural patterns mapped in, sir. That is all." Smugly: "True, that's a mighty big 'all.' The pattern of an individual is complex beyond imagination, and dynamic rather than static; our math boys call it n-dimensional. We will have to develop methods for scanning it without harm to the subject, recording it, and transferring it to a different matrix, whether that matrix be photonic-electronic or molecular-organic." Drawing breath, then portentously: "Consider the benefits, right here on Earth, of having such a capability."

"I don't know about that," said the commentator. "Maybe you could plant a copy of my personality somewhere else; but *I'd* go on in this same old body, wouldn't I?"

"It would hardly be your exact personality anyhow," admitted the spokesman. "The particular matrix would . . . um . . . determine so much of the functioning. The important thing, from the viewpoint of extrasolar exploration, is that this will give us machines which are not mere robots, but which have such human qualities as motivation and self-programming.

"At the same time, they'll have the advantages of robots. For example, they can be switched off in transit; they won't experience those empty years between stars; they'll arrive sane."

"Some of us wonder if they'll have departed sane. But look," the commentator challenged, "if your machines that you imagine you can program to be people, if they're that good, then why have them manufacture artificial flesh-and-blood people at the end of a trip?"

"Only where circumstances justify it," said the spokesman. "Under some conditions, organic bodies will be preferable. Testing the habitability of a planet is just the most obvious possibility. Consider how your body heals its own wounds. In numerous respects it's actually stronger, more durable, than metal or plastic."

"Why give them the same minds—if I may speak of minds in this connection—the same as the machines?"

"A matter of saving mass." The spokesman smirked at his own wit. "We know the psychoneural scanner will be far too large and fragile to carry along. The apparatus which impresses a pattern on the androids will have to use pre-existent data banks. It can be made much lighter than would otherwise be necessary, if those are the same banks already in use."

He lifted a finger. "Besides, our psychologists think this will have a reinforcing effect. I'd hardly dare call the relationship, ha, ha, parental—"

"Nor I," said the commentator. "I'd call it something like obscene or ghastly.")

When Joel and I, together, month after month guide these chemistries to completion, and when —O climax outcrying the seven thunders!—we send ourselves into the sleeping bodies—maybe, for us at least, it is more than making love ever was.

Joel and Mary were on their honeymoon when he told her of his wish.

Astronauts and ranking engineers could afford to go where air and water were clean, trees grew instead of walls, birdsong resounded instead of traffic, and one's fellow man was sufficiently remote that one could feel benign toward him. Doubtless that was among the reasons why politicians got re-elected by gnawing at the space program.

This evening the west was a fountain of gold above a sea which far out shimmered purple, then broke upon the sands in white thunder. Behind, palms made traces on a blue where Jupiter had kindled. The air was mild, astir with odors of salt and jasmine.

They stood, arms around each other's waists, her head leaned against him, and watched the sun leave. But when he told her, she stepped from him and he saw terror.

"Hey, what's wrong, darling?" He seized her hands.

"No," she said. "You mustn't."

"What? Why ever not? You're working for it too!"

The sky-glow caught tears. "For somebody else to go, that's fine. It, it'd be like winning a war—a just war, a triumph—when somebody else's man got to do the dying. Not you," she pleaded.

"But . . . good Lord," he tried to laugh, "it won't be me, worse luck. My satisfaction will be strictly vicarious. Supposing I'm accepted, what do I sacrifice? Some time under a scanner; a few cells for chromosome templates. Why in the cosmos should you care?"

"I don't know. It'd be . . . oh, I never thought about it before, never realized the thing might strike home like this—" She swallowed. "I guess it's . . . I'd think, there's a Joel, locked for the rest

of his existence inside a machine . . . and there's a
Joel in the flesh, dying some gruesome death, or
marooned forever."

Silence passed before he replied, slowly: "Why
not think, instead, there's a Joel who's glad to pay
the price and take the risk—" he let her go and
swept a gesture around heaven—"for the sake of
getting out yonder?"

She bit her lip. "He'd even abandon his wife."

"I hoped you'd apply also."

"No. I couldn't face it. I'm too much a, an Earthling. This is all too dear to me."

"Do you suppose I don't care for it? Or for you?"
He drew her to him.

They were quite alone. On grass above the
strand, they won to joy again.

"After all," he said later, "the question won't get
serious for years and years."

I don't come back fast. They can't just ram a lifetime into a new body. That's the first real thought
I have, as I drift from a cave where voices echoed
on and on, and then slowly lights appeared,
images, whole scenes, my touch on a control
board, Dad lifting me to his shoulder which is way
up in the sky, leaves above a brown secret pool,
Mary's hair tickling my nose, a boy who stands on
his head in the schoolyard, a rocket blastoff that
shakes my bones with its sound and light, Mother
giving me a fresh-baked ginger cookie, Mother laid
out dead and the awful strangeness of her and
Mary holding my hand very tight, Mary, Mary,
Mary.

No, that's not her voice, it's another woman's,
whose, yes, Korene's, and I'm being stroked and
cuddled more gently than I ever knew could be. I
blink to full consciousness, free-fall afloat in the
arms of a robot.

"Joel," she murmurs. "Welcome."

It crashes in on me. No matter the slow awaken-
ing: suddenly this. I've taken the anesthetic before
they wheel me to the scanner, I'm drowsing dizzily
off, then *now* I have no weight, metal and
machinery cram everywhere in around me, those
are not eyes I look into but glowing optical
sensors, "Oh, my God," I say, "it happened to me."

This me. Only I'm Joel! Exactly Joel, nobody
else.

I stare down the nude length of my body and
know that's not true. The scars, the paunch, the
white hairs here and there on the chest are gone.
I'm smooth, twenty years in age, though with half
a century inside me. I snap after breath.

"Be calm," says Korene.

And the ship speaks with my voice: "Hi, there.
Take it easy, pal. You've got a lot of treatment and
exercise ahead, you know, before you're ready for
action."

"Where are we?" breaks from me.

"Sigma Draconis," Korene says. "In orbit
around the most marvelous planet—intelligent
life, friendly, and their art is beyond describing,
'beautiful' is such a weak little word—"

"How are things at home?" I interrupt. "I mean,
how were they when you . . . we . . . left?"

"You and Mary were still going strong, you at
age seventy," she assures me. "Likewise the children and grandchildren." *Ninety years ago.*

I went under, in the laboratory, knowing a
single one of me would rouse on Earth and return
to her. I am not the one.

I didn't know how hard that would lash.

Korene holds me close. It's typical of her not to
be in any hurry to pass on the last news she had of
her own self. I suppose, through the hollowness
and the trying to cry in her machine arms, I
suppose that's why my body was programmed
first. Hers can take this better.

"It's not too late yet," she begged him. "I can still swing the decision your way."

Olaf's grizzled head wove back and forth. "No. How many times must I tell you?"

"No more," she sighed. "The choices will be made within a month."

He rose from his armchair, went to her where she sat, and ran a big ropy-veined hand across her cheek. "I am sorry," he said. "You are sweet to want me along. I hate to hurt you." She could imagine the forced smile above her. "But truly, why would you want a possible millennium of my grouchiness?"

"Because you are Olaf," Korene answered.

She got up likewise, stepped to a window, and stood looking out. It was a winter night. Snow lay hoar on roofs across the old city, spires pierced an uneasy glow, a few stars glimmered. Frost put shrillness into the rumble of traffic and machines. The room, its warmth and small treasures, felt besieged.

She broke her word by saying, "Can't you see, a personality inside a cybernet isn't a castrated cripple? In a way, we're the ones caged, in these ape bodies and senses. There's a whole new universe to become part of. Including a universe of new closenesses to me."

He joined her. "Call me a reactionary," he growled, "or a professional ape. I've often explained that I like being what I am, too much to start over as something else."

She turned to him and said low: "You'd also start over as what you were. We both would. Over and over."

"No. We'd have these aged minds."

She laughed forlornly. "'If youth knew, if age could.'"

"We'd be sterile."

"Of necessity. No way to raise children on any likely planet. Otherwise—Olaf, if you refuse, I'm going regardless. With another man. I'll always wish he were you."

He lifted a fist. "All right, God damn it!" he shouted. "All right! I'll tell you the real reason why I won't go under your bloody-scanner! I'd die too envious!"

It is fair here beyond foretelling: beyond understanding, until slowly we grow into our planet.

For it isn't Earth. Earth we have forever laid behind us, Joel and I. The sun is molten amber, large in a violet heaven. At this season its companion has risen about noon, a gold-bright star which will drench night with witchery under the constellations and three swift moons. Now, toward the end of day, the hues around us— intensely green hills, tall blue-plumed trees, rainbows in wings which jubilate overhead—are become so rich that they fill the air; the whole world glows. Off across the valley, a herd of beasts catches the shiningness on their horns.

We took off our boots when we came back to camp. The turf, not grass nor moss, is springy underfoot, cool between the toes. The nearby forest breathes out fragrances; one of them recalls rosemary. Closer is smoke from the fire Korene built while we were exploring. It speaks to my nostrils and the most ancient parts of my brain: of autumn leaves burning, of blazes after dark in what few high solitudes remained on Earth, of hearths where I sat at Christmas time with the children.

"Hello, dears," says my voice out of the machine. (It isn't the slim fleet body she uses aboard ship; it's built for sturdiness, is the only awkward sight in all the landscape.) "You seem to have had a pleasant day."

"Oh, my, oh, my!" Arms uplifted, I dance. "We *must* find a name for this planet. Thirty-six Ophiuchi B Two is ridiculous."

"We will," says Joel in my ear. His palm falls on my flank. It feels like a torch.

"I'm on the channel too," says the speaker with his voice. "Uh, look, kids, fun's fun, but we've got to get busy. I want you properly housed and supplied long before winter. And while we ferry the stuff, do the carpenteering, et cetera, I want more samples for us to analyze. So far you've just found some fruits and such that're safe to eat. You need meat as well."

"I hate to think of killing," I say, when I am altogether happy.

"Oh, I reckon I've got enough hunter instinct for both of us," says Joel, my Joel. Breath gusts from him, across me. "Christ! I never guessed how good elbow room and freedom would feel."

"Plus a large job," Korene reminds: the study of a world, that she and her Joel may signal our discoveries back to a Sol we can no longer see with our eyes alone; that in the end, they may carry back what we have gathered, to an Earth that perhaps will no longer want it.

"Sure. I expect to love every minute." His clasp on me tightens. Waves shudder outward, through me. "Speaking of love—"

The machine grows still. A shadow has lengthened across its metal, where firelight weaves reflected. The flames talk merrily. A flying creature cries like a trumpet.

"So you have come to that," says Korene at last, a benediction.

"Today," I declare from our glory.

There is another quietness.

"Well, congratulations," says Korene's Joel. "We, uh, we were planning a little wedding present for you, but you've caught us by surprise."

Mechanical tendrils reach out. Joel releases me to take them in his fingers. "All the best, both of you. Couldn't happen to two nicer people, even if I am one of them myself, sort of. Uh, well, we'll break contact now, Korene and I. See you in the morning?"

"Oh, no, oh, no," I stammer, between weeping and laughter, and cast myself on my knees to embrace this body whose two spirits brought us to life and will someday bury us. "Stay. We want you here, Joel and I. You, you are us." *And more than us and pitifully less than us.* "We want to share with you."

The priest mounted to his pulpit. Tall in white robes, he waited there against the shadows of the sanctuary; candles picked him out and made a halo around his hood. When silence was total in the temple, he leaned forward. His words tolled forth to the faces and the cameras:

"Thou shalt have none other gods but me, said the Lord unto the childen of Israel. Thou shalt love thy neighbor as thyself, said Christ unto the world. And sages and seers of every age and every faith warned against *hubris*, that overweening pride which brings down upon us immortal anger.

"The Tower of Babel and the Flood of Noah may be myths. But in myth lies a wisdom of the race which goes infinitely beyond the peerings and posturings of science. Behold our sins today and tremble.

"Idolatry: man's worship of what he alone has made. Uncharity: man's neglect, yes, forsaking of his brother in that brother's need, to whore after mere adventure. *Hubris:* man's declaration that he can better the work of God.

"You know what I mean. While the wretched of Earth groan in their billions for succor, treasure is spewed into the barrenness of outer space.

Little do the lords of lunacy care for their fellow mortals. Nothing do they care for God.

"'To follow knowledge like a sinking star, Beyond the utmost bound of human thought' is a pair of lines much quoted these days. Ulysses, the eternal seeker. May I remind you, those lines do not refer to Homer's wanderer, but to Dante's, who was in hell for breaking every constraint which divine Providence had ordained.

"And yet how small, how warm and understandable was his sin! His was not that icy arrogance which today the faceless engineers of the interstellar project urge upon us. Theirs is the final contempt for God and for man. In order that we may violate the harmony of the stars, we are to create, in metal and chemicals, dirty caricatures of a holy work; we are actually to believe that by our electronic trickery we can breathe into them souls."

Nat the rhesus monkey runs free. The laboratory half of the cabin is barred to him; the living quarters, simply and sturdily equipped, don't hold much he can harm. He isn't terribly mischievous anyway. Outdoors are unlimited space and trees where he can be joyful. So, when at home with Korene and Joel, he almost always observes the restrictions they have taught him.

His wish to please may stem from memory of loneliness. It was a weary while he was caged on the surface, after he had been grown in the tank. (His body has, in fact, existed longer than the two human ones.) He had no company save rats, guinea pigs, tissue cultures, and the like—and, of course, the machine which tended and tested him. That that robot often spoke, petted and played games, was what saved his monkey sanity. When at last living flesh hugged his own, what hollow within him was suddenly filled?

What hollow in the others? He skips before their feet, he rides on their shoulders, at night he shares their bed.

But today is the third of cold autumn rains. Though Korene has given to this planet of Eighty-two Eridani the name Gloria, it has its seasons, and now spins toward a darker time. The couple have stayed inside, and Nat gets restless. No doubt, as well, the change in his friends arouses an unease.

There ought to be cheer. The cabin is amply large for two persons. It is more than snug, it is lovely, in the flowing grain of its timbers and the crystal-glittering stones of its fireplace. Flames dance on the hearth; they laugh; a bit of their smoke escapes to scent the air like cinnamon; through the brightness of fluorescent panels, their light shimmers off furnishings and earthenware which Joel and Korene made together in the summer which is past—off the racked reels of an audiovisual library and a few beloved pictures— off twilit panes where rain sluices downward. Beyond a closed door, wind goes *brroo-oom*.

Joel sits hunched at his desk. He hasn't bathed or shaved lately, his hair is unkempt, his coverall begrimed and sour. Korene has maintained herself better; it is dust in the corners and un-washed dishes in a basin which bespeak what she has neglected while he was trying to hunt. She sprawls on the bed and listens to music, though the ringing in her ears makes that hard.

Both have grown gaunt. Their eyes are sunken, their mouths and tongues are sore. Upon the dried skin of hands and faces, a rash has appeared.

Joel casts down his slide rule. "Damn, I can't think!" he nearly shouts. "Screw those analyses! What good are they?"

Korene's reply is sharp. "They just might show what's gone wrong with us and how to fix it."

"Judas! When I can't even sleep right—" He twists about on his chair to confront the inactive robot. "You! You damned smug machines, where are you? What're you doing?"

A tic goes ugly along Korene's lip. "They're busy, yonder in orbit," she says. "I suggest you follow their example."

"Yah! Same as you?"

"Quite—anytime you'll help me keep our household running, Sir Self-Appointed Biochemist." She starts to lift herself but abandons the effort. Tears of self-pity trickle forth. "Olaf wouldn't have turned hysterical like you."

"And Mary wouldn't lie flopped-out useless," he says. However, the sting she has given sends him back to his labor. Interpreting the results of gas chromatography on unknown compounds is difficult at best. When he has begun to hallucinate —when the graphs he has drawn slide around and intertwine as if they were worms—

A crash resounds from the pantry. Korene exclaims. Joel jerks erect. Flour and the shards of a crock go in a tide across the floor. After them bounds Nat. He stops amidst the wreckage and gives his people a look of amazed innocence. Dear me, he all but says, how did this happen?

"You lousy little sneak!" Joel screams. "You know you're not allowed on the shelves!" He storms over to stand above the creature. "How often—" Stooping, he snatches Nat up by the scruff of the neck. A thin tone of pain and terror slips between his fingers.

Korene rises. "Let him be," she says.

"So he can finish the . . . havoc?" Joel hurls the monkey against the wall. The impact is audible. Nat lies twisted and wailing.

Silence brims the room, inside the wind. Korene gazes at Joel, and he at his hands, as if they confronted these things for the first time. When at last she speaks, it is altogether without tone. "Get out. Devil. Go."

"But," he stammers. "But, I didn't mean."

Still she stares. He retreats into new anger. "That pest's been driving me out of my skull! You know he has! We may be dead because of him, and yet you gush over him till I could puke!"

"Right. Blame him for staying healthy when we didn't. I find depths in you I never suspected before."

"And I in you," he jeers. "He's your baby, isn't he? The baby you've been tailored never to bear yourself. Your spoiled brat."

She brushes past him and kneels beside the animal.

Joel utters a raw kind of bark. He lurches to the door, hauls it open, disappears as if the dusk has eaten him. Rain and chill blow in.

Korene doesn't notice. She examines Nat, who pants, whimpers, watches her with eyes that are both wild and dimming. Blood mats his fur. It becomes clear that his back is broken.

"My pretty, my sweet, my bouncy-boy, please don't hurt. Please," she sobs as she lifts the small form. She carries him into the laboratory, prepares an injection, cradles him and sings a lullaby while it does its work.

Afterward she brings the body back to the living room, lies down holding it, and cries herself into a half-sleep full of nightmares.

—Her voice rouses her, out of the metal which has rested in a corner. She never truly remembers, later, what next goes on between her selves. Words, yes; touch; a potion for her to drink; then the blessing of nothingness. When she awakens, it is day and the remnant of Nat is gone from her.

So is the robot. It returns while she is leaving the bed. She would weep some more if she had the strength; but at least, through a headache she can think.

The door swings wide. Rain has ended. The

world gleams. Here too are fall colors, beneath a lucent sky where wandersongs drift from wings beating southward. The carpet of the land has turned to sallow gold, the forest to bronze and red and a purple which bears tiny flecks like mica. Coolness streams around her.

Joel enters, half leaning on the machine, half upheld by it. Released, he crumples at her feet. From the throat which is not a throat, his voice begs:

"Be kind to him, will you? He spent the night stumbling around the woods till he caved in. Might've died, if a chemosensor of ours hadn't gotten the spoor."

"I wanted to," mumbles the man on the floor. "After what I did."

"Not his fault," says the ship anxiously, as if his identity were also involved and must clear itself of guilt. "He wasn't in his right mind."

The female sound continues: "An environmental factor, you see. We have finally identified it. You weren't rational either, girl. But never blame yourself, or him." Hesitation. "You'll be all right when we've taken you away from here."

Korene doesn't observe how unsteady the talking was, nor think about its implications. Instead, she sinks down to embrace Joel.

"How could I do it?" he gasps upon her breast.

"It wasn't you that did," says Korene in the robot, while Korene in the woman holds him close and murmurs.

—They are back aboard ship, harnessed weightless. Thus far they haven't asked for explanations. It was enough that their spirits were again together, that the sadness and the demons were leaving them, that they slept unhaunted and woke to serenity. But now the soothing drugs have worn off and healing bodies have, afresh, generated good minds.

They look at each other, whisper, and clasp

hands. Joel says aloud, into the metal which encloses them: "Hey. You two."

His fellow self does not answer. Does it not dare? Part of a minute goes by before the older Korene speaks. "How are you, my dears?"

"Not bad," he states. "Physically."

How quiet it grows.

Until the second Korene gives challenge. "Hard news for us. Isn't that so?"

"Yes," her voice sighs back.

They stiffen. "Go on," she demands.

The answer is hasty. "You were suffering from pellagra. That was something we'd never encountered before; not too simple to diagnose, either, especially in its early stages. We had to ransack our whole medical data bank before we got a clue as to what to look for in the cell and blood samples we took. It's a deficiency disease, caused by lack of niacin, a B vitamin."

Protest breaks from Joel. "But hell, we knew the Glorian biochemistry doesn't include B complex! We took our pills."

"Yes, of course. That was one of the things which misled us, along with the fact that the animals throve on the same diet as yours. But we've found a substance in the native food—all native food; it's as integral to life as ATP is on Earth—a material that seemed harmless when we made the original analyses—" pain shrills forth— "when we decided we could create you—"

"It acts with a strictly human-type gene," the ship adds roughly. "We've determined which one, and don't see how to block the process. The upshot is release of an enzyme which destroys niacin in the bloodstream. Your pills disguised the situation at first, because the concentration of antagonist built up slowly. But equilibrium has been reached at last, and you'd get no measurable help from swallowing extra doses; they'd break down before you could metabolize them."

"Mental disturbances are one symptom," Korene says from the speaker. "The physical effects in advanced cases are equally horrible. Don't worry. You'll get well and stay well. Your systems have eliminated the chemical, and here is a lifetime supply of niacin."

She does not need to tell them that here is very little which those systems can use a fuel, nor any means of refining the meats and fruits on which they counted.

The ship gropes for words. "Uh, you know, this is the kind of basic discovery, I think, the kind of discovery we had to go into space to make. A piece of genetic information we'd never have guessed in a million years, staying home. Who knows what it'll be a clue to? Immortality?"

"Hush," warns his companion. To the pair in the cabin she says low, "We'll withdraw, leave you alone. Come out in the passageway when you want us . . . . Peace." A machine cannot cry, can it?

For a long while, the man and the woman arc mute. Finally, flatly, he declares, "What rations we've got should keep us, oh, I'd guess a month."

"We can be thankful for that." When she nods, the tresses float around her brow and cheekbones.

"Thankful! Under a death sentence?"

"We knew . . . our selves on Earth knew, some of us would die young. I went to the scanner prepared for it. Surely you did likewise."

"Yes. In a way. Except it's happening to me." He snaps after air. "And you, which is worse. This you, the only Korene that this I will ever have. Why *us*?"

She gazes before her, then astonishes him with a smile. "The question which nobody escapes. We've been granted a month."

He catches her to him and pleads, "Help me. Give me the guts to be glad."

—The sun called Eighty-two Eridani rises in white-gold radiance over the great blue rim of the planet. That is a blue as deep as the ocean of its winds and weather, the ocean of its tides and waves, surging aloft into flame and roses. The ship orbits on toward day. Clouds come aglow with morning light. Later they swirl in purity above summer lands and winter lands, storm and calm, forest, prairie, valley, height, river, sea, the flocks upon flocks which are nourished by this world their mother.

Korene and Joel watch it through an hour, side by side and hand in hand before a screen, afloat in the crowdedness of machinery. The robot and the ship have kept silence. A blower whirrs its breeze across their bare skins, mingling for them their scents of woman and man. Often their free hands caress, or they kiss; but they have made their love and are now making their peace.

The ship swings back into night. Opposite, stars bloom uncountable and splendid. She stirs. "Let us," she says.

"Yes," he replies.

"You could wait," says the ship. His voice need not be so harsh; but he does not think to control it. "Days longer."

"No," the man tells him. "That'd be no good," seeing Korene starve to death; for the last food is gone. "Damn near as bad as staying down there," and watching her mind rot while her flesh corrupts and withers.

"You're right," the ship agrees humbly. "Oh, Christ, if we'd thought!"

"You couldn't have, darling," says the robot with measureless gentleness. "No one could have."

The woman strokes a bulkhead, tenderly as if it were her man, and touches her lips to the metal.

He shakes himself. "Please, no more things

we've talked out a million times," he says. "Just goodbye."

The robot enfolds him in her clasp. The woman joins them. The ship knows what they want, it being his wish too, and *Sheep May Safely Graze* brightens the air.

The humans float together. "I want to say," his words stumble, "I never stopped loving Mary, and missing her, but I love you as much, Korene, and, and thanks for being what you've been.

"I wish I could say it better," he finishes.

"You don't need to," she answers, and signals the robot.

They hardly feel the needle. As they float embraced, toward darkness, he calls drowsily, "Don't grieve too long, you there. Don't ever be afraid o' making more lives. The universe'll always surprise us."

"Yes." She laughs a little through the sleep which is gathering her in. "Wasn't that good of God?"

We fare across the light-years and the centuries, life after life, death after death. Space is our single home. Earth has become more strange to us than the outermost comet of the farthest star.

For to Earth we have given:

Minds opened upon endlessness, which therefore hold their own world, and the beings upon it, very precious.

A knowledge of natural law whereby men may cross the abyss in the bodies their mothers gave them, short years from sun to sun, and planets unpeopled for their taking, so that their kind will endure as long as the cosmos.

A knowledge of natural law whereby they have stopped nature's casual torturing of them through sickness, madness, and age.

The arts, histories, philosophies and faiths and

things once undreamable, of a hundred sentient races; and out of these, an ongoing renaissance which does not look as if it will ever die.

From our gifts have sprung material wealth at each man's fingertips, beyond the grasp of any whole Earthbound nation; withal, a growing calm and wisdom, learned from the manyfoldedness of reality. Each time we return, strife seems less and fewer seem to hate their brothers or themselves.

But does our pride on behalf of them beguile us? They have become shining enigmas who greet us graciously, neither thrust us forth again nor seek to hold us against our wills. Though finally each of us never comes back, they make no others. Do they need our gifts any longer? Is it we the wanderers who can change and grow no more?

Well, we have served; and one service will remain to the end. Two in the deeps, two and two on the worlds, we alone remember those who lived, and those who died, and Olaf and Mary.

EPILOGUE

I

His name was a set of radio pulses. Converted into equivalent sound waves, it would have been an ugly squawk; so because he, like any consciousness, was the center of his own coordinate system, let him be called Zero.

He was out hunting that day. Energy reserves were low in the cave. That other who may be called One—being the most important dweller in Zero's universe—had not complained. But there was no need to. He also felt a dwindling potential. Accumulators grew abundantly in their neighborhood, but an undue amount of such cells must be processed to recharge One while she was creating. Motiles had more concentrated energy. And, of course, they were more highly organized. Entire parts could be taken from the body of a motile, needing little or no reshaping for One to use. Zero himself, though the demands on his functioning were much less, wanted a more easily assimilated charge than the accumulators provided.

In short, they both needed a change of diet.

Game did not come near the cave any more. The past hundred years had taught that it was unsafe. Eventually, Zero knew, he would have to move. But the thought of helping One through mile upon mile, steep, overgrown, and dangerous, made him delay. Surely he could still find large motiles within a few days' radius of his present home.

With One's help he fastened a carrier rack on his shoulders, took weapons in hand, and set forth.

That was near sunset. The sky was still light when he came on spoor: broken earthcrystals not yet healed, slabs cut from several boles, a trace of lubricant. Tuning his receptors to the highest sensitivity, he checked all the bands commonly made noisy by motiles. He caught a low-amplitude conversation between two persons a hundred miles distant, borne this far by some freak of atmospherics; closer by he sensed the impulses of small scuttering things, not worth chasing; a flier jetted overhead and filled his perception briefly with static. But no vibration of the big one. It must have passed this way days ago and now be out of receptor-shot.

Well, he could follow the trail, and catch up with the clumsy sawyer in time. It was undoubtedly a sawyer—he knew these signs—and therefore worth a protracted hunt. He ran a quick check on himself. Every part seemed in good order. He set into motion, a long stride which must eventually overhaul anything on treads.

Twilight ended. A nearly full moon rose over the hills like a tiny cold lens. Night vapors glowed in masses and streamers against a purple-black sky where stars glittered in the optical spectrum and which hummed and sang in the radio range. The forest sheened with alloy, flashed with icy speckles of silicate. A wind blew through the radiation-absorber plates overhead, setting them to ringing against each other; a burrower whirred, a grubber crunched through lacy crystals, a river brawled chill and loud down a ravine toward the valley below.

As he proceeded, weaving among trunks and girders and jointed rods with the ease of long practice, Zero paid most attention to his radio receptors. There was something strange in the

upper communication frequencies tonight, an
occasional brief note . . . set of notes, voice, drone,
like nothing he had heard before or heard tell
of . . . But the world was a mystery. No one had
been past the ocean to the west or the mountains
to the east. Finally Zero stopped listening and concentrated on tracking his prey. That was difficult,
with his optical sensors largely nullified by the
darkness, and he moved slowly. Once he tapped
lubricant from a cylinder growth and once he
thinned his acids with a drink of water. Several
times he felt polarization in his energy cells and
stopped for a while to let it clear away: he rested.

Dawn paled the sky over distant snowpeaks, and
gradually turned red. Vapors rolled up the slopes
from the valley, tasting of damp and sulfide. Zero
could see the trail again, and began to move
eagerly.

Then the strangeness returned—louder.

Zero slid to a crouch. His lattice swiveled
upward. Yes, the pulses did come from above.
They continued to strengthen. Soon he could
identify them as akin to the radio noise associated
with the functioning of a motile. But they did not
sense like any type he knew. And there was something else, a harsh flickering overtone, as if he also
caught leakage from the edge of a modulated
short-wave beam—

The sound struck him.

At first it was the thinnest of whistles, high and
cold above the dawn clouds. But within seconds it
grew to a roar that shook the earth, reverberated
from the mountains, and belled absorber plates
until the whole forest rang. Zero's head became an
echo chamber; the racket seemed to slam his brain
from side to side. He turned dazzled, horrified
sensors heavenward. And he saw the thing
descending.

For a moment, crazily, he thought it was a flier.

It had the long spindle-shaped body and the air-fins. But no flier had ever come down on a tail of multicolored flame. No flier blocked off such a monstrous portion of sky. When the thing must be two miles away!

He felt the destruction as it landed, shattered frames, melted earthcrystals, a little burrower crushed in its den, like a wave of anguish through the forest. He hurled himself flat on the ground and hung on to sanity with all four hands. The silence which followed, when the monster had settled in place, was like a final thunderclap.

Slowly Zero raised his head. His perceptions cleared. An arc of sun peered over the sierra. It was somehow outrageous that the sun should rise as if nothing had happened. The forest remained still, hardly so much as a radio hum to be sensed. The last echoes flew fading between the hills.

A measure of resolution: this was no time to be careful of his own existence. Zero poured full current into his transmitter. *"Alarm, alarm! All persons receiving, prepare to relay. Alarm!"*

Forty miles thence, the person who may as well be called Two answered, increasing output intensity the whole time: "Is that you, Zero? I noticed something peculiar in the direction of your establishment. What is the matter?"

Zero did not reply at once. Others were coming in, a surge of voices in his head, from mountaintops and hills and lowlands, huts and tents and caves, hunters, miners, growers, searakers, quarriers, toolmakers, suddenly become a unity. But he was flashing at his own home: "Stay inside, One. Conserve energy. I am unharmed, I will be cautious, keep hidden and stand by for my return."

"Silence!" called a stridency which all recognized as coming from Hundred. He was the oldest of them, he had probably gone through a total of half a dozen bodies. Irreversible polarization had slowed his thinking a little, taken the edge off, but the wisdom of his age remained and he presided over their councils. "Zero, report what you have observed."

The hunter hesitated. "That is not easy. I am at—" He described the location. ("Ah, yes," murmured Fifty-Six, "near that large galena lick.") "The thing somewhat resembles a flier, but enormous, a hundred feet long or more. It came down about two miles north of here on an incandescent jet and is now quiet. I thought I overheard a beamed signal. If so, the cry was like nothing any motile ever made."

"In these parts," Hundred added shrewdly. "But the thing must have come from far away. Does it look dangerous?"

"Its jet is destructive," Zero said, "but nothing that size, with such relatively narrow fins, could glide about. Which makes me doubt it is a predator."

"Lure accumulators," said Eight.

"Eh? What about them?" asked Hundred.

"Well, if lure accumulators can emit signals powerful enough to take control of any small motile which comes near and make it enter their grinders, perhaps this thing has a similar ability. Then, judging from its size, its lure must have tremendous range and close up could overpower large motiles. Including even persons?"

Something like a shiver moved along the communication band.

"It is probably just a grazer," said Three. "If so—" His overt signal trailed off, but the thought continued in all their partly linked minds: *A motile that big! Megawatt-hours in its energy cells. Hundreds or thousands of usable parts. Tons of metal. Hundred, did your great-grandcreator recall any such game, fabulous millennia ago?*

No.

If it is dangerous, it must be destroyed or driven off. If not, it must be divided among us. In either case: attacked!

Hundred rapped the decision forth. "All male persons take weapons and proceed to rendezvous at Broken Glade above the Coppertaste River. Zero, stalk as close as seems feasible, observe what you can, but keep silence unless something quite unforeseeable occurs. When we are gathered, you can describe details on which we may base a specific plan. Hasten!"

The voices toned away in Zero's receptor circuits. He was alone again.

The sun cleared the peaks and slanted long rays between the forest frames. Accumulators turned the black faces of their absorber plates toward it and drank thirstily of radiation. The mists dissipated, leaving boles and girders ashine with moisture. A breeze tinkled the silicate growths underfoot. For a moment Zero was astonishingly conscious of beauty. The wish that One could be here beside him, and the thought that soon he might be fused metal under the monster's breath, sharpened the morning's brightness.

Purpose congealed in him. Further down was a turmoil of frank greed. In all the decades since his activation there had been no such feast as this quarry should provide. Swiftly, he prepared himself. First he considered his ordinary weapons. The wire noose would never hold the monster, nor did he think the iron hammer would smash delicate moving parts (it did not seem to have any), or the steel bolts from his crossbow pierce a thin plate to short out a crucial circuit. But the clawed, spearheaded pry bar might be of use. He kept it in one hand while two others unfastened the fourth and laid it with his extra armament in the carrier rack. Thereupon they deftly hooked his cutting torch in its place. No one used this artificial device except for necessary work, or to finish off a big motile whose cells could replace the tremendous energy expended by the flame, or in cases of dire need. But if the monster attacked him, that would surely constitute dire need. His only immediate intention was to spy on it.

Rising, he stalked among shadows and sun reflections, his camouflage-painted body nearly invisible. Such motiles as sensed him fled or grew very still. Not even the great slasher was as feared a predator as a hunting person. So it had been since that ancient day when some forgotten savage genius made the first crude spark gap and electricity was tamed.

Zero was about halfway to his goal, moving slower and more carefully with each step, when he perceived the newcomers.

He stopped dead. Wind clanked the branches above him, drowning out any other sound. But his electronic sensors told him of . . . two . . . three moving shapes, headed from the monster. And their emission was as alien as its own.

In a different way. Zero stood for a long time straining to sense and to understand what he sensed. The energy output of the three was small, hardly detectable even this close; a burrower or skitterer used more power to move itself. The output felt peculiar, too, not really like a motile's: too simple, as if a mere one or two circuits oscillated. Flat, cold, activityless. But the signal output, on the other hand—it *must* be signal, that radio chatter—why, that was a shout. The things made such an uproar that reporters tuned at minimum could pick them up five miles away. As if they did not know about game, predators, enemies.

Or as if they did not care.

A while more Zero paused. The eeriness of this

advent sent a tingle through him. It might be said
he was gathering courage. In the end he gripped
his pry bar more tightly and struck off after the
three.

They were soon plain to his optical and radar
senses among the tall growths. He went stock-still
behind a frame and watched. Amazement shocked
his very mind into silence. He had assumed, from
their energy level, that the things were small. But
they stood more than half as big as he did! And yet
each of them had only one motor, operating at a
level barely sufficient to move a person's arm.
That could not be their power source. But what
was?

Thought returned to him. He studied their outlandishness in some detail. They were shaped not
altogether unlike himself, though two-armed,
hunchbacked, and featureless. Totally unlike the
monster, but unquestionably associated with it.
No doubt it had sent them forth as spy eyes, like
those employed by a boxroller. Certain persons
had been trying for the last century or so to
develop, from domesticated motiles, similar
assistants for hunting persons. Yes, a thing as big
and awkward as the monster might well need
auxiliaries.

Was the monster than indeed a predator? Or
even—the idea went like a lightning flash through
Zero's entire circuitry—a thinker? Like a person?
He struggled to make sense of the modulated
signals between the three bipeds. No, he could not.
But—

Wait!

Zero's lattice swung frantically back and forth.
He could not shake off the truth. That last signal
had come from the monster, hidden by a mile of
forest. From the monster to the bipeds. And were
they answering?

The bipeds were headed south. At the rate they

were going, they might easily come upon traces of habitation, and follow those traces to the cave where One was, long before Hundred's males had gathered at Broken Glade.

The monster would know about One.

Decision came. Zero opened his transmitter to full output, but broadcast rather than beamed in any degree. He would give no clue where those were whom he called. *"Attention, attention!* Tone in on me: direct sensory linkage. I am about to attempt capture of these motiles."

Hundred looked through his optics, listened with his receptors, and exclaimed, "No, wait, you must not betray our existence before we are ready to act."

"The monster will soon learn of our existence in any event," Zero answered. "The forest is full of old campsites, broken tools, traps, chipped stones, slag heaps. At present I should have the advantage of surprise. If I fail and am destroyed, that ought still to provide you with considerable data. Stand alert!"

He plunged from behind the girders.

The three had gone past. They sensed him and spun about. He heard a jagged modulation of their signal output. A reply barked back, lower in frequency. The voice of the monster? There was no time to wonder about that. Slow and clumsy though they were, the bipeds had gotten into motion. The central one snatched a tube slung across its back. Pounding toward them, through shattering crystals and clangorous branches, Zero thought, *I have not yet made any overtly hostile move, but* — The tube flashed and roared.

An impact sent Zero staggering aside. He went to one knee. Ripped circuits overwhelmed him with destruction signals. As the pain throbbed toward extinction, his head cleared enough to see that half his upper left arm was blown off.

The tube was held steady on him. He rose. The
knowledge of his danger flared in him. A second
biped had its arms around the third, which was
tugging a smaller object from a sheath.

Zero discharged full power through his
effectors. Blurred to view by speed, he flung himself to one side while his remaining left hand
threw the pry bar. It went meteorlike across a
shaft of sunlight and struck the tube. The tube was
pulled from the biped's grasp, slammed to the
ground and buckled.

Instantly Zero was upon the three of them. He
had already identified their communication
system, a transmitter and antenna actually
outside the skin! His one right hand smashed
across a biped's back, tearing the radio set loose.
His torch spat with precision. Fused, the
communicator of a second biped went dead.

The third one tried to escape. Zero caught it in
four strides, plucked off its antenna, and carried it
wildly kicking under one arm while he chased the
other two. When he had caught the second, the
first stood its ground and battered forlornly at
him with its hands. He lashed them all together
with his wire rope. As a precaution, he emptied
the carrier rack of the one which had shot him.
Those thin objects might be dangerous even with
the tube that had launched them broken. He
stuffed the bipeds into his own carrier.

For a moment, then, he lingered. The forest held
little sonic noise except the wind in the
accumulators. But the radio spectrum clamored.
The monster howled; Zero's own broadcast rolled
between sky and mountainside, from person to
person and so relayed across the land.

"No more talk now," he finished his report. "I
do not want the monster to track me. I have
prevented these auxiliaries from communicating
with it. Now I shall take them to my cave for

study. I hope to present some useful data at the rendezvous."

"This may frighten the monster off," Seventy-Two said.

"So much the better," Hundred answered.

"In that case," Zero said, "I will at least have brought back something from my hunt."

He snapped off his transmission and faded into the forest shadows.

II

The boat had departed from the spaceship on a mere whisper of jets. Machinery inboard hummed, clicked, murmured, sucked in exhausted air and blew out renewed; busied itself with matters of warmth and light, computation and propulsion. But it made no more than a foundation for silence.

Hugh Darkington stared out the forward port. As the boat curved away from the mother ship's orbit, the great hull gleamed across his sky—fell astern and rapidly dwindled until lost to view. The stars which it had hidden sprang forth, icy-sharp points of glitter against an overwhelming blackness.

They didn't seem different to him. They were, of course. From Earth's surface the constellations would be wholly alien. But in space so many stars were visible that they made one chaos, at least to Darkington's eyes. Captain Thurshaw had pointed out to him, from the ship's bridge, that the Milky Way had a new shape, this bend was missing and that bay had not been there three billion years ago. To Darkington it remained words. He was a biologist and had never paid much attention to astronomy. In the first numbness of loss and isolation, he could think of nothing which mattered less than the exact form of the Milky Way.

Still the boat spiraled inward. Now the moon drifted across his view. In those eons since the *Traveler* left home, Luna had retreated from Earth: not as far as might have been predicted, because (they said) Bering Straits had vanished with every other remembered place; but nonetheless, now it was only a tarnished farthing. Through the ship's telescopes it had looked like itself. Some new mountains, craters, and maria, some thermal erosion of old features, but Thurshaw could identify much of what he once knew. It was grotesque that the moon should endure when everything else had changed.

Even the sun. Observed through a dimmer screen, the solar disc was bloated and glaring. Not so much in absolute terms, perhaps. Earth had moved a little closer, as the friction of interplanetary dust and gas took a millennial toll. The sun itself had grown a little bigger and hotter, as nuclear reactions intensified. In three billion years such things became noticeable even on the cosmic scale. To a living organism they totaled doomsday.

Darkington cursed under his breath and clenched a fist till the skin stretched taut. He was a thin man, long-faced, sharp-featured, his brown hair prematurely sprinkled with gray. His memories included beautiful spires above an Oxford quad, wonder seen through a microscope, a sailboat beating into the wind of Nantucket which blew spray and a sound of gulls and church bells at him, comradeship bent over a chessboard or hoisting beer steins, forests hazy and ablaze with Indian summer: and all these things were dead. The shock had worn off, the hundred men and women aboard the *Traveler* could function again, but home had been amputated from their lives and the stump hurt.

Frederika Ruys laid her own hand on his and squeezed a little. Muscle by muscle he untensed himself, until he could twitch a smile in response to hers. "After all," she said, "we knew we'd be gone a long time. That we might well never come back."

"But we'd have been on a living planet," he mumbled.

"So we can still find us one," declared Sam Kuroki from his seat at the pilot console. "There're no less than six G-type stars within fifty light-years."

"It won't be the same," Darkington protested.

"No," said Frederika. "In a way, though, won't it be more? We, the last humans in the universe, starting the race over again?"

There was no coyness in her manner. She wasn't much to look at, plump, plain, with straight yellow hair and too wide a mouth. But such details had ceased to matter since the ship ended time acceleration. Frederika Ruys was a brave soul and a skilled engineer. Darkington felt incredibly lucky that she had picked him.

"Maybe we aren't the last, anyhow," Kuroki said. His flat features broke in one of his frequent grins; he faced immensity with a sparrow's cockiness. "Ought to've been other colonies than ours planted, oughtn't there? Of course, by now their descendants 'ud be bald-headed dwarfs who sit around thinking in calculus."

"I doubt that," Darkington sighed. "If humans had survived anywhere else in the galaxy, don't you think they would at least have come back and . . . and reseeded this with life? The mother planet?" He drew a shaken breath. They had threshed this out a hundred times or more while the *Traveler* orbited about unrecognizable Earth, but they could not keep from saying the obvious again and again, as a man must keep touching a wound on his body. "No, I think the war really did begin soon after we left. The world situation was all set to explode."

That was why the *Traveler* had been built, and even more why it had departed in such haste, his mind went on. Fifty couples scrambling off to settle on Tau Ceti II before the missiles were unleashed. Oh, yes, officially they were a scientific team, and one of the big foundations had paid for the enterprise. But in fact, as everyone knew, the hope was to insure that a fragment of civilization would be saved, and someday return to help rebuild. (Even Panasia admitted that a total war would throw history back a hundred years; Western governments were less optimistic.) Tension had mounted so horribly fast in the final months that no time was taken for a really careful check of the field drive. So new and little understood an engine ought to have had scores of test flights before starting out under full power. But . . . well . . . next year might be too late. And exploratory ships *had* visited the nearer stars, moving just under the speed of light, their crews experiencing only a few weeks of transit time. Why not the *Traveler?*

"The absolute war?" Frederika said, as she had done so often already. "Fought until the whole world was sterile? No. I won't believe it."

"Not in that simple and clean-cut a way," Darkington conceded. "Probably the war did end with a nominal victor: but he was more depopulated and devastated than anyone had dared expect. Too impoverished to reconstruct, or even to maintain what little physical plant survived. A downward spiral into the Dark Ages."

"M-m-m, I dunno," Kuroki argued. "There were

a lot of machines around. Automation, especially. Like those self-reproducing, sun-powered, mineral-collecting sea rafts. And a lot of other self-maintaining gadgets. I don't see why industry couldn't be revived on such a base."

"Radioactivity would have been everywhere," Darkington pointed out. "Its long-range effect on ecology . . . Oh, yes, the process may have taken centuries, as first one species changed or died, and then another dependent on it, and then more. But how could the human survivors recreate technology when biology was disintegrating around them?" He shook himself and stiffened his back, ashamed of his self pity of a minute ago, looking horror flatly in the face. "That's my guess. I could be wrong, but it seems to fit the facts. We'll never know for certain, I suppose."

Earth rolled into sight. The planetary disc was still edged with blueness darkening toward black. Clouds still trailed fleecy above shining oceans; they gleamed upon the darkness near the terminator as they caught the first light before sunrise. Earth was forever fair.

But the continental shapes were new, speckled with hard points of reflection upon black and ocher where once they had been softly green and brown. There were no polar caps; sea level temperatures ranged from eighty to two hundred degrees Fahrenheit. No free oxygen remained: the atmosphere was nitrogen, its oxides, ammonia, hydrogen sulfide, sulfur dioxide, carbon dioxide, and steam. Spectroscopes had found no trace of chlorophyll or any other complex organic compound. The ground cover, dimly glimpsed through clouds, was metallic.

This was no longer Earth. There was no good reason why the *Traveler* should send a boat and three highly unexpendable humans down to look at its lifelessness. But no one had suggested

leaving the Solar System without such a final visit.
Darkington remembered being taken to see his
grandmother when she was dead. He was twelve
years old and had loved her. It was not her in the
box, that strange unmeaningful mask, but where
then was she?

"Well, whatever happened seems to be three
billion years in the past," Kuroki said, a little too
loudly. "Forget it. We got troubles of our own."

Frederika's eyes had not left the planet. "We
can't ever forget, Sam," she said. "We'll always
wonder and hope—they, the children at
least—hope that it didn't happen to them too
cruelly." Darkington started in surprise as she
went on murmuring, very low, oblivious of the
men:

> "to tell you of the ending of the day.
> And you will see her tallness with surprise,
> and looking into gentle, shadowed eyes
> protest: it's not that late; you have to stay
> awake a minute more, just one, to play
> with yonder ball. But nonetheless you rise
> so they won't hear her say, 'A baby cries,
> but you are big. Put all your toys away.'

> "She lets you have a shabby bear in bed,
> though frankly doubting that you two can go
> through dream-shared living rooms or wingless
>   flight.
> She tucks the blankets close beneath your head
> and smooths your hair and kisses you, and so
> goes out, turns off the light. 'Good night. Sleep
>   tight.'"

Kuroki glanced around at her. The plaid shirt
wrinkled across his wide shoulders. "Pomes yet,"
he said. "Who wrote that?"

"Hugh," said Frederika. "Didn't you know he

published poetry? Quite a bit. I admired his work long before I met him."

Darkington flushed. Her interest was flattering, but he regarded *Then Death Will Come* as a juvenile effort.

However, his embarrassment pulled him out of sadness. (On the surface. Down beneath, it would always be there, in every one of them. He hoped they would not pass too much of it on to their children. Let us not weep eternally for Zion.) Leaning forward, he looked at the planet with an interest that mounted as the approach curve took them around the globe. He hoped for a few answers to a hell of a lot of questions.

For one thing, why, in three billion years, had life not re-evolved? Radioactivity must have disappeared in a few centuries at most. The conditions of primordial Earth would have returned. Or would they? What had been lacking this time around?

He woke from his brown study with a jerk as Kuroki said, "Well, I reckon we can steepen our trajectory a bit." A surprising interval had passed. The pilot touched controls and the mild acceleration increased. The terrestrial disc, already enormous, swelled with terrifying velocity, as if tumbling down upon them.

Then, subtly, it was no longer to one side or above, but was beneath; and it was no longer a thing among the stars but the convex floor of bowl-shaped creation. The jets blasted more strongly. Kuroki's jaws clenched till knots of muscle stood forth. His hands danced like a pianist's.

He was less the master of the boat, Darkington knew, than its helper. So many tons, coming down through atmospheric turbulence at such a velocity, groping with radar for a safe landing spot, could not be handled by organic brain and nerves. The boat's central director—essentially a computer whose input came from the instruments and whose efferent impulses went directly to the controls—performed the basic operations. Its task was fantastically complex: very nearly as difficult as the job of guiding the muscles when a man walks. Kuroki's fingers told the boat, "Go that way," but the director could overrule him.

"I think we'll settle among those hills." The pilot had to shout now, as the jets blasted stronger. "Want to come down just east of the sunrise line, so we'll have a full day ahead of us, and yonder's the most promising spot in this region. The lowlands look too boggy."

Darkington nodded and glanced at Frederika. She smiled and made a thumbs-up sign. He leaned over, straining against his safety harness, and brushed his lips across hers. She colored with a pleasure that he found oddly moving.

Someday, on another planet—that possibly hadn't been born when they left Earth—

He had voiced his fears to her, that the engine would go awry again when they started into deep space, and once more propel them through time, uncontrollably until fuel was exhausted. A full charge in the tanks was equivalent to three billion years, plus or minus several million; or so the physicists aboard had estimated. In six billion A.D. might not the sun be so swollen as to engulf them when they emerged?

She had rapped him across the knuckles with her slide rule and said no, you damned biologist, but you'll have to take my word for it because you haven't got the math. I've studied it as far as differential equations, he said. She grinned and answered that then he'd never had a math course. It seemed, she said, that time acceleration was readily explained by the same theory which underlay the field drive. In fact, the effect had been

demonstrated in laboratory experiments. Oh, yes,
I know about that, he said; reactive thrust is
rotated through a fourth dimension and gets
applied along the temporal rather than a spatial
axis. You do not know a thing about it, she said, as
your own words have just proved. But never mind.
What happened to us was that a faulty manifold
generated the t-acceleration effect in our engine.
Now we've torn everything down and rebuilt from
scratch. We know it'll work right. The tanks are
recharged. The ship's ecosystem is in good order.
Any time we want, we can take off for a younger
sun, and travel fifty light-years without growing
more than a few months older. After which, seeing
no one else was around, she sought his arms; and
that was more comforting than her words.

A last good-by to Grandmother Earth, he
thought. *Then we can start the life over again that
we got from her.*

The thrust upon him mounted. Toward the end
he lay in his chair, now become a couch, and concentrated on breathing.

They reached ground.

Silence rang in their ears for a long while.
Kuroki was the first to move. He unstrapped his
short body and snapped his chair back upright.
One hand unhooked the radio microphone,
another punched buttons. "Boat calling *Traveler*,"
he intoned. "We're okay so far. Come in, *Traveler*.
Hello, hello."

Darkington freed himself, stiffly, his flesh
athrob, and helped Frederika rise. She leaned on
him a minute. "Earth," she said. Gulping: "Will
you look out the port first, dearest? I find I'm not
brave enough."

He realized with a shock that none of them had
yet glanced at the landscape. Convulsively, he
made the gesture.

He stood motionless for so long that finally she
raised her head and stared for herself.

III

They did not realize the full strangeness before
they donned spacesuits and went outside. Then,
saying very little, they wandered about looking
and feeling. Their brains were slow to develop the
gestalts which would allow them really to see
what surrounded them. A confused mass of detail
could not be held in the memory, the underlying
form could not be abstracted from raw sense
impressions. A tree is a tree, anywhere and any-
when, no matter how intricate its branching or
how oddly shaped its leaves and blossoms. But
what is a—thick shaft of gray metal, planted in the
sand, central to a labyrinthine skeleton of straight
and curved girders, between which run still more
enigmatic structures embodying helices and
toruses and Mobius strips and less familiar
geometrical elements; the entire thing some fifty
feet tall; flaunting at the top several hundred thin
metal plates whose black sides are turned toward
the sun?

When you have reached the point of being able
to describe it even this crudely, then you *have*
apprehended it.

Eventually Darkington saw that the basic structure was repeated, with infinite variation of size
and shape, as far as he could see. Some specimens
tall and slender, some low and broad, they
dominated the hillside. The deeper reaches were
made gloomy by their overhang, but sun speckles
flew piercingly bright within those shadows as the
wind shook the mirror faces of the plates. That
same wind made a noise of clanking and clashing
and far-off deep booming, mile after metal mile.

There was no soil, only sand, rusty red and
yellow. But outside the circle which had been

devastated by the boat's jets, Darkington found
the earth carpeted with prismatic growths, a few
inches high, seemingly rooted in the ground. He
broke one off for closer examination and saw tiny
crystals, endlessly repeated, in some transparent
siliceous material: like snowflakes and
spiderwebs of glass. It sparkled so brightly,
making so many rainbows, that he couldn't well
study the interior. He could barely make out at the
center a dark clump of . . . wires, coils,
transistors? *No*, he told himself, *don't be silly*. He
gave it to Frederika, who exclaimed at its beauty.

He himself walked across an open stretch,
hoping for a view even vaguely familiar. Where
the hillside dropped too sharply to support
anything but the crystals—they made it one dazzle
of diamonds—he saw eroded contours, the remote
white sword of a waterfall, strewn boulders and a
few crags like worn-out obelisks. The land rolled
away into blue distances; a snowcapped mountain
range guarded the eastern horizon. The sky overhead was darker than in his day, faintly greenish
blue, full of clouds. He couldn't look near the
fierce big sun.

Kuroki joined him. "What d'you think, Hugh?"
the pilot asked.

"I hardly dare say. You?"

"Hell, I can't think with that bloody boiler
factory clattering at me." Kuroki grimaced behind
his faceplate. "Turn off your sonic mike and let's
talk by radio."

Darkington agreed. Without amplification, the
noise reached him through his insulated helmet as
a far-off tolling. "We can take it for granted," he
said, "that none of this is accidental. No minerals
could simply crystallize out like this."

"Don't look manufactured to me, though."

"Well, said Darkington, "you wouldn't expect
them to turn out their products in anything like a

human machine shop."

"Them?"

"Whoever . . . whatever . . . made this. For whatever purpose."

Kuroki whistled. "I was afraid you'd say something like that. But we didn't see a trace of—cities, roads, anything—from orbit. I know the cloudiness made seeing pretty bad, but we couldn't have missed the signs of a civilization able to produce stuff on this scale."

"Why not? If the civilization isn't remotely like anything we've ever imagined?"

Frederika approached, leaving a cartful of instruments behind. "The low and medium frequency radio spectrum is crawling," she reported. "You never heard so many assorted hoots, buzzes, whirrs, squeals, and whines in your life."

"We picked up an occasional bit of radio racket while in orbit," Kuroki nodded. "Didn't think much about it, then."

"Just noise," Frederika said hastily. "Not varied enough to be any kind of, of communication. But I wonder what's doing it?"

"Oscillators," Darkington said. "Incidental radiation from a variety of—oh, hell, I'll speak plainly —machines."

"But—" Her hand stole toward his. Glove grasped glove. She wet her lips. "No, Hugh, this is absurd. How could any one be capable of making . . . what we see . . . and not have detected us in orbit and—and done something about us?"

Darkington shrugged. The gesture was lost in his armor. "Maybe they're biding their time. Maybe they aren't here at the moment. The whole planet could be an automated factory, you know. Like those ocean mineral harvesters we had in our time"—it hurt to say that—"which Sam mentioned on the way down. Somebody may come around periodically and collect the production."

"Where do they come from?" asked Kuroki in a rough tone.

"I don't know, I tell you. Let's stop making wild guesses and start gathering data."

Silence grew between them. The skeleton towers belled. Finally Kuroki nodded. "Yeah. What say we take a little stroll? We may come on something."

Nobody mentioned fear. They dared not.

Re-entering the boat, they made the needful arrangements. The *Traveler* would be above the horizon for several hours yet. Captain Thurshaw gave his reluctant consent to an exploration on foot. The idea conflicted with his training, but what did survey doctrine mean under these conditions? The boat's director could keep a radio beam locked on the ship and thus relay communication between Earth and orbit. While Kuroki talked, Darkington and Frederika prepared supplies. Not much was needed. The capacitor pack in each suit held charge enough to power thermostat and air renewer for a hundred hours, and they only planned to be gone for three or four. They loaded two packboards with food, water, and the "buckets" used for such natural functions as eating, but that was only in case their return should be delayed. The assorted scientific instruments they took were more to the point. Darkington holstered a pistol. When he had finished talking, Kuroki put the long tube of a rocket gun and a rackful of shells on his own back. They closed their helmets anew and stepped out.

"Which way?" Frederika asked.

"Due south," Darkington said after studying the terrain. "We'll be following this long ridge, you see. Harder to get lost." There was little danger of that, with the boat emitting a continuous directional signal. Nonetheless they all had

compasses on their wrists and took note of land-
marks as they went.

The boat was soon lost to view. They walked
among surrealistic rods and frames and spirals,
under ringing sheet metal. The crystals crunched
beneath their tread and broke sunlight into hot
shards of color. But not many rays pushed
through the tangle overhead; shadows were dense
and restless. Darkington began to recognize unrelated types of structure. They included long,
black, seemingly telescopic rods, fringed with thin
plates; glassy spheres attached to intricate grids;
cables that looped from girder to girder.
Frequently a collapsed object was seen crumbling
on the ground.

Frederika looked at several disintegrated
specimens, examined others in good shape, and
said: "I'd guess the most important material, the
commonest, is an aluminum alloy. Though—see
here—these fine threads embedded in the core
must be copper. And this here is probably
manganese steel with a protective coating of . . .
um . . . something more inert."

Darkington peered at the end of a broken strut
through a magnifying glass. "Porous," he said.
"Good Lord, are these actually capillaries to
transport water?"

"I thought a capillary was a hairy bug with lots
of legs that turned into a butterfly," said Kuroki.
He ducked an imaginary fist. "Okay, okay, somebody's got to keep up morale."

The boat's radio relayed a groan from the
monitor aboard the ship. Frederika said patiently,
"No, Sam, the legs don't turn into a butterfly—,"
but then she remembered there would never again
be bravely colored small wings on Earth and
banged a hand against her faceplate as if she had
been about to knuckle her eyes.

Darkington was still absorbed in the specimen

he held. "I never heard of a machine this finely constructed," he declared. "I thought nothing but a biological system could—"

"Stop! Freeze!"

Kuroki's voice rapped in their earphones. Darkington laid a hand on his pistol butt. Otherwise only his head moved, turning inside the helmet. After a moment he saw the thing too.

It stirred among shadows, behind a squat cylinder topped with the usual black-and-mirror plates. Perhaps three feet long, six or eight inches high . . . It came out into plain view. Darkington glimpsed a slim body and six short legs of articulated dull metal. A latticework swiveled at the front end like a miniature radio-radar beamcaster. Something glinted beadily beneath, twin lenses? Two thin tentacles held a metal sliver off one of the great stationary structures. They fed it into an orifice, and sparks shot back upward—

"Holy Moses," Kuroki whispered.

The thing stopped in its tracks. The front-end lattice swung toward the humans. Then the thing was off, unbelievably fast. In half a second there was nothing to see.

Nobody moved for almost a minute. Finally Frederika clutched Darkington's arm with a little cry. The rigidness left him and he babbled of experimental robot turtles in the early days of cybernetic research. Very simple gadgets. A motor drove a wheeled platform, steered by a photoelectric unit that approached light sources by which the batteries might be recharged and, when this was done, became negatively phototropic and sought darkness. An elementary feedback circuit. But the turtles had shown astonishing tenacity, had gone over obstacles or even around . . . .

"That beast there was a good deal more complicated," she interrupted.

"Certainly, certainly," Darkington said. "But—"

"I'll bet it heard Sam talk on the radio, spotted us with radar—or maybe eyes, if those socketed glass things were eyes—and took off."

"Very possibly, if you must use anthropomorphic language. However—"

"It was eating that strut." Frederika walked over to the piece of metal which the runner had dropped. She picked it up and came stiffly back with it. "See, the end has been ground away by a set of coarse emery wheels or something. You couldn't very well eat alloy with teeth like ours. You have to grind it."

"Hey," Kuroki objected. "Let's not go completely off the deep end."

"What the hell's happened down there?" called the man aboard the *Traveler*.

They resumed walking, in a dreamlike fashion, as they recounted what they had seen. Frederika concluded: "This . . . this arrangement might conceivably be some kind of automated factory—chemosynthetic or something—if taken by itself. But not with beasts like that one running loose."

"Now wait," Darkington said. "They could be maintenance robots, you know. Clear away rubbish and wreckage."

"A science advanced enough to build what we see wouldn't use such a clumsy system of maintenance," she answered. "Get off your professional caution, Hugh, and admit what's obvious."

Before he could reply, his earphones woke with a harsh jabber. He stopped and tried to tune in—it kept fading out, he heard it only in bursts—but the bandwidth was too great. What he did hear sounded like an electronic orchestra gone berserk. Sweat prickled his skin.

When the sound had stopped: "Okay," breathed Kuroki, "you tell me."

"Could have been a language, I suppose," said

Frederika, dry-throated. "It wasn't just a few simple oscillations like that stuff on the other frequencies."

Captain Thurshaw himself spoke from the orbiting ship. "You better get back to the boat and sit prepared for quick blastoff."

Darkington found his nerve. "No, sir. If you please. I mean, uh, if there are intelligences . . . if we really do want to contact them . . . now's the time. Let's at least make an effort."

"Well—"

"We'll take you back first, of course, Freddie."

"Nuts," said the girl. "I stay right here."

Somehow they found themselves pushing on. Once, crossing an open spot where only the crystals stood, they spied something in the air. Through binoculars, it turned out to be a metallic object shaped vaguely like an elongated manta. Apparently it was mostly hollow, upborne by air currents around the fins and propelled at low speed by a gas jet. "Oh, sure," Frederika muttered. "Birds."

They re-entered the area of tall structures. The sonic amplifiers in their helmets were again tuned high, and the clash of plates in the wind was deafening. Like a suit of armor, Darkington thought idiotically. Could be a poem in that. Empty armor on a wild horse, rattling and tossing as it was galloped down an inexplicably deserted city street—symbol of—

The radio impulses that might be communication barked again in their earphones. "I don't like this," Thurshaw said from the sky. "You're dealing with too many unknowns at once. Return to the boat and we'll discuss further plans."

They continued walking in the same direction, mechanically. *We don't seem out of place here ourselves, in this stiff cold forest,* Darkington thought. *My god, let's turn around. Let's assert our dignity as organic beings. We aren't mounted on rails!*

"That's an order," Thurshaw stated.

"Very well, sir," Kuroki said. "And, uh, thanks."

The sound of running halted them. They whirled. Frederika screamed.

"What's the matter?" Thurshaw shouted. "What's the matter?" The unknown language ripped across his angry helplessness.

Kuroki yanked his rocket gun loose and put the weapon to his shoulder. "Wait!" Darkington yelled. But he grabbed at his own pistol. The on-comer rushed in a shower of crystal splinters, whipping rods and loops aside. Its gigantic weight shuddered in the ground.

Time slowed for Darkington, he had minutes or hours to tug at his gun, hear Frederika call his name, see Juroki take aim and fire. The shape was mountainous before him. Nine feet tall, he estimated in a far-off portion of his rocking brain, three yards of biped four-armed monstrosity, head horned with radio lattice, eyes that threw back sunlight in a blank glitter, grinder orifice and—The rocket exploded. The thing lurched and half fell. One arm was in ruins.

"Ha!" Kuroki slipped a fresh shell into his gun. "Stay where you are, you!"

Frederika, wildly embracing Darkington, found time to gasp, "Sam, maybe it wasn't going to do any harm," and Kuroki snapped, "Maybe it was. Too goddam big to take chances with." Then everything smashed.

Suddenly the gun was knocked spinning by a hurled iron bar they hadn't even noticed. And the giant was among them. A swat across Kuroki's back shattered his radio and dashed him to earth. Flame spat and Frederika's voice was cut short in Darkington's receivers.

He pelted off, his pistol uselessly barking. "Run, Freddie!" he bawled into his sonic microphone.

"I'll try and—" The machine picked him up. The
pistol fell from his grasp. A moment later,
Thurshaw's horrified oaths were gone:
Darkington's radio antenna had been plucked out
by the roots. Frederika tried to escape, but she
was snatched up just as effortlessly. Kuroki, back
on his feet, stood where he was and struck with
ludicrous fists. It didn't take long to secure him
either. Hog-tied, stuffed into a rack on the shoulders of the giant, the three humans were borne off
southward.

IV

At first Zero almost ran. The monster must have
known where its auxiliaries were and something
of what had happened to them. Now that contact
was broken, it might send forth others to look for
them, better armed. Or it might even come itself,
roaring and burning through the forest. Zero fled.

Only the monster's voice, raggedly calling for its
lost members, pursued him. After a few miles he
crouched in a rod clump and strained his
receptors. Nothing was visible but thickly
growing accumulators and bare sky. The monster
had ceased to shout. Though it still emitted an unmodulated signal, distance had dwindled this
until the surrounding soft radio noise had almost
obliterated that hum.

The units Zero had captured were making considerable sound-wave radiation. If not simply the
result of malfunction in their damaged
mechanism, it must be produced by some
auxiliary system which they had switched on
through interior controls. Zero's sound receptors
were not sensitive enough to tell him whether the

emission was modulated. Nor did he care. Certain low forms of motile were known to have well-developed sonic parts, but anything so limited in range was useless to him except as a warning of occurrences immediately at hand. A person needed many square miles to support himself. How could there be a community of persons without the effortless ability to talk across transhorizon distances?

Irrelevantly, for the first time in his century and a half of existence, Zero realized how few persons he had ever observed with his own direct optics. How few he had touched. Now and then, for this or that purpose, several might get together. A bride's male kin assisted her on her journey to the groom's dwelling. Individuals met to exchange the products of their labor. But still—this rally of all functional males at Broken Glade, to hunt the monster, would be the greatest assemblage in tradition. Yet not even Hundred had grasped its uniqueness.

For persons were always communicating. Not only practical questions were discussed. In fact, now that Zero thought about it, such problems were the least part of discourse. The major part was ritual, or friendly conversation, or art. Zero had seldom met Seven as a physical entity, but the decades in which they criticized each other's poetry had made them intimate. The abstract tone constructions of Ninety-six, the narratives of Eighty, the speculations about space and time of Fifty-nine—such things belonged to all.

Direct sensory linkage, when the entire output of the body was used to modulate the communication band, reduced still further the need for physical contact. Zero had never stood on the seashore himself. But he had shared consciousness with Fourteen, who lived there. He had perceived the slow inward movement of waves, their susurrus, the salt in the air; he had experienced the smearing of grease over his skin to protect it from corrosion, drawing an aquamotile from a net and feasting. For those hours, he and the searaker had been one. Afterward he had shown Fourteen the upland forest . . . .

What am I waiting for? Consciousness of his here-and-now jarred back into Zero. The monster had not pursued. The units on his back had grown quiescent. But he was still a long way from home. He rose and started off again, less rapidly but with more care to obliterate his traces.

As the hours passed, his interior sensors warned him increasingly of a need for replenishment. About midday he stopped and unloaded his three prizes. They were feebly squirming and one of them had worked an arm loose. Rather than lash them tight again, he released their limbs and secured them by passing the rope in successive loops around their middles and a tall stump, then welding everything fast with his torch.

That energy drain left him ravenous. He scouted the forest in a jittery spiral until he found some accumulators of the calathiform sort. A quick slash with his pry bar exposed their spongy interiors, rich with energy storage cells and mineral salts. They were not very satisfying eaten unprocessed, but he was too empty to care. With urgency blunted, he could search more slowly and thoroughly. Thus he found the traces of a burrow, dug into the sand, and came upon a female digger. She was heavy with a half-completed new specimen and he caught her easily. This too would have been better if treated with heat and acid, but even raw materials tasted good in his grinder.

Now to get something for One. Though she, better than he, could slow down her functioning when nourishment was scarce, a state of coma while the monster was abroad could be dangerous.

After hunting for another hour, Zero had the good luck to start a rotor. It crashed off among the rods and crystals, faster than he could run, but he put a crossbow bolt through its hub. Dismembered and packed into his carrier, it made an immensely cheering burden.

He returned to his prizes. Moving quickly in comparison to the windy clatter of the forest, he came upon them unobserved. They had quit attempting to escape—he saw the wire was shiny where they had tried to saw it on a sharp rock—and were busy with other tasks. One of them had removed a box-like object from its back and inserted its head (?) and arms through gasketed holes. A second was just removing a similar box from its lower section. The third had plugged a flexible tube from a bottle into its face.

Zero approached. "Let me inspect those," he said, before thinking how ridiculous it was to address them. They shrank away from him. He caught the one with the bottle and unplugged the tube. Some liquid ran out. Zero extended his chemical sensor and tasted cautiously. Water. Very pure. He did not recall ever having encountered water so free of dissolved minerals.

Thoughtfully, he released the unit. It stoppered the tube. So, Zero reflected, they required water like him, and carried a supply with them. That was natural; they (or, rather, the monster they served) could not know where the local springs and streams were. But why did they suck through a tube? Did they lack a proper liquid-ingestion orifice? Evidently. The small hole in the head, into which the tube had fitted, had automatically closed as the nipple was withdrawn.

The other two had removed their boxes. Zero studied these and their contents. There were fragments of mushy material in both, vaguely similar to normal body sludge. Nourishment or waste? Why such a clumsy system? It was as if the interior mechanism must be absolutely protected from contact with the environment.

He gave the boxes back and looked more thoroughly at their users. They were not quite so awkward as they seemed at first. The humps on their backs were detachable carriers like his. Some of the objects dangling at their waists or strapped to their arms must also be tools. (Not weapons or means of escape, else they would have used them before now. Specialized artificial attachments, then, analogous to a torch or a surgical ratchet.) The basic bipedal shape was smoother than his own, nearly featureless except for limb joints. The head was somewhat more complicated, though less so than a person's. Upon the cylindrical foundation grew various parts, including the sound-wave generators which babbled as he stood there watching. The face was a glassy plate, behind which moved . . . what? Some kind of jointed, partly flexible mechanism.

There was no longer any possibility of radio communication with –or through—them. Zero made a few experimental gestures, but the units merely stirred about. Two of them embraced. The third waved its arms and made sonic yelps. All at once it squatted and drew geometrical shapes in the sand, very much like the courtship figures drawn by a male dunerunner.

So . . . they not only had mechanical autonomy, like the spy eyes of a boxroller, but were capable of some independent behavior. They were more than simple remote-control limbs and sensors of the monster. Most probably they were domesticated motiles.

But if so, then the monster race had modified their type even more profoundly than the person race had modified the type of its own tamed motiles down in the lowlands. These bipeds were

comically weak in proportion to size; they lacked
grinders and liquid-ingestion orifices; they used
sonics to a degree that argued their radio abilities
were primitive; they required ancillary apparatus;
in short, they were not functional by themselves.
Only the care and shelter furnished by their
masters allowed them to remain long in existence.

*But what are the masters? Even the monster may
well be only another motile. Certainly it appeared
to lack limbs. The masters may be persons like us,
come from beyond the sea or the mountains with
skills and powers transcending our own.*

*But then what do they want? Why have they not
tried to communicate with us? Have they come to
take our land away?*

The question was jolting. Zero got hastily into
motion. With his rack loaded, he had no room for
his prizes. Besides, being crammed into it for
hours was doubtless harmful to them; they moved
a good deal more strongly now, after a rest, than
when he first took them out. He simply left them
tied together, cut the wire loose from the stump,
and kept that end in one hand. Since he continued
to exercise due caution about leaving a trail, he
did not move too fast for them to keep up. From
time to time they would stagger and lean on each
other for support—apparently their energy cells
polarized more quickly than his—but he found
they could continue if he let them pause a while,
lie down, use their curious artifacts.

The day passed. At this time of year, not long
past the vernal equinox, the sun was up for about
twenty hours. After dark, Zero's captives began
stumbling and groping. He confirmed by direct
sense perception that they had no radar. If they
ever did, that part had been wrecked with their
communicators. After some thought, he fashioned
a rough seat from a toppled bole and nudged them
to sit upon it. Thus he carried them in two hands.

They made no attempt to escape, emitted few sounds, obviously they were exhausted. But to his surprise, they began to stir about and radiate sonics when he finally reached home and set them down. He welded the end of their rope to an iron block he kept for emergencies.

Part of him reflected that their mechanism must be very strange indeed, maybe so strange that they would not prove ingestible. Obviously their cells went to such extremes of polarization that they became comatose, which a person only did in emergencies. To them, such deactivation appeared to be normal, and they roused spontaneously.

He dismissed speculation. One's anxious voice had been rushing over him while he worked. "What has happened? You are hurt! Come closer, let me see, oh, your poor arm! Oh, my dear!"

"Nothing serious," he reassured her. "I shot a rotor. Prepare yourself a meal before troubling about me."

He lowered himself to the cave floor beside her great beautiful bulk. The glow globes, cultivated on the rough stone walls, shed luster on her skin and on the graceful tool tendrils that curled forth to embrace him. His chemical sensor brought him a hint of solvents and lubricants, an essence of femaleness. The cave mouth was black with night, save where one star gleamed bright and somehow sinister above the hills. The forest groaned and tolled. But here he had light and her touch upon his body. He was home.

She unshipped the rack from his shoulders but made no motion toward the food-processing cauldron. Most of her tools and all her attention were on his damaged. Arm. "We must replace everything below the elbow," she decided; and, as a modulation: "Zero, you brave clever adored fool, why did you hazard yourself like that? Do you not understand, even yet, without you my world would be rust?"

"I am sorry . . . to take so much from the new one," he apologized.

"No matter. Feed me some more nice large rotors like this and I will soon replace the loss, and finish all the rest too." Her mirth fluttered toward shyness. "I want the new one activated soon myself, you know, so we can start another."

The memory of that moment last year, when his body pattern flowed in currents and magnetic fields through hers, when the two patterns heterodyned and deep within her the first crystallization took place, glowed in him. Sensory linkage was a wan thing by comparison.

What they did together now had a kindred intimacy. When she had removed the ruined forearm and he had thrust the stump into her repair orifice, a thousand fine interior tendrils enfolded it, scanning, relaying, and controlling. Once again, more subtly than in reproduction, the electro-chemical-mechanical systems of One and Zero unified. The process was not consciously controllable; it was a female function; One was at this moment no different from the most primitive motile joined to her damaged mate in a lightless burrow.

It took time. The new person which her body was creating within itself was, of course, full size and, as it happened, not far from completion. (Had the case been otherwise, Zero would have had to wait until the new one did in fact possess a well-developed arm.) But it was not yet activated; its most delicate and critical synaptic pathways were still only half-finished, gradually crystallizing out of solution. A part could not lightly nor roughly be removed.

But in the end, One's functions performed the task. Slowly, almost reluctantly, Zero withdrew

his new hand. His mind and hers remained inter-
twined a while longer. At last, with a shaky little
overtone of humor, she exclaimed, "Well, how do
your fingers wiggle? Is everything good? Then let
us eat. I am famished!"

Zero helped her prepare the rotor for consumption. They threw the damaged forearm into the
cauldron too. While they processed and shared the
meal, he recounted his experiences. She had
shown no curiosity about the three bipeds. Like
most females, she lacked any great interest in the
world beyond her home, and had merely assumed
they were some new kind of wild motile. As he
talked, the happiness died in her. "Oh, no," she
said, "you are not going out to fight the lightning
breather, are you?"

"Yes, we must." He knew what image terrified
her, himself smashed beyond hope of reconstruction, and added in haste: "If we leave it free, no
tradition or instinct knows what it may do. But
surely, at the very least, so large a thing will cause
extensive damage. Even if it is only a grazer, its
appetite   will   destroy   untold   acres   of
accumulators; and it may be a predator. On the
other hand, if we destroy it, what a hoard of
nourishment! Your share and mine will enable us
to produce a dozen new persons. The energy will
let me range for hundreds of miles, thus gaining
still more food and goods for us."

"If the thing can be assimilated," she said
doubtfully. "It could be full of hydrofluoric acid
or something, like a touch-me-not."

"Yes, yes. For that matter, the flier may be the
property of intelligent beings: which does not
necessarily mean we will not destroy and consume
it. I intend to find out about that aspect right now.
If the monster's auxiliaries are ingestible, the
monster itself is almost sure to be."

"But if not—Zero, be careful!"

"I will. For your sake also." He stroked her and felt an answering vibration. It would have been pleasant to sit thus all night, but he must soon be on his way to rendezvous. And first he must dissect at least one specimen. He took up his pry bar and approached the three units.

V

Darkington awoke from a nightmare-ridden half-sleep when he was dumped on the cave floor. He reached for Frederika and she came to him. For a space there was nothing but their murmuring.

Eventually they crouched on the sand and looked about. The giant that captured them had welded the free end of the wire rope to an immovable chunk of raw iron. Darkington was attached at that side, then the girl, and Kuroki on the outer end. They had about four feet of slack from one to the next. Nothing in the kit remaining to them would cut those strands.

"Limestone cave, I guess," Kuroki croaked. Behind the faceplate he was gaunt, bristly, and sunken-eyed. Frederika didn't look much better. They might not have survived the trip here if the robot hadn't carried them the last few hours. Nonetheless an odd, dry clarity possessed Darkington's brain. He could observe and think as well as if he had been safe on shipboard. His body was one enormous ache, but he ignored that and focused on comprehending what had happened.

Here near the entrance, the cave was about twenty feet high and rather more wide. A hundred feet deeper inward, it narrowed and ended. That area was used for storage: a junk shop of mech-

anical and electronic parts, together with roughly
fashioned metal and stone tools that looked
almost homelike. The walls were overgrown with
thin wires that sprouted scores of small crystalline globes. These gave off a cool white light that
made the darkness outside appear the more
elemental.

"Yes, a cave in a sheer hillside," said Frederika.
"I saw that much. I kept more or less conscious all
the way here, trying to keep track of our route.
Not that that's likely to do us much good, is it?"
She hugged her knees. "I've got to sleep soon—oh,
but I have to sleep!"

"We got to get in touch." Kuroki's voice rose.
(Thank heaven and some ages-dead engineer that
sound mikes and earphones could be switched on
by shoving your chin against the right button!
With talk cut off, no recourse would have remained but to slip quietly into madness.) "God damn it,
I tried to show that tin nightmare we're intelligent. I drew diagrams and—" He checked himself.
"Well, probably its builders don't monitor it. We'll
have another go when they show up."

"Let's admit the plain facts, Sam," Frederika
said tonelessly. "There aren't any builders. There
never were any."

"Oh, no." The pilot gave Darkington a beggar's
look. "You're the biologist, Hugh. Do you believe
that?"

Darkington bit his lip. "I'm afraid she's right."

Frederika's laugh barked at them. "Do you
know what that big machine is, there in the middle
of the cave? The one the robot is fooling around
with? I'll tell you. His wife!" She broke off.
Laughter echoed too horribly in their helmets.

Darkington gazed in that direction. The second
object had little in common with the biped shape,
being low and wide—twice the bulk—and
mounted on eight short legs which must lend very

little speed or agility. A radio lattice, optical lenses, and arms (two, not four) were similar to the biped's. But numerous additional limbs were long goosenecks terminating in specialized appendages. Sleek blued metal covered most of the body.

And yet, the way those two moved—

"I think you may be right about that also," Darkington said at last.

Kuroki beat the ground with his fist and swore. "Sorry, Freddie," he gulped. "But won't you, for God's sake, explain what you're getting at? This mess wouldn't be so bad if it made some sense."

"We can only guess," Darkington said.

"Well, guess, then!"

"Robot evolution," Frederika said. "After man was gone, the machines that were left began to evolve."

"No," said Kuroki, "that's nuts. Impossible!"

"I think what we've seen would be impossible any other way," Darkington said. "Metallic life couldn't arise spontaneously. Only carbon atoms make the long hookups needed for the chemical storage of biological information. But electronic storage is equally feasible. And ... before the *Traveler* departed ... self-reproducing machines were already in existence."

"I think the sea rafts must have been the important ones." Frederika spoke like someone in dream. Her eyes were fixed wide and unblinking on the two robots. "Remember? They were essentially motorized floating boxes, containing metallurgic processing plants and powered by solar batteries. They took dissolved minerals out of sea water, magnesium, uranium, whatever a particular raft was designed for. When it had a full cargo, it went to a point on shore where a depot received its load. Once empty, it returned to open waters for more. It had an inertial navigation device, as well as electronic sensors and various homeostatic systems, so it could cope with the normal vicissitudes of its environment.

"And it had electronic templates which bore full information on its own design. They controlled mechanisms aboard, which made any spare part that might be needed. Those same mechanisms also kept producing and assembling complete duplicate rafts. The first such outfit cost hundreds of millions of dollars to manufacture, let alone the preliminary research and development. But once made, it needed no further investment. Production and expansion didn't cost anyone a cent.

"And after man was gone from Earth . . . all life had vanished . . . the sea rafts were still there, patiently bringing their cargoes to crumbling docks on barren shores, year after year after meaningless year—"

She shook herself. The motion was violent enough to be seen in armor. "Go on, Hugh," she said, her tone turned harsh. "If you can."

"I don't know any details," he began cautiously. "You should tell me how mutation was possible to a machine. But if the templates were actually magnetic recordings on wire or tape, I expect that hard radiation would affect them, as it affects an organic gene. And for a while there was certainly plenty of hard radiation around. The rafts started making imperfect duplicates. Most were badly designed and, uh, foundered. Some, though, had advantages. For instance, they stopped going to shore and hanging about for decades waiting to be unloaded. Eventually some raft was made which had the first primitive ability to get metal from a richer source than the ocean: namely, from other rafts. Through hundreds of millions of years, an ecology developed. We might as well call it an ecology. The land was reconquered. Wholly new *types* of machine proliferated. Until today, well, what we've seen."

"But where's the energy come from?" Kuroki demanded.

"The sun, I suppose. By now, the original solar battery must be immensely refined. I'd make a guess at dielectric storage on the molecular level, in specialized units—call them cells—which may even be of microscopic size. Of course, productivity per acre must be a good deal lower than it was in our day. Alloys aren't as labile as amino acids. But that's offset to a large extent by their greater durability. And, as you can see in this cave, by interchangeability."

"Huh?"

"Sure. Look at those spare parts stacked in the rear. Some will no doubt be processed, analogously to our eating and digesting food. But others are probably being kept for use as such. Suppose you could take whole organs from animals you killed and install them in yourself to replace whatever was wearing out. I rather imagine that's common on today's Earth. The 'black box' principle was designed into most machines in our own centruy. It would be inherited."

"Where's the metal come from in the first place?"

"From lower types of machine. Ultimately from sessile types that break down ores, manufacture the basic alloys, and concentrate more dielectric energy than they use. Analogous to vegetation. I daresay the, uh, metabolism involves powerful reagents. Sulfuric and nitric acids in glass-lined compartments must be the least of them. I doubt if there are any equivalent of microbes, but the ecology seems to manage quite well without. It's a grosser form of existence than ours. But it works. It works."

"Even sex." Frederika giggled a little crazily.

Darkington squeezed her gauntleted hand until she grew calmer. "Well," he said, "quite probably in the more complex machines, reproduction has

become the specialty of one form while the other
specializes in strength and agility. I daresay there
are corresponding psychological differences."

"Psychological?" Kuroki bridled. "Wait a
minute! I know there is—was—a lot of loose talk
about computers being electronic brains and such
rot, but—"

"Call the phenomenon what you like," Darkington shrugged. "But that robot uses tools which are
made, not grown. The problem is how to convince
it that *we* think."

"Can't it see?" Frederika exclaimed. "We use
tools too. Sam drew mathematical pictures. What
more does it want?"

"I don't know enough about this world to even
guess," Darkington said tiredly. "But I
suppose ... well ... we might once have seen a
trained ape doing all sorts of elaborate things,
without ever assuming it was more than an ape.
No matter how odd it looked."

"Or maybe the robot just doesn't give a damn,"
Kuroki said. "There were people who wouldn't
have."

"If Hugh's guess about the 'black box' is right,"
Frederika added slowly, "then the robot race must
have evolved as hunters, instead of hunting being
invented rather late in their evolution. As if men
had descended from tigers instead of simians.
How much psychological difference would that
make?"

No one replied. She leaned forlornly against
Darkington. Kuroki turned his eyes from them,
perhaps less out of tact than loneliness. His girl
was several thousand miles away, straight up,
with no means for him to call her and say goodby.

Thurshaw had warned the insistent volunteers
for this expedition that there would be no rescue.
He had incurred sufficient guilt in letting three
people—three percent of the human race—risk

themselves. If anything untoward happened, the *Traveler* would linger a while in hopes the boat could somehow return. But in the end the *Traveler* would head for the stars. Kuroki's girl would have to get another father for the boy she might name Sam.

I wish to hell Freddie were up there with her, Darkington thought. *Or do I? Isn't that simply what I'm supposed to wish?*

God! Cut that out. Start planning!

His brain spun like wheels in winter mud. What to do, what to do, what to do? His pistol was gone, so were Kuroki's rockets, nothing remained but a few tools and instruments. At the back of the cave there were probably stored some weapons with which a man could put up a moment's fight. (Only a moment, against horror, of sitting in your own fearstink until the monster approached or the air-renewal batteries grew exhausted and you strangled.) The noose welded around his waist, ending in a ton of iron, choked off any such dreams. They must communicate, somehow, anyhow, plead, threaten, promise, wheedle. But the monster hadn't cared about the Pythagorean theorem diagrammed in sand. What next, then? How did you say "I am alive" to something that was not alive?

Though what was aliveness? Were proteins inherently and unescapably part of any living creature? If the ancient sea rafts had been nothing except complicated machines, at what point of further complication had their descendants come to life? *Now stop that, you're a biologist, you know perfectly well that any such question is empirically empty, and anyhow it has nothing to do with preserving the continuity of certain protein chemistries which are irrationally much loved.*

"I think it talks by radio." Kuroki's slow voice sounded oddly through the thudding in Darkington's head. "It probably hasn't got any notion that sound waves might carry talk. Maybe it's even deaf. Ears wouldn't be any too useful in that rattletrap jungle. And our own radios are busted." He began to fumble in the girl's pack. "I'm not feeling you up, Freddie. Your spacesuit isn't exactly my type. But I think I could cobble together one working set from the pieces of our three, if I can borrow some small tools and instruments. Once we make systematic noises on its talk band, the robot might get interested in trying to savvy us."

"Sam," she said faintly, "for that idea you can feel me up all you want."

"I'll take a rain check." He could actually chuckle, Darkington heard. "I'm sweaty enough in this damn suit to pass for a rainstorm just by myself."

He began to lay out the job. Darkington, unable to help, ashamed that he had not thought of anything, turned attention back to the robots. They were coupled together, ignoring him.

Frederika dozed off. How slowly the night went. But Earth was old, rotating as wearily as . . . as himself . . . . He slept.

A gasp awoke him.

The monster stood above them. Tall, tall, higher than the sky, it bestrode their awareness and looked down with blank eyes upon Kuroki's pitiful, barely begun work. One hand was still a torch and another hand had been replaced. It was invulnerable and soulless as a god. For an instant Darkington's half-aroused self groveled before it.

Then the torch spat, slashed the wire rope across, and Kuroki was pulled free.

Frederika cried out. "Sam!"

"Not . . . so eager . . . pal," the pilot choked in the robot's arms. "I'm glad you like me, but . . . ugh . . . careful!"

With a free hand, the robot twisted experimentally at Kuroki's left leg. The suit joints turned. Kuroki shrieked. Darkington thought he heard the leg bones leave their sockets.

"No! You filthy machine!" He plunged forward. The rope stopped him cold. Frederika covered her faceplate and begged Kuroki to be dead.

He wasn't, yet. He wasn't even unconscious. He kept on screaming as the robot used a prying tool to drag the leg off his armor. Leakseal compound flowed from between the fabric layers and preserved the air in the rest of his suit.

The robot dropped him and sprang back, frantically fanning itself. A whiff of oxygen, Darkington realized amidst the red and black disintegration of his sanity. Oxygen was nearly as reactive as fluorine, and there had been no free oxygen on Earth since—Kuroki's agony jerked toward silence.

The robot reapproached with care, squatted above him, poked at the exposed flesh, tore loose a chunk for examination and flung it aside. The metal off a joint seemed better approved.

Darkington realized vaguely that Frederika lay on the ground close to Kuroki and wept. The biologist himself was even nearer. He could have touched the robot as well as the body. Instead, though, he retreated, mumbling and mewing.

The robot had clearly learned a lesson from the gas, but was just as clearly determined to go on with the investigation. It stood up, moved a cautious distance away, and jetted a thin, intensely blue flame from its torch hand. Kuroki's corpse was divided across the middle.

Darkington's universe roared and exploded. He lunged again. The rope between him and Frederika was pulled across the firebeam. The strands parted like smoke.

The robot pounced at him, ran into the oxygen

gushing from Kuroki's armor, and lurched back.
Darkington grabbed the section of rope that joined
him to the block. The torch was too bright to look
at. If he touched its flame, that was the end of him
too. But there was no chance to think about such
matters. Blindly and animally, he pulled his leash
across the cutting jet.

He was free.

"Get out, Freddie!" he coughed, and ran straight
toward the robot. No use trying to run from a
thing that could overtake him in three strides. The
torch had stopped spitting fire, but the giant
moved in a wobbly, uncertain fashion, still dazed
by the oxygen. By pain? Savagely, in the last spark
of awareness, Darkington hoped so. *"Get out,
Freddie!"*

The robot staggered in pursuit of him. He
dodged around the other machine, the big one that
they had called female. To the back of the cave. A
weapon to fight with, gaining a moment where
Frederika might escape. An extra pry bar lay on
the floor. He snatched it and whirled. The huge
painted shape was almost upon him.

He dodged. Hands clashed together just above
his helmet. He pelted back to the middle of the
cave. The female machine was edging into a
corner. But slow, awkward—

Darkington scrambled on top of it.

An arm reached from below to pluck him off. He
snarled and struck with the pry bar. The noise
rang in the cave. The arm sagged, dented. This
octopod had nothing like the biped's strength. Its
tool tendrils, even more frail, curled away from
him.

The male robot loomed close. Darkington
smashed his weapon down on the radio lattice at
his feet. It crumpled. He brandished the bar and
howled senselessly, "Stand back, there! One step
more and I'll give her the works! I'll kill her!"

The robot stopped. Monstrous it bulked, an engine that could tear apart a man and his armor, and raised its torch hand.

"Oh no," Darkington rasped. He opened a bleeder valve on his suit, kneeling so the oxygen would flow across the front end of the thing on which he rode. Sensors ought to be more vulnerable than skin. He couldn't hear if the she-robot screamed as Kuroki had done. That would be on the radio band. But when he gestured the male back, it obeyed.

"Get the idea?" he panted, not a communication but as hatred. "You can split my suit open with your flame gun, but my air will pour all over this contraption here. Maybe you could knock me off her by throwing something, but at the first sign of any such move on your part, I'll open my bleeder valve again. She'll at least get a heavy dose of oxy. And meanwhile I'll punch the sharp end of this rod through one of those lenses. Understand? Well, then, stay where you are, machine!"

The robot froze.

Frederika came near. She had slipped the loop of cable joining her to Kuroki off what was left of his torso. The light shimmered on her faceplate so Darkington couldn't see through, and her voice was strained out of recognition. "Hugh, oh, Hugh!"

"Head back to the boat," he ordered. Rationality was returning to him.

"Without you? No."

"Listen, this is not the place for grandstand heroics. Your first duty is to become a mother. But what I hope for, personally, is that you can return in the boat and fetch me. You're no pilot, but they can instruct you by radio from the ship if she's above the horizon. The general director does most of the work in any event. You land here, and I can probably negotiate a retreat for myself."

"But—but—the robot needed something like twenty hours to bring us here. And it knew the way better than I do. I'll have to go by compas and guess, mostly. Of course, I won't stop as often as it did. No more than I have to. But still—say twenty hours for me—you can't hold out that long!"

"I can damn well try," he said. "You got any better ideas?"

"All right, then. Good-by, Hugh. No, I mean so long. I love you."

He grunted some kind of answer, but didn't see her go. He had to keep watching the robot.

VI

"Zero!" his female called, just once, when the unit sprung upon her back. She clawed at it. The pry bar smashed across her arm. He felt the pain-surge within her sensors, broadcast through her communicator, like a crossbow bolt in his body.

Wildly, he charged. The enemy unit crashed the bar down on One's lattice. She shrilled in anguish. Affected by the damage that crippled her radar, her communicator tone grew suddenly, hideously different. Zero slammed himself to a halt.

Her sobbing, his own name blindly repeated, overwhelmed the burning in him where the corrosive gas had flowed. He focused his torch to narrow beam and took careful aim.

The unit knelt, fumbling with its free hand. One screamed again, louder. Her tendrils flailed about. Numbly, Zero let his torch arm droop. The unit rose and poised its weapon above her lenses. A single strong thrust downward through the glass could reach her brain. The unit gestured him back. He obeyed.

"Help," One cried. Zero could not look at the wreckage of her face. There was no escaping her distorted voice. "Help, Zero. It hurts so much."

"Hold fast," he called in his uselessness. "I cannot do anything. Not now. The thing is full of poison. That is what you received." He managed to examine his own interior perceptions. "The pain will abate in a minute . . . from such a small amount. But if you got a large dose—I do not know. It might prove totally destructive. Or the biped might do ultimate mechanical damage before I could prevent it. Hold fast, One mine. Until I think of something."

"I am afraid," she rattled. "For the new one."

"Hold fast," he implored. "If that unit does you any further harm, I will destroy it slowly. I expect it realizes as much."

The other functional biped came near. It exchanged a few ululations with the first, turned and went quickly from the cave. "It must be going back to the flying monster," said One. The words dragged from her, now and then she whimpered as her perceptions of damage intensified, but she could reason again. "Will it bring the monster here?"

"I cannot give chase," said Zero unnecessarily. "But—" He gathered his energy. A shout blasted from his communicator. *"Alarm, alarm! All persons receiving, prepare to relay. Alarm!"*

Voices flashed in his head, near and far, and it was as if they poured strength into him. He and One were not alone in a night cave, a scuttling horror on her back and the taste of poison only slowly fading. Their whole community was here.

He reported the situation in a few phrases. "You have been rash," Hundred said, shaken. "May there be no further penalties for your actions."

"What else would you have had him do?" defended Seven. "We cannot deal randomly with a thing as powerful as the monster. Zero took upon himself the hazards of gathering information. Which he has succeeded in, too."

"Proving the danger is greater than we imagined," shuddered Sixteen.

"Well, that is a valuable datum."

"The problem now is, what shall we do?" Hundred interrupted. "Slow though you say it is, I expect the auxiliary that escaped can find the monster long before we can rendezvous and get up into the hills."

"Until it does, though, it cannot communicate, its radio being disabled," Zero said. "So the monster will presumably remain where it is, ignorant of events. I suggest that those persons who are anywhere near this neighborhood strike out directly toward that area. They can try to head off the biped."

"You can certainly capture it in a few minutes," Hundred said.

"I cannot leave this place."

"Yes, you can. The thing that has seized your female will not logically do anything more to her, unprovoked, lest she lose her present hostage value."

"How do you know?" Zero retorted. "In fact, I believe if I captured its companion, this unit would immediately attack One. What hope does it have except in the escape of the other, that may bring rescue?"

"Hope is a curious word to use in connection with an elaborated spy eye," Seven said.

"If it is," Zero said. "Their actions suggest to me that these bipeds are more than unthinking domesticated motiles."

"Let be!" Hundred said. "There is scant time to waste. We may not risk the entire community for the sake of a single member. Zero, go fetch back that biped."

Unmodulated radio buzzed in the night. Finally Zero said, "No." One's undamaged hand reached toward him, but she was too far away for them to touch each other. Nor could she caress him with radar.

"We will soon have you whole again," he murmured to her. She did not answer, with the community listening.

Hundred surrendered, having existed long enough to recognize unbendable negation. "Those who are sufficiently near the monster to reach it before dawn, report," he directed. When they had finished—about thirty all told—he said, "Very well, proceed there. Wherever feasible, direct your course to intercept the probable path of the escaped unit. If you capture it, inform us at once. The rest of us will rendezvous as planned."

One by one the voices died out in the night, until only Hundred, who was responsible, and Seven, who was a friend, were in contact with Zero. "How are you now, One?" Seven asked gently.

"I function somewhat," she said in a tired, uneven tone. "It is strange to be radar blind. I keep thinking that heavy objects are about to crash into me. When I turn my optics that way, there isn't anything." She paused. "The new one stirred a little bit just now. A motor impulse pathway must have been completed. Be careful, Zero," she begged. "We have already taken an arm tonight."

"I cannot understand your description of the bipeds' interior," Hundred said practically. "Soft, porous material soaked in sticky red liquid; acrid vapors—How do they *work?* Where is the mechanism?"

"They are perhaps not functional at all," Seven proposed. "They may be purely artificial devices, powered by chemical action."

"Yet they act intelligently," Zero argued. "If the monster—or the masters—do not have them under direct control—and certainly there is no radio involved—"

"There may be other means than radio to monitor an auxiliary," Seven said. "We know so little, we persons."

"In that case," Zero answered, "the monster has known about this cave all the time. It is watching me at this moment, through the optics of that thing on One's back."

"We must assume otherwise," Hundred said.

"I do," Zero said. "I act in the belief that these bipeds are out of contact with the flier. But if nevertheless they perform as they have been doing, then they certainly have independent function, including at least a degree of intelligence." A thought crashed through him, so stunning that he could not declare it at once. Finally: "They may be the monster's masters! It may be the auxiliary, they the persons!"

"No, no, that is impossible," Hundred groaned. Seven's temporary acceptance was quicker; he had always been able to leap from side to side of a discussion. He flashed:

"Let us assume that in some unheard-of fashion, these small entities are indeed the domesticators, or even the builders, of that flying thing. Can we negotiate with them?"

"Not after what has happened," Zero said bleakly. He was thinking less about what he had done to them than what they had done to One.

Seven continued: "I doubt it myself, on philosophical grounds. They are too alien. Their very functioning is deadly: the destruction wrought by their flier, the poison under their skins. Eventually, a degree of mutual comprehension may be achieved. But that will be a slow and painful process. Our first responsibility is to our own form of existence. Therefore we must unmistakably get the upper hand, before we even try to talk with them." In quick excitement, he added, "And I think we can."

Zero and Hundred meshed their intellects with his. The scheme grew like precipitation in a supersaturated pond. Slow and feeble, the strangers were only formidable by virtue of highly developed artifacts (or, possibly, domesticated motiles of radically modified type): the flier, the tube which had blown off Zero's arm, and other hypothetical weapons. But armament unused is no threat. If the flier could be immobilized—

Of course, presumably there were other dwarf bipeds inside it. Their voices had been heard yesterday. But Zero's trip here had proven that they lacked adequate nighttime senses. Well, grant them radar when in an undamaged condition. Radar can be confused, if one knows how.

Hundred's orders sprang forth across miles to the mountaineers now converging on the flier: "Cut the heaviest accumulator strands you can find in the forest. Twist them into cables. Under cover of darkness, radar window, and distraction objects, surround the monster. We believe now that it may not be sentient, only a flier. Weld your cables fast to deeply founded boles. Then, swiftly, loop them around the base of the flier. Tie it down!"

"No," said Twenty-nine, aghast. "We cannot weld the cables to its skin. It would annihilate us with one jetblast. We would have to make nooses first and—"

"So make the nooses," Zero said. "The monster is not a perfectly tapered spindle. The jets bulge out at the base. Slip the nooses around the body just above the jets. I hardly think it can rise then, without tearing its own tubes out."

"Easy for you to say, Zero, safe in your cave."

"If you knew what I would give to have matters otherwise—"

Abashed, the hunters yielded. Their mission was

not really so dangerous. The nooses—two should be ample if the cable was heavy—could be laid in a broad circle around the area which the jets had flattened and devastated. They could be drawn tight from afar, and would probably slip upward by themselves, coming to rest just above the tubes, where the body of the flier was narrowest. If a cable did get stuck on something, someone would have to dash close and free it. A snort of jetfire during those few seconds would destroy them. But quite probably the flier, or its masters, could be kept from noticing him.

"And when we do have the monster leashed, what then?" asked Twenty-nine.

"We will do what seems indicated," Hundred said. "If the aliens do not seem to be reaching a satisfactory understanding with us—if we begin to entertain any doubts—we can erect trebuchets and batter the flier to pieces."

"That might be best," said Zero, with a revengeful look at One's rider.

"Proceed as ordered," said Hundred.

"But what about us?" Zero asked. "One and myself?"

"I shall come to you," Seven said. "If nothing else, we can stand watch and watch. You mentioned that the aliens polarize more easily than we do. We can wait until it drops from exhaustion."

"Good," said Zero. Hope lifted in him as if breaking through a shell. "Did you hear, One? We need only wait."

"Pain," she whispered. Then, resolutely: "I can minimize energy consumption. Comatose, I will not sense anything . . ." He felt how she fought down terror, and guessed what frightened her: the idea that she might never be roused.

"I will be guarding you all the time," he said. "You and the new one."

"I wish I could touch you, Zero—" Her radiation

dimmed, second by second. Once or twice consciousness returned, kicked upward by fear; static gasped in Zero's perception; but she slipped again into blackness.

When she was quite inert, he stood staring at the unit on her. No, the entity. Somewhere behind that glass and horrible tissue, a brain peered back at him. He ventured to move an arm. The thing jerked its weapon aloft. It seemed indeed to have guessed that the optics were her most vulnerable spot. With immense care, Zero let his arm fall again. The entity jittered about, incapable of his own repose. Good. Let it drain its energy the faster.

He settled into his own thoughts. Hours wore away. The alien paced on One's broad back, sat down, sprang up again, slapped first one hand and then another against its body, made long noises that might possibly be intended to fight off coma. Sometimes it plugged the water tube into its face. Frequently Zero saw what looked like a good chance to catch it off guard—with a sudden rush and a flailing blow, or an object snatched off the floor and thrown, or even a snap shot with his torch—but he decided not to take the hazard. Time was his ally.

Besides, now that his initial rage had abated, he began to hope he might capture the entity undamaged. Much more could be learned from a functional specimen than from the thing which lay dismembered near the iron block. Faugh, the gases it was giving off! Zero's chemical sensor retracted in disgust.

The first dawnlight grayed the cave mouth.

"We have the flier!" Twenty-nine's exuberant word made Zero leap where he stood. The alien scrambled into motion. When Zero came no closer, it sagged again. "We drew two cables around its body. No trouble whatsoever. It never

stirred. Only made the same radio hum. It still has
not moved."

"I thought—" someone else in his party
ventured. "Not long ago . . . was there not a
gibberish signal from above?"

"There might well be other fliers above the
clouds," agreed Hundred from the valley. "Have a
care. Disperse yourselves. Remain under cover.
The rest of us will have rendezvoused by early
afternoon. At that time we will confer afresh.
Meanwhile, report if anything happens. And . . .
good work, hunters.

Twenty-nine offered a brief sensory linkage.
Thus Zero saw the place: the cindered blast area,
and the upright spindle shining in the first long
sunlight, and the cables that ran from its waist to
a pair of old and mighty accumulator boles. Yes,
the thing was captured for certain. Wind blew
over the snowpeaks, set forest to chiming and
scattered the little sunrise clouds. He had rarely
known his land so beautiful.

The perception faded. He was in his cave again.
Seven called: "I am getting close now, Zero. Shall I
enter?"

"No, best not. You might alarm the alien into
violence. I have watched its movements the whole
night. They grow more slow and irregular each
hour. It must be near collapse. Suppose you wait
just outside. When I believe it to be comatose, I
will have you enter. If it does not react to the sight
of you, we will know it has lost consciousness."

"If it is conscious," mused Seven. "Despite our
previous discussion, I cannot bring myself to
believe quite seriously that these are anything but
motiles or artifacts. Very ingenious and complex,
to be sure . . . but *aware*, like a person?"

The unit made a long series of sonic noises. They
were much weaker than hitherto. Zero allowed
satisfaction to wax in him. Nevertheless, he would

not have experienced this past night again for any profit.

Several hours later, a general alarm yanked his attention back outward. "The escaped auxiliary has returned! It has entered the flier!"

"What? You did not stop it?" Hundred demanded.

Twenty-nine gave the full report. "Naturally, after the change of plan, we were too busy weaving cables and otherwise preparing ourselves to beat the forest for the dwarf. After the flier was captured, we dispersed ourselves broadly as ordered. We made nothing like a tight circle around the blasted region. Moreover, our attention was directed at the flier, in case it tried to escape, and at the sky in case there should be more fliers. Various wild motiles were about, which we ignored, and the wind has gotten very loud in the accumulators. Under such circumstances, you will realize that probability actually favored the biped unit passing between us and reaching the open area unobserved.

"When it was first noticed, no person was close enough to reach the flier before it did. It slid a plate aside in one of the jacks which support the flier and pulled a switch. A portal opened in the body above and a ladder was extruded. By that time, a number of us had entered the clearing. The unit scrambled up the ladder. We hesitated, fearing a jetblast. None came. But how could we have predicted that? When at last we did approach, the ladder had been retracted and the portal was closed. I pulled the switch myself but nothing happened. I suppose the biped, once inside, deactivated that control by means of a master switch."

"Well, at least we know where it is," Hundred said. "Disperse again, if you have not already done so. The biped may try to escape, and you do not want to get caught in the jet-blast. Are you certain the flier cannot break your cables?"

"Quite certain. Closely observed, the monster—the flier seems to have only a skin of light alloy. Nor would I expect it to be strong against the unnatural kind of stresses imposed by our tethers. If it tries to rise, it will pull itself in two."

"Unless," said Fourteen, as he hastened through valley mists toward Broken Glade, "some biped emerges with a torch and cuts the cables."

"Just let it dare!" said Twenty-nine, anxious to redeem his crew's failure.

"It may bring strong weapons," Zero warned.

"Ten crossbows are cocked and aimed at that portal. If a biped shows itself, we will fill it with whetted steel."

"I think that will suffice," Zero sid. He looked at the drooping shape upon One. "They are not very powerful, these things. Ugly, cunning, but weak."

Almost as if it knew it was being talked about, the unit reeled to its feet and shook the pry bar at him. Even Zero would detect the dullness in its noises. *Another hour*, he thought, *and One will be free.*

Half that time had gone by when Seven remarked from outside, "I wonder why the builders . . . whoever the ultimate intelligences are behind these manifestations . . . why have they come?"

"Since they made no attempt to communicate with us," Zero said in renewed grimness, "we must assume their purpose is hostile."

"And?"

"Teach them to beware of us."

He felt already the pride of victory. But then the monster spoke.

Up over the mountains rolled the voice, driven by the power which hurled those hundreds of tons through the sky. Roaring and raging through the radio spectrum, louder than lightning, enormous enough to shake down moon and stars, blasted that shout. Twenty-nine and his hunters yelled as the volume smote their receptors. Their cry was lost, drowned, engulfed by the tide which seethed off the mountainsides. Here and there, where some accumulator happened to resonate, blue arcs of flame danced in the forest. Thirty miles distant, Zero and Seven still perceived the noise as a clamor in their heads. Hundred and his followers in the valley stared uneasily toward the ranges. On the seashore, females called, "What is that? What is that?" and aquamotiles dashed themselves about in the surf.

Seven forgot all caution. He ran into the cave. The enemy thing hardly moved. But neither Zero nor Seven observed that. Both returned to the entrance and gazed outward with terror.

The sky was empty. The forest rang in the breeze. Only that radio roar from beyond the horizon told of anything amiss. "I did not believe—" stammered Seven. "I did not expect—a tone that loud—"

Zero, who had One to think about, mustered decisiveness. "It is not hurting us," he said. "I am glad not to be as close as the hunters are, but even they should be able to endure it for a while. We shall see. Come, let us two go back inside. Once we have secured our prisoner—"

The monster began to talk.

No mere outrageous cry this time, but speech. Not words, except occasionally. A few images. But such occurrences were coincidental. The monster spoke in its own language, which was madness.

Seized along every radio receptor channel there was in him, total sensory and mental linkage, Zero became the monster.

DITditditditDAHdit-nulnulnulnul-ditditDAH-dah & the vector sum: infinitesimals infinitely-added from nul-to-INFINITY, dit—ditdit—DA—

ditditditnul (gammacolored chaos, *bang* goes a
universe scattering stars&planets&bursts-of-fire
BLOCK   THAT   NEUTRON   BLOCK   THAT
NEUTRON BLOCK THAT BLOCK THAT BLOCK
THAT NEUTRON) one-one***nononul—DATTA—
ditditchitterchitterchitter burning suns & moons,
burning stars & brains, burningburningburning
Burning DahditDahditDahdit give me fifty million
logarithms this very microsecond or you will Burn
ditditditdit—DAYADHVAM—DAMYATA

and one long wild logarithmic spiral down
spacetimeenergy continuum of potentialgradient
Xproduct i,j,k but multiply Time by the velocity of
light in nothingness and the square root of minus
one (two, three, four, five, six CHANGE for duo-
decimal computation   zzzzzzzzz)

buzzzzzzzzzzZ

integral over sigma of del cross H d sigma
equals one over c times integral over sigma partial
of E with respect to t dot d sigma but correct for
nonsphericalshapentropicoordinatetransform-
ationtop&quantumelectrodynamicchargelectri-
calephaselagradientemperature rising to burning
Burning BURNING

dit-dit-chitterchitterchitter from eyrie to blind
gnawer and back again O help the trunk is burningburningburning THEREFORE ANNUL in the
name of the seven thunders

Everything-that-has-been, break up the roots of
existence and strike flat the thick rotundity o' the
world RRRIP spacetime across and throw it on the
unleaping primordial energy for now all that was
& will be, the very fact that it once *did* exist, is
canceled and torn to pieces and Burning
                                Burning
                                Burning
                                Burning

As the sun fell down the bowl of sky, and the sky
cracked open, and the mountains ran like rivers

forming faces that gaped and jeered, and the moon rose in the west and spat the grisliness of what he had done at him, Zero ran. Seven did not; could not; lay by the cave entrance, which was the gate of all horrors and corruptions, as if turned to salt. And when God descended, still shouting in His tongue which was madness, His fiery tail melted Seven to a pool.

Fifty million years later the star called Wormwood ascended to heaven; and a great silence fell upon the land.

Eventually Zero returned home. He was not surprised to find that the biped was gone. Of course it had been reclaimed by its Master. But when he saw that One was not touched, he stood mute for a long while indeed.

After he roused her, she—who had been awake when the world was broken and refashioned— could not understand why he led her outside to pray that they be granted mercy, now and in the hour of their dissolution.

VII

Darkington did not regain full consciousness until the boat was in space. Then he pulled himself into the seat beside Frederika. "How did you do it?" he breathed.

Her attention remained focused on piloting. Even with the help of the director and radio instructions from the ship, it was no easy task for a novice. Absently, she answered, "I scared the robots away. They'd made the boat fast, you see. With cables too thick to pull apart. I had to go back out and cut them with a torch. But I'd barely gotten inside ahead of the pack. I didn't expect

they would let me emerge. So I scared them off.
After that, I went out, burned off the cables, and
flew to get you."

"Barely in time," he shuddered. "I was about
the pass out. I did keel over once I was aboard." A
time went by with only the soft rushing noise of
brake jets. "Okay," he said, "I give up. I admit
you're beautiful, a marvel of resourcefulness, and
I can't guess how you shooed away the enemy. So
tell me."

The director shut off the engine. They floated
free. She turned her face, haggard, sweaty,
begrimed, and dear, toward him and said diffi-
dently, "I didn't have any inspiration. Just a guess
and nothing to lose. We knew for pretty sure that
the robots communicated by radio. I turned the
boat's 'caster on full blast, hoping the sheer
volume would be too much for them. Then something else occurred to me. If you have a radio
transceiver in your head, hooked directly into
your nervous system, would that be sort of like
telepathy? I mean, it seems more direct somehow
than routing everything we say through a larynx.
Maybe I could confuse them by emitting
unfamiliar signals. Not any old signals, of course.
They'd be used to natural radio noise. But—well—
the boat's general director includes a pretty
complicated computer, carrying out millions of
operations per second. Information is conveyed,
not noise; but at the same time, it didn't seem to
me like information that a bunch of semisavages
could handle.

"Anyhow, there was no harm in trying. I hooked
the broadcaster in parallel with the effector circuits, so the computer's output not only
controlled the boat as usual but also modulated
the radio emission. Then I assigned the computer
a good tough problem in celestial navigation, put
my armor back on, summoned every ounce of

nerve I had, and went outside. Nothing happened. I cut the cables without seeing any trace of the robots. I kept the computer 'talking' while I jockeyed the boat over in search of the cave. It must have been working frantically to compensate for my clumsiness; I hate to imagine what its output 'sounded' like. Felt like? Well, when I'd landed, I opened the airlock and, and you came inside, and—" Her fists doubled. "Oh, God, Hugh! How can we tell Sam's girl?"

He didn't answer.

With a final soft impulse, the boat nudged against the ship. As grapnels made fast, the altered spin of the vessels put Earth back in view. Darkington looked at the planet for minutes before he said:

"Good-by. Good luck."

Frederika wiped her eyes with hands that left streaks of dirt in the tears. "Do you think we'll ever come back?" she wondered.

"No," he said. "It isn't ours any more."

STARFOG

"From another universe. Where space is a
shining cloud, two hundred light-years across,
roiled by the red stars that number in the many
thousands, and where the brighter suns are
troubled and cast forth great flames. Your spaces
are dark and lonely."

Daven Laure stopped the recording and asked
for an official translation. A part of *Jaccavrie's*
computer scanned the molecules of a plugged-in
memory cylinder, identified the passage, and
flashed the Serievan text onto a reader screen.
Another part continued the multitudinous tasks of
planetary approach. Still other parts waited for
the man's bidding, whatever he might want next. A
Ranger of the Commonalty traveled in a very
special ship.

And even so, every year, a certain number did
not come home from their missions.

Laure nodded to himself. Yes, he'd understood
the woman's voice correctly. Or, at least, he
interpreted her sentences approximately the same
way as did the semanticist who had interviewed
her and her fellows. And this particular statement
was as difficult, as ambiguous as any which they
had made. Therefore: (a) Probably the linguistic
computer on Serieve had done a good job of un-
raveling their basic language. (b) It had accurately
encoded its findings—vocabulary, grammar,

tentative reconstruction of the underlying world-view—in the cylinders which a courier had brought to Sector HQ. (c) The reencoding, into his own neurones, which Laure underwent on his way here, had taken well. He had a working knowledge of the tongue which—among how many others?—was spoken on Kirkasant.

"Wherever that may be," he muttered.

The ship weighed his words for a nanosecond or two, decided no answer was called for, and made none.

Restless, Laure got to his feet and prowled from the study cabin, down a corridor to the bridge. It was so called largely by courtesy. *Jaccavrie* navigated, piloted, landed, lifted, maintained, and, if need be, repaired and fought for herself. But the projectors here offered a full outside view. At the moment, the bulkheads seemed cramped and barren. Laure ordered the simulacrum activated.

The bridge vanished from his eyes. Had it not been for the G-field underfoot, he might have imagined himself floating in space. A crystal night enclosed him, unwinking stars scattered like jewels, the frosty glitter of the Milky Way. Large and near, its radiance stopped down to preserve his retinas, burned the yellow sun of Serieve. The planet itself was a growing crescent, blue banded with white, rimmed by a violet sky. A moon stood opposite, worn golden coin.

But Laure's gaze strayed beyond, toward the deeps and then, as if in search of comfort, the other way, toward Old Earth. There was no comfort, though. They still named her Home, but she lay in the spiral arm behind this one, and Laure had never seen her. He had never met anyone who had. None of his ancestors had, for longer than their family chronicles ran. Home was a half-remembered myth; reality was here, these stars on the fringes of this civilization.

Serieve lay near the edge of the known. Kirkasant lay somewhere beyond.

"Surely not outside of spacetime," Laure said.

"If you've begun thinking aloud, you'd like to discuss it," *Jaccavrie* said.

He had followed custom in telling the ship to use a female voice and, when practical, idiomatic language. The computer had soon learned precisely what pattern suited him best. That was not identical with what he liked best; such could have got disturbing on a long cruise. He found himself more engaged, inwardly, with the husky contralto that had spoken in strong rhythms out of the recorder than he was with the mezzo-soprano that now reached his ears.

"Well . . . maybe so," he said. "But you already know everything in the material we have aboard."

"You need to set your thoughts in order. You've spent most of our transit time acquiring the language."

"All right, then, let's run barefoot through the obvious." Laure paced a turn around the invisible deck. He felt its hardness, the vibration back through his sandals, he sensed the almost subliminal beat of driving energies, he caught a piny whiff of air as the ventilators shifted to another part of their odor-temperature-ionization cycle; but still the stars blazed about him, and their silence seemed to enter his bones. Abruptly, harshly, he said: "Turn that show off."

The ship obeyed. "Would you like a planetary scene?" she asked. "You haven't yet looked at those tapes from the elf castles on Jair that you bought—"

"Not now." Laure flung himself into a chair web and regarded the prosaic metal, instruments, manual override controls that surrounded him. "This will do."

"Are you feeling well? Why not go in the diagnoser and let me check you out? We've time before we arrive."

The tone was anxious. Laure didn't believe that emotion was put on. He refrained from anthropomorphizing his computer, just as he did those non-human sophonts he encountered. At the same time, he didn't go along with the school of thought which claimed that human-sensibility terms were absolutely meaningless in such connections. An alien brain, or a cybernetic one like *Jaccavrie*'s, could think; it was aware; it had conation. Therefore it had analogies to his.

Quite a few Rangers were eremitic types, sane enough but basically schizoid. That was their way of standing the gaff. It was normal for them to think of their ships as elaborate tools. Daven Laure, who was young and outgoing, naturally thought of his as a friend.

"No, I'm all right," he said. "A bit nervous, nothing else. This could turn out to be the biggest thing I . . . you and I have tackled yet. Maybe one of the biggest anyone has, at least on this frontier. I'd've been glad to have an older man or two along." He shrugged. "None available. Our service should increase its personnel, even if it means raising dues. We're spread much too thin across— how many stars?"

"The last report in my files estimated ten million planets with a significant number of Commonalty members on them. As for how many more there may be with which these have reasonably regular contact—"

"Oh, for everything's sake, come off it!" Laure actually laughed, and wondered if the ship had planned things that way. But, regardless, he could begin to talk of this as a problem rather than a mystery.

"Let me recapitulate," he said, "and you tell me
if I'm misinterpreting matters. A ship comes to
Serieve, allegedly from far away. It's like nothing
anybody has ever seen, unless in historical works.
(They haven't got the references on Serieve to
check that out, so we're bringing some from HQ.)
Hyperdrive, gravity control, electronics, yes, but
everything crude, archaic, bare-bones. Fission
instead of fusion power, for example . . . and
human piloting!

"That is, the crew seem to be human. We have
no record of their anthropometric type, but they
don't look as odd as people do after several generations on some planets I could name. And the
linguistic computer, once they get the idea that it's
there to decipher their language and start cooper-
ating with it, says their speech appears to have
remote affinities with a few that we know, like
ancient Anglic. Preliminary semantic analysis
suggests their abstractions and constructs aren't
quite like ours, but do fall well inside the human
psych range. All in all, then, you'd assume they're
explorers from distant parts."

"Except for the primitive ship," *Jaccavrie*
chimed in. "One wouldn't expect such technological backwardness in any group which had maintained any contact, however tenuous, with the
general mass of the different human civilizations.
Nor would such a slow, underequipped vessel
pass through them without stopping, to fetch up in
this border region."

"Right. So . . . if it isn't a fake . . . their gear
bears out a part of their story. Kirkasant is an ex-
ceedingly old colony . . . yonder." Laure pointed
toward unseen stars. "Well out in the Dragon's
Head sector, where we're barely beginning to
explore. Somehow, somebody got that far, and in
the earliest days of interstellar travel. They settled
down on a planet and lost the trick of making
spaceships. Only lately have they regained it."

"And come back, looking for the companionship of their own kind." Laure had a brief, irrational vision of *Jaccavrie* nodding. Her tone was so thoughtful. She would be a big, calm, dark-haired woman, handsome in middle age though getting somewhat plump . . . "What the crew themselves have said, as communication got established, seems to bear out this idea. Beneath a great many confused mythological motifs, I also get the impression of an epic voyage, by a defeated people who ran as far as they could."

"But Kirkasant!" Laure protested. "The whole situation they describe. It's impossible."

"Might not that Vandange be mistaken? I mean, we know so little. The Kirkasanters keep talking about a weird home environment. Ours appears to have stunned and bewildered them. They simply groped on through space till they happened to find Serieve. Thus might their own theory, that somehow they blundered in from an altogether different continuum, might it not conceivably be right?"

"Hm-m-m. I guess you didn't see Vandange's accompanying letter. No, you haven't, it wouldn't've been plugged into your memory. Anyway, he claims his assistants examined that ship down to the bolt heads. And they found nothing, no mechanism, no peculiarity, whose function and behavior weren't obvious. He really gets indignant. Says the notion of interspace-time transference is mathematically absurd. I don't have quite his faith in mathematics, myself, but I must admit he has one common-sense point. If a ship could somehow flip from one entire cosmos to another . . . why, in five thousand years of interstellar travel, haven't we gotten some record of it happening?"

"Perhaps the ships to which it occurs never come back."

"Perhaps. Or perhaps the whole argument is

due to misunderstanding. We don't have any good grasp of the Kirkasanter language. Or maybe it's a hoax. That's Vandange's opinion. He claims there's no such region as they say they come from. Not anywhere. Neither astronomers nor explorers have ever found anything like a . . . a space like a shining fog, crowded with stars—"

"But why should these wayfarers tell a falsehood?" *Jaccavrie* sounded honestly puzzled.

"I don't know. Nobody does. That's why the Serievan government decided it'd better ask for a Ranger."

Laure jumped up and started pacing again. He was a tall young man, with the characteristic beardlessness, fair hair and complexion, slightly slanted blue eyes of the Fircland mountaineers on New Vixen. But since he had trained at Starborough, which is on Aladir not far from Irontower City, he affected a fashionably simple gray tunic and blue hose. The silver comet of his calling blazoned his left breast.

"I don't know," he repeated. There rose in him a consciousness of that immensity which crouched beyond this hull. "Maybe they are telling the sober truth. We don't dare not know."

When a mere few million people have an entire habitable world to themselves, they do not often build high. That comes later, along with formal wilderness preservation, disapproval of fecundity, and inducements to emigrate. Pioneer towns tend to be low and rambling. (Or so it is in that civilization wherein the Commonalty operates. We know that other branches of humanity have their distinctive ways, and hear rumors of yet stranger ones. But so vast is the galaxy—these two or three spiral arms, a part of which our race has to date thinly occupied—so vast, that we cannot even keep track of our own culture, let alone anyone else's.)

Pelogard, however, was founded on an island off the Branzan mainland, above Serieve's arctic circle: which comes down to almost 56°. Furthermore, it was an industrial center. Hence most of its buildings were tall and crowded. Laure, standing by the outer wall of Ozer Vandange's office and looking forth across the little city, asked why this location had been chosen.

"You don't know?" responded the physicist. His inflection was a touch too elaborately incredulous.

"I'm afraid not," Laure confessed. "Think how many systems my service has to cover, and how many individual places within each system. If we tried to remember each, we'd never be anywhere but under the neuroinductors."

Vandange, seated small and bald and prim behind a large desk, pursed his lips. "Yes, yes," he said. "Nevertheless, I should not think an *experienced* Ranger would dash off to a planet without temporarily mastering a few basic facts about it."

Laure flushed. An experienced Ranger would have put this conceited old dustbrain in his place. But he himself was too aware of youth and awkwardness. He managed to say quietly, "Sir, my ship has complete information. She needed only scan it and tell me no precautions were required here. You have a beautiful globe and I can understand why you're proud of it. But please understand that to me it has to be a way station. My job is with those people from Kirkasant, and I'm anxious to meet them."

"You shall, you shall," said Vandage, somewhat mollified. "I merely thought a conference with you would be advisable first. As for your question, we need a city here primarily because updwelling ocean currents make the arctic waters mineral-rich. Extractor plants pay off better than they would farther south."

Despite himself, Laure was interested. "You're

getting your minerals from the sea already? At so early a stage of settlement?"

"This sun and its planets are poor in heavy metals. Most local systems are. Not surprising. We aren't far, here, from the northern verge of the spiral arm. Beyond is the halo—thin gas, little dust, ancient globular clusters very widely scattered. The interstellar medium from which stars form has not been greatly enriched by earlier generations."

Laure suppressed his resentment at being lectured like a child. Maybe it was just Vandage's habit. He cast another glance through the wall. The office was high in one of the buildings. He looked across soaring blocks of metal, concrete, glass, and plastic, interlinked with trafficways and freight cables, down to the waterfront. There bulked the extractor plants, warehouses, and sky-docks. Cargo craft moved ponderously in and out. Not many passenger vessels flitted between. Pelogard must be largely automated.

The season stood at late spring. The sun cast brightness across a gray ocean that a wind rumpled. Immense flocks of seabirds dipped and wheeled. Or were they birds? They had wings, any-how, steely blue against a wan sky. Perhaps they cried or sang, into the wind skirl and wave rush; but Laure couldn't hear it in this enclosed place.

"That's one reason I can't accept their yarn," Vandange declared.

"Eh?" Laure came out of his reverie with a start.

Vandange pressed a button to opaque the wall. "Sit down. Let's get to business."

Laure eased himself into a lounger opposite the desk. "Why am I conferring with you?" he counterattacked. "Whoever was principally working with the Kirkasanters had to be a semanticist. In short, Paeri Ferand. He consulted specialists on your university faculty, in anthropology, history, and so forth. But I should think your own role as a physicist was marginal. Yet you're the one taking up my time. Why?"

"Oh, you can see Ferand and the others as much as you choose," Vandage said. "You won't get more from them than repetitions of what the Kirkasanters have already told. How could you? What else have they got to go on? If nothing else, an underpopulated world like ours can't maintain staffs of experts to ferret out the meaning of every datum, every inconsistency, every outright lie. I had hoped, when our government notified your sector, headquarters, the Rangers would have sent a real team, instead of—" He curbed himself. "Of course, they have many other claims on their attention. They would not see at once how important this is."

"Well," Laure said in his annoyance, "if you're suspicious, if you think the strangers need further investigation, why bother with my office? It's just an overworked little outpost. Send them on to a heart world, like Sarnac, where the facilities and people really can be had."

"It was urged," Vandange said. "I, and a few others who felt as I do, fought the proposal bitterly. In the end, as a compromise, the government decided to dump the whole problem in the lap of the Rangers. Who turn out to be, in effect, you. Now I must persuade you to be properly cautious. Don't you see, if those ... beings ... have some hostile intent, the very worst move would be to send them on—let them spy out our civilization—let them, perhaps, commit nuclear sabotage on a vital center, and then vanish back into space." His voice grew shrill. "That's why we've kept them here so long, on one excuse after the next, here on our home planet. We feel responsible to the rest of mankind!"

"But what—" Laure shook his head. He felt a sense of unreality. "Sir, the League, the troubles, the Empire, its fall, the Long Night . . . every such thing—behind us. In space and time alike. The people of the Commonalty don't get into wars."

"Are you quite certain?"

"What makes *you* so certain of any menace in— one antiquated ship. Crewed by a score of men and women. Who came here openly and peacefully. Who, by every report, have been struggling to get past the language and culture barriers and communicate with you in detail—what in cosmos' name makes you worry about them?"

"The fact that they are liars."

Vandange sat awhile, gnawing his thumb, before he opened a box, took out a cigar and puffed it into lighting. He didn't offer Laure one. That might be for fear of poisoning his visitor with whatever local weed he was smoking. Scattered around for many generations on widely differing planets, populations did develop some odd distributions of allergy and immunity. But Laure suspected plain rudeness.

"I thought my letter made it clear," Vandange said. "They insist they are from another continuum. One with impossible properties, including visibility from ours. Conveniently on the far side of the Dragon's Head, so that we don't see it here. Oh, yes," he added quickly, "I've heard the arguments. That the whole thing is a misunderstanding due to our not having an adequate command of their language. That they're really trying to say they came from—well, the commonest rationalization is a dense star cluster. But it won't work, you know. It won't work at all."

"Why not?" Laure asked.

"Come, now. Come, now. You must have learned

some astronomy as part of your training. You must know that some things simply do not occur in the galaxy."

"Uh—"

"They showed us what they alleged were lens-and-film photographs taken from, ah, inside their home universe." Vandange bore down heavily on the sarcasm. "You saw copies, didn't you? Well, now, where in the real universe do you find that kind of nebulosity—so thick and extensive that a ship can actually lose its bearings, wander around lost, using up its film among other supplies, until it chances to emerge in clear space? For that matter, assuming there were such a region, how could anyone capable of building a hyperdrive be so stupid as to go beyond sight of his beacon stars?"

"Uh . . . I thought of a cluster, heavily hazed, somewhat like the young clusters of the Pleiades type."

"So did many Serievans," Vandange snorted. "Please use your head. Not even Pleiadic clusters contain that much gas and dust. Besides, the verbal description of the Kirkasanters sounds like a globular cluster, insofar as it sounds like anything. But not much. The ancient red suns are there, crowded together, true. But they speak of far too many younger ones.

"And of far too much heavy metal at home. Which their ship demonstrates. Their use of alloying elements like aluminum and beryllium is incredibly parsimonious. On the other hand, electrical conductors are gold and silver, the power plant is shielded not with lead but with inert-coated osmium, and it burns plutonium which the Kirkasanters assert was mined!

"They were astonished that Serieve is such a light-metal planet. Or claimed they were astonished. I don't know about that. I do know that this whole region is dominated by light elements. That its interstellar spaces are relatively free of dust and gas, the Dragon's Head being the only exception and it merely in transit through our skies. That all this is even more true of the globular clusters, which formed in an ultratenuous medium, mostly before the galaxy had condensed to its present shape—which, in fact, practically don't *occur* in the main body of the galaxy, but are off in the surrounding halo!"

Vandange stopped for breath and triumph.

"Well." Laure shifted uneasily in his seat and wished *Jaccavrie* weren't ten thousand kilometers away at the only spaceport. "You have a point. There are contradictions, aren't there? I'll bear what you said in mind when I, uh, interview the strangers themselves."

"And you will, I trust, be wary of them," Vandange said.

"Oh, yes. Something queer does seem to be going on."

In outward appearance, the Kirkasanters were not startling. They didn't resemble any of the human breeds that had developed locally, but they varied less from the norm than some. The fifteen men and five women were tall, robust, broad in chest and shoulders, slim in waist. Their skins were dark coppery reddish, their hair blue-black and wavy; males had some beard and mustache which they wore neatly trimmed. Skulls were dolichocephalic, faces disharmonically wide, noses straight and thin, lips full. The total effect was handsome. Their eyes were their most arresting feature, large, long-lashed, luminous in shades of gray, or green, or yellow.

Since they had refused—with an adamant politeness they well knew how to assume—to let cell samples be taken for chromosome analysis,

Vandange had muttered to Laure about nonhumans in surgical disguise. But that the Ranger classed as the fantasy of a provincial who'd doubtless never met a live xeno. You couldn't fake so many details, not and keep a viable organism. Unless, to be sure, happenstance had duplicated most of those details for you in the course of evolution . . .

Ridiculous, Laure thought. *Coincidence isn't that energetic.*

He walked from Pelogard with Demring Lodden, captain of the *Makt,* and Demring's daughter, navigator Graydal. The town was soon behind them. They found a trail that wound up into steeply rising hills, among low, gnarly trees which had begun to put forth leaves that were fronded and colored like old silver. The sun was sinking, the air noisy and full of salt odors. Neither Kirkasanter appeared to mind the chill.

"You know your way here well," Laure said clumsily.

"We should," Demring answered, "for we have been held on this sole island, with naught to do but ramble it when the *reyad* takes us."

"Reyad?" Laure asked.

"The need to . . . search," Graydal said. "To track beasts, or find what is new, or be alone in wild places. Our folk were hunters until not so long ago. We bear their blood."

Demring wasn't to be diverted from his grudge. "Why are we thus confined?" he growled. "Each time we sought an answer, we got an evasion. Fear of disease, need for us to learn what to expect— Ha, by now I'm half minded to draw my gun, force my way to our ship, and depart for aye!"

He was erect, grizzled, deeply graven of countenance and bleak of gaze. Like his men, he wore soft boots, a knee-length gown of some fine-scaled leather, a cowled cloak, a dagger and an energy

pistol at his belt. On his forehead sparkled a
diamond that betokened authority.

"Well, but, Master," Graydal said, "here today
we deal with no village witchfinders. Daven Laure
is a king's man, with power to act, knowledge and
courage to act rightly. Has he not gone off alone
with us because you said you felt stifled and spied
on in the town? Let us talk as freefolk with him."

Her smile, her words in the husky voice that
Laure remembered from his recordings, were
gentle. He felt pretty sure, though, that as much
steel underlay her as her father, and possibly
whetted sharper. She almost matched his height,
her gait was tigerish, she was herself weaponed
and diademmed. Unlike Laure's close cut or Demring's short bob, her hair passed through a
platinum ring and blew free at full length. Her
clothes were little more than footgear, fringed
shorts, and thin blouse. However attractive, the
sight did not suggest seductive feminity to the
Ranger—when she wasn't feeling the cold that
struck through his garments. Besides, he had
already learned that the sexes were mixed aboard
the *Makt* for no other reason than that women
were better at certain jobs than men. Every female
was accompanied by an older male relative. The
Kirkasanters were not an uncheerful folk, on the
whole, but some of their ideals looked austere.

Nonetheless, Graydal had lovely strong
features, and her eyes, under the level brows,
shone amber.

"Maybe the local government was
overcautious," Laure said, "but don't forget, this
is a frontier settlement. Not many light-years
hence, in that part of the sky you came from,
begins the unknown. It's true the stars are comparatively thin in these parts—average distance
between them about four parsecs—but still, their
number is too great for us to do more than feel our

way slowly forward. Especially when, in the
nature of the case, planets like Serieve must
devote most of their effort to developing themselves. So, when one is ignorant, one does best to
be careful."

He flattered himself that was a well-composed
conciliatory speech. It wasn't as oratorical as one
of theirs, but they had lung capacity for a thinner
atmosphere than this. He was disappointed when
Demring said scornfully, *"Our* ancestors were not
so timid."

"Or else their pursuers were not," Graydal
laughed.

The captain looked offended. Laure hastily
asked: "Have you no knowledge of what
happened?"

"No," said the girl, turned pensive. "Not in
truth. Legends, found in many forms across all
Kirkasant, tell of battle, and a shipful of people
who fled far until at last they found haven. A few
fragmentary records—but those are vague, save
the Baorn Codex; and it is little more than a com-
pendium of technical information which the
Wisemen of Skribent preserved. Even in that
case"—she smiled again—"the meaning of most
passages was generally obscure until after our
modern scientists had invented the thing
described for themselves."

"Do you know what records remain in Homeland?" Demring asked hopefully.

Laure sighed and shook his head. "No. Perhaps
none, by now. Doubtless, in time, an expedition
will go from us to Earth. But after five thousand
trouble-filled years—And your ancestors may not
have started from there. They may have belonged
to one of the first colonies."

In a dim way, he could reconstruct the story.
There had been a fight. The reasons—personal,

familial, national, ideological, economic, whatever they were—had dropped into the bottom of the millennia between then and now. (A commentary on the importance of any such reasons.) But someone had so badly wanted the destruction of someone else that one ship, or one fleet, hounded another almost a quarter way around the galaxy.

Or maybe not, in a literal sense. It would have been hard to do. Crude as they were, those early vessels could have made the trip, if frequent stops were allowed for repair and resupply and refilling of the nuclear converters. But to this day, a craft under hyperdrive could only be detected within approximately a light-year's radius by the instantaneous "wake" of space-pulses. If she lay doggo for a while, she was usually unfindable in the sheer stupendousness of any somewhat larger volume. That the hunter should never, in the course of many months, either have overhauled his quarry or lost the scent altogether, seemed conceivable but implausible.

Maybe pursuit had not been for the whole distance. Maybe the refugees had indeed escaped after a while, but—in blind panic, or rage against the foe, or desire to practice undisturbed a brand of utopianism, or whatever the motive was—they had continued as far as they possibly could, and hidden themselves as thoroughly as nature allowed.

In any case, they had ended in a strange part of creation: so strange that numerous men on Serieve did not admit it existed. By then, their ship must have been badly in need of a complete overhaul, amounting virtually to a rebuilding. They settled down to construct the necessary industrial base. (Think, for example, how much plant you must have before you make your first transistor.) They did not have the accumulated experience of later generations to prove how impossible this was.

Of course they failed. A few score—a few hundred at absolute maximum, if the ship had been rigged with suspended-animation lockers—could not preserve a full-fledged civilization while coping with a planet for which man was never meant. And they had to content themselves with that planet. Once into the Cloud Universe, even if their vessel could still wheeze along for a while, they were no longer able to move freely about, picking and choosing.

Kirkasant was probably the best of a bad lot. And Laure thought it was rather a miracle that man had survived there. So small a genetic pool, so hostile an environment . . . but the latter might well have saved him from the effects of the former. Natural selection must have been harsh. And, seemingly, the radiation background was high, which led to a corresponding mutation rate. Women bore from puberty to menopause, and buried most of their babies. Men struggled to keep them alive. Often death harvested adults, too, entire families. But those who were fit tended to survive. And the planet did have an unfilled ecological niche: the one reserved for intelligence. Evolution galloped. Population exploded. In one or two millennia, man was at home on Kirkasant. In five, he crowded it and went looking for new planets.

Because culture had never totally died. The first generation might be unable to build machine tools, but could mine and forge metals. The next generation might be too busy to keep public schools, but had enough hard practical respect for learning that it supported a literate class. Succeeding generations, wandering into new lands, founding new nations and societies, might war with each other, but all drew from a common tradition and looked to one goal: reunion with the stars.

Once the scientific method had been created afresh, Laure thought, progress must have been more rapid than on Earth. For the natural philosophers knew certain things were possible, even if they didn't know how, and this was half the battle. They must have got some hints, however oracular, from the remnants of ancient texts. They actually had the corroded hulk of the ancestral ship for their studying. Given this much, it was not too surprising that they leaped in a single lifetime from the first moon rockets to the first hyperdrive craft—and did so on a basis of wildly distorted physical theory, and embarked with such naiveté that they couldn't find their way home again!

All very logical. Unheard of, outrageously improbable, but in this big a galaxy the strangest things are bound to happen now and again. The Kirkasanters could be absolutely honest in their story.

If they were.

"Let the past tend the past," Graydal said impatiently. "We've tomorrow to hunt in."

"Yes," Laure said, "but I do need to know a few things. It's not clear to me how you found us. I mean, you crossed a thousand light-years or more of wilderness. How did you come on a speck like Serieve?"

"We were asked that before," Demring said, "but then we could not well explain, few words being held in common. Now you show a good command of the Hobrokan tongue, and for our part, albeit none of these villagers will take the responsibility of putting one of us under your educator machine . . . in talking with technical folk, we've gained various technical words of yours."

He was silent awhile, collecting phrases. The three people continued up the trail. It was wide

enough for them to walk abreast, somewhat
muddy with rain and melted snow. The sun was so
far down that the woods walled it off; twilight
smoked from the ground and from either side,
though the sky was still pale. The wind was dying
but the chill deepening. Somewhere behind those
dun trunks and ashy-metallic leaves, a voice went
"K-kr-r-r-*ruk!*" and, above and ahead, the sound of
a river became audible.

Demring said with care: "See you, when we
could not find our way back to Kirkasant's sun,
and at last had come out in an altogether different
cosmos, we thought our ancestors might have
originated there. Certain traditional songs hinted
as much, speaking of space as dark for instance;
and surely darkness encompassed us now, and
immense loneliness between the stars. Well, but in
which direction might Homeland lie? Casting
about with telescopes, we spied afar a black cloud,
and thought, if the ancestors had been in flight
from enemies, they might well have gone through
such, hoping to break their trail."

"The Dragon's Head Nebula," Laure nodded.

Graydal's wide shoulders lifted and fell. "At
least it gave us something to steer by," she said.

Laure stole a moment's admiration of her
profile. "You had courage," he said. "Quite aside
from everything else, how did you know this civilization had not stayed hostile to you?"

"How did we know it ever was in the first
place?" she chuckled. "Myself, insofar as I believe
the myths have any truth, I suspect our ancestors
were thieves or bandits, or—"

"Daughter!" Demring hurried on, in a scandal-
ized voice: "When we had fared thus far, we found
the darkness was dust and gas such as pervade the
universe at home. There was simply an absence of
stars to make them shine. Emerging on the
far side, we tuned our neutrino detectors. Our

reasoning was that a highly developed civilization would use a great many nuclear power plants. Their neutrino flux should be detectable above the natural noise level—in this comparatively empty cosmos—across several score light-years or better, and we could home on it."

First they sound like barbarian bards, Laure thought, *and then like radionicians. No wonder a dogmatist like Vandange can't put credence in them.*

Can I?

"We soon began to despair," Graydal said. "We were nigh to the limit—"

"No matter," Demring interrupted.

She looked steadily first at one man, then the other, and said, "I dare trust Daven Laure." To the Ranger: "Belike no secret anyhow, since men on Serieve must have examined our ship with knowledgeable eyes. We were nigh to our limit of travel without refueling and refurbishing. We were about to seek for a planet not too unlike Kirkasant where— But then, as if by Valfar's Wings, came the traces we sought, and we followed them here.

"And here were humans!"

"Only of late has our gladness faded as we begin to see how they temporize and keep us half prisoner. Wholly prisoner, maybe, should we try to depart. Why will they not rely on us?"

"I tried to explain that when we talked yesterday," Laure said. "Some important men don't see how you could be telling the truth."

She caught his hand in a brief, impulsive grasp. Her own was warm, slender, and hard. "But you are different?"

"Yes." He felt helpless and alone. "They've, well, they've called for me. Put the entire problem in the hands of my organization. And my fellows have so much else to do that, well, I'm given broad discretion."

Demring regarded him shrewdly. "You are a young man," he said. "Do not let your powers paralyze you."

"No. I will do what I can for you. It may be little."

The trail rounded a thicket and they saw a rustic bridge across the river, which ran seaward in foam and clangor. Halfway over, the party stopped, leaned on the rail and looked down. The water was thickly shadowed between its banks, and the woods were becoming a solid black mass athwart a dusking sky. The air smelled wet.

"You realize," Laure said, "it won't be easy to retrace your route. You improvised your navigational coordinates. They can be transformed into ours on this side of the Dragon's Head, I suppose. But once beyond the nebula, I'll be off my own charts, except for what few listed objects are visible from either side. No one from this civilization has been there, you see, what with millions of suns closer to our settlements. And the star sights you took can't have been too accurate."

"You are not going to take us to Homeland, then," Demring said tonelessly.

"Don't you understand? Homeland, Earth, it's so far away that I myself don't know what it's like anymore!"

"But you must have a nearby capital, a more developed world than this. Why do you not guide us thither, that we may talk with folk wiser than these wretched Serievans?"

"Well . . . uh . . . Oh, many reasons. I'll be honest, caution is one of them. Also, the Commonalty does not have anything like a capital, or— But yes, I could guide you to the heart of civilization. Any of numerous civilizations in this galactic arm." Laure took a breath and slogged on. "My decision, though, under the circumstances, is that first I'd better see your world Kirkasant.

After that . . . well, certainly, if everything is all right, we'll establish regular contacts, and invite your people to visit ours, and— Don't you like the plan? Don't you want to go home?"

"How shall we, ever?" Graydal asked low.

Laure cast her a surprised glance. She stared ahead of her and down, into the river. A fish— some kind of swimming creature—leaped. Its scales caught what light remained in a gleam that was faint but startling against those murky waters. She didn't seem to notice, though she cocked her head instinctively toward the splash that followed.

"Have you not listened?" she said. "Did you not hear us? How long we searched in the fog, through that forest of suns, until at last we left our whole small bright universe and came into this great one that has so much blackness in it—and thrice we plunged back into our own space, and groped about, and came forth without having found trace of any star we knew—" Her voice lifted the least bit. "We are lost, I tell you, eternally lost. Take us to your home, Daven Laure, that we may try to make ours there."

He wanted to stroke her hands, which had clenched into fists on the bridge rail. But he made himself say only: "Our science and resources are more than yours. Maybe we can find a way where you cannot. At any rate, I'm duty bound to learn as much as I can, before I make report and recommendation to my superiors."

"I do not think you are kind, forcing my crew to return and look again on what has gone from them," Demring said stiffly. "But I have scant choice save to agree." He straightened. "Come, best we start back toward Pelogard. Night will soon be upon us."

"Oh, no rush," Laure said, anxious to change the subject. "An arctic zone, at this time of year— We'll have no trouble."

"Maybe you will not," Graydal said. "But Kirkasant after sunset is not like here."

They were on their way down when dusk became night, a light night where only a few stars gleamed and Laure walked easily through a clear gloaming. Graydal and Demring must needs use their energy guns at minimum intensity for flashcasters. And even so, they often stumbled.

Makt was three times the size of *Jaccavrie*, a gleaming torpedo shape whose curve was broken by boat housings and weapon turrets. The Ranger vessel looked like a gig attending her. In actuality, *Jaccavrie* could have outrun, outmaneuvered, or outfought the Kirkasanter with ludicrous ease. Laure didn't emphasize that fact. His charges were touchy enough already. He had suggested hiring a modern carrier for them, and met a glacial negative. This craft was the property and bore the honor of the confederated clans that had built her. She was not to be abandoned.

Modernizing her would have taken more time than increased speed would save. Besides, while Laure was personally convinced of the good intentions of Demring's people, he had no right to present them with up-to-date technology until he had proof they wouldn't misuse it.

One could not accurately say that he resigned himself to accompanying them in his ship at the plodding pace of theirs. The weeks of travel gave him a chance to get acquainted with them and their culture. And that was not only his duty but his pleasure. Especially, he found, when Graydal was involved.

Some time passed before he could invite her to dinner *à deux*. He arranged it with what he felt sure was adroitness. Two persons, undisturbed, talking socially, could exchange information of the subtle kind that didn't come across in committee. Thus he proposed a series of private

meetings with the officers of *Makt*. He began with
the captain, naturally; but after a while came the
navigator's turn.

Jaccavrie phased in with the other vessel, laid
alongside and made air-lock connections in a
motion too smooth to feel. Graydal came aboard
and the ships parted company again. Laure
greeted her according to the way of Kirkasant,
with a handshake. The clasp lasted a moment.
"Welcome," he said.

"Peace between us." Her smile offset her
formalism. She was in uniform—another obsolete
aspect of her society—but it shimmered gold and
molded itself to her.

"Won't you come to the saloon for a drink
before we eat?"

"I shouldn't. Not in space."

"No hazard," said the computer in an amused
tone. "I operate everything anyway."

Graydal had tensed and clapped hand to gun at
the voice. She had relaxed and tried to laugh. "I'm
sorry. I am not used to . . . you." She almost
bounded on her way down the corridor with
Laure. He had set the interior weight at one
standard G. The Kirkasanters maintained theirs
fourteen percent higher, to match the pull of their
home world.

Though she had inspected this ship several
times already, Graydal looked wide-eyed around
her. The saloon was small but sybaritic. "You do
yourself proud," she said amidst the draperies,
music, perfumes, and animations.

He guided her to a couch. "You don't sound
quite approving," he said.

"Well—"

"There's no virtue in suffering hardships."

"But there is in the ability to endure them." She
sat too straight for the form-fitter cells to make
her comfortable.

"Think I can't?"

Embarrassed, she turned her gaze from him, toward the viewscreen, on which flowed a color composition. Her lips tightened. "Why have you turned off the exterior scene?"

"You don't seem to like it, I've noticed." He sat down beside her. "What will you have? We're fairly well stocked."

"Turn it on."

"What?"

"The outside view." Her nostrils dilated. "It shall not best me."

He spread his hands. The ship saw his rueful gesture and obliged. Space leaped into the screen, star-strewn except where the storm-cloud mass of the dark nebula reared ahead. He heard Graydal suck in a breath and said quickly, "Uh, since you aren't familiar with our beverages, I suggest daiquiris. They're tart, a little sweet—"

Her nod was jerky. Her eyes seemed locked to the screen. He leaned close, catching the slight warm odor of her, not quite identical with the odor of other women he had known, though the difference was too subtle for him to name. "Why does that sight bother you?" he asked.

"The strangeness. The aloneness. It is so absolutely alien to home. I feel forsaken and—" She filled her lungs, forced detachment on herself, and said in an analytical manner: "Possibly we are disturbed by a black sky because we have virtually none of what you call night vision." A touch of trouble returned. "What else have we lost?"

"Night vision isn't needed on Kirkasant, you tell me," Laure consoled her. "And evolution there worked fast. But you must have gained as well as atrophied. I know you have more physical strength, for instance, than your ancestors could've had." A tray with two glasses extended from the side. "Ah, here are the drinks."

She sniffed at hers. "It smells pleasant," she
said. "But are you sure there isn't something I
might be allergic to?"

"I doubt that. You didn't react to anything you
tried on Serieve, did you?"

"No, except for finding it overly bland."

"Don't worry," he grinned. "Before we left, your
father took care to present me with one of your
saltshakers. It'll be on the dinner table."

Jaccavrie had analyzed the contents. Besides
sodium and potassium chloride—noticeably less
abundant on Kirkasant than on the average
planet, but not scarce enough to cause real trouble
—the mixture included a number of other salts.
The proportion of rare earths and especially
arsenic was surprising. An ordinary human who
ingested the latter element at that rate would lose
quite a few years of life expectancy. Doubtless the
first refugee generations had, too, when
something else didn't get them first. But by now
their descendants were so well adapted that food
din't taste right without a bit of arsenic trioxide.

"We wouldn't have to be cautious—we'd know
in advance what you can and cannot take— if you'd
permit a chromosome analysis," Laure hinted.
"The laboratory aboard this ship can do it."

Her cheeks turned more than ever coppery. She
scowled. "We refused before," she said.

"May I ask why?"

"It . . . violates integrity. Humans are not to be
probed into."

He had encountered that attitude before, in
several guises. To the Kirkasanter—at least, to the
Hobrokan clansman; the planet had other cultures
—the body was a citadel for the ego, which by
right should be inviolable. The feeling, so basic
that few were aware of having it, had led to the
formation of reserved, often rather cold person-

alities. It had handicapped if not stopped the
progress of medicine. On the plus side, it had
made for dignity and self-reliance; and it had
caused this civilization to be spared professional
gossips, confessional literature, and
psychoanalysis.

"I don't agree," Laure said. "Nothing more is
involved than scientific information. What's
personal about a DNA map?"

"Well . . . maybe. I shall think on the matter."
Graydal made an obvious effort to get away from
the topic. She sipped her drink, smiled, and said,
'Mm-m-m, this *is* a noble flavor."

"Hoped you'd like it. I do. We have a custom in
the Commonalty—" He touched glasses with her.

"Charming. Now we, when good friends are together, drink half what's in our cups and then
exchange them."

"May I?"

She blushed again, but with pleasure. "Certainly. You honor me."

"No, the honor is mine." Laure went on, quite
sincere: "What your people have done is
tremendous. What an addition to the race you'll
be!"

Her mouth drooped. "If ever my folk may be
found."

"Surely—"

"Do you think we did not try?" She tossed off
another gulp of her cocktail. Evidently it went fast
to her unaccustomed head. "We did not fare forth
blindly. Understand that *Makt* is not the first ship
to leave Kirkasant's sun. But the prior ones went
to nearby stars, stars that can be seen from home.
They are many. We had not realized how many
more are in the Cloud Universe, hidden from eyes
and instruments, a few light-years farther on. We,
our ship, we intended to take the next step. Only
the next step. Barely beyond that shell of suns we

could see from Kirkasant's system. We could find
our way home again without trouble. Of course we
could! We need but steer by those suns that were
already charted on the edge of instrumental perception. Once we were in their neighborhood, our
familiar part of space would be visible."

She faced him, gripping his arm painfully hard,
speaking in a desperate voice. "What we had not
known, what no one had known, was the impre-
cision of that charting. The absolute magnitudes,
therefore the distances and relative positions of
those verge-visible stars ... had not been
determined as well as the astronomers believed.
Too much haze, too much shine, too much variability. Do you understand? And so, suddenly, our
tables were worthless. We thought we could
identify some suns. But we were wrong. Flitting
toward them, we must have bypassed the volume
of space we sought ... and gone on and on, more
hopelessly lost each day, each endless day—

"What makes you think you can find our
home?"

Laure, who had heard the details before, had
spent the time admiring her and weighing his
reply. He sipped his own drink, letting the sour-
ness glide over his palate and the alcohol slightly,
soothingly burn him, before he said: "I can try. I
do have instruments your people have not yet
invented. Inertial devices, for example, that work
under hyperdrive as well as at true velocity. Don't
give up hope." He paused. "I grant you, we might
fail. Then what will you do?"

The blunt question, which would have driven
many women of his world to tears, made her rally.
She lifted her head and said—haughtiness rang
through the words: "Why, we will make the best of
things, and I do not think we will do badly."

Well, he thought, *she's descended from nothing*

*but survivor types. Her nature is to face trouble
and whip it.*

"I'm sure you will succeed magnificently," he
said. "You'll need time to grow used to our ways,
and you may never feel quite easy in them, but—"

"What are you marriages like?" she asked.

"Uh?" Laure fitted his jaw back into place.

She was not drunk, he decided. A bit of drink, together with these surroundings, the lilting music,
odors and pheromones in the air, had simply
lowered her inhibitions. The huntress in her was
set free, and at once attacked whatever had been
most deeply perturbing her. The basic reticence
remained. She looked straight at him, but she was
fiery-faced, as she said:

"We ought to have had an equal number of men
and women along on *Makt*. Had we known what
was to happen, we would have done so. But now
ten men shall have to find wives among foreigners.
Do you think they will have much difficulty?"

"Uh, why no. I shouldn't think they will," he
floundered. "They're obviously superior types,
and then, being exotic—glamorous . . . "

"I speak not of amatory pleasure. But . . . what I
overheard on Serieve, a time or two . . . did I mis-
comprehend? Are there truly women among you
who do not bear children?"

"On the older planets, yes, that's not
uncommon. Population control—"

"We shall have to stay on Serieve, then, or
worlds like it." She sighed. "I had hoped we might
go to the pivot of your civilization, where your real
work is done and our children might become
great."

Laure considered her. After a moment, he
understood. Adapting to the uncountably many
aliennesses of Kirkasant had been a long and cruel
process. No blood line survived which did not do
more than make up its own heavy losses. The will

to reproduce was a requirement of existence. It, too, became an instinct.

He remembered that, while Kirkasant was not a very fertile planet, and today its population strained its resources, no one had considered reducing the birthrate. When someone on Serieve had asked why, Demring's folk had reacted strongly. The idea struck them as obscene. They didn't care for the notion of genetic modification or exogenetic growth either. And yet they were quite reasonable and noncompulsive about most other aspects of their culture.

Culture, Laure thought. *Yes. That's mutable. But you don't change your instincts; they're built into your chromosomes. Her people must have children.*

"Well," he said, "you can find women who want large families on the central planets, too. If anything, they'll be eager to marry your friends. They have a problem finding men who feel as they do, you see."

Graydal dazzled him with a smile and held out her glass. "Exchange?" she proposed.

"Hoy, you're way ahead of me." He evened the liquid levels. "Now."

They looked at each other throughout the little ceremony. He nerved himself to ask, "As for you women, do you necessarily have to marry within your ship?"

"No," she said. "It would depend on . . . whether any of your folk . . . might come to care for one of us."

"That I can guarantee!"

"I would like a man who travels," she murmured, "if I and the children could come along."

"Quite easy to arrange," Laure said.

She said in haste: "But we are buying grief, are we not? You told me perhaps you can find our planet for us."

"Yes. I hope, though, if we succeed, that won't be the last I see of you."

"Truly it won't."

They finished their drinks and went to dinner. *Jaccavrie* was also an excellent cook. And the choice of wines was considerable. What was said and laughed at over the table had no relevance to anyone but Laure and Graydal.

Except that, at the end, with immense and tender seriousness, she said: "If you want a cell sample from me . . . for analysis . . . you may have it."

He reached across the table and took her hand. "I wouldn't want you to do anything you might regret later," he said.

She shook her head. The tawny eyes never left him. Her voice was slow, faintly slurred, but bespoke complete awareness of what she was saying. "I have come to know you. For you to do this thing will be no violation."

Laure explained eagerly: "The process is simple and painless, as far as you're concerned. We can go right down to the lab. The computer operates everything. It'll give you an anesthetic spray and remove a small sample of flesh, so small that tomorrow you won't be sure where the spot was. Of course, the analysis will take a long while. We don't have all possible equipment aboard. And the computer does have to devote most of her—most of its attention to piloting and interior work. But at the end, we'll be able to tell you—"

"Hush." Her smile was sleepy. "No matter. If you wish this, that's enough. I ask only one thing."

"What?"

"Do not let a machine use the knife, or the needle, or whatever it is. I want you to do that yourself."

" . . . Yes. Yonder is our home sky." The physicist Hirn Oran's son spoke slow and hushed.

Cosmic interference seethed across his radio
voice, nigh drowning it in Laure's and Graydal's
earplugs.

"No," the Ranger said. "Not off there. We're
already in it."

"What?" Silvery against rock, the two space-
armored figures turned to stare at him. He could
not see their expressions behind the faceplates,
but he could imagine how astonishment flickered
above awe.

He paused, arranging words in his mind. The
star noise in his receivers was like surf and fire.
The landscape overwhelmed him.

Here was no simple airless planet. No planet is
ever really simple, and this one had a stranger
history than most. Eons ago it was apparently a
subjovian, with a cloudy hydrohelium and
methane atmosphere and an immense shell of ice
and frozen gases around the core; for it orbited its
sun at a distance of almost a billion and a half
kilometers, and though that primary was bright,
at this remove it could be little more than a spark.

Until stellar evolution — hastened, Laure
believed, by an abnormal infall of cosmic material
—took the star off the main sequence. It swelled,
surface cooling to red but total output growing so
monstrous that the inner planets were consumed
On the farther ones, like this, atmosphere fled into
space. Ice melted; the world-ocean boiled; each
time the pulsations of the sun reached a
maximum, more vapor escaped. Now nothing
remained except a ball of metal and rock, hardly
larger than a terrestrial-type globe. As the
pressure of the top layers was removed, frightful
tectonic forces must have been liberated. Mountains—the younger ones with crags like sharp
teeth, the older ones worn by meteorite and
thermal erosion—rose from a cratered plain of
gloomy stone. Currently at a minimum, but none-

theless immense, a full seven degrees across, blue
core surrounded and dimmed by the tenuous
ruddy atmosphere, the sun smoldered aloft.

Its furnace light was not the sole illumination.
Another star was passing sufficiently near at the
time that it showed a perceptible disk ... in a
stopped-down viewscreen, because no human eye
could directly confront that electric cerulean
intensity. The outsider was a B_8 newborn out of
dust and gas, blazing with an intrinsic radiance of
a hundred Sols.

Neither one helped in the shadows cast by the
pinnacled upthrust which Laure's party was in-
vestigating. Flashcasters were necessary.

But more was to see overhead, astride the dark.
Stars in thousands powdered the sky, brilliant
with proximity. And they were the mere fringes of
the cluster. It was rising as the planet turned,
partly backgrounding and partly following the
sun. Laure had never met a sight to compare. For
the most part, the individuals he could pick out in
that enormous spheroidal cloud of light were
themselves red: long-lived dwarfs, dying giants
like the one that brooded over him. But many
glistened exuberant golden, emerald, sapphire.
Some could not be older than the blue which
wandered past and added its own harsh hue to this
land. All those stars were studded through a soft
glow that pervaded the entire cluster, a nacreous
luminosity into which they faded and vanished,
the fog wherein his companions had lost their
home but which was a shining beauty to behold.

"You live in a wonder," Laure said.

Graydal moved toward him. She had had no
logical reason to come down out of *Makt*'s orbit
with him and Hirn. The idea was simply to break
out certain large ground-based instruments that
Jaccavrie carried, for study of their goal before
traveling on. Any third party could assist. But she

had laid her claim first, and none of her shipmates argued. They knew how often she and Laure were in each other's company.

"Wait until you reach our world," she said low. "Space is eldritch and dangerous. But once on Kirkasant— We will watch the sun go down in the Rainbow Desert; suddenly, in that thin air, night has come, our shimmering star-crowded night, and the auroras dance and whisper above the stark hills. We will see great flying flocks rise from dawn mists over the salt marshes, hear their wings thunder and their voices flute. We will stand on the battlements of Ey, under the banners of those very knights who long ago rid the land of the firearms, and watch the folk dance welcome to a new year—"

"If the navigator pleases," said Hirn, his voice sharpened by an unadmitted dauntedness, "we will save our dreams for later and attend now to the means of realizing them. At present, we are supposed to choose a good level site for the observing apparatus. But, ah, Ranger Laure, may I ask what you meant by saying we are already back in the Cloud Universe?"

Laure was not as annoyed to have Graydal interrupted as he might normally have been. She'd spoken of Kirkasant so often that he felt he almost been there himself. Doubtless it had its glories, but by his standards it was a grim, dry, storm-scoured planet where he would not care to stay for long at a time. Of course, to her it was beloved home; and he wouldn't mind making occasional visits if— No, chaos take it, there was work on hand!

Part of his job was to make explanations. He said: "In your sense of the term, Physicist Hirn, the Cloud Universe does not exist."

The reply was curt through the static. "I disputed that point on Serieve already, with Vandange and others. And I resented their implication that we of *Makt* were either liars or incompetent observers."

"You're neither," Laure said quickly. "But communications had a double barrier on Serieve. First, an imperfect command of your language. Only on the way here, spending most of my time in contact with your crew, have I myself begun to feel a real mastery of Hobrokan. The second barrier, though, was in some ways more serious: "Vandange's stubborn preconceptions, and your own."

"I was willing to be convinced."

"But you never got a convincing argument. Vandange was so dogmatically certain that what you reported having seen was impossible, that he didn't take a serious look at your report to see if it might have an orthodox explanation after all. You naturally got angry at this and cut the discussions off short. For your part, you had what you had always been taught was a perfectly good theory, which your experiences had confirmed. You weren't going to change your whole concept of physics just because the unlovable Ozer Vandange scoffed at it."

"But we were mistaken," Graydal said. "You've intimated as much, Daven, but never made your meaning clear."

"I wanted to see the actual phenomenon for myself, first," Laure said. "We have a proverb— so old that it's reputed to have originated on Earth —'It is a capital mistake to theorize in advance of the data.' But I couldn't help speculating, and what I see shows my speculations were along the right lines."

"Well?" Hirn challenged.

"Let's start with looking at the situation from your viewpoint," Laure suggested. "Your people sent millennia on Kirkasant. You lost every hint, except a few ambiguous traditions, that things might be different elsewhere. To you, it was natural that the night sky should be like a gently shining mist, and stars should crowd thickly around. When you developed the scientific method again, not many generations back, perforce you studied the universe you knew. Ordinary physics and chemistry, even atomistics and quantum theory, gave you no special problems. But you measured the distances of the visible stars as light-months—at most, a few light-years—after which they vanished in the foggy background. You measured the concentration of that fog, that dust and fluorescing gas. And you had no reason to suppose the interstellar medium was not equally dense everywhere. Nor had you any hint of receding galaxies.

"So your version of relativity made space sharply curved by the mass packed together throughout it. The entire universe was two or three hundred light-years across. Stars condensed and evolved—you could witness every stage of that—but in a chaotic fashion, with no particular overall structure. It's a wonder to me that you went on to gravitics and hyperdrive. I wish I were scientist enough to appreciate how different some of the laws and constants must be in your physics. But you did plow ahead. I guess the fact you knew these things were possible was important to your success. Your scientists would keep fudging and finagling, in defiance of theoretical niceties, until they made something work."

"Um-m-m . . . as a matter of fact, yes," Hirn said in a slightly abashed tone. Graydal snickered.

"Well, then *Makt* lost her way, and emerged into the outer universe, which was totally strange," Laure said. "You had to account somehow for what you saw. Like any scientists, you stayed with accepted ideas as long as feasible—a perfectly

correct principle which my people call the razor of
Occam. I imagine that the notion of contiguous
space-times with varying properties looks quite
logical if you're used to thinking of a universe
with an extremely small radius. You may have
been puzzled as to how you managed to get out of
one 'bubble' and into the next, but I daresay you
cobbled together a tentative explanation."

"I did," Hirn said. "If we postulate a multi-
dimensional—"

"Never mind," Laure said. "That's no longer
needful. We can account for the facts much more
simply."

"How? I have been pondering it. I think I can
grasp the idea of a universe billions of light-years
across, in which the stars form galaxies. But our
home space—"

"Is a dense star cluster. And as such, it has no
definite boundaries. That's what I meant by saying
we are already in it. In the thin verge, at least."
Laure pointed to the diffuse, jeweled
magnificence that was rising higher above these
wastes, in the wake of the red and blue suns.
"Yonder's the main body, and Kirkasant is somewhere there. But this system here is associated.
I've checked proper motions and I know."

"I could have accepted some such picture while
on Serieve," Hirn said. "But Vandange was so
insistent that a star cluster like this cannot be."
Laure visualized the sneer behind his faceplate. "I
thought that he, belonging to the master
civilization, would know whereof he spoke."

"He does. He's merely rather unimaginative,"
Laure said. "You see, what we have here is a
globular cluster. That's a group made up of stars
close together in a roughly spherical volume of
space. I'd guess you have a quarter million,
packed into a couple of hundred lightyears'
diameter.

"But globular clusters haven't been known like

this one. The ones we do know lie mostly well off the galactic plane. The space within them is much clearer than in the spiral arms, almost a perfect vacuum. The individual members are red. Any normal stars of greater than minimal mass have gone off the main sequence long ago. The survivors are metal-poor. That's another sign of extreme age. Heavy elements are formed in stellar cores, you know, and spewed back into space. So it's the younger suns, coalescing out of the enriched interstellar medium, that contain a lot of metal. All in all, everything points to the globular clusters being relics of an embryo stage in the galaxy's life.

"Yours, however—! Dust and gas so thick that not even a giant can be seen across many parsecs. Plenty of mainsequence stars, including blues which cannot be more than a few million years old, they burn out so fast. Spectra, not to mention planets your explorers visited, showing atomic abundances far skewed toward the high end of the periodic table. A background radiation too powerful for a man like me to dare take up permanent residence in your country.

"Such a cluster shouldn't be!"

"But it is," Graydal said.

Laure made bold to squeeze her hand, though little of that could pass through the gauntlets. "I'm glad," he answered.

"How do you explain the phenomenon?" Hirn asked.

"Oh, that's obvious . . . now that I've seen the things and gathered some information on its path," Laure said. "An improbable situation, maybe unique, but not impossible. This cluster happens to have an extremely eccentric orbit around the galactic center of mass. Once or twice a gigayear, it passes through the vast thick clouds that surround that region. By gravitation, it sweeps up immense quantities of stuff. Meanwhile, I suppose, perturbation causes some of its senior members to drift off. You might say it's periodically rejuvenated.

"At present, it's on its way out again. Hasn't quite left our spiral arm. It passed near the galactic midpoint just a short while back, cosmically speaking; I'd estimate less than fifty million years. The infall is still turbulent, still condensing out into new stars like that blue giant shining on us. Your home sun and its planets must be a product of an earlier sweep. But there've been twenty or thirty such since the galaxy formed, and each one of them was responsible for several generations of giant stars. So Kirkasant has a lot more heavy elements than the normal planet, even though it's not much younger than Earth. Do you follow me?"

"Hm-m-m . . . perhaps. I shall have to think." Hirn walked off, across the great tilted block on which the party stood, to its edge, where he stopped and looked down into the shadows below. They were deep and knife sharp. The mingled light of red and blue suns, stars, starfog played eerie across the stone land. Laure grew aware of what strangeness and what silence—under the hiss in his ears—pressed in on him.

Graydal must have felt the same, for she edged close until their armors clinked together. He would have liked to see her face. She said: "Do you truly believe we can enter that realm and conquer it?"

"I don't know," he said, slow and blunt. "The sheer number of stars may beat us."

"A large enough fleet could search them, one by one."

"If it could navigate. We have yet to find out whether that's possible."

"Suppose. Did you guess a quarter million suns in the cluster? Not all are like ours. Not even a majority. On the other coin side, with visibility as low as it is, space must be searched back and forth, light-year by light-year. We of *Makt* could die of eld before a single vessel chanced on Kirkasant."

"I'm afraid that's true."

"Yet an adequate number of ships, dividing the task, could find our home in a year or two."

"That would be unattainably expensive, Graydal."

He thought he sensed her stiffening. "I've come on this before," she said coldly, withdrawing from his touch. "In your Commonalty they count the cost and the profit first. Honor, adventure, simple charity must run a poor second."

"Be reasonable," he said. "Cost represents labor, skill, and resources. The gigantic fleet that would go looking for Kirkasant must be diverted from other jobs. Other people would suffer need as a result. Some might suffer sharply."

"Do you mean a civilization as big, as productive as yours could not spare that much effort for a while without risking disaster?"

She's quick on the uptake, Laure thought. *Knowing what machine technology can do on her single impoverished world, she can well guess what it's capable of with millions of planets to draw on. But how can I make her realize that matters aren't that simple?"*

"Please, Graydal," he said. "Won't you believe I'm working for you? I've come this far, and I'll go as much farther as need be, if something doesn't kill us."

He heard her gulp. "Yes. I offer apology. *You* are different."

"Not really. I'm a typical Commonalty member. Later, maybe, I can show you how our civilization

works, and what an odd problem in political
economy we've got if Kirkasant is to be redis-
covered. But first we have to establish that
locating it is physically possible. We have to make
long-term observations from here, and then enter
those mists, and— One trouble at a time, I beg
you!"

She laughed gently. "Indeed, my friend. And you
will find a way." The mirth faded. It had never
been strong.

"Won't you?" The reflection of clouded stars
glistened on her faceplate like tears.

Blindness was not dark. It shone.

Standing on the bridge, amidst the view of
space, Laure saw nimbus and thunderheads. They
piled in cliffs, they eddied and streamed, their
color was a sheen of all colors overlying white—
mother-of-pearl—but here and there they
darkened with shadows and grottoes; here and
there they glowed dull red as they reflected a
nearby sun. For the stars were scattered about in
their myriads, dominantly ruby and ember, some
yellow or candent, green or blue. The nearest were
clear to the eye, a few showing tiny disks, but the
majority were fuzzy glows rather than lightpoints.
Such shimmers grew dim with distance until the
mist engulfed them entirely and nothing remained
but mist.

A crackling noise beat out of that roiling form-
lessness, like flames. Energies pulsed through his
marrow. He remembered the old, old myth of the
Yawning Gap, where fire and ice arose and out of
them the Nine Worlds, which were doomed in the
end to return to fire and ice; and he shivered.

"Illusion," said *Jaccavrie*'s voice out of
immensity.

"What?" Laure started. It was as if a mother
goddess had spoken.

She chuckled. Whether deity or machine, she had the great strength of ordinariness in her. "You're rather transparent to an observer who knows you well," she said. "I could practically read your mind."

Laure swallowed. "The sight, well, a big, marvelous, dangerous thing, maybe unique in the galaxy. Yes, I admit I'm impressed."

"We have much to learn here."

"Have you been doing so?"

"At a near-capacity rate, since we entered the denser part of the cluster." *Jaccavrie* shifted to primness. "If you'd been less immersed in discussions with the Kirkasanter navigation officer, you might have got running reports from me."

"Destruction!" Laure swore. "I was studying her notes from their trip outbound, trying to get some idea of what configuration to look for, once we've learned how to make allowances for what this material does to starlight— Never mind. We'll have our conference right now, just as you requested. What'd you mean by 'an illusion'?"

"The view outside," answered the computer. "The concentration of mass is not really as many atoms per cubic centimeter as would be found in a vaporous planetary atmosphere. It is only that, across light-years, their absorption and reflection effects are cumulative. The gas and dust do, indeed, swirl, but not with anything like the velocity we think we perceive. That is due to our being under hyperdrive. Even at the very low pseudospeed at which we are feeling our way, we pass swiftly through varying densities. Space itself is not actually shining; excited atoms are fluorescing. Nor does space roar at you. What you hear is the sound of radiation counters and other instruments which I've activated. There are no real, tangible currents working on our hull, making it quiver. But when we make quantum microjumps across strong interstellar magnetic fields, and those fields vary according to an extraordinarily complex pattern, we're bound to interact noticeably with them.

"Admittedly the stars are far thicker than appears. My instruments can detect none beyond a few parsecs. But what data I've gathered of late leads me to suspect the estimate of a quarter million total is conservative. To be sure, most are dwarfs—"

"Come off that!" Laure barked. "I don't need you to explain what I knew the minute I saw this place."

"You need to be drawn out of your fantasizing," *Jaccavrie* said. "Though you recognize your daydreams for what they are, you can't afford them. Not now."

Laure tensed. He wanted to order the view turned off, but checked himself, wondered if the robot followed that chain of his impulses too, and said in a harshened voice: "When you go academic on me like that, it means you're postponing news you don't want to give me. We have troubles."

"We can soon have them, at any rate," *Jaccavrie* said. "My advice is to turn back at once."

"We can't navigate," Laure deduced. Though it was not unexpected, he nonetheless felt smitten.

"No. That is, I'm having difficulties already, and conditions ahead of us are demonstrably worse."

"What's the matter?"

"Optical methods are quite unsuitable. We knew that from the experience of the Kirkasanters. But nothing else works, either. You recall, you and I discussed the possibility of identifying supergiant stars through the clouds and using them for beacons. Though their light be diffused and absorbed, they should produce other effects—they should be powerful neutrino sources, for instance

—that we could use."

"Don't they?"

"Oh, yes. But the effects are soon smothered. Too much else is going on. Too many neutrinos from too many different sources, to name one thing. Too many magnetic effects. The stars are so close together, you see; and so many of them are double, triple, quadruple, hence revolving rapidly and twisting the force lines; and irradiation keeps a goodly fraction of the interstellar medium in the plasma state. Thus we get electromagnetic action of every sort, plus synchrotron and betatron radiation, plus nuclear collision, plus—"

"Spare me the complete list," Laure broke in. "Just say the noise level is too high for your instruments."

"And for any instruments that I can extrapolate as buildable," *Jaccavrie* replied. "The precision their filters would require seems greater than the laws of atomistics would allow."

"What about your inertial system? Bollixed up, too?"

"It's beginning to be. That's why I asked you to come take a good look at what's around us and what we're headed into, while you listen to my report." The robot was not built to know fear, but Laure wondered if she didn't spring back to pedantry as a refuge: "Inertial navigation would work here at kinetic velocities. But we can't traverse parsecs except hyperdrive. Inertial and gravitational mass being identical, too rapid a change of gravitational potential will tend to cause uncontrollable precession and nutation. We can compensate for that in normal parts of space. But not here. With so many stars so closely packed, moving among each other on paths too complex for me to calculate, the variation rate is becoming too much."

"In short," Laure said slowly, "if we go deeper

into this stuff, we'll be flying blind."

"Yes. Just as *Makt* did."

"We can get out into clear space time, can't we? You can follow a more or less straight line till we emerge."

"True. I don't like the hazards. The cosmic ray background is increasing considerably."

"You have screen fields."

"But I'm considering the implications. Those particles have to originate somewhere. Magnetic acceleration will only account for a fraction of their intensity. Hence the rate of nova production in this cluster, and of supernovae in the recent past, must be enormous. This in turn indicates vast numbers of lesser bodies—neutron stars, rogue planets, large meteoroids, thick dust banks —things that might be undetectable before we blunder into them."

Laure smiled at her unseen scanner. "If anything goes wrong, you'll react fast," he said. "You always do."

"I can't guarantee we won't run into trouble I can't deal with."

"Can you estimate the odds on that for me?"

Jaccavrie was silent. The air sputtered and sibilated. Laure found his vision drowning in the starfog. He needed a minute to realize he had not been answered. "Well?" he said.

"The parameters are too uncertain." Overtones had departed from her voice. "I can merely say that the probability of disaster is high in comparison to the value for travel through normal regions of the galaxy."

"Oh, for chaos' sake!" Laure's laugh was uneasy. "That figure is almost too small to measure. We knew before we entered this nebula that we'd be taking a risk. Now what about coherent radiation from natural sources?"

"My judgment is that the risk is out of

proportion to the gain," *Jaccavrie* said. "At best, this is a place for scientific study. You've other work to do. Your basic—and dangerous—fantasy is that you can satisfy the emotional cravings of a few semibarbarians."

Anger sprang up in Laure. He gave it cold shape: "My order was that you report on coherent radiation."

Never before had he pulled the rank of his humanness on her.

She said like dead metal: "I have detected some in the visible and short infrared, where certain types of star excite pseudoquasar processes in the surrounding gas. It is dissipated as fast as any other light."

"The radio bands are clear?"

"Yes, of that type of wave, although—"

"Enough. We'll proceed as before, toward the center of the cluster. Cut this view and connect me with *Makt.*"

The hazy suns vanished. Laure was alone in a metal compartment. He took a seat and glowered at the outercom screen before him. What had gotten into *Jaccavrie*, anyway? She'd been making her disapproval of this quest more and more obvious over the last few days. She wanted him to turn around, report to IIQ, and leave the Kirkasanters there for whatever they might be able to make of themselves in a lifetime's exile. Well . . . her judgments were always conditioned by the fact that she was a Ranger vessel, built for Ranger work. But couldn't she see that his duty, as well as his desire, was to help Graydal's people?

The screen flickered. The two ships were so differently designed that it was hard for them to stay in phase for any considerable time, and thus hard to receive the modulation imposed on space-pulses. After a while the image steadied to show a face. "I'll switch you to Captain Demring," the communications officer said at once. In his folk, such lack of ceremony was as revealing of strain as haggardness and dark-rimmed eyes.

The image wavered again and became the Old Man's. He was in his cabin, which had direct audiovisual connections, and the background struck Laure anew with outlandishness. What history had brought forth the artistic conventions of that bright-colored, angular-figured tapestry? What song was being sung on the player, in what language, and on what scale? What was the symbolism behind the silver mask on the door?

Worn but indomitable, Demring looked forth and said, "Peace between us. What occasions this call?"

"You should know what I've learned," Laure said. "Uh, can we make this a three-way with your navigator?"

"Why?" The question was machine steady.

"Well, that is, her duties—"

"She is to help carry out decisions," Demring said. "She does not make them. At maximum, she can offer advice in discussion." He waited before adding, with a thrust: "And you have been having a great deal of discussion already with my daughter, Ranger Laure."

"No . . . I mean, yes, but—" The younger man rallied. He did have psych training to call upon, although its use had not yet become reflexive in him. "Captain," he said, "Graydal has been helping me understand your ethos. Our two cultures have to see what each other's basics are if they're to cooperate, and that process begins right here, among these ships. Graydal can make things clearer to me, and I believe grasps my intent better, than anyone else of your crew."

"Why is that?" Demring demanded.

Laure suppressed pique at his arrogance—he

was her father—and attempted a smile. "Well, sir, we've gotten acquainted to a degree, she and I. We can drop formality and just be friends."

"That is not necessarily desirable," Demring said.

Laure recollected that, throughout the human species, sexual customs are among the most variable. And the most emotionally charged. He put himself inside Demring's prejudices and said with what he hoped was the right slight note of indignation: "I assure you nothing improper has occurred."

"No, no." The Kirkasanter made a brusque, chopping gesture. "I trust her. And you, I am sure. Yet I must warn that close ties between members of radically different societies can prove disastrous to everyone involved."

Laure might have sympathized as he thought, *He's afraid to let down his mask—is that why their art uses the motif so much?—but underneath, he is a father worrying about his little girl.* He felt too harassed. First his computer, now this! He said coolly, "I don't believe our cultures are that alien. They're both rational-technological, which is a tremendous similarity to begin with. But haven't we got off the subject? I wanted you to hear the findings this ship has made."

Demring relaxed. The unhuman universe he could cope with. "Proceed at will, Ranger."

When he had heard Laure out, though, he scowled, tugged his beard, and said without trying to hide distress: "Thus we have no chance of finding Kirkasant by ourselves."

"Evidently not," Laure said. "I'd hoped that one of my modern locator systems would work in this cluster. If so, we could have zigzagged rapidly between the stars, mapping them, and had a fair likelihood of finding the group you know within months. But as matters stand, we can't establish an accurate enough grid, and we have nothing to tie any such grid to. Once a given star disappears in the fog, we can't find it again. Not even by straight-line backtracking, because we don't have the navigational feedback to keep on a truly straight line."

"Lost." Demring stared down at his hands, clenched on the desk before him. When he looked up again, the bronze face was rigid with pain. "I was afraid of this," he said. "It is why I was reluctant to come back at all. I feared the effect of disappointment on my crew. By now you must know one major respect in which we differ from you. To us, home, kinfolk, ancestral graves are not mere pleasures. They are an important part of our identities. We are prepared to explore and colonize, but not to be totally cut off." He straightened in his seat and turned the confession into a strategic datum by finishing dry-voiced: "Therefore, the sooner we leave this degree of familiarity behind us and accept with physical renunciation the truth of what has happened to us— the sooner we get out of this cluster—the better for us."

"No," Laure said. "I've given a lot of thought to your situation. There *are* ways to navigate here."

Demring did not show surprise. He, too, must have dwelt on contingencies and possibilities. Laure sketched them nevertheless:

"Starting from outside the cluster, we can establish a grid of artificial beacons. I'd guess fifty thousand, in orbit around selected stars, would do. If each has its distinctive identifying signal, a spaceship can locate herself and lay a course. I can imagine several ways to make them. You want them to emit something that isn't swamped by natural noise. Hyperdrive drones, shuttling automatically back and forth, would be detectable in a light-year's radius. Coherent radio broadcasters on the right bands should be detectable at the same distance or better. Since the stars hereabouts are only light-weeks or light-months apart, an electromagnetic network wouldn't take long to complete its linkups. No doubt a real engineer, turned loose on the problem, would find better answers than these."

"I know," Demring said. "We on *Makt* have discussed the matter and reached similar conclusions. The basic obstacle is the work involved, first in producing that number of beacons, then— more significantly—in planting them. Many manyears, much shipping, must go to that task, if it is to be accomplished in a reasonable time."

"Yes."

"I like to think," said Demring, "that the clans of Hobrok would not haggle over who was to pay the cost. But I have talked with men on Serieve. I have taken heed of what Graydal does and does not relay of her conversations with you. Yours is a mercantile civilization."

"Not exactly," Laure said. "I've tried to explain—"

"Don't bother. We shall have the rest of our lives to learn about your Commonalty. Shall we turn about, now, and end this expedition?"

Laure winced at the scorn but shook his head. "No, best we continue. We can make extraordinary findings here. Things that'll attract scientists. And with a lot of ships buzzing around—"

Demring's smile had no humor. "Spare me, Ranger. There will never be that many scientists come avisiting. And they will never plant beacons throughout the cluster. Why should they? The chance of one of their vessels stumbling on Kirkasant is negligible. They will be after unusual stars and planets, information on magnetic fields and plasmas and whatever else is readily studied. Not even the anthropologists will have any strong impetus to search out our world. They have many others to work on, equally strange to them, far more accessible."

"I have my own obligations," Laure said. "It was a long trip here. Having made it, I should recoup some of the cost to my organization by gathering as much data as I can before turning home."

"No matter the cost to my people?" Demring said slowly. "That they see their own sky around them, but nonetheless are exiles—for weeks longer?"

Laure lost his patience. "Withdraw if you like, Captain," he snapped. "I've no authority to stop you. But I'm going on. To the middle of the cluster, in fact."

Demring retorted in a cold flare: "Do you hope to find something that will make you personally rich, or only personally famous?" He reined himself in at once. "This is no place for impulsive acts. Your vessel is undoubtedly superior to mine. I am not certain, either, that *Makt*'s navigational equipment is equal to finding that advanced base where we must refuel her. If you continue, I am bound in simple prudence to accompany you, unless the risks you take become gross. But I urge that we confer again."

"Any time, Captain." Laure cut his circuit.

He sat then, for a while, fuming. The culture barrier couldn't be that high. Could it? Surely the Kirkasanters were neither so stupid nor so perverse as not to see what he was trying to do for them. Or were they? Or was it his fault? He'd concentrated more on learning about them than on teaching them about him. Still, Graydal, at least, should know him by now.

The ship sensed an incoming call and turned

Laure's screen back on. And there she was. Gladness lifted in him until he saw her expression.

She said without greeting, winter in the golden gaze: "We officers have just been given a playback of your conversation with my father. What is your" (outphasing occurred, making the image into turbulence, filling the voice with staticlike ugliness, but he thought he recognized) "intention?" The screen blanked.

"Maintain contact," Laure told *Jaccavrie*.

"Not easy in these gravitic fields," the ship said.

Laure jumped to his feet, cracked fist in palm, and shouted, "Is everything trying to brew trouble for me? Bring her back or so help me, I'll scrap you!"

He got a picture again, though it was blurred and watery and the voice was streaked with buzzes and whines, as if he called to Graydal across light-years of swallowing starfog. She said —was it a little more kindly?—"We're puzzled. I was deputed to inquire further, since I am most . . . familiar . . . with you. If our two craft can't find Kirkasant by themselves, why are we going on?"

Laure understood her so well, after the watches when they talked, dined, drank, played music, laughed together, that he saw the misery behind her armor. For her people—for herself—this journey among mists was crueler than it would have been for him had he originated here. He belonged to a civilization of travelers; to him, no one planet could be the land of lost content. But in them would always stand a certain ridge purple against sunset, marsh at dawn, ice cloud walking over wind-gnawed desert crags, ancient castle, wingbeat in heaven . . . and always, always, the dear bright nights that no other place in man's universe knew.

They were a warrior folk. They would not settle

down to be pitied; they would forge something powerful for themselves in their exile. But he was not helping them forget their uprootedness.

Thus he almost gave her his true reason. He halted in time and, instead, explained in more detail what he had told Captain Demring. His ship represented a considerable investment, to be amortized over her service life. Likewise, with his training, did he. The time he had spent coming hither was, therefore, equivalent to a large sum of money. And to date, he had nothing to show for that expense except confirmation of a fairly obvious guess about the nature of Kirkasant's surroundings.

He had broad discretion—while he was in service. But he could be discharged. He would be, if his career, taken as a whole, didn't seem to be returning a profit. In this particular case, the profit would consist of detailed information about a unique environment. You could prorate that in such terms as: scientific knowledge, with its potentialities for technological progress; spacefaring experience; public relations—

Graydal regarded him in a kind of horror. "You cannot mean . . . we go on . . . merely to further your private ends," she whispered. Interference gibed at them both.

"No!" Laure protested. "Look, only look, I want to help you. But you, too, have to justify yourselves economically. You're the reason I came so far in the first place. If you're to work with the Commonalty, and it's to help you make a fresh start, you have to show that that's worth the Commonalty's while. Here's where we start proving it. By going on. Eventually, by bringing them a bookful of knowledge they didn't have before."

Her gaze upon him calmed but remained aloof. "Do you think that is right?"

"It's the way things are, anyhow," he said.

"Sometimes I wonder if my attempts to explain
my people to you haven't glided right off your
brain."

"You have made it clear that they think of
nothing but their own good," she said thinly.

"If so, I've failed to make anything clear." Laure
slumped in his chair web. Some days hit a man
with one club after the next. He forced himself to
sit erect again and say:

"We have a different ideal from you. Or no,
that's not correct. We have the same set of ideals.
The emphases are different. You believe the
individual ought to be free and ought to help his
fellowman. We do, too. But you make the service
basic, you give it priority. We have the opposite
way. You give a man, or a woman, duties to the
clan and the country from birth. But you protect
his individuality by frowning on slavishness and
on anyone who doesn't keep a strictly private side
to his life. We give a person freedom, within a
loose framework of common-sense prohibitions.
And then we protect his social aspect by frowning
on greed, selfishness, callousness."

"I know," she said. "You have—"

"But maybe you haven't thought how we *must*
do it that way," he pleaded. "Civilization's gotten
too big out there for anything but freedom to
work. The Commonalty isn't a government. How
would you govern ten million planets? It's a
private, voluntary, mutual-benefit society, open to
anyone anywhere who meets the modest
standards. It maintains certain services for its
members, like my own space rescue work. The
services are widespread and efficient enough that
local planetary governments also like to hire
them. But I don't speak for my civilization.
Nobody does. You've made a friend of me. But
how do you make friends with ten million times a
billion individuals?"

"You've told me before," she said.

And it didn't register. Not really. Too new an idea for you, I suppose, Laure thought. He ignored her remark and went on:

"In the same way, we can't have a planned interstellar economy. Planning breaks down under the sheer mass of detail when it's attempted for a single continent. History is full of cases. So we rely on the market, which operates as automatically as gravitation. Also as efficiently, as impersonally, and sometimes as ruthlessly—but we didn't make this universe. We only live in it."

He reached out his hands, as if to touch her through the distance and the distortion. "Can't you see? I'm not able to help your plight. Nobody is. No individual quadrillionaire, no foundation, no government, no consortium could pay the cost of finding your home for you. It's not a matter of lacking charity. It's a matter of lacking resources for that magnitude of effort. The resources are divided among too many people, each of whom has his own obligations to meet first.

"Certainly, if each would contribute a pittance, you could buy your fleet. But the tax mechanism for collecting that pittance doesn't exist and can't be made to exist. As for free-will donations—how do we get your message across to an entire civilization, that big, that diverse, that busy with its own affairs?—which include cases of need far more urgent than yours.

"Graydal, we're not greedy where I come from. We're helpless."

She studied him at length. He wondered, but could not see through the ripplings, what emotions passed across her face. Finally she spoke, not altogether ungently, though helmeted again in the reserve of her kindred, and he could not hear anything of it through the buzzings except: " . . . proceed, since we must. For a while, anyhow. Good watch, Ranger.''

The screen blanked. This time he couldn't make the ship repair the connection for him.

At the heart of the great cluster, where the nebula was so thick as to be a nearly featureless glow, pearl-hued and shot with rainbows, the stars were themselves so close that thousands could be seen. The spaceships crept forward like frigates on unknown seas of ancient Earth. For here was more than fog; here were shoals, reefs, and riptides. Energies travailed in the plasma. Drifts of dust, loose planets, burnt-out suns lay in menace behind the denser clouds. Twice *Makt* would have met catastrophe had not *Jaccavrie* sensed the danger with keener instruments and cried a warning to sheer off.

After Demring's subsequent urgings had failed, Graydal came aboard in person to beg Laure that he turn homeward. That she should surrender her pride to such an extent bespoke how worn down she and her folk were. "What are we gaining worth the risk?" she asked shakenly.

"We're proving that this is a treasure house of absolutely unique phenomena," he answered. He was also hollowed, partly from the long travel and the now constant tension, partly from the half estrangement between him and her. He tried to put enthusiasm in his voice. "Once we've reported, expeditions are certain to be organized. I'll bet the foundations of two or three whole new sciences will get laid here."

"I know. Everything astronomical in abundance, close together and interacting." Her shoulders drooped. "But our task isn't research. We can go back now, we could have gone back already, and carried enough details with us. Why do we not?"

"I want to investigate several planets yet, on the

ground, in different systems," he told her. "Then we'll call a halt."

"What do they matter to you?"

"Well, local stellar spectra are freakish. I want to know if the element abundances in solid bodies correspond."

She stared at him. "I do not understand you," she said. "I thought I did, but I was wrong. You have no compassion. You led us, you lured us so far in that we can't escape without your ship for a guide. You don't care how tired and tormented we are. You can't, or won't, understand why we are anxious to live."

"I am myself," he tried to grin. "I enjoy the process."

The dark head shook. "I said you won't understand. We do not fear death for ourselves. But most of us have not yet had children. We do fear death for our bloodlines. We *need* to find a home, forgetting Kirkasant, and begin our families. You, though, you keep us on this barren search—why? For your own glory?"

He should have explained then. But the strain and weariness in him snapped: "You accepted my leadership. That makes me responsible for you, and I can't be responsible if I don't have command. You can endure another couple of weeks. That's all it'll take."

And she should have answered that she knew his motives were good and wished simply to hear his reasons. But being the descendant of hunters and soldiers, she clicked heels together and flung back at him: "Very well, Ranger. I shall convey your word to my captain."

She left, and did not again board *Jaccavrie*.

Later, after a sleepless "night," Laure said, "Put me through to *Makt*'s navigator."

"I wouldn't advise that," said the woman-voice

of his ship.

"Why not?"

"I presume you want to make amends. Do you know how she—or her father, or her young male shipmates that must be attracted to her—how they will react? They are alien to you, and under intense strain."

"They're human!"

Engines pulsed. Ventilators whispered. "Well?" said Laure.

"I'm not designed to compute about emotions, except on an elementary level," *Jaccavrie* said. "But please recollect the diversity of mankind. On Reith, for example, ordinary peaceful men can fall into literally murderous rages. It happens so often that violence under those circumstances is not a crime in their law. A Talatto will be patient and cheerful in adversity, up to a certain point: after which he quits striving, contemplates his God, and waits to die. You can think of other cultures. And they are within the ambience of the Commonalty. How foreign might not the Kirkasanters be?"

"Um-m-m—"

"I suggest you obtrude your presence on them as little as possible. That makes for the smallest probability of provoking some unforeseeable outburst. Once our task is completed, once we are bound home, the stress will be removed, and you can safely behave toward them as you like."

"Well . . . you may be right." Laure stared dull-eyed at a bulkhead. "I don't know. I just don't know."

Before long, he was too busy to fret much. *Jaccavrie* went at his direction, finding planetary systems that belonged to various stellar types. In each, he landed on an airless body, took analytical readings and mineral samples, and gave the larger worlds a cursory inspection from a distance.

He did not find life. Not anywhere. He had expected that. In fact, he was confirming his whole guess about the inmost part of the cluster.

Here gravitation had concentrated dust and gas till the rate of star production became unbelievable. Each time the cluster passed through the clouds around galactic center and took on a new load of material, there must have been a spate of supernovae, several per century for a million years or more. He could not visualize what fury had raged; he scarcely dared put his estimate in numbers. Probably radiation had sterilized every abode of life for fifty light-years around. (Kirkasant must, therefore, lie farther out—which fitted in with what he had been told, that the intersteller medium was much denser in this core region than in the neighborhood of the vanished world.)

Nuclei had been cooked in stellar interiors, not the two, three, four star-generations which have preceded the majority of the normal galaxy—here, a typical atom might well have gone through a dozen successive supernova explosions. Transformation built on transformation. Hydrogen and helium remained the commonest elements, but only because of overwhelming initial abundance. Otherwise the lighter substances had mostly become rare. Planets were like nothing ever known before. Giant ones did not have thick shells of frozen water, nor did smaller ones have extensive silicate crusts. Carbon, oxygen, nitrogen, sodium, aluminum, calcium were all but lost among . . . iron, gold, mercury, tungsten, bismuth, uranium and transuranics— On some little spheres Laure dared not land. They radiated too fiercely. A heavily armored robot might someday set foot on them, but never a living organism.

The crew of *Makt* didn't offer to help him. Irrational in his hurt, he didn't ask them. *Jaccavrie*

could carry on any essential communication with
their captain and navigator. He toiled until he
dropped, woke, fueled his body, and went back to
work. Between stars, he made detailed analyses of
his samples. That was tricky enough to keep his
mind off Graydal. Minerals like these could have
formed nowhere but in this witchy realm.

Finally the ships took orbit around a planet that
had atmosphere. "Do you indeed wish to make
entry there?" the computer asked. "I would not
recommend it."

"You never recommend anything I want to do,"
Laure grunted. "I know air adds an extra factor to
reckon with. But I want to get some idea of
element distribution at the surface of objects like
that." He rubbed bloodshot eyes. "It'll be the last.
Then we go home."

"As you wish." Did the artificial voice actually
sigh? "But after this long a time in space, you'll
have to batten things down for an aerodynamic
landing."

"No, I won't. I'm taking the sled as usual. You'll
stay put."

"You are being reckless. This isn't an airless
globe where I can orbit right above the mountaintops and see everything that might happen to you.
Why, if I haven't misgauged, the ionosphere is so
charged that the sled radio can't reach me."

"Nothing's likely to go wrong," Laure said. "But
should it, you can't be spared. The Kirkasanters
need you to conduct them safely out."

"I—"

"You heard your orders." Laure proceeded to
discuss certain basic precautions. Not that he felt
they were necessary. His objective looked peaceful—dry, sterile, a stone spinning around a star.

Nevertheless, when he departed the main hatch
and gunned his gravity sled to kill velocity, the
view caught at his breath.

Around him reached the shining fog. Stars and stars were caught in it, illuminating caverns and tendrils, aureoled with many-colored fluorescences. Even as he looked, one such point, steely blue, multiplied its brilliance until the intensity hurt his eyes. Another nova. Every stage of stellar evolution was so richly represented that it was as if time itself had been compressed— cosmos, what an astrophysical laboratory!

(For unmanned instruments, as a general rule. Human flesh couldn't stand many months in a stretch of the cosmic radiation that sleeted through these spaces, the synchrotron and betatron and Cerenkov quanta that boiled from particles hurled in the gas across the intertwining magnetism of atoms and suns. Laure kept glancing at the cumulative exposure meter on his left wrist.)

The solar disk was large and lurid orange. Despite thermostating in the sled, Laure felt its heat strike at him through the bubble and his own armor. A stepdown viewer revealed immense prominences licking flame-tongues across the sky, and a heartstoppingly beautiful corona. A Type K shouldn't be that spectacular, but there were no normal stars in sight—not with this element distribution and infall.

Once the planet he was approaching had been farther out. But friction with the nebula, over gigayears, was causing it to spiral inward. Surface temperature wasn't yet excessive, about 50° C., because the atmosphere was thin, mainly noble gases. The entire world hadn't sufficient water to fill a decent lake. It rolled before him as a gloom little relieved by the reddish blots of gigantic dust storms. Refracted light made its air a fiery ring.

His sled struck that atmosphere, and for a while he was busy amidst thunder and shudder, helping the autopilot bring the small craft down. In the end, he hovered above a jumbled plain. Mountains bulked bare on the near horizon. The rock was black and brown and darkly gleaming. The sun stood high in a deep purple heaven. He checked with an induction probe, confirmed that the ground was solid—in fact, incredibly hard—and landed.

When he stepped out, weight caught at him. The planet had less diameter than the least of those on which men live, but was so dense that gravity stood at 1.22 standard G. An unexpectedly strong wind shoved at him. Though thin, the air was moving fast. He heard it wail through his helmet. From afar came a rumble, and a quiver entered his boots and bones. Landslide? Earthquake? Unseen volcano? He didn't know what was or was not possible here. Nor, he suspected, did the most expert planetologist. Worlds like this had not hitherto been trodden.

Radiation from the ground was higher than he liked. Better do his job quickly. He lugged forth apparatus. A power drill for samples—he set it up and let it work while he assembled a pyroanalyzer and fed it a rock picked off the chaotic terrain. Crumbled between alloy jaws, flash heated to vapor, the mineral gave up its fundamental composition to the optical and mass spectrographs. Laure studied the printout and nodded in satisfaction. The presence of atmosphere hadn't changed matters. This place was loaded with heavy metals and radioactives. He'd need a picture of molecular and crystalline structures before being certain that they were as easily extractable as he'd found them to be on the other planets; but he had no reason to doubt it.

Well, he thought, aware of hunger and aching feet, *let's relax awhile in the cab, catch a meal and a nap, then go check a few other spots, just to make*

sure they're equally promising; and then—
The sky exploded.

He was on his belly, faceplate buried in arms
against that flash, before his conscious mind knew
what had happened. Rangers learn about nuclear
weapons. When, after a minute, no shock wave
had hit him, no sound other than a rising wind, he
dared sit up and look.

The sky had turned white. The sun was no
longer like an orange lantern but molten brass. He
couldn't squint anywhere near it. Radiance
crowded upon him, heat mounted even as he
climbed erect. *Nova,* he thought in his rocking
reality, and caught Graydal to him for the moment
he was to become a wisp of gas.

But he remained alive, alone, on a plain that
now shimmered with light and mirage. The wind
screamed louder still. He felt how it pushed him,
and how the mass of the planet pulled, and how
his mouth was dry and his muscles taunted for a
leap. The brilliance pained his eyes, but was not
unendurable behind a self-adapting faceplate and
did not seem to be growing greater. The infrared
brought forth sweat on his skin, but he was not
being baked.

Steadiness came. Something almighty strange
was happening. It hadn't killed him yet, though. As
a check, with no hope of making contact, he tuned
his radio. Static brawled in his earplugs.

His heart thudded. He couldn't tell whether he
was afraid or exhilarated. He was, after all, quite a
young man. But the coolness of his training came
upon him. He didn't stop feeling. Wildness
churned beneath self-control. But he did
methodically begin to collect his equipment, and
to reason while he acted.

*Not a nova burst. Main sequence stars don't go
nova. They don't vary in seconds, either . . . but*

then, every star around here is abnormal. Perhaps, if I'd checked the spectrum of this one, I'd have seen indications that it was about to move into another phase of a jagged output cycle. Or perhaps I wouldn't have known what the indications meant. Who's studied astrophysics in circumstances like these?

What had occurred might be akin to the Wolf-Rayet phenomenon, he thought. The stars around him did not evolve along ordinary lines. They had strange compositions to start with. And then matter kept falling into them, changing that composition, increasing their masses. That must produce instability. Each spectrum he had taken in this heart of the cluster showed enormous turbulence in the surface layers. So did the spots, flares, prominences, coronas he had seen. Well, the turbulence evidently went deeper than the photospheres. Actual stellar cores and their nuclear furnaces might be affected. Probably every local sun was a violent variable.

Even in the less dense regions, stars must have peculiar careers. The sun of Kirkasant had apparently been stable for five thousand years—or several million, more likely, since the planet had well-developed native life. But who could swear it would stay thus? Destruction! The place had to be found, had to, so that the people could be evacuated if need arose. You can't let little children fry—

Laure checked his radiation meter. The needle climbed ominously fast up the dial. Yonder sun was spitting X rays, in appreciable quantity, and the planet had no ozone layer to block them. He'd be dead if he didn't get to shelter—for choice, his ship and her forcescreens—before the ions arrived. Despite its density, the globe had no magnetic field to speak of, either, to ward them off. Probably the core was made of stuff like osmium and uranium. Such a weird blend might well be solid rather than molten. *I don't know about that. I do know I'd better get my tail out of here.*

The wind yelled. It began driving ferrous dust against him, borne from somewhere else. He saw the particles scud in darkling whirls and heard them click on his helmet. Doggedly, he finished loading his gear. When at last he entered the sled cab and shut the air lock, his vehicle was trembling under the blast and the sun was reddened and dimmed by haze.

He started the motor and lifted. No sense in resisting the wind. He was quite happy to be blown toward the night side. Meanwhile he'd gain altitude, then get above the storm, collect orbital velocity and—

He never knew what happened. The sled was supposedly able to ride out more vicious blows than any this world could produce. But who could foretell what this world was capable of? The atmosphere, being thin, developed high velocities. Perhaps the sudden increased irradiation had triggered paroxysm in a cyclone cell. Perhaps the dust, which was conductive, transferred energy into such a vortex at a greater rate than one might believe. Laure wasn't concerned about meteorological theory.

He was concerned with staying alive, when an instant blindness clamped down upon him with a shriek that nigh tore the top off his skull, and he was whirled like a leaf and cast against a mountainside.

The event was too fast for awareness, for anything but reaction. His autopilot and he must somehow have got some control. The crash ruined the sled, ripped open its belly, scattered its cargo, but did not crumple the cab section. Shock harness kept the man from serious injury. He was momentarily unconscious, but came back with no worse than an aching body and blood in his mouth.

Wind hooted. Dust went hissing and scouring. The sun was a dim red disk, though from time to time a beam of pure fire struck through the storm and blazed off metallic cliffsides.

Laure fumbled with his harness and stumbled out. Half seen, the slope on which he stood caught at his feet with cragginess. He had to take cover. The beta particles would arrive at any moment, the protons, within hours, and they bore his death.

He was dismayed to learn the stowed equipment was gone. He dared not search for it. Instead, he made his clumsy way into the murk.

He found no cave—not in his waterless land—but by peering and calculating (odd how calm you can grow when your life depends on your brain) he discovered in what direction his chances were best, and was rewarded. A one-time landslide had piled great slabs of rock on each other. Among them was a passage into which he could crawl.

Then nothing to do but lie in that narrow space and wait.

Light seeped around a bend, with the noise of the storm. He could judge thereby how matters went outside. Periodically he crept to the entrance of his dolmen and monitored the radiation level. Before long it had reached such a count that— space armor, expert therapy, and all—an hour's exposure would kill him.

He must wait.

Jaccavrie knew the approximate area where he intended to set down. She'd come looking as soon as possible. Flitting low, using her detectors, she'd find the wrecked sled. More than that she could not do unaided. But he could emerge and call her. Whether or not they actually saw each other in this mountainscape, he could emit a radio signal for her to home on. She'd hover, snatch him with a forcebeam, and reel him in.

But . . . this depended on calm weather. *Jaccavrie* could overmaster any wind. But the dust would blind both her and him. And deafen and mute them; it was conducive, radio could not get through. Laure proved that to his own satisfaction by experimenting with the miniradar built into his armor.

So everything seemed to depend on which came first, the end of the gale or the end of Laure's powerpack. His air renewer drew on it. About thirty hours' worth of charge remained before he choked on his own breath. If only he'd been able to grab a spare accumulator or two, or better still, a hand-cranked recharger! They might have rolled no more than ten meters off. But he had decided not to search the area. And by now, he couldn't go back. Not through the radiation.

He sighed, drank a bit from his water nipple, ate a bit through his chow lock, wished for a glass of beer and a comfortable bed, and went to sleep.

When he awoke, the wind had dropped from a full to a half gale; but the dust drift was so heavy as to conceal the glorious starfog night that had fallen. It screened off some of the radiation, too, though not enough to do him any good. He puzzled over why the body of the planet wasn't helping more. Finally he decided that ions, hitting the upper air along the terminator, produced secondaries and cascades which descended everywhere.

The day-side bombardment must really have got fierce!

Twenty hours left. He opened the life-support box he had taken off his shoulder rack, pulled out the sanitary unit, and attached it. Men don't die romantically, like characters on a stage. Their bodies are too stubborn.

So are their minds. He should have been putting his thoughts in order, but he kept being disturbed by recollections of his parents, of Graydal, of a funny little tavern he'd once visited, of a gaucherie he'd rather forget, of some money owing to him, of Graydal— He ate again, and drowsed again, and the wind filled the air outside with dust, and time closed in like a hand.

Ten hours left. No more?

Five. Already?

What a stupid way to end. Fear fluttered at the edge of his perception. He beat it. The wind yammered. How long can a dust storm continue, anyhow? Where'd it come from? Daylight again, outside his refuge, colored like blood and brass. The charged particles and X rays were so thick that some diffused in to him. He shifted cramped muscles, and drank the stench of his unwashed skin, and regretted everything he had wanted and failed to do.

A shadow cast on the cornering rock. A rustle and slither conducted to his ears. A form, bulky and awkward as his own, crawling around the tunnel bend. Numb, shattered, he switched on his radio. The air was fiarly clear in here and he heard her voice through the static: " . . . you are, you are alive! Oh, Valfar's Wings upbear us, you live!"

He held her while she sobbed, and he wept, too. "You shouldn't have," he stammered. "I never meant for *you* to risk yourself—"

"We dared not wait," she said when they were calmer. "We saw, from space, that the storm was enormous. It would go on in this area for days. And we didn't know how long you had to live. We only knew you were in trouble, or you'd have been back with us. We came down. I almost had to fight my father, but I won and came. The hazard wasn't so great for me. Really, no, believe me. She protected me till we found your sled. Then I did have to go out afoot with a metal detector to find you. Because you were obviously sheltered somewhere, and so you could only be detected at closer range than she can come. But the danger wasn't that great, Daven. I can stand much more radiation than you. I'm still well inside my tolerance, won't even need any drugs. Now I'll shoot off this flare, and she'll see, and come so close that we can make a dash— You are all right, aren't you? You swear it?"

"Oh, yes," he said slowly. "I'm fine. Better off than ever in my life." Absurdly, he had to have the answer, however footling all questions were against the fact that she had come after him and was here and they were both alive. "We? Who's your companion?"

She laughed and clinked her faceplate against his. "*Jaccavrie*, of course. Who else? You didn't think your womenfolk were about to leave you alone, did you?"

The ships began their trek homeward. They moved without haste. Best to be cautious until they had emerged from the nebula, seen where they were, and aimed themselves at the Dragon's Head.

"My people and I are pleased at your safety," said Demring's image in the outercom screen. He spoke under the obligation to be courteous, and could not refrain from adding: "We also approve your decision not to investigate that planet further."

"For the first, thanks," Laure answered. "As for the second—" He shrugged. "No real need. I was curious about the effects of an atmosphere, but my computer has just run off a probability analysis of the data I already have, which proves that no more are necessary for my purposes."

"May one inquire what your purposes are?"

"I'd like to discuss that first with your navigator. In private."

The green gaze studied Laure before Demring said, unsmiling: "You have the right of command. And by our customs, she having been instrumental in saving your life, a special relationship exists. But again I counsel forethought."

Laure paid no attention to that last sentence. His pulse was beating too gladly. He switched off as soon as possible and ordered the best dinner his ship could provide.

"Are you certain you want to make your announcement through her?" the voice asked him. "And to her in this manner?"

"I am. I think I've earned the pleasure. Now I'm off to make myself presentable for the occasion. Carry on." Laure went whistling down the corridor.

But when Graydal boarded, he took both her hands and they looked long in silence at each other. She had strewn jewels in her tresses, turning them to a starred midnight. Her clothes were civilian, a deep blue that offset coppery skin, amber eyes, and suppleness. And did he catch the least woodsy fragrance of perfume?

"Welcome," was all he could say at last.

"I am so happy," she answered.

They went to the saloon and sat down on the couch together. Daiquiris were ready for them. They touched glasses. "Good voyage," he made the old toast, "and merry landing."

"For me, yes." Her smile faded. "And I hope for the rest. How I hope."

"Don't you think they can get along in the outside worlds?"

"Yes, undoubtedly." The incredible lashes fluttered. "But they will never be as fortunate as . . . as I think I may be."

"You have good prospects yourself?" The blood roared in his temples.

"I am not quite sure," she replied shyly.

He had intended to spin out his surprise at length, but suddenly he couldn't let her stay troubled, not to any degree. He cleared his throat and said, "I have news."

She tilted her head and waited with that relaxed alertness he liked to see. He wondered how foolish the grin was on his face. Attempting to recover dignity, he embarked on a roundabout introduction.

"You wondered why I insisted on exploring the cluster center, and in such detail. Probably I ought to have explained myself from the beginning. But I was afraid of raising false hopes. I'd no guarantee that things would turn out to be the way I'd guessed. Failure, I thought, would be too horrible for you, if you knew what success would mean. But I was working on your behalf, nothing else.

"You see, because my civilization is founded on individualism, it makes property rights quite basic. In particular, if there aren't any inhabitants or something like that, discoverers can claim ownership within extremely broad limits.

"Well, we . . . you . . . our expedition has met the requirements of discovery as far as those planets are concerned. We've been there, we've proven what they're like, we've located them as well as might be without beacons—"

He saw how she struggled not to be too sanguine. "That isn't a true location," she said. "I can't imagine how we will ever lead anybody back to precisely those stars."

"Nor can I," he said. "And it doesn't matter. Because, well, we took an adequate sample. We can be sure now that practically every star in the cluster heart has planets that are made of heavy elements. So it isn't necessary, for their

exploitation, to go to any particular system. In
addition, we've learned about hazards and so
forth, gotten information that'll be essential t)
other people. And therefore"—he chuckled—' I
guess we can't file a claim on your entire Cloud
Universe. But any court will award you ... us ...
a fair share. Not specific planets, since they can't
be found right away. Instead, a share of everything. Your crew will draw royalties on the richest
mines in the galaxy. On millions of them."

She responded with thoughtfulness rather than
enthusiasm. "Indeed? We did wonder, on *Makt*, if
you might not be hoping to find abundant metals.
But we decided that couldn't be. For why would
anyone come here for them? Can they not be had
more easily, closer to home?"

Slightly dashed, he said, "No. Especially when
most worlds in this frontier are comparatively
metal-poor. They do have some veins of ore, yes.
And the colonists can extract anything from the
oceans, as on Serieve. But there's a natural limit
to such a process. In time, carried out on the scale
that'd be required when population has grown ...
it'd be releasing so much heat that p'anetary
temperature would be affected."

"That sounds farfetched."

"No. A simple calculation will prove it. According to historical records, Earth herself ran into the
problem, and not terribly long after the industrial
era began. However, quite aside from remote
prospects, people will want to mine these cluster
worlds immediately. True, it's a long haul, and
operations will have to be totally automated. But
the heavy elements that are rare elsewhere are so
abundant here as to more than make up for those
extra costs." He smiled. "I'm afraid you can't
escape your fate. You're going to be ... not
wealthy. To call you 'wealthy' would be like calling a supernova 'luminous.' You'll command more

resources than many whole civilizations have done."

Her look upon him remained grave. "You did this for us? You should not have. What use would riches be to us if we lost you?"

He remembered that he couldn't have expected her to carol about this. In her culture, money was not unwelcome, but neither was it an important goal. So what she had just said meant less than if a girl of the Commonalty had spoken. Nevertheless, joy kindled in him. She sensed that, laid her hand across his, and murmured, "But your thought was noble."

He couldn't restrain himself any longer. He laughed aloud. "Noble?" he cried. "I'd call it clever. Fiendishly clever. Don't you see? I've given you Kirkasant back!"

She gasped.

He jumped up and paced exuberant before her. "You could wait a few years till your cash reserves grow astronomical and buy as big a fleet as you want to search the cluster. But it isn't needful. When word gets out, the miners will come swarming. They'll plant beacons, they'll have to. The grid will be functioning within one year, I'll bet. As soon as you can navigate, identify where you are and where you've been, you can't help finding your home—in weeks!"

She joined him, then, casting herself into his arms, laughing and weeping. He had known of emotional depth in her, beneath the school reserve. But never before now had he found as much warmth as was hers.

Long, long afterward, air locks linked and she bade him good night. "Until tomorrow," she said.

"Many tomorrows, I hope."

"And I hope. I promise."

He watched the way she had gone until the locks

closed again and the ships parted company. A
little drunkenly, not with alcohol, he returned to
the saloon for a nightcap.

"Turn off that color thing," he said. "Give me an
outside view."

The ship obeyed. In the screen appeared stars,
and the cloud from which stars were being born.
"Her sky," Laure said. He flopped on to the couch
and admired.

"I might as well start getting used to it," he said.
"I expect I'll spend a lot of vacation time, at least,
on Kirkasant."

"Daven," said *Jaccavrie*.

She was not in the habit of addressing him thus,
and so gently. He started. "Yes?"

"I have been—" Silence hummed for a second.
"I have been wondering how to tell you. Any
phrasing, any inflection, could strike you as something I computed to produce an effect. I am only a
machine."

Though unease prickled him, he leaned forward
to touch a bulkhead. It trembled a little with her
engine energy. "And I, old girl," he said. "Or else
you also are an organism. We're both people."

"Thank you," said the ship, almost too low to be
heard.

Laure braced himself. "What did you have to tell
me?"

She forgot about keeping her voice humanized.
The words clipped forth: "I finished the
chromosome analysis some time ago. Thereafter I
tried to discourage certain tendencies I noticed in
you. But now I have no way to avoid giving you the
plain truth. They are not human on that planet."

"What?" he yelled. The glass slipped from his
hand and splashed red wine across the deck.
"You're crazy! Records, traditions, artifacts,
appearance, behavior—"

The ship's voice came striding across his. "Yes,

they are human descended. But their ancestors had to make an enormous adaptation. The loss of night vision is merely indicative. The fact that they can, for example, ingest heavy metals like arsenic unharmed might be interpreted as simple immunity. But you will recall that they find unarsenated food tasteless. Did that never suggest to you that they have developed a metabolic requirement for the element? And you should have drawn a conclusion from their high tolerance for ionizing radiation. It cannot be due to their having stronger proteins, can it? No, it must be because they have evolved a capacity for extremely rapid and error-free repair of chemical damage from that source. This in turn is another measure of how different their enzyme system is from yours.

"Now the enzymes, of course, are governed by the DNA of the cells, which is the molecule of heredity—"

"Stop," Laure said. His speech was as flat as hers. "I see what you're at. You are about to report that your chromosome study proved the matter. My kind of people and hers can't reproduce with each other."

"Correct," *Jaccavrie* said.

Laure shook himself, as if he were cold. He continued to look at the glowing fog. "You can't call them nonhuman on that account."

"A question of semantics. Hardly an important one. Except for the fact that Kirkasanters apparently are under an instinctual compulsion to have children."

"I know," Laure said.

And after a time: "Good thing, really. They're a high-class breed. We could use a lot of them."

"Your own genes are above average," *Jaccavrie* said.

"Maybe. What of it?"

Her voice turned alive again. "I'd like to have grandchildren," she said wistfully.

Laure laughed. "All right," he said. "No doubt one day you will." The laughter was somewhat of a victory.

More Bestselling Science Fiction from Pinnacle/Tor